RESCUE FROM PLANET PLEASURE

Mario Acevedo

WordFire Press
Colorado Springs, Colorado

RESCUE FROM PLANET PLEASURE
Copyright © 2015 Mario Acevedo

All rights reserved. No part of this book may be reproduced or transmitted in any form or by any electronic or mechanical means, including photocopying, recording or by any information storage and retrieval system, without the express written permission of the copyright holder, except where permitted by law. This novel is a work of fiction. Names, characters, places and incidents are either the product of the author's imagination, or, if real, used fictitiously.

ISBN: 978-1-61475-307-0

Cover by Eric Matelski

Art Director Kevin J. Anderson

Book Design by RuneWright, LLC
www.RuneWright.com

Published by
WordFire Press, an imprint of
WordFire, Inc.
PO Box 1840
Monument CO 80132

Kevin J. Anderson & Rebecca Moesta, Publishers

WordFire Press Trade Paperback Edition May 2015
Printed in the USA
wordfirepress.com

RESCUE FROM PLANET PLEASURE

"Acevedo is a very disturbed man—and I mean that in the absolute finest sense of the term."

—Tim Dorsey

"... horror fan's perfect vacation read."

—Publisher's Weekly

"Decidedly good, clean, unwholesome fun."

—Baltimore Sun

"The most imaginative story I've read in months ... trashy ... silly and so much fun."

—Seattle Stranger

"Gleefully debunks vampire lore and creates new rules of the game."

—La Bloga

"A comedic approach to vampirism."

—Baltimore Sun

"A sassy, fast, fun read."

—Boulder Camera

"A witty, fast-paced, detective tale that also manages to update vampire lore in clever and imaginative ways."

—El Paso Times

"Part hard-boiled private eye, part soft-core porn, and part pure humor."

—Statesman Journal, Oregon

"A high-speed, well-crafted romp through the forests of the night."

—Booklist

Dedication

*To my critique group,
for constantly reminding me of the error of my ways.*

Chapter One

"Felix, it's up to you to save the world."

The voice blurted through the receiver of a Princess telephone. It had been in a box of junk that lay beside my coffin and started to ring and kept ringing until I answered the goddamned thing.

The clock radio on my bookshelf said 2:12 p.m., the best naptime for us vampires. I resented the interruption of the telephone—*an unconnected telephone*, no less. This was supposed to be the start of a long overdue break from work, a staycation during which I was all set to do nothing but kick back, drink bloody cocktails, and get laid.

I settled into the quilted satin lining of my coffin, receiver to ear, hoping I was dreaming. My coffin lay on a heavy table in the back room of my office. "Who *is* this?" The *fuck*, as in *who-the-fuck-is-this*, was implied.

"*Chale*, who else could it be ... *pendejo?*"

The *pendejo* cinched it. *Coyote*.

"It's been awhile," I drawled sleepily. Years since we parted ways in Los Angeles after the ancient trickster had helped me bring down a *nidus*—vampire nest—of renegade bloodsuckers. "What do you need ... money?"

"*Vato*, you need to get here right away and save the world."

"Save? From what?"

"But first you have to go to outer space."

Okay, maybe I was dreaming. I was about to drop the phone and nod off when he mentioned: "Rescue Carmen and bring her home."

Carmen? The name bored through the fog of sleepiness like a searchlight and illuminated the memories of the most bodacious female vampire who ever lived.

Years ago, I had lost Carmen to an alien gangster, a short, round scumbag by the name of Clayborn. He had approached our government with a deal: alien technology for earth women. Why earth women? *Female intuition.* Human females were valued as empathetic companions. Think highly compassionate pets.

According to Clayborn, the aliens recognized Carmen's psychic powers, took her captive, teleported her to an interspace cruiser, and whisked her to an auction, where she fetched top alien dollar. Jolie and I snagged Clayborn before he could flee Earth. We were about to go all Gitmo on his double-crossing ass when agents from the Galactic Union came to arrest him. Not surprisingly, he was a wanted fugitive back on his home turf. Since finding and returning Carmen was no concern of the alien cops, Jolie obliged them by decapitating Clayborn and handing over his corpse.

All this happened because our government and their cronies in Cress Tech International had gotten kissy-faced with Clayborn and schemed to make billions from extraterrestrial technology. They had kidnapped victims for the aliens, even going as far as crashing a commuter jet—killing dozens—to hide the disappearance of abducted women.

I sat up. "You found Carmen?"

"*Simón.* The *Araneum* asked me—"

"Wait a minute, you and the Araneum?" The Araneum—the secret worldwide network of vampires—had long ago grabbed Coyote by his skinny neck and tossed his scruffy carcass out of their ranks.

"They need me. I need you. Things are going bad for us vampires, *ese*. We need Carmen to fight back."

"Against who?"

"Phaedra."

My jumbled thoughts snapped into place. If the Araneum was in cahoots with Coyote, then a very bad prediction was about to come true.

To say Phaedra was trouble would be to say that Hitler caused a little mischief. Phaedra was a scheming teenage wench with incredible psychic powers. I'd saved her from zombies once. Mortally wounded during our escape from the zombie animator's lair, I had reluctantly turned her into a vampire to keep her from dying. Last time I saw Phaedra, she had pinned my ass to the floor with a blast of psychic energy. She vowed to destroy the Araneum and set herself up as queen of the undead bloodsuckers. Then she disappeared. Now she was back and apparently ready to fulfill her promise of conquest.

But if Phaedra was on the rampage, I hadn't heard anything. "What's happened?"

"It's bad. *Bien cagada*. She's organized an undead rebellion. Started to pick off the Araneum and they can't stop her. It's *vampiro contra vampiro*."

"Hold on," I said. "Give me a minute to catch up. How does Carmen fit into this?"

Coyote answered, "Carmen is the only vampire powerful enough to stop Phaedra."

"There's me."

"Felix, sometimes you're a funny guy. But no joking, *por favor*."

"Carmen is light years away. How are we?—"

"Not we, you. And Jolie."

Jolie? "Since when have you known Jol?—"

"She's on the way to get you. Should be there soon."

A knock sounded on the hall door.

"Soon is right."

"Then we'll talk later. Be careful, *ese*." The line went dead.

I dropped the handset onto its cradle and let the phone fall back into the box.

The knock turned into pounding. My office is on the second floor of the Oriental Theater in the Denver Highlands. If anyone wanted to get up here, I'd have to buzz them in. That an uninvited guest was at my door was not a good omen. Just as I reached under my pillow for a Colt Python .357 Magnum and its load of hollow-point silver bullets, a woman hollered.

"Goddamn it, Felix, open the fucking door."

No mistaking the charm in that dainty voice. Jolie.

Revolver in hand, I climbed out of the coffin, slid off the table and left the back room to answer the hall door. Standing to one side—in case it wasn't Jolie—I extended my fangs and talons, threw the deadbolt, and turned the knob. I tried to appear as badass as I could in my bare feet and pajamas. The door popped open.

Jolie entered, wearing Joe Rocket armored riding leathers and heavy biker boots. Very much the deadly vampire enforcer who once had orders to kill me but didn't.

Apprehension sparked over the penumbra of her aura, orange as fire. The *tapetum lucidum* of her unmasked eyes were radioactive red with urgency. Coppery hair pulled into a ponytail and gathered in a leather tail tamer. Face slathered with Dermablend and makeup to dampen the many freckles and darken her anemic undead complexion. She carried a flip-up motorcycle helmet in her gloved hand. "Let's go. We need to burn asphalt."

"It's good to see you, too." Jolie and I shared a lot, mostly heartache over Carmen.

"Yeah, yeah. We'll exchange the how-have-you-beens when we get to Coyote's."

"Which is where?"

"Fajada Butte."

"Which is where?"

"Northwest New Mexico."

People call New Mexico the Land of Enchantment. Having grown up there, I knew the northwest section more as the Land of Nothing, unless you get a boner for lots of sky and dirt. There's a reason the place is uninhabited.

The phone rang again. I retracted my fangs and claws, returned to the back room, and plucked the handset from the box. I answered though I knew who it had to be.

Coyote, of course. "Hey *vato*, you mentioned money earlier."

I wish I hadn't.

"I need some *ficha*. Pay you back when the *vieja's* welfare check comes. *Gracias.*"

The phone died once more before I could say no. Mooching bastard.

Jolie entered the back room. Her aura crackled with urgency. Dropping the handset once again into the box, I gave her and her motorcycle getup another once-over. "So you're on a bike. I'm following you?"

"Like hell. You're riding bitch on my wheels."

"Think again." One, I wasn't riding a motorcycle when I could be busting the miles on the comfy seats of my Cadillac. Two, I don't ride bitch.

"Felix, we can't waste time. Phaedra is close. We gotta go. *Now*." Jolie tapped her wrist impatiently. "Unless your car can cruise at a hundred fifty plus, you're riding with me."

"On what, a rocket sled?"

"Practically." She walked by my coffin, looked into the box and retrieved the Princess phone. "What's with the vintage crap?"

"Found that in the alley. My mom owned a phone like it. Back when she was alive."

"Oh." Jolie set the phone down. She plucked a small backpack from under the table and flung it at me. "Pack your shit and let's go." She tromped into my front room and helped herself to a 500ml bag of human blood from the office mini-fridge.

The backpack wouldn't hold much. "I take it we won't be gone for long."

She fanged a hole in the top of the bag, inserted a straw and drank. "With luck, a few days."

"How about with no luck?"

"Then it won't matter. We'll be dead."

Chapter Two

"As of this moment," Jolie shouted from the front room, "consider yourself behind enemy lines."

Really? Then *was* I out of the loop. When I had gone to bed, my number one concern was that my liquor cabinet was getting a little bare. Now I was packing for a trip to save the world via a detour into outer space, *and* my office was within the blast radius of a brewing vampire civil war.

"If things have gotten this bad, why wasn't I warned?"

"The Araneum tried but their messenger crows never got through."

That gave me pause. A crow visited about once a week to bring a new assignment or to deliver a rebuke. Then again, the last time I saw Phaedra, she brandished a necklace of crow heads and dismissed the Araneum's omnipotence. "Just how far behind enemy—"

Jolie snapped her fingers. "Chop, chop, Felix. Less talk, more getting the hell out of here."

"When did you meet Coyote?"

"We haven't met. He called me out of the blue to warn that a couple of rogue vampires were coming to off me. After I took care of them, Coyote called again and explained what was going on and to fetch you." She snapped her fingers again. "Come on, Felix. Let's *go*!"

I changed out of my pajamas. Put on cargo pants, a work shirt, hiking boots, leather jacket. Since I frequently crashed in my office, I kept extra clothes here. Searching through them, I stuffed a toiletry bag and cell phone charger into the backpack, plus bags of blood and a box of ammo. I tucked the Colt magnum into a holster sewn inside my jacket. After locking up, I followed Jolie downstairs and out to the front sidewalk.

At the curb, a white Suzuki Hayabusa leaned against its kickstand, headlamp and air scoops pinched into an angry squint, the machine looking sleek and menacing, like a jet fighter minus the wings. The Hayabusa is the fastest production motorcycle in the world and even though this crotch rocket was standing still, I could see a tornado of speeding tickets swirling in its wake.

The bike had no panniers or touring bags attached, which begged the question: "Where's your stuff?"

Jolie slapped a pocket on the butt cheek of her riding pants. "VISA card is all the luggage I need. Or I"—she made air quotes—"'borrow' when I need to."

I gave the motorcycle another rueful look. "We take my Cadillac," I said, "and I promise to make that car haul ass 'til we get to Fajada Butte or the engine seizes. In the meantime, we'll have air conditioning. GPS. iTunes. *Cup holders.*"

Jolie pulled the helmet over her head, not paying any mind to my words. She snatched an open-face helmet with a bubble visor that had been hidden behind the windscreen, said, "Catch," and tossed it.

I examined my helmet, the blemished orange metal-flake surface, the frayed webbing, the scratched visor. "How much did you pay for this at the thrift store? A whole dollar?"

"And you're worth every penny." She yanked the front of her helmet down, clicked it into place, and slid her sunglasses through the visor port. "Ready?" She cinched her gloves, threw a leg over the seat, tilted the Suzuki upright off its stand, and pressed the ignition button. The engine snarled and settled into a low growl.

My turn. Helmet on. Sunglasses on. My dark shades made her aura invisible.

The rear footrests were above the angled exhaust pipes. To mount the bike, I had to fold my legs until I practically squatted on the tiny pillion.

Jolie gave the throttle a slight twist and we rolled from the curb. She lifted her boots and tucked her legs against the engine. I leaned into her, my arms around her waist, my ass tilted upward. Very much the bitch position.

She cruised toward the highway, me spooning against her. Long ago, we spent time like this, only naked with nothing between us but post-sex funk and regrets for what we let happen to Carmen.

On the highway, Jolie accelerated to a clip that had us breezing through metro traffic. The drive to northwest New Mexico would take us through the town of Durango in southwest Colorado. No matter which way you go, it's a confusion of highways. Direct routes were impossible because every road has to contend with an inconvenient feature of nature's landscaping called the Rocky Mountains.

Jolie headed south from Denver, then off the interstate onto Highway 285. We were going fast but nowhere near the hundred fifty plus she had bragged about.

Her left thumb touched a switch by the clutch lever. Red and blue lights strobed along the front fairing. I lifted my head and panned to the rear of the bike and noticed similar lights.

Jolie gave me the elbow. Hard. *Quit moving.*

I shouted, "You think those lights will fool the cops?"

"Like I'm worried," she shouted back.

True. Any cop who stopped us would get the zap hypnosis. He—or she—would be lucky if all we did was snack on their necks.

The cars in front of us eased to the right lane to make way. Jolie molded herself to the gas tank and I clutched her waist. She cranked the engine into a howl and the bike kicked forward. Traffic and terrain whooshed by in a smear of colors. Her ponytail hung out the back of her helmet and the slipstream made it slap my visor. A peek over her shoulder at the speedometer showed the needle arcing past one forty.

She didn't slow for the corner. The bike leaned close to the road, our knees grazing a pube's width distance from the asphalt blurring past.

The rear tire hitched when it began to slide. Using vampire-quick reflexes, Jolie expertly worked the throttle and wiggled her hips, snapping the tire firmly back on the road.

And so we zoomed through the mountains, a white blur with red and blue lights warning other drivers to keep clear. I thought about the trip to New Mexico. What was so special about Fajada Butte? How were Jolie and I getting Carmen back home? How had Coyote located Carmen? Was she okay? Who was holding her prisoner? Once we got her back to earth, how was she going to stop Phaedra? What the fuck was I thinking? Outer space? Back to Earth?

We stopped for gas in Gunnison, worked the cramps out of our legs and each sucked down a bag of blood. I said, "You mentioned that Phaedra put the hurt out on Araneum. How?"

"It happened pretty quickly. Like a coup."

"How is that possible?"

"An inside job. Vampires turned against the Araneum."

"Family joined Phaedra?"

Jolie swung a leg back over the Hayabusa. "Seems that way."

"And all this time I've been doing my PI day job, clueless?"

"Maybe Phaedra saved you for last." Jolie started the Suzuki and fastened her helmet. "As dessert."

Minutes later, we were on Highway 550, clipping south through the San Juan National Forest, my mind back to sifting the questions. The Araneum was on the ropes? This explained why a messenger crow hasn't visited me in … a couple of months. Usually, not hearing from the Araneum was a good thing. This time though, not hearing from the Araneum was a very bad thing.

A black dot appeared before us and streaked past.

Jolie decelerated to one-twenty, to eighty, fifty, coasted at thirty and raised her head.

The black streak returned and slowed. It was a crow fluttering towards us and dive-bombed in front of the bike, then wheeled away, cawing.

The crow was telling us something. Had the Araneum sent it?

My vampire sense—the braiding of my six senses and intuition—tingled the nape of my neck. I glanced left, right, then behind us. A dark blue Ford Mustang followed at speed and gained on us.

"We got company," I yelled to Jolie.

Her helmet twitched toward the left rearview mirror. "Got 'em."

"What's the plan?"

"Let them try and catch us." Jolie hunched back down over the gas tank and redlined the engine.

I pressed my chest against her back, the hard shape of the Colt revolver in my jacket reassuring.

The highway poked through a tunnel blasted in the rock, an ideal place for an ambush. We screamed through. Nothing happened. I caught a one-two beat of relief, then we slalomed around curves to enter a stretch named the Million Dollar Highway for its breathtaking mountainous views ... at normal speed. At this velocity we didn't concern ourselves about anything except for the road in front of us and the Mustang on our tail.

A quarter of a mile ahead, a pickup truck sat parked on the right shoulder. As we closed on it, someone stood on the bed, watching us, holding something at chest level. The device was square and shiny, the size of a shoebox.

A vibration rang my nerves, then tore up my spine and smashed into my skull, like a thousand brass cymbals crashing together.

White light exploded inside my head, blanking out my vision. The motorcycle slipped away. I became weightless, disoriented, floating through nothingness.

Chapter Three

I found myself bouncing along the asphalt. Butt first. Then one shoulder. A double slap of pain.

The fog in my head vanished, and my vision burst into Technicolor brilliance, blue sky and white clouds whirling above.

The back of my helmet rebounded against the road. The visor snapped loose and my sunglasses flew off. Something squished between my back and the pavement.

My brain clicked into vampire survival mode, and my synapses sparked at hyper-speed. Time slowed. Microseconds became milliseconds. Milliseconds became seconds. The blur of the crash sharpened into slow-motion focus.

Jolie pancaked beside me, landing on her back, arms and legs spread out, her aura a twirling pool of orange fire.

We spun down the road like hockey pucks. The Suzuki tumbled alongside us, somersaulting, chewing against the guardrail, disintegrating into a cascade of plastic and metal.

Close behind us, the Mustang charged through the motorcycle debris. An orange aura shimmered around the driver. *Vampire!* And red from the front passenger. Human. He aimed a shotgun out his window, no doubt hunting for Jolie and me. Though my mind was super-aware, I couldn't make out his face behind the gaping snout of that twelve-gauge cannon.

Jolie had the best shot at the Mustang so I yelled to her, "You take out the car. I'll get the pickup."

Her helmeted head tracked the guy with the shotgun as she pivoted down the asphalt, unzipping her jacket, reaching with both hands across her chest to draw a brace of Kimber .45 pistols. Her boot heels sparked across the pavement. As she swung around like a gun turret, she aimed at the Mustang, squeezing the triggers so quickly that the semi-auto volleys came out like burps from a submachine gun.

The marble-sized slugs zinged toward the Mustang in a swarm of lead. Steam geysered from the punctured radiator. Bullet holes stitched the windshield in front of the driver. The shooter's face tore up so fast that he remained scowling even as bullets mulched flesh and bone.

The Mustang swerved. The front wheels locked up, the nose end of the big muscle car digging into the asphalt, the chassis pitching forward. The air bags exploded against the driver and passenger. The car flipped between Jolie and me, tilting, pinwheeling, flinging parts, smashing over the remains of the motorcycle, and crunched upside down.

Jolie and I had slowed our spinning. The slides of her empty Kimbers were locked back, smoke hula-hooping from the exposed barrels and her boot heels. My backside burned from the friction as I continued to slide down the road. Jolie scrambled to reload her .45's.

We were almost to the pickup truck parked on the shoulder. Tendrils of alarm whipped from the red aura surrounding the man in the bed. He wore a hat and a brown duster and held a cube of polished steel bars framing a box of layered glass.

I experienced a flash of recognition about the device, but first it was my turn for payback.

I yanked my jacket open, and at lightning speed, had the magnum out and blasting.

Bullets cleaved through the device he was holding. It broke apart in a spray of glass. Slugs hammered the man, doubling him over. Blood spurted from his chest. His aura vanished like a snuffed match flame and he fell from view into the bed. The truck pulled away, kicking dirt. It fishtailed across the pavement and accelerated up the highway. The driver's aura glowed red in the rear cab window. The pickup rounded the curve and disappeared.

Heels dragging across the pavement, I finally spun to a halt. My mind slowed to normal speed.

Jolie catapulted onto her feet and limped toward the Mustang. She tossed her helmet and gloves aside. The leather on the spine, shoulder blades, and elbows of her jacket was worn to the Kevlar armor underneath. She reloaded the Kimbers with a pair of fresh magazines she fished from a jacket pocket.

The car lay on its battered roof, the shattered remains of the windows looking like the nubs of broken teeth, the wheels twisted like mangled paws.

Bones and joints aching, I struggled upright. The tattered backpack dangled from my shoulders. A smear of blood spiraled from where I had first landed to where I had come to rest—the red stain was from the bags of blood that had popped inside the backpack. The rest of the items—my toiletry bag, cell phone charger, and ammo—were scattered amid random parts of car and motorcycle.

I gathered loose cartridges from the pavement and replaced the spent shells in my magnum. After ditching my helmet, I joined Jolie where she crouched beside the Mustang. She stared at the slack bodies of the driver and shooter hanging from their safety belts, blood dripping from the bullet holes uglifying their faces. The spent airbags draped like used condoms. Neither of our attackers had auras. Fangs shone in the driver's mouth.

I asked, "He look familiar?"

His blood was starting to turn into brown flakes.

Jolie shook her head and shoved her pistols into the holsters inside her jacket. She pointed at him. "We got a vampire." She swung her finger to the shooter. "And a human."

"Plus the two humans in the pickup," I added. I knew where Jolie was going with this. Vampire relations with mortals were strictly controlled. We could feed on them, exploit them, but their awareness of us and the supernatural world, the Great Secret, was limited to those humans who chose to become *chalices*—willing suppliers of blood. Their knowledge of the undead was a guarded secret, and any revelations would be punished by turning or by death.

I put my revolver away and pulled the shotgun from inside the car. "These clowns were Phaedra's soldiers. So she does have an army and vampire traitors are among them."

The shotgun was a Mossberg Tactical Semi-Auto. I worked the action and ejected a round, which I snatched in mid-air. I clawed it open, not surprised the shell was loaded with silver buckshot packed in garlic powder. I winced at the poisonous odor. "These guys knew they were going after vampires."

Jolie noted, "I doubt any of these humans were chalices."

"Meaning," I said, bending the barrel of the shotgun and sent it twirling over the trees like a boomerang, "whoever was behind the attack wasn't afraid of betraying the Great Secret." Protecting the Great Secret was the reason for the existence of the Araneum.

Talons extended, Jolie reached in, cut the safety belts, and let the bodies fall into heaps. "Let's see who these douchebags are." She retrieved their wallets and tossed one to me.

I opened it and looked inside. The ID was a Colorado driver's license, but the colors were off and the photo was blurry. "So we got a name, won't do much good as this ID is fake. There's not much else. No credit cards. No business cards. No receipts."

"Same here," Jolie replied.

I pulled out a stack of crisp hundred dollar notes. "Plenty of these, though."

Jolie plucked them from my hand, added them to the Benjamins she withdrew from the other wallet, and folded the cash into a side pocket of her riding pants. "For my expenses," she explained.

We tossed both wallets back inside the car.

Jolie crouched again and retrieved a cell phone. The screen was cracked, the back missing, and its components fell loose. "Not getting anything from this." She threw the phone into the weeds. "What about checking the registration? Running the plates?"

"Why waste our time? These guys were expendable. We need to worry about the next crew sent our way." I pointed to the trail of debris. "Who knew we were making this trip?"

"It was a last-minute plan between Coyote and me."

Jolie hadn't set the trap for herself. Which meant?—

"I know what you're thinking," she blurted. "No way could it be Coyote."

I couldn't believe that either. "Then I'll bet the guys in the Mustang had my place under surveillance. They must've arranged an ambush with the pickup."

Jolie had tuned me out. She was panning the desolate highway, eyes first drawn north toward the tunnel we'd gone through, then south where the pavement inclined and curved out of sight behind the rocks and ponderosas. The road had been plowed across the side of a mountain, rising on the left and dropping on the right into a wooded and rocky draw. I got the impression someone watched us, not close, but from a great distance.

As a vampire, I have no beating heart. Instead, a *kundalini noir*—the black serpent of supernatural energy—animates my undead body. Paranoia made my kundalini noir vibrate like a tuning fork.

"Come on," she said. "Let's get rid of the evidence before someone stops and gets too nosey."

We each grasped a wheel on one side of the Mustang, heaved together, and rolled the car over. Sunlight slanted through the twisted windshield frame. As this light lingered across the driver, his skin darkened and shriveled and burst into flame. His head resembled a burning charcoal briquette.

Once death finally claimed a vampire, the sun would consume his undead flesh. Jolie and I backed away, though not afraid for our safety. Clothing and sunscreen protected us from the sun's deadly rays. We kept our distance out of awe and terror at this preview of every vampire's inevitable demise.

Smoke filled the interior and billowed from the broken windows and seams in the car body. The vampire's hands withered and broke apart. His smoldering head deflated like a collapsing soufflé and crumbled into ash. After a moment there was nothing left of him but a pile of clothes covered in undead dust.

Jolie sighed. "Fuck, I always hate to see this."

"Show's over," I said. "Back to work."

We straightened the wheels so they wobbled more-or-less straight when we pushed the coupe past the guardrail and off the road. The car teeter-tottered over the edge. The rear bumper swung upwards, and the Mustang bounced down the slope, flattening a path through the brush, smashing saplings, and vanishing into the thicket. The car ripped and thrashed through the brush until it crashed with a loud *krump* that echoed across the hills. A cloud of dust billowed over the treetops below.

We talked as we tidied the littered wreckage of the Suzuki, tossing the larger pieces down the hillside, and collected my scattered belongings and her helmet and gloves.

Jolie thumped her palm against the side of her head. "What the hell caused that mental whammy? A ray gun?"

I reflected on the device the man in the truck had aimed at us. When I recognized what the device was, an icy hook twisted my guts. "No. A psychotronic projector."

Jolie halted in mid-pitch, an exhaust pipe in hand, and perked an eyebrow. "A what?"

I punted my helmet into the draw. "The aliens on the Roswell UFO had brought it. They were testing it to see if they could psychically control humans. I destroyed the original at Rocky Flats."

"So the aliens are back?"

"Can't say for sure. Phaedra has psychic powers and maybe discovered how to make one. Or she's cut a deal with the aliens. Have you met Phaedra?"

Jolie threw the exhaust pipe down the slope. "Haven't had that pleasure. Remember back in Morada? When she gave us the slip?" Jolie referred to our assignment in southern Colorado when we had been ordered to stem an outbreak of zombies. Afterwards, when we tried to find Phaedra, the treacherous newly-turned bloodsucker had disappeared. She later returned to my apartment in Denver with the severed head of another vampire enforcer and told me her quest was to destroy the Araneum. After giving me a demonstration of her special supernatural power—a psychic mind blast—she again vanished.

"Count yourself lucky," I said. "She doesn't need a projector. She can conjure those mental blasts on her own."

"How?"

"Don't know. She was dying of Huntington's chorea when I met her. It's a disease that causes voids in the brain. Maybe that allowed her to develop psychic powers. She could project her thoughts into your dreams and consciousness. Plus she had discovered a portal into the psychic plane, and that gave her the ability to see from place to place. After I turned her, she learned how to read minds and focus her psychic powers into a mental howitzer. Trust me, what we experienced a few minutes ago was the BB gun version."

We found our sunglasses and put them back on.

"Is it possible she read my mind," Jolie asked, "or yours, or Coyote's, and learned about our trip?"

"It is possible. But you can detect her mental trespassing. Feels like a hallucination controlled by someone else. I haven't felt anything like that recently."

"Me either," she replied. "What about Coyote?"

"Good luck to Phaedra. Reading his mind would be like snorkeling in a sewer."

Jolie surveyed the surrounding mountains. "And she's out there. What does she want?"

"Long term? Take charge of the vampires."

"She's welcome to that headache. But why?"

I shrugged. "Arrogance. Ambition. Could be she's simply fucking nuts."

"What about short term?"

"Get rid of you and me. And she could know about our plan to get Carmen."

We stood quiet. The wind rustled through the trees. I wondered about the details of our mission, uncertain and overwhelmed by the tasks ahead. Meeting Coyote. Rescuing Carmen. Stopping Phaedra. I was sure Jolie's thoughts were spinning around the same axis.

I broke the silence. "What's next?"

"Get to New Mexico. *Pronto.*" She gestured that I follow her behind a clump of tall mountain grass. She unbuckled and kicked away her boots and peeled off her jacket and riding pants, stripping to a green tank top and black yoga pants. Shrugged loose her cross-draw holsters and pistols. She had a gymnast's build: a wide back and shoulders, small firm breasts, muscular thighs, and a world-class bubble butt. She unfastened the leather tail tamer and raked a hand through her hair to loosen the tresses.

She cocked an ear to the north. "Car's coming. Hide." Standing in her socks, she straightened her shoulders and puffed her chest, adding an unimpressive inch to her less than voluptuous chest.

I scrunched low behind the grass. "What are you doing?"

She angled her buns toward the road. "Hoping for an ass man." She extended a thumb.

"What if it's another hit?"

"Then they're fucked. Felix, keep your goddamn head down."

I flattened myself below the slope, fangs and nerves primed, hand on the grip of my revolver, just in case.

A throaty engine cruised to a halt. A window scrolled down. Jolie mumbled. A door lock clicked. The door opened and closed. The car growled and pulled away.

Irritation raked through me. Had she left me? No sooner had I thought that, the car's tires chirped to a stop. The car idled for a moment, then whined in reverse and halted beside my grassy blind. The horn honked.

I raised my head. A silver Porsche Panamera Turbo S with Texas plates rumbled next to the shoulder, Jolie at the wheel.

"Bring our stuff," she hollered.

I scooped up our things and rushed to the car.

Jolie wiped blood from the corners of her mouth. The owner of the car, a big meaty guy, was sprawled across the rear seat like a slab of prime rib, medium rare. The fang marks on his neck were fading. I tossed our gear in the back next to the unconscious Texan.

I settled into the front seat and raised my window. Refrigerated air whooshed from the vents. "Much better."

Jolie took in the interior, the sweeping lines of brushed steel, exotic woods, and cream-colored leather. "How much do you think this go-kart cost?"

"A hundred and fifty grand. Maybe one seventy-five."

"How fast does it go?"

"This is the top of the Panamera line. I'm sure it will move along."

Jolie eased the Porsche onto the highway. "Ever hear the expression 'drive it like you stole it'?"

"Can't say that I have."

"Then let me demonstrate." She grinned and floored the accelerator.

Chapter Four

We were thirty minutes along a miserable stretch of dirt road, the last leg of our trip to Fajada Butte. Shadows from a late afternoon sun slanted across the landscape, making the features of Chaco Canyon pop in dramatic relief. We'd taken the highway south from Farmington, New Mexico, then a one-lane service route that looped northwest, and now followed this washboard trail that was beating our Porsche Panamera to scrap iron. With every scrape and bone-jarring bump, pieces rattled loose from the car and tumbled into the dust behind us.

We'd made great time on the highway, the Porsche and its turbocharged 550 horsepower engine howled along at one hundred thirty miles per hour. Time from Durango through Farmington to the last turnoff: one hour, twenty minutes.

Though I had plenty of questions about our mission, we hadn't talked much because Jolie had driven with NASCAR focus as we zigzagged through traffic.

That was then. Now we crept along at fifteen miles per hour, our maximum possible speed as we bottomed out the shocks on countless potholes along the narrow, corrugated path. Dense, weedy shrubs clawed the Porsche's paint job. Rocks seemed to leap up from the ground and smash against the frame, as if the native spirits took glee at pummeling this masterpiece of white man engineering into junk.

Jeeps and pickups chattered past the opposite way, the passengers giving us the stink eye for trashing this expensive automobile.

Ordinarily, subjecting any machine to such abuse would've made me groan in shame. But this wasn't my car, and if the owner of this Porsche didn't have insurance, then boo hoo for him. Besides, served him right for stopping for a hitchhiker like Jolie. He remained on the back seat, asleep, kept unconscious by our grazing on his blood and the enzymes we had pumped into him.

Jolie's face was a placid mask behind her sunglasses even as she fought to control a steering wheel that vibrated like a paint shaker. When I'd met her years ago in Key West, she and Carmen were cruising on choppers, wearing denim cutoffs and cowboy boots, looking hotter than the neon colors of their bikini tops. Jolie was definitely a good-time girl who complemented Carmen's brassy outlandishness.

Jolie enjoyed a public brawl almost as much as a bout of casual sex. She was older than me by two centuries, maybe three. I wasn't sure because all women, even the undead, are circumspect about revealing their true age. The Araneum put her sinister talents to use as an enforcer. She was more than an exceptional specimen of womankind and a powerful female vampire; she was a weapon.

We were going to need all of those talents to rescue Carmen from the aliens, however that was to happen, and then in our fight against Phaedra.

Jolie took her foot off the gas, and the Porsche coasted to a bumpy stop. "Warning light came on."

"Which one?"

"Take your pick."

I stared through the dusty windshield at the hills around distant Chaco Canyon. Long way to walk. I got out, hoping I could jury-rig what had busted and coax a few more miles out of the Porsche.

The bodywork appeared to have been whipped with chains by a car-hating sadist. Everything below the beltline had been gnawed to tatters. Nothing remained of the left outside mirror. The right hung from its stub like a loose eyeball. Remnants of the front fascia were jammed inside both forward wheel wells. Tumbleweeds and a prickly pear clung to where the front bumper had been.

Something puddled beneath the engine, and I crouched to look. Oil streamed from the belly pan and pooled on the dirt.

"What do you think?" Jolie shouted from her side. "Can you fix it?"

My diagnosis in three words. "No. Goddamn. Way."

I straightened and looked about to take stock of where we were. Sagebrush and clumps of grass dotted the low hills surrounding us. To the north, Fajada Butte was still too far away to pick out from the rugged cliffs of Chaco Canyon. I checked the GPS on my cell phone.

Jolie yelled, "What's our location?"

The phone had no signal, and I tucked it back into my pocket. "Someplace between nowhere and lost."

I spied a tower to the left, a hundred meters off the road and along a gentle rise. The tower looked about thirty-feet high and was painted beige to blend in with the desert. At first I wished it was a cellular phone mast, hoping that modern technology was finally creeping into this part of New Mexico. But the tower lacked the standard pillow-shaped cell-phone antennae, and I had gotten no signal.

Scanning the horizon, I spotted another one to the north, a spike against the rugged backdrop and possibly another one farther out. Hard to tell at this distance.

I lifted my sunglasses for a better peek but it didn't help.

Looking south, I saw another tower. And way south, another shimmering in the haze. And farther still, one more. I should've spotted them from the road, but I hadn't been paying attention to anything except feeling the potholes sucker punch my kidneys.

The towers should've followed the meandering chicken-scratch path—the most convenient way to haul and erect them. And they weren't in a straight line. The towers seemed planted in an arc. Facing northwest. Centered on ... Fajada Butte.

Where Coyote wanted to meet.

Jolie climbed out the driver's door. She buckled back into her motorcycle boots and walked toward me.

I asked, "What do you know about Fajada Butte?"

A hand up to shade her face, Jolie swiveled at the hips to study the towers. "It's a big fucking rock sticking out of the desert. Plus a Navajo spiritual center. An Anasazi Stonehenge. A New-Age psychic vortex. UFO landing platform. No surprise that weird things are supposed to happen there. My turn for a question. Is it me or is there something strange about these towers?"

"Definitely strange. For a couple of reasons. One, they're oriented toward Fajada Butte. Two, they're here." I started hiking to the closest tower, Jolie at my heels.

The tower jutted from a rocky, sandy slope. A flat rectangular box sat on top of the tower. Each side of the box was about two-feet square and angled slightly to the inside of the arc.

Up close, I could see the tower was a metal post roughly a foot in diameter with small lift rings welded up its side. I kicked dirt from the base and exposed a concrete footing. These towers were here to stay.

I circled the tower and discovered a postcard-sized placard attached at eye level. The placard listed a serial number, followed by what I figured were technical specs, and this: Property of Cress Tech International.

"The plot thickens."

"What do you mean?" Jolie read the placard over my shoulder.

"Remember Hilton Head?"

"How could I forget?"

That was where we had lost Carmen to the aliens. The hotel complex on the island disguised a safe room for Clayborn. "The alien facility on Hilton Head was built and operated by Cress Tech International." I pointed to what was written on the placard. "The same people who erected these."

Jolie backtracked from the tower. "Fuck me."

"Hold that thought." I also stepped back and kept my eyes fixed to the box mounted on the tower. The box had a transparent prism on top.

My kundalini noir tingled and not in a good way.

"Now what?" Jolie had been watching me, sunglasses raised to read my aura. I'm sure it sparked with plenty of dismay.

"I know what that box is. A psychotronic diviner."

"How is that different from the projector those bastards had on the truck?"

"This one only detects psychic energy transmissions. The Araneum gave me a copy that I had used to home in on Phaedra back before I turned her."

Jolie lowered her shades. She spread her arms to encompass the tower array. "So this was built to detect psychic energy?"

"I'm guessing more." I stared at the diviner and paged through my memory for details. "Here's what I remember. The Roswell UFO had been taken to Rocky Flats for study. The Araneum built a psychotronic diviner from plans sketched by a Doctor Milan Blavatsky, one of the Rocky Flats scientists assigned to reverse engineer the alien technology."

"The government knows about psychic energy?"

"For decades, I'm sure. Mostly to experiment with one crackpot scheme after another. Remote viewing. Mind reading."

"But these work?" Jolie jabbed at the psychotronic diviner. "Right?"

"They do."

"Can they detect us?"

"Not unless they found a way to improve them. And even if they did, their surveillance would be cluttered with signals. Everything with an aura transmits psychic energy. Me. You. The rabbits. The birds. Even plants. What the diviners detect are bursts of concentrated psychic energy."

"Felix, the closer we get to Fajada Butte, the clearer the answers are supposed to get. But look at what we have in this crazy-ass bitch of a mystery." Jolie counted on her fingers. "Psychic energy. That murderous wench, Phaedra. Vampire assassins. A super-secret government contractor."

"And Carmen in outer space."

"Yeah, that." Visibly exasperated, she brandished one hand, all five fingers extended. "Is there anything else?"

"*Chale locita*, don't forget me." The voice surprised us from behind.

Talons and fangs extending, Jolie and I whipped about.

"Hey, *vatos*. 'Bout time you showed up." It was Coyote.

Chapter Five

Imagine a scrawny, mangy coyote. Imagine the tricky, thieving look in its eyes. Now turn that coyote into a human form.

That's Coyote.

The last time I saw him, back in Los Angeles, he had cleaned up his act—literally. With a haircut and a shave, a tailored dress shirt with pearl snaps, pressed jeans, Mexican cowboy boots. No surprise the reason for that transformation was an ex-porn star with J-cup breasts.

Now he appeared as I remembered him best, dressed like he'd stolen clothes from the Salvation Army and then scrambled through a barbed wire fence. A stained and tattered denim jacket over a threadbare plaid shirt, a pair of jeans even more ragged than his jacket, dirty cross trainers with his toes pushing through the sides. I'd have to ask him what had happened to his girlfriend with the big hooters.

A wispy mustache darkened his upper lip and a spot above his chin. Nubby hairs poked from his jaw. He adjusted a frayed baseball cap so that it sat farther back on his head. His complexion resembled the leather in the pocket of an old catcher's mitt.

I removed my sunglasses and studied his aura. The glowing orange sheath bubbled serenely like the liquid in a lava lamp.

Coyote was over five hundred years old. The bastard son of a Jewish conquistador (on the lam in the New World from the Inquisition) and Doña Marina a.k.a. La Malinche—the indigenous maiden who became Hernán Cortés' interpreter, advisor, and concubine—Coyote considered himself the very first Mexican.

His dark, almost black, eyes reflected a wariness and cunning from being on the lookout for centuries, always suspect and so hunted like his animal namesake.

"So you're Coyote?" Jolie asked.

"All day and tomorrow, *chiquita*."

She tilted her head. "Where the fuck did you come from?"

"I knew you'd be here." He walked between us toward the tower.

Jolie stepped close behind him. "You didn't answer my question."

"There are more important things to know." He began stamping his foot around the base of the tower.

"What are you doing?" I asked.

He rapped a knuckle against the steel pole and it echoed hollow. "These things have a sigmoidoscope inside."

Sigmoidoscope? I was surprised he could pronounce all the syllables. "You mean like for a colonoscopy?"

Coyote halted and stared at me, the shine in his eyes dulling with confusion. Blobs in his aura formed into question marks. His ability to manipulate his aura was one of his many tricks.

"Felix means an up-your-butt examination," Jolie explained.

The creases around Coyote's eyes deepened when he grinned. "A butt check?" He thumped the tower again. "With one of these? You're a funny guy, *ese*. Kind of freaky but that's your business." The question marks turned into exclamation points then dissolved back into random blobs.

"Then what are you—"

"An earthquake detector *chingadera*." He returned to stamping around the tower.

"A seismograph?"

Coyote rolled his eyes at Jolie. "Now he gets it. That's what I said." He chuckled and whispered to himself. "Butt check. *Que pendejadas.*"

Now I was confused. Jolie shrugged and gave me a WTF look.

Coyote started down the slope toward the Porsche. Jolie and I trotted after him.

"Are those towers earthquake detectors?" She sounded disappointed.

"No *chica*. They are exactly what you think they are."

Jolie shot me a second WTF look.

"Get used to it," I said.

Coyote reached the Porsche. He stuck his head through the driver's window. He sniffed and bent lower. Jolie and I watched him inhale deeply as if he was taking in the aroma of a fragrant flower. Pleasure sparked through his aura. He straightened and turned to Jolie. "This is where you sat."

She crossed her arms and tapped one foot. Her aura crackled with the same annoyance that matched her tight frown. The low angle of the afternoon sun cut into my eyes and I put my sunglasses back on.

Coyote craned his neck to check out the owner of the Porsche, still unconscious in the backseat. Coyote licked his lips. "Shame to waste all that blood. Oh well."

He crossed his arms and blinked *I-Dream-of-Jeannie* style. The trunk popped open. He chuckled. "And they say you can't learn nothing from the television."

Jolie and I were so rushed to get to Fajada Butte that we hadn't examined the trunk. It contained matching Gucci luggage in masculine black leather with gold trim—two suitcases and a wheeled carry-on.

A briefcase that I had gone through before sat on the front seat. Didn't contain much of interest. Business papers. A laptop with porn.

Coyote unzipped the carry-on and told Jolie and me to search the suitcases.

I ran my hand through suits and trousers. "What are we looking for?"

He stuffed socks inside his jacket. "Whatever looks worth keeping."

"The driver has a nice watch...."

Coyote already had the gold Rolex on his wrist. And wore the Texan's Ray-Bans.

Jolie held up a box of Trojans and rattled a prescription bottle of Cialis. "The guy wears a wedding ring. What makes me think he wasn't on the way to see his wife?"

"These?" I showed her a pair of banana hammocks—one in red satin and the other in gold lamé.

She winced and shut her eyes. "I'm getting a visual of that Texan that I don't need."

Coyote snatched the underwear from my hand. "No time for fooling around." He shoved both man panties into his pocket. Now I was getting a visual I didn't need.

"Now we go." Coyote left the car and proceeded up the hill for a moment before stopping to address me. "Hey, you owe me money."

I didn't but so what as far as Coyote was concerned. Hint that you might spring him a few bills and he'd turn that offer into an ironclad debt. I handed him the $320 I had lifted from the Texan's wallet.

"I was expecting more but thanks anyway, *ese*. I know you're good for the rest." He folded the bills and slipped them down the front of his pants. He patted where he'd just stashed the money. "Give the old lady a reason to go treasure hunting."

"More like salvage diving," Jolie quipped. She put her pistol holsters and jacket on.

I stuffed whatever of mine I could fit into the pockets of my jacket—some makeup, contacts, spare ammo. The rest—including Jolie's fancy-ass motorcycle helmet—we left in the car.

Jolie and I hustled to catch up with Coyote.

She asked, "Where are we going?"

"Away from here."

She turned to me. "Is he always this talkative?"

"He's a real chatterbox today." I threw a regretful glance back to the forlorn Porsche. What remained of its sleek lines was covered in dust and scratches, the high-performance wheels mired in the sand, and the trunk gaped open with clothes and luggage spilling out. The poor car looked like I felt after a bad weekend.

Jolie's initial dose of amnesia enzymes had wiped clean the driver's memory from the moment before he met her, and the pleasure enzymes we had pumped into him during our feeding had kept his mind blank of everything but pleasant dreams.

"What about the driver?" Jolie asked.

Coyote waved off her concern. "Somebody will come by tomorrow morning. They'll take care of him. *Gabachos* get lost around here all the time."

We continued up the rise and past the towers. Jolie and I marched along in graceless un-vampiric steps across the uneven, hardscrabble ground and its checkerboard patches of wickedly thorny plants. As bad as the washboard road had been, at least it was a defined trail through this desert wilderness.

Jolie halted to pick cholla spines out of her pants. "Coyote, how far are we walking?"

"Not far. I got a ride."

Out here? But he sounded confident and I wanted to believe him.

We wandered around outcroppings and cactus, down and up dips and reached the crest. Looking across the reverse side, I saw clusters of piñon, scrub oak, and juniper following the edges of a shallow gully.

Coyote slid down a steep narrow wash to the gully floor and into the shadows beneath the trees. Jolie and I followed him, our asses bumping over rocks and broken sticks. Once at the bottom, I noticed that something shifted ahead, rustling branches and tearing shrubs. Coyote continued straight to the source of the noise.

It was a little burro hitched with a frayed sisal rope to the branch of an oak. The small beast placidly chewed buffalo grass and twitched its ears at our approach. The remainder of the rope had been knotted into a bridle and reins.

"This is Rayo." Coyote stroked the burro's neck and loosened the rope from the branch.

"Means lightning," I explained to Jolie.

The burro's withers were almost at my waist, meaning Rayo was small for a pack animal. Coyote grasped the reins, put an arm around the burro's neck, and whipped a leg over. He adjusted his posture and sat straight. The toes of his cross trainers almost touched the ground. The burro-Coyote combo looked top heavy but Rayo didn't seem to mind. He just kept munching the grass and twitching his ears.

I looked to the other trees and didn't see any more burros. "You said we had a ride."

"I said *I* had a ride. Attention to detail, *ese*." Coyote gestured to the shrubs around us. "So unless you two find a couple of burritos of your own, you better keep walking." He tugged on the reins, pointing Rayo in the direction we had been hiking, and clucked. The little burro lurched into a quick rhythmic gait. Coyote rode with his elbows up and head bobbling on his neck.

Jolie exhaled a deep, regretful sigh. "Our quest to save Carmen from the aliens and stop Phaedra has come to this. Mr. Third World on a donkey."

We jogged after Coyote. He led us on a path that meandered around and under the trees, where we had to pick our way past low branches, cactus, and spiny weeds.

"Going forward will be easier if we either follow the middle of the gully or the ridgeline." Jolie said this loud so Coyote couldn't ignore her pissed-off lilt.

But he acted like he hadn't heard her. Instead, every few minutes he would check the Texan's Rolex, which was interesting since I thought he seldom cared if it was morning or afternoon, yesterday or today.

"You late for an appointment?" Jolie asked, still sounding pissed.

"Me?"

"There another vampire on a burro checking his watch?"

Coyote tugged on the reins and halted. He panned the gully. "Not that I can see." He flicked the reins and Rayo went back to his trot.

We kept on. Coyote's obsession with checking the time made me read my watch as well. It seemed we'd been hiking over this God forsaken terrain for hours but it had been only forty minutes. A low rhythmic drone echoed toward us. Coyote popped the reins and shouted, "*Vamonos*, Rayo."

The little burro bolted into the middle of the gully, Coyote's arms, legs, and head bouncing like they were held together with loose springs. He yelled over his shoulder. "Stay under the trees."

The drone grew loud and became the sound of rotor blades and turbine engines. Coyote continued into the gully, the burro high-stepping over the sand.

Jolie grabbed my arm and hauled me under a thick growth of branches. She swiveled her head to pinpoint the approaching sound, looking alert and wary as a hunted wolf.

The noise echoed louder and an instant later, a UH-60 Blackhawk zoomed into view high and to our right. The black helicopter swerved when the crew must've spotted Coyote and it entered a banking descent over the gully.

Coyote acted oblivious to the approaching aircraft. Its cargo doors were open, and men in tactical uniforms—Kevlar helmets, armored vests, cargo pants bloused into combat boots, ammo pouches and radios and holsters strapped to their legs and torsos—stood on platforms behind the wheels. They carried M4 carbines equipped with grenade launchers. A sensor turret under the nose of the Blackhawk rotated toward Coyote. A red laser shot from the turret and locked onto him.

Chapter Six

The UH-60 circled like a shark sniffing its prey, descending, slowing to hover beside Coyote and his burro. The laser remained locked on him.

The helicopter was a dark, almost black green. I couldn't read any markings on the fuselage or tail. The laser went out and the helicopter dropped low enough to kick up a wall of dust that reduced Coyote and Rayo to dusky silhouettes.

At the instant the helicopter's wheels touched ground, three men bounded out and advanced on Coyote, carbines at the ready.

Jolie tensed and reached to cross draw her pistols. Against her, the crew from the helicopter had little chance. Against the both of us, they had none. But when the helicopter had appeared, Coyote had ridden into the open and ordered Jolie and me to stay under cover. So I had to trust that he knew what he was doing. I grasped Jolie's elbow and hauled her down and behind a juniper.

The men drew close to Coyote. One of them gestured—the leader no doubt, asking questions. Coyote waved a hand. The three men froze for an instant, then turned for the UH-60 and boarded. The pilot cranked the engines to maximum volume, and the helicopter hopped upward in a tornado of dust and sand.

Jolie and I waited for the helicopter to disappear over the rim of the gully before we ran to Coyote. He spit dirt and Rayo hacked cartoony puffs of dust.

"What was that about?" I brushed sand from Coyote's shoulders.

He removed his dust-smeared sunglasses, revealing clean circles around his eyes. "They were listening, *ese*. When I stamped my feet around the tower, they heard."

The seismograph in the tower. When Coyote disturbed the dirt around its base he had triggered a signal.

"Why would they use a seismograph? Wouldn't it be easier to mount a camera on the tower?"

Coyote put his hands in front of his eyes like he was holding binoculars. "Maybe they *were* watching."

I thought back to Coyote's insistence that we leave the Porsche and his constant checking the time on his stolen Rolex. "You were timing the arrival of the helicopter, weren't you?"

Coyote winked. "Say *vato*, you might yet get a gold star."

Jolie palmed one of the .45s and kept her eyes on the horizon. "What did those guys ask about?"

Coyote shrugged. "A little of this, a little of that."

"What did you tell them?"

Coyote waved his hand like he'd done with the men and mimicked Alec Guinness doing Obi-Wan Kenobi. "These are not the droids you are looking for."

"A Jedi mind trick?"

"More like an old Indian trick. From an old *indio*. Me."

"I thought you were Mexican."

"If you're Mexican you're part Indian. And part Spaniard. Part eagle. Dog. Snake. Parts from whatever no one else wants." Coyote put his sunglasses back on. They were now immaculately clean.

"Who does the helicopter belong to?"

"You know."

I was about to answer that I didn't, then remembered the towers were property of Cress Tech International.

Jolie must've been thinking the same thing because she said, "That's nuts. Why are such heavily armed guards from Cress Tech protecting those towers? This is public land."

Coyote tugged the burro's reins and urged the animal forward. "Too many questions. *Soy muy cansado* and I want to get home. Come along unless you want to spend the night out here."

We hustled through the gully. Coyote rode with his head and shoulders drooping. The toes of his shoes hung low enough to snag the creosote and grass, and I expected to see him eventually tumble off the burro.

The sky darkened, azure to indigo. Long shadows fell over us, and the air-cooled. We put away our sunglasses and used vampiric night vision to pick our way through the gloom. Critters dashed around us, their tiny bodies swaddled in glowing auras.

The walls of the gully flattened and we ran in the open toward a mesa a quarter of mile to the west. The sky became velvet black and set off the brilliance of the Milky Way that hung above like a sash of diamonds.

"Wonder which one of those is where we'll find Carmen?" Jolie pointed to the stars.

I scoped the celestial vista horizon to horizon. "Take your pick."

"Light from most stars is centuries old." Jolie dropped her arm and sighed as if humbled by the majesty of the heavens. "Even the closest, Proxima Centauri, is over four light years away."

"You an amateur astronomer?"

"I've been thinking a lot about Carmen."

The sadness in the mumbled reply told me that Jolie loved Carmen with more depth and in a way that I never did. My thoughts about Carmen pivoted around the guilt I carried for not preventing the aliens from kidnapping her. But more than guilt that gnawed at me. I felt incomplete without her, and that loss would never begin to heal as long as I suspected she was alive.

Coyote halted the burro. "You want to know where to find Carmen?" Without raising his head, he lifted an arm and jabbed his index finger to the Milky Way about midway above the horizon. "A planet orbiting that star."

Jolie and I stared at the spot, unable to pick out one star from the dazzling cluster.

"You sure about that?" I asked.

"*Vato*, I've never been more sure of anything in my long *chingada vida*." He lowered his arm and jerked his legs to spur the burro forward.

It had been years since I'd been under a sky so dark and yet so bright with stars. I began thinking about my immortality. Theoretically, I could outlive any star. In fact, I could be walking this same ground long after our sun had gone super nova, boiled the oceans, and then cooled into a big cinder. The thought depressed me. What would be the point of living on a big empty rock?

Maybe none of us were supposed to survive that long. The end, when it came, no matter how gruesome, would be a welcome escape from a bleak and far more terrible future. Better to die fighting than waste away twiddling our thumbs into infinity.

Pondering what lay on the other side of forever made my head hurt. I pulled my mind back and set it to scan the landscape for signs of trouble and pick at the knot of questions around the task to rescue Carmen and stop Phaedra.

How were Jolie and I going to get to that planet? Who held Carmen prisoner? Would they simply let her walk away? How were we to return home? And once all that happened, how would we defeat Phaedra? When was Coyote going to clue us in?

We reached the mesa. Coyote and his burro stutter-stepped over a narrow path that wound up the cliff. Jolie and I followed along the tight switchbacks. The hard-packed dirt often crumbled beneath our feet and we scrambled to avoid sliding over cactus and sharp rocks. The trail dead-ended at the bottom of a steep, sandy wash.

I expected Coyote to stop the burro, thinking he might have taken a wrong turn.

Instead, the burro scaled the trough as if that ground was level pavement and the rest of the world was at an angle. Coyote could walk up the pitched slope using vampiric levitation, but not Rayo. Unless he was a supernatural creature.

"Is Rayo a shape-shifter?" I asked. "Maybe one of the local skin walkers?"

Coyote muttered, "*Vato*, if you had the power to change shape, would you turn into a burro and let me ride you?"

"Maybe Rayo lost a bet."

The burro chuffed and brayed.

Coyote stroked its neck. "You insulted him, *ese*. Rayo takes pride in his work. He's a better burro than most people are human."

Jolie and I planted our feet in the wash and stepped upward. The long day and the anxiety stressed my kundalini noir, and I found myself straining to reach the top.

Coyote and Rayo stepped over the rim and out of view. Jolie beat me to the top and waited.

Once I climbed out of the wash and onto the mesa, I sniffed a desert breeze scented with grilled onions, peppers, corn, and goat meat. Add some Type B Positive and I'd be a happy vampire.

Tiny yellow squares—the windows of a distant home—beckoned along the rim of the mesa. A feather of smoke twisted from the squat dwelling.

The trail followed the rim of the mesa. To our right sprawled the valley west of Chaco Canyon, a carpet of dull grays and beiges blurred together. Way to the south, tiny points of light crawled along the service road.

We approached the dwelling. Two adobe structures sat on either side of a doublewide. A wire fence enclosed a yard behind the closest adobe building. Chickens clucked inside a coop. Goats bleated. A wooden fence surrounded a second yard behind the doublewide. Scrub, junipers, and a few scraggy cedars grew across the mesa on the far side of the buildings.

A mongrel hound barked but didn't advance beyond the circle of light cast by a bare bulb above the front door of the doublewide. Wise dog. The high desert had all kinds of predators—coyotes, mountain lions, and wolves—that would snack on its canine hide.

"What's this place?" Jolie asked.

"Home," Coyote grumbled.

"You don't seem too pleased about it."

A long trek across the wilderness. Getting accosted by a helicopter and its crew of goons. If this was my home, I'd be glad to be on familiar turf.

A voice slithered through the gloom, sounding eerie and forbidding, even to me, an undead bloodsucking killer.

"*Donde estan mis hijos?*"

Any kid with a drop of Mexican blood recognized the cry. It was *La Llorona*, the ghost woman who had drowned her children and who now prowled rivers, streams, and lakes for victims. She'd lure you into the water and drown you, hoping to trade your soul for those of her lost children.

What was La Llorona doing up here, so far away from water?

She cried out again, her piercing voice now closer and louder.

Coyote yelled back. "Okay mom, I heard you. Shut up already."

Chapter Seven

Coyote's mother? The feared La Llorona?

Two auras materialized in the distance, about halfway to the houses at the far rim of the mesa. One was roughly the size of a human woman. The other was shaped ... well, like something definitely not human. Their auras floated like glowing blobs, fluctuating colors: red to orange to yellow to green to blue to indigo to violet and then back through the spectrum.

Every living creature emits an aura, and the color reveals where the creature manifests its psychic awareness. The red chakra resides at the base of the spine and shows a preoccupation with material concerns. The orange resides in the sacral plexus and shows a connection from the material to the psychic world. The other chakras continue up the spine and through the head. Yellow is transformation. Green, compassion. Blue, inspiration. Indigo, illumination. Violet, oneness with the universe.

Humans, not surprisingly, have a red aura. We vampires exist on the orange plane as do most supernatural creatures. Werewolves flicker between red and orange. I've only met a few creatures with a yellow aura, extraterrestrials among them. And only one creature with a green aura, a forest dryad I'd had an affair with and who was later murdered by another vampire. But this was the first time I've ever seen a creature whose aura not only reached the rare indigo and violet chakras but also cycled through their aura colors like lights on a theater marquee.

Coyote and his burro continued to lead us forward. Spikes of anxiety poked from the penumbra of his orange aura. Rayo's aura remained a steady red.

I nodded to the one shaped like a woman. "That's your mom?"

"Unfortunately," groaned Coyote.

"What's that thing with her?"

"You'll see."

If Coyote's mother could shift her psychic awareness to the violet plane, then she must be an incredibly spiritual creature. But that didn't square with her reputation as La Llorona. Someone that enlightened wouldn't spend her free time drowning strangers.

She cried out again, and goose bumps returned to my arms.

Jolie sidled close. "What's going on?"

I explained about La Llorona.

"And she's Coyote's mom? She drowned him?"

Coyote had once briefly given me the lowdown of his life. "Not that I know."

Jolie said, "I thought Coyote's mom was La Malinche."

"That too."

"But she drowned her kids?"

"I don't think so. History says La Malinche had a daughter and another son. They would've been step-siblings to Coyote though I'm sure they never knew each other. Besides acting as Cortes' booty call, she was also his translator and was a big reason the Spaniards got the drop on the Aztecs. That's why in Mexico La Malinche is a synonym for traitor. In one myth, her punishment is being doomed to walk the earth as La Llorona."

"And the drowned kids?"

"A metaphor for the indigenous people she betrayed to the Conquistadores."

Jolie's aura sparked in annoyance. "Figures. Spanish men raped and pillaged Mexico, and it's an Indian woman who's pinned with the blame."

Our two parties halted, facing each other. Coyote introduced Jolie and me. La Malinche, La Llorona, whatever her name was, stood to our left. She looked petite and healthy considering she was over five centuries old. And between you and me, her delicate features—big shiny eyes rimmed with thick lashes, a well-proportioned nose, wide mouth with a plump lower lip—made her a real MILF. Much too pretty to be Coyote's mother. Or rather, Coyote was too homely to be her son. Her flowing dark hair and gauzy garments fluttered dramatically despite the calm air.

She stared at us, then at Coyote, then back at us, smiling awkwardly as if waiting for an introduction. Finally she frowned, "Coyote, where are your manners, *cabezon*?" She waved at Jolie and me. "I am Doña Marina."

Her companion resembled a velociraptor crossed with a gorilla—a lizard's snout, beady eyes, plenty of sharp teeth, long muscular arms with fearsome clawed hands. His crinkled metallic suit seemed to be made of faceted bits of pewter that undulated like they were connected with magnets. As a vampire, I was introduced to all kinds of weird shit.

He bowed. "*El Cucuy*."

I translated for Jolie. "The boogieman."

They stood at eye level.

"The boogieman?" Her brow knitted. "I thought you would be taller."

"I hear that a lot."

"How can you change your aura colors?" she asked.

Coyote's mother answered. "When you've lived as long as we have, you learn a few things." She made her aura glow like a stack of illuminated Lifesavers then fused the colors into a brilliant white light. Her aura dimmed to an orange that matched ours.

"Hmmm ... interesting," Jolie remarked. "What should I call you? Doña Marina? I'm not fond of either La Malinche or La Llorona."

Coyote's mother smiled. Her aura flashed a pleasant green. "Marina is fine." She beckoned Jolie close. "What a nice girl you are. *Mijo*," Marina said to Coyote, "you could learn from her. Some class for starters."

Coyote spurred the burro forward. "*Vamanos*, Rayo. Let's go find some tequila and forget we have family."

Marina braided her arm with Jolie's, and they walked together. "I bet a girl like you doesn't drink tequila." Marina's voice rose as she said this, obviously for Coyote's benefit.

Jolie's aura bubbled, the equivalent of a blush. Marina acted as if she didn't notice. Truth was, I've seen Jolie drink enough tequila in one sitting to drown the Mexican navy.

"Hey *mijo*," Marina said, "it's a long walk back to the house."

"Mom," he replied wearily, "you want to ride the burro?"

"No. But you could've asked."

"I never ask because you never say yes."

"See what I put up with up?" Yellow spines covered Marina's aura. "What is the greater shame? Being cursed as La Llorona or enduring the pain of such a thoughtless son?"

A plume extended from Coyote's aura, fashioned itself into an out-sized pistol, and shot him in the head. The plume dissolved into confetti and disappeared.

El Cucuy and I fell in behind Jolie and Marina. He leaned toward me and whispered, "Awkward."

Marina looked over her shoulder at me. "You're here to help Coyote?"

"I am, though I'm not sure how."

"He's very scared by this," she whispered, "but don't tell him I said so."

Coyote flicked the reins and made Rayo trot ahead.

"I don't know what 'this' is," I said.

"*This* has to do with Fajada Butte," Marina replied. "That's all I know."

"We're here because of a war."

"As if that's a surprise. Tell me when there is no war."

"A vampire war."

"How does that change anything? One side killing another."

"You're talking like we wished for this trouble. If we don't fight, we'll be annihilated. Maybe you as well."

"I don't think so." Her body and aura shrank to a point of light and disappeared. I blinked and searched the darkness. A moment later, a tiny light appeared to our right and grew into a column of flame. A figure materialized inside the fire. Marina.

"Very Biblical," Jolie offered, "but probably not much good against Phaedra."

"Why does it have to be Coyote?" Marina's pleading voice sounded like any mother who grieved as a child marched off to battle. Even the ugly ones.

"Why does it have to be any of us?" I answered.

Jolie pointed at El Cucuy. "What's your business in this war?"

He raised his hands and shook them. "Keep me out of this. I'm only here to keep Marina company."

We reached the doublewide. A rust-colored cur—a dust mop on legs—lunged at Coyote, barking and wagging its tail.

He reached for the dog. "Che, come here."

"Che?" I asked. "Odd name for a dog."

"Why, *vato*? What else could I name him? He's a red dog."

The door opened. A woman appeared in silhouette behind a screen door. Red aura. Human. Hair cut short and spiky. She stepped barefoot onto the small wooden porch and propped the screen door against her plump hip. "You finally made it, slowpoke," she said to Coyote.

He introduced Jolie and me. She was his girlfriend. Rainelle Tewa.

"You're Felix?" she asked. "The one with Coyote's money?"

I gave him the stink eye.

Rainelle was a stocky woman and on the busty side, though she was hardly the over-endowed queen that was Coyote's last *amante*. She was dark skinned. Round face with almond eyes. A patchwork dress and bangles on her wrists made her look especially Hopi Bohemian. I wondered if Rainelle was Coyote's chalice but she didn't wear a scarf or a collar that would've identified her as a vampire's feedbag.

She hip-checked the door and held it wide. "You guys come inside. Doña Marina," she said to Coyote's mom, "you want to join us?"

She replied no.

"Cucuy?"

"I'll hang out with her. We need to practice scaring people."

Marina eased into the night, her aura dimming as she screeched, "*Donde estan mis hijos?*"

El Cucuy sauntered beside her and howled, "Bleah! Boo! Booga! Booga!"

Coyote rode Rayo into the pen around the first adobe building, let the burro loose with the dog, and returned. He stepped through the door and Rainelle scolded him. "Wipe your feet."

"You're sounding like my mother."

"Then you should listen to her."

The doublewide creaked and shifted as we entered through a tiny kitchen. Every doublewide I'd ever been in had a unique odor, and this one was no different. A greasy cooking smell clotted the air.

Second-hand furniture—a threadbare sofa, chipped and battered chairs, bookcases sagging with knickknacks, a coffee table covered in rings from the bottoms of cups—crowded the worn carpet of a living room lined with fake-wood vinyl paneling.

A heavy-set man filled a wingback chair like a hermit crab in its shell. He had ruddy, peeling skin and bushy Elvis sideburns. A Peterbilt trucker's cap. A turquoise bolo tie with a Zia sun cinched the collar of a western shirt. His eyelids drooped, and his head bobbed to whatever tune played through the earbuds that climbed like a vine from the pocket of his canvas vest. Coyote didn't introduce him—or us—and up close, the guy reeked of peyote.

Jolie sat next to me on the sofa.

Rainelle brought a baking pan covered with a dishtowel and set it on the coffee table. She made more trips and brought soup bowls filled with grilled cobs of corn, sliced peppers, onion, and chunks of goat meat.

Coyote slapped the trucker's knee with a length of thin copper tubing. The trucker cracked his eyelids, loosened his bolo tie, and spread his shirt collar to bare his neck. He tilted his head to one side.

Coyote gestured that Jolie bring one of the bowls. He spit on one end of the tubing and screwed it into the trucker's neck. He held the other end of the tube over the bowl. Blood flowed out the tubing like a thick sauce and drenched the food. My bowl was next. Rainelle held the last bowl for Coyote.

When his bowl was filled, Coyote popped the tube from the trucker's neck, then licked his thumb and mashed it over the hole. Vampiric enzymes would heal the wound. He sucked out the blood remaining in the tube. A moment later he pulled his thumb from the trucker's neck, and the wound had scabbed over.

The trucker raised one hand and rubbed his fingertips together.

Coyote looked at me and pointed to the hand.

I pulled out my wallet and slapped two fifties into the trucker's palm. First time that I'd ever paid a chalice.

He stuffed the money into a vest pocket, pulled a pair of sunglasses from another pocket, and put them on. He settled into the chair and resumed bobbing his head.

The blood steamed in our bowls. Rainelle uncovered the pan to offer loaves of fry bread. She tore the bread into pieces and handed them to Jolie and me. "Hurry, eat, before it gets cold."

I slathered blood over a corncob like it was melted butter.

Jolie folded the meat and vegetables into the blood. "When do we start our mission to get Carmen?"

Coyote squeezed next to me on the sofa and shoveled a spoon into his bowl. A warm meal. Back at home. Back with his woman. He should've been content. But his aura percolated with dread.

"Tomorrow we'll visit Fajada Butte and I'll explain what you need to know."

Chapter Eight

We sopped the last bit of blood with fry bread and handed our empty bowls to Rainelle.

It was two in the morning, and our biorhythms were thoroughly messed up. As vampires, creatures of the night and all that, we're supposed to keep nocturnal hours. But we live among humans, and to get anything done, we have to abide by their day-job schedules. Venturing into the sunlight wears us out, and after a few days, vampires need to recuperate by sleeping during the day, preferably in a coffin.

Coyote said we were welcome to crash in his doublewide, as if we had much choice. He and Rainelle slept in the master bedroom. The second bedroom was stuffed with a pirate's booty of clothes, footwear (many still in boxes), small appliances (some also in boxes), and electronics.

That left the living room with the trucker-chalice passed out on the armchair. His rosy-red aura pulsed so serenely it could've purred. Jolie called dibs on the sofa, which left me the carpet. Rainelle brought pillows and blankets, all marked with the Motel 6 logo. Jolie and I stripped to our skivvies. She folded those muscular shanks of hers under a blanket, then shoved her .45s under a pillow. I tucked my magnum under mine.

With every snore, the trucker-chalice ratcheted down the armchair until his ass scooted off the edge of the cushion, leaving the nape of his neck hooked on the seat back.

Jolie and I tried our best to ignore his snoring until we could no longer stand his loud-as-a-chainsaw rumblings. At the same instant, we bolted to our feet and each of us grabbed one of his arms. We hauled him to the door of the living room. I kicked it open. We pitched the trucker-chalice off the porch onto a stack of hay bales, where he collapsed like a broken marionette, still snoring and smacking his lips.

The cool night air beckoned for vampiric mischief. But we had a long day tomorrow so we closed the door and lay down to sleep.

Early in the morning, Rainelle woke me as she padded through the living room. I lay on the floor and watched her pull the curtains tight so no outside light could peek through.

Coyote must have taught her the precautions needed to protect us vampires. It was at dawn that the sun's rays were at their deadliest and even the thickest layers of sunscreen weren't much help. The best protection was to remain indoors with the windows covered by thick opaque curtains, behind which us brave monsters hid like trapdoor spiders.

I glanced at my watch. Still another hour until dawn. I pulled the blanket over my head and went back to sleep.

It seemed like a moment later when something hit me. "Hey, *ese.*" Coyote was tapping my shoulder with his shoe. "Get up."

Yawning, I curled upright and smelled coffee brewing. Jolie sat on the sofa, moist hair pinned back, and was busily applying a foundation of Dermablend. My watch read 9:42 a.m., well into the safe zone of morning.

Coyote set cups of black coffee and a creamer with goat's blood on the coffee table. Rainelle offered fry bread fresh out of the toaster.

Jolie asked Coyote about his mom.

He snorted dismissively. "It'll be another hour before she comes home. Probably doing the Walk of Shame."

Jolie quirked an eyebrow at me. *With El Cucuy?*

I shrugged. *None of our business.*

After breakfast, Jolie visited the second bedroom and sorted through the clothes. She traded her leather touring pants for jeans and her motorcycle boots for a pair of cross trainers. But she kept her Joe Rocket jacket. Gotta look badass.

A half hour later she and I were bouncing in the bed of a battered Ford 150. Slathered in sunscreen. Sunglasses on. Pistols cleaned, oiled, and loaded. Extra ammo in our pockets. With Rainelle at the helm, the pickup clattered toward the rim of the mesa. Coyote sat next to her, his window open and the breeze batting his collar and the ragged strands of hair that poked from under his ball cap. The Rolex glittered on his thin wrist, and the over-sized Ray-Bans on his bony, dark face made him look like an emaciated fly.

The sky was an unspoiled blue. I breathed the fragrant sage and the homey smell from wood fires. Our problems seemed distant, and I wondered if it would be a crime if we played hooky from saving the world.

We passed a line of fence posts made of discarded car bumpers and drive shafts. The pickup dropped off the edge of the mesa onto a road steep as an Olympic toboggan run. Rainelle jiggled the steering wheel and kept us on course—barely—as we caromed down the slope. I was almost pitched out and Jolie clutched my arm. Seconds later, I returned the favor. I comforted myself by hoping this ride might be the most dangerous leg of today's journey.

I caught Rainelle checking her hair in the rearview. For her, this suicide drop was just another day at the ranch.

At the bottom of the hill, the road forked with a trail that meandered over the rolling, open ground. Rainelle gunned the engine and followed the bumpy trail. The truck shook so hard I was certain it was going to fall apart, and Jolie and I were tossed about like ping-pong balls in a raffle cage.

Miles later, Rainelle ran out of trail and halted on the top of a shallow hill. Even with a 4x4, this desert would murder anything on wheels. Coyote climbed out, as did Jolie and I, grateful for steady earth beneath our feet. Our destination, Fajada Butte, loomed miles ahead, a wrinkled truncated thumb rising from the desert floor. With a wave, Rainelle shifted into reverse, swung the truck between two cactuses, ground the gears, and rumbled away.

Jolie took off her sunglasses and polished the lenses with her t-shirt. She put them back on and faced Coyote. "Now you're going to tell us how we're going to get Carmen?"

"No point to it." He started walking, all sharp angles and baggy clothes, like an animated scarecrow. "Not until we get to the butte."

Jolie and I fell in step behind him. She asked, "If this is so goddamn important, why don't you fill in the details?"

He didn't answer and started to trot.

I asked, "Where's your burro?"

"Rayo's on sabbatical, *ese*."

We jogged over rocks and crusted sand, but Fajada Butte didn't appear to be getting any closer. The sun rose directly overhead, and its autumn light beamed on us bright and barely warm.

A thirst itched my throat, and I realized that none of us had brought water or blood. Unless Coyote knew of a stash of hemoglobin, we were in for long, miserable foray through this wilderness.

A rumble echoed across the openness. The sky was too clear for the sound to be thunder. The rumble deepened and grew into a menacing *thump, thump, thump*.

Helicopter.

At any moment, I expected to see another Blackhawk pop over the horizon. Not sure of how to react, I took my cue from Coyote, and he continued, unconcerned.

Jolie swiveled her head to get a bearing on the noise.

A rotor disk climbed from behind a hill to our left. The disk rose and lifting beneath it appeared the transmission hump, then the engine pods, then a helicopter big as a locomotive. A gigantic CH-53 Sea Dragon roared straight for us.

Another glance at Coyote. He kept jogging, and so did we.

The immense helicopter cruised at a hundred feet in altitude and at a slow, even speed, maybe thirty miles an hour. Long lattice booms stuck from each side of the fuselage. Each boom was tipped with a large psychotronic diviner that slewed left and right in a steady, synchronized tempo.

The Sea Dragon gained on us. The ground trembled. The aircraft grew huge and terrifyingly loud, a twenty-ton storm cloud of metal and noise.

Its crew remained hidden behind the canopy, and I didn't see anyone leaning out a side window. The helicopter was the same color as the Blackhawk from yesterday, a green so dark that the machine seemed to be in shadow no matter what angle you looked at it. A sensor turret on the chin made jerky movements to lock on each of us as if taking snapshots.

The Sea Dragon roared overhead and blotted out the sun. Its shadow flashed across the ground. Rotorwash swept the dirt. I tipped my head and covered my face. When I looked back up, the helicopter was receding from us, its shadow hurdling over the ground beneath it.

Jolie brushed dust from her face and jacket. She shouted to Coyote. "What the hell was that about?"

He didn't break stride or reply.

Jolie picked up a rock, threw it, and it ricocheted by his feet. "Hey, I'm talking to you."

Coyote kept his pace at a relentless trot.

Jolie picked up another rock, then dropped it. "Why is he such an asshole?" She turned to me. "What do you think is going on?"

"I'm guessing Cress Tech."

"What was the helicopter doing?"

"A survey of some kind. Didn't you notice the strange equipment hanging out the sides of the fuselage?"

"Survey? For what?"

"Something psychic."

"Is that a guess?"

"Pretty much."

"Don't know about you," she replied, "but I don't like risking my ass for a bunch of goddamn guesses."

"Me either. But it seems somebody, and by that somebody I mean Uncle Sam, is paying Cress Tech buttloads of money to do psychic research here. First the towers with the psychotronic diviners, then the armed helicopter response team. The chopper that just flew by is the biggest one in the Navy inventory and keeping it in the air ain't cheap."

The CH-53 shrank into the distance. The appearance of the big helicopter made me consider worrisome thoughts.

Human awareness of the psychic world was limited to glimpses revealed in dreams, synchronicity, premonitions, and out-of-body experiences—all fleeting and unreliable. Say the word psychic and most would reply with charlatan. Psychic phenomena remained as mysterious to us as electricity was to the Romans. But if the government unlocked the secrets of the psychic world, what then?

"You're being quiet," Jolie said. "What's on your mind?"

"Nothing good. Since I know humans all too well, I'm gonna say the military helicopters and heavily-armed guards pretty much cinches that the government takes the psychic world real seriously. Harnessing psychic power could be much like the invention of the electric light bulb, radar, computers. Once humans figure out how to access and control the psychic world, then the bean counters and lawyers will get to work."

"That's fucking scary," Jolie replied. "If that happens, then when you dream, expect to pay for access to the psychic plane like paying for an Internet connection, plus all the related bullshit. Paranormal pop-up ads. Subconscious spam."

She shaded her brow and scanned the horizon. A Cress Tech tower materialized in the distant haze.

"Remember Phaedra's sketches?" Jolie asked. We had found the drawings in her home soon after she'd disappeared. "She had drawn the psychic plane as an enormous room lined with doors. She could see and project her thoughts through those doors. What if it's possible for someone to physically travel through them?"

I answered, "Coyote did a lot of strange disappearing acts when we were together in Los Angeles. One time he opened my car door and dropped into traffic. I was sure he was gonna get trampled by the cars behind me, but when I looked back, he was gone."

Jolie turned towards me. Her eyebrows arched over the tops of her sunglasses.

"Later," I continued, "renegade vampires blew up Coyote's pickup—hoping to get me—and instead incinerated him. Or so I thought until three days later, when he showed up in the back seat of my car, famished and covered in soot. After mooching a meal and beer, he disappeared again." I snapped my fingers. "Just like that. I had looked away for a second and then he was gone, like he'd never been there. Nothing left except for discarded burrito wrappers and empty bottles of Löwenbräu."

"And don't forget Marina's disappearing act," Jolie added. She stared at Coyote. "So it's no wild leap to say they know how to transport through the psychic plane?"

I knew he was listening. I talked loud to engage him. "What worries me is what if the government also finds out how? I don't know much about psychic powers, but what I've seen scares the hell out of me."

"No shit," Jolie added. "Don't forget Phaedra's mind blasts."

Coyote stopped abruptly, faced us, and scowled. "You two *pendejos* sure talk a lot. And you're forgetting about another bunch of *culeros* fucking things up."

Jolie and I halted. *Who?*

"The aliens." Coyote scratched his crotch and resumed his run. "And you're right about me being in a hurry. *Vatos*, it's a race against catastrophe."

Jolie and I stared at Coyote as he trotted away. We were now close enough to Fajada Butte that against the horizon, the rocky formation looked as big as my fist.

I thought back to what he had just said. *Aliens.*

Great.

Or course I knew that at some point our operation involved the aliens. After all, they held Carmen captive.

But the whole *cabronada*—the aliens, Phaedra, and Cress Tech—pivoted around the psychic world.

About the only thing I could piece together—from my experience with Coyote's Houdini hocus-pocus—was that access to the psychic world might open shortcuts between points in deep space.

We reached the narrow dirt road we'd been on yesterday. Thin clouds of dust blossomed to the south and to the northeast. I wondered—but not too much—about what had happened to the Texan and his Porsche sedan.

We came across a barbed-wire fence with a placard from the National Park Service that warned against trespassing onto Fajada Butte. Coyote levitated to scale the wires like he was walking up steps and dropped to the other side. Jolie bent her knees and sprang over the fence as if her legs were super Pogo sticks. I followed Coyote's less athletic example.

He glanced to the sun, put his hand up as if to gauge the sun's height above the horizon, and then checked his Rolex. He started running with Jolie and me at his heels.

A quarter of a mile farther, we scrambled down Chaco Wash and up the other side. Fajada Butte loomed before us, imposing and portending mystic secrets, like another Mt. Sinai.

In Spanish, *fajada* means *banded*, and the eroded columns of stone that made up the face of the butte resembled a tall band or a girdle. A sloped skirt of dirt and rock circled its base. A lop-sided dome with a flat-topped crown topped the summit.

"How tall do you think?"

Jolie raised her sunglasses and squinted. "At least three hundred feet."

Coyote read his watch and ran faster. Jolie and I sped behind him.

We reached the bottom of the rocky slope and veered to the right around the southern side of the butte. Coyote picked up the pace. Normally his attention drifted like a leaf in the breeze, and it disturbed me to see him so focused. We were obviously on a schedule, but for what?

"Hey Coyote," Jolie blurted, "what exactly is the hur—"

I elbowed her and shook my head. *Don't bother.*

Coyote bounded over the rough ground and talus with the agility of his namesake. He paused at the bottom of the butte only long enough to again read his watch, then turned his ball cap around and shimmied up a crack between the hundred-foot-tall sandstone columns like a caffeinated lizard.

After the long hike I was ready for a break, but I wasn't going to let a wizened five-hundred-year-old vampire put me to shame.

Something smacked my head. It was Jolie using me for a springboard to leap high into the gap between another set of columns.

"C'mon, Felix. You're moving like an old man."

For humans, a free climb between the eroded sandstone columns would've been very dangerous but thanks to vampire levitation, we easily skittered upward.

Once above the columns, we scrambled up the rocky, rounded slope to a tall step of sandstone, climbed that and arrived at the base of the butte's crown. We were treated to a spectacular high-rise view of the basin—a sprawling blanket of beiges with stripes of olive and viridian—with Chaco Wash unwinding to the northwest and south, and the mesas to the east and north marbled in reds and grays. At the southern end of the wash where it curved around a mesa, the ancient Chaco Ruins looked like tiny, broken rectangles made of dirt.

Coyote didn't slow for sightseeing. He scampered toward the crown to approach three sandstone slabs set parallel and edgewise against the broad face of the rock wall. He cut another nervous glance to his Rolex.

He ducked into a shaded gap between the slabs and the wall, pointed to me, and beckoned with a quick pump of his arm.

I crouched beside him, Jolie looking over my shoulder.

Two spiral petroglyphs had been carved into the rock wall at waist level. The small one on the left was maybe four or five inches in diameter. The other was larger, at least a foot wide. Both carvings were well eroded and projected a prehistoric eeriness. A vertical blade of sunlight shining between the slabs sliced across the right side of the larger spiral.

Coyote pressed his hand against the center of the larger petroglyph and skipped his fingertips across the spiral grooves as if counting. He spread his hand and held it under the sliver of light, his palm flat against the rock. He looked at his watch and ordered, "Quickly, *vato*. Put your left hand on mine."

Confused by what he was doing, I hesitated. "What?"

He slapped his hand against the petroglyph. The light crept across the knuckle of his index finger. "Do it now!"

Extending my arm, I leaned over him and placed my hand over his.

He looked at Jolie. "We'll be right back."

Back from where?

The sliver of light draped across the back of my hand and warmed my skin. The light grew brighter, brighter still, and I blinked.

Coyote pushed up from under me. Cars honked all around us.

We were at the corner of a busy street and an interstate on-ramp.

Chapter Nine

I stood straight, paralyzed in disbelief. One second I was in New Mexico, on top of Fajada Butte. And the next ...

I took in the landmarks. An auto body shop straight ahead. A plain, rather ratty, two-story apartment building across the street. Behind me, the signs on the closest lamppost said: Van Nuys Boulevard, and Westbound Ramp for the Golden State Highway.

Pacoima, California.

California was where I had first met Coyote, in a parking garage not far from here. For an instant, it felt like the years between then and now had gone *poof*. An astonished glance at my watch told me that only minutes had passed since I last checked the time.

Coyote dropped his sunglasses into a chest pocket of his denim jacket. His tapetum lucidum glowed a supernatural red. I was about to offer a spare set of contacts to hide his vampire eyes when his irises miraculously dulled to a very human dark brown. His ball cap was still turned backwards and he rotated the cap by the bill to shade his face. "You hungry, *vato*?"

"Did you move us through the psychic plane?"

"Explanations later. Right now, let's eat. *Vamanos.*" He pimp-strolled up the sidewalk past the jumbled mosaic of commercial signs and storefronts that lined Van Nuys.

I took a hesitant step forward, still not convinced that the world around me was real. A low-rider blasting the percussive beats of *reggaeton* cruised by. The air reeked of car exhaust and warm asphalt. If I was imagining this, it was a pretty damn good dream. I eased into my stride and caught up with Coyote.

We passed a Catholic Church surrounded by an acre of parking lot. Then hoofed past mom-and-pop restaurants, nail salons, cell phone stores, fast food joints—the usual mishmash of American suburban sprawl.

At Laurel Canyon, we hustled across the street toward a *carneceria*-liquor store. A turquoise-colored awning shaded the front door, and an electronic buzzer announced our entrance. The air carried the heavy, humid smell of raw meat. Coyote headed through an aisle with shelves of canned beans and chili on the left and cases of beer on the right. A row of glass cases packed with ice and slabs of beef and pork lined the back wall. I stopped to replace my sunglasses with contacts.

A heavy-set man with a Pancho Villa mustache stood behind a case. He did a double take at our approach and hustled around the case toward us, his thick mitts wiping stains on a butcher's apron. "*Oye*, Coyote. Long time, *compa*."

When was Coyote last here?

"Yeah, I've been busy," he said.

The butcher lifted an eyebrow.

"*Tu sabes*," Coyote explained, "going here, going there. Gathering material for my novel."

Laughter rumbled in my gut, and I strained so hard to keep from guffawing that my belly hurt.

Coyote shot me an especially dirty stink-eye. He then introduced me to the butcher—Gustavo.

"Here for lunch, Coyote?" he asked.

Coyote smiled. "*Símon.*"

Gustavo backed up a step and plucked a receipt tacked to a corkboard. "First, you gotta settle up your tab. Nineteen fifty."

Coyote pointed to me. Having resigned myself to the fact that I'd become his personal ATM, I reached for my wallet. He asked, "How about two cups of boar's blood and six pork tamales?"

"The total then is thirty one *bolas*," Gustavo replied.

I counted out the bills. Gustavo took the money and disappeared through a swinging door into a back room. He returned with fresh tamales in a Ziploc bag and two Styrofoam cups with plastic lids.

Coyote took the receipt and mumbled something about "for tax purposes."

Gustavo bid us goodbye and tended to the customers queuing behind us. On the way out I bought a six-pack of ice-cold Carta Blanca.

I found a table around back between the service entrance and the Dumpster. After upending a couple of plastic crates to use as chairs, I brushed cigarette butts off the table. Couldn't say much about the ambience but we had privacy. Coyote pulled the tamales out of the Ziploc and stacked them on top. I shared the opener on my scout knife so we could crack open our beers.

"Isn't Gustavo suspicious that you're a vampire? Who else would order blood?"

"Nah. He just thinks I'm a little weird. Imagine that." Coyote guzzled a Carta Blanca.

"Start explaining how we got here." I removed the lid from my Styrofoam cup. Steam curled from the warm blood. I peeled the cornhusk from a tamale and dipped it in the blood. "You could've told me we were about to teleport."

"Don't tell, show. Right, *ese?*" A grin wormed onto his face. "That's something I've learned from writing my novel. Besides, if I would've told you, you wouldn't have believed me or understood how going from there to here works." While Coyote talked, he was chomping on his second tamale and starting another beer.

"I still don't understand, but I believe."

Coyote wiped blood from his chin and licked his fingers. His second beer was already a dead soldier. "Then we're halfway there."

"So you understand how this teleportation works?"

"*Claro.* Remember when you and Jolie were discussing Phaedra's drawing?" So Coyote had been eavesdropping.

I replied, "The one of a giant room lined with doors?"

He dunked a third tamale into his cup of blood. "What we just did was go from one door, across the psychic plane, and through another door."

I shucked my second tamale. "How did you know where we were going?"

He upended beer number three and chugged. He put the bottle down and burped. "I used the Sun Dagger."

"The petroglyph we put our hands on? That's its name?"

"Now. It's been called lots of things by lots of different people." Coyote returned to chewing, drinking, and swallowing.

"Then that petroglyph was a portal?"

Coyote shoved the last of his third tamale into his mouth. He chewed as he talked. "Portal?" He chuckled and spit bits of bloody tamale. "You've been watching too many scientific fiction movies."

"Then what would you call it?"

Coyote tipped the Carta Blanca to his lips and greedily emptied it. He set the bottle aside and grabbed a fourth and held it in his hands, his eyes focused faraway. He brought his attention to the present and shrugged. "Portal, I guess. It opens into a tunnel, *ese*. A tunnel that's always shifting through space. One end is on top of Fajada Butte and the other moving around."

I imagined the tunnels as wormholes, a darling topic of quantum mechanics and science fiction. I recalled that Coyote had kept referring to his watch before using the Sun Dagger. "And depending on the time, the other end opens to a different location?"

"You got it, bro." Coyote reached for the fifth Carta Blanca.

I snatched the bottle for myself. Since I had paid for lunch, I deserved at least two beers and two tamales to his four of each. "How do you know the schedule?"

"I got it figured out."

"And you'll show me?"

"In time."

"Why didn't we bring Jolie?"

"You know how it is when you bring a *ruca* along. I wanted this to be just us *vatos*." Coyote leaned into his chair and unbuckled his belt. He stuck both hands inside his pants and scratched. "You bring a girl and you gotta act Miss Manners and shit." He fastened his belt and sniffed his fingers. He grasped the last bit of my tamale. "You gonna eat this?"

"Not anymore."

He dipped the tamale into my cup of blood.

"You can have that too."

Coyote smiled. "Thanks, *vato*. You're a decent *camarada*." He munched the last of the tamale and slurped the remaining blood from both cups.

I cleared the table and pitched our trash into the Dumpster. Coyote started for the sidewalk.

A lot of questions still pinged in my head. "But you don't need a petroglyph to teleport. Remember the last time we were here? One time, you tumbled out of my car and disappeared. And the other time, when your truck was blown up, you vanished and then returned from wherever you had gone."

"Doors are everywhere. And I have the magic key right here." He tapped his temple and his fingertip gave a hollow metallic *thunk, thunk* against his skull.

"Then why did we need the Sun Dagger?"

"I didn't need the Sun Dagger. *You* needed the Sun Dagger."

Coyote's convoluted explanation tied my thoughts into knots. What I needed was another drink. Of something stronger than Mexican beer.

"How do we get back?"

"The same way we got here. Only backwards."

Did I say a drink? Make that many drinks. From a very large bottle.

Instead of walking south on Van Nuys toward our arrival point, we headed north. Cars and trucks rushed by.

Coyote suddenly pushed me off the sidewalk and into the path of a large delivery truck. A jolt of panic stung my nerves. I was just about to summon vampire speed to bound out of the way when he dove off the curb and slammed into my belly. I dropped backwards and pictured the truck squashing the both of us into the asphalt.

My shoulders hit sand and I sprawled under bright sunlight. Coyote stumbled past me. I lay on my back and stared past the edges of the sandstone slabs on Fajada Butte.

Jolie stepped close and looked down on me. "Where the hell have you guys been?"

I rolled to my feet and brushed dirt from my clothes. I wasn't as confused as I was angry.

Coyote braced an arm against one of the slabs and beamed a Cheshire Cat grin. "Like I told you. Backwards."

I looked back Jolie and said, "Pacoima."

She sniffed. "And you guys had lunch while I sat on this rock?"

I fanned my hands. "Don't yell at me, I didn't make the travel arrangements."

Coyote read his Rolex and said to Jolie, "Your turn." He ducked under the slab and crouched against the petroglyph.

She chuffed. "We better go someplace awesome." She saluted *sayonara* and joined Coyote.

I crouched to get a better look at them. "Where are you guys going?"

"Just hold down the fort, *ese*." Coyote put his hand where the beam of light sliced across the Sun Dagger. "We'll be back soon."

Jolie placed her hand over his. They dissolved into the wall, and a blink later, they were gone.

Even though I knew what to expect, I grimaced in amazement. *Holyfreakin'shit.*

Chapter Ten

Until Coyote and Jolie returned, I had nothing to do but study the view. I spotted the muted gleam of the Cress Tech towers facing the butte. The closest of the towers was at least a mile away and the sunlight reflecting off the psychotronic diviner on top made the device shine like a metal button in the dusty haze. I counted eleven towers in one arc to the west and five more in another arc to the east. The towers were placed about a half-mile apart. The two arcs could be just the start of a large circle that had yet to be filled in. By my guess a total of twenty-four towers would be needed to complete its circumference.

I mused over what Cress Tech was using the psychotronic diviners for. They detected psychic transmissions, and years ago I had used one to find Phaedra.

And these? Did they detect our teleportation through the Sun Dagger?

I thought about that as I sat in the shade and waited for Coyote and Jolie to return.

And waited. One hour. Two. Three.

Coyote and I had been gone half an hour. Where did he and Jolie go? What if they got stuck at their destination? Or were they caught in a supernatural traffic jam inside the psychic plane?

The sun dipped toward the western horizon, and a long shadow bled from the butte across Chaco Canyon.

I heard Jolie laughing. Then a snicker from Coyote. A tote bag full of clothes flew from between the stone slabs and landed beside me in the dirt. Both of them emerged from between the slabs. Jolie wore a lime-green bikini and pink flip-flops. She carried a plastic hurricane cup with a long bendy straw. Coyote still wore his same clothes and palmed a half-eaten hoagie in one hand and a tallboy of PBR in the other.

Jolie perched her sunglasses on her head. Her eyes sizzled with excitement. "That was fucking awesome." I could smell rum on her breath.

"The hell you go?" I asked.

She showed me the side of her cup where it said: Key West.

"We go to Pacoima," I grumbled to Coyote, "for a quick lunch. And you take Jolie for happy hour in Key West?"

Coyote replied through a mouthful of sandwich. "*Vato*, what can I say? She looks better than you in a bikini."

Jolie shucked her flip-flops and pulled her jeans, t-shirt, and jacket from the tote bag. She yanked them over her bikini and sat on the ground to tie her cross trainers.

The throb of an approaching helicopter echoed toward us.

Coyote straightened and swiveled his head to locate the sound. "We can't let them find us up here." He pointed to the side of the butte. "Go. Go. Get off this hill."

My thoughts zinged to the towers and their psychotronic diviners. Our jumps through the psychic world must have triggered an alarm.

With me in the lead, we dashed off the top of the butte and slid down a chute between the stone columns along its face. When we reached the bottom, we'd have to scramble for a hiding place as far from the butte as we could get.

A Blackhawk appeared, cruising below us, prowling low and slow.

I braced my arms and legs against the sides of the chute. Jolie and Coyote piled on top of me.

The helicopter landed at the edge of the butte's rocky skirt, a hundred meters from us, blocking our escape. Armed men hopped out and fanned from the machine.

These goons were as well equipped as Navy SEALs but I couldn't say if they were military, or special police, or contractors. But whoever they were, I was sure they either worked directly for or answered to Cress Tech International.

The Blackhawk lifted into the air and flew off. The men shouted to each other and hustled along the slope, moving past in a loose formation that told me they didn't realize we were here.

"Back up," I whispered. We had passed a deep groove that we could retreat into. The drumming of the helicopter blades masked the sounds of rocks crumbling from the sandstone as we inched back up. The groove was about five feet deep and ten feet high, and we packed ourselves into it. Luckily, our side of the butte was in shadow that grew darker by the minute.

Another helicopter circled above.

"Shit," Jolie whispered. "I left my stuff up there."

"You Coyote?" I asked. "What about the beer can?"

"I crushed it and put it in my pocket. It's worth money."

A whole nickel. Perhaps.

For their troubles, the helicopter crews would find a tote bag, ladies flip-flops, and a plastic hurricane cup from Key West. Let Cress Tech try to make sense about how that stuff got up there.

The Blackhawks made pass after pass as twilight gathered. Laser beams from their chin turrets traced the ground. They landed repeatedly, dropped off ground teams, circled, landed at another spot, and picked them up to repeat the procedure along the ground surrounding the butte. For all the noise and excitement, the effect was very much Keystone Cops.

Since it looked like we might be stuck here for the night, we slowed our metabolisms to conserve energy. This would also cool our bodies to near ambient temperatures and reduce the likelihood that we'd be discovered by thermal viewers. We kept our sunglasses on to hide our reflective eyes at the expense of losing our night vision and the ability to see auras.

Another two helicopters arrived and doubled the chaos. One of the men in SWAT gear wandered along the bottom of the butte in front of us. He had slung his carbine under one arm and walked like he'd lost much of his enthusiasm. He halted before us and shined a flashlight along the stone columns. I tensed. We were maybe fifty feet above him, but should he spot us, I'd dive on him, hopefully before he could cry for help.

He swept the beam left and right, up and down. He turned it off, unzipped his pants, and took a whiz that was a bit too aromatic. He gave himself a shake, zipped up and strode away.

The helicopters kept orbiting. A half dozen Humvees arrived. They scurried over the ground, rocks popped from under their tires, dirt plumed the air, headlamps and searchlights swept in flaming arcs through the fog of dust.

Cress Tech was here because we had tripped an alarm. But their haphazard response told me they had been caught unaware. Maybe they were hoping for a minor psychotronic blip and we must've spooked them by gonging the alarm big time. I didn't know what they expected to find—not us, for sure—and with typical macho thinking, they had dispatched lots of guns to greet the supernatural. Foolish humans.

The hours passed with glacial slowness, and we remained as motionless as the rock. Jerusalem crickets and beetles inched up our sleeves and pants, over our faces, and into our ears and nostrils. No need to flinch or scratch. We vampires spend a lot of time in crypts and are used to creepy-crawlies.

Finally, when the night was inky black and cool, the helicopters landed, the men climbed in and flew away. The Humvees drove off in a long dust cloud, a carnival parade of flashing lights and sweeping headlamps.

We waited and listened for stay-behinds. I piqued my ears for the *scritch* of Velcro, the creak of a boot on the ground, the metallic click from a gun. No sound except for the flapping of owl wings. I willed life back into my limbs, and we untangled ourselves. I beat the bugs from my clothes. Jolie snorted a centipede out her nose. Coyote munched on something.

We removed our sunglasses and panned the area for suspicious auras. Nothing but desert critters trying to make their living.

My watch read 4:40 a.m.

"What now?" Jolie asked. Our side of the butte faced east, and if we lingered here, the morning light would fry us like chorizo.

"Home." Coyote slithered over me, slid down the chute and let himself fall. He hit the ground running.

Jolie and I dropped after him. We sprinted over the rough slope and headed west. Using the cover of gloom, we weren't worried about getting noticed as we ran fast as antelopes. If someone did spot us, then we'd be another one of those strange desert phenomena that New Mexico is famous for.

Coyote chose a path over the lowest ground between the two closest towers. Our auras glowed like paper lanterns. But if the psychotronic diviners did spot us, we'd be long gone before Deputy Dawg arrived.

Coyote scrambled over the edge of Chaco Wash, followed by Jolie, then me at her heels. He jumped from outcropping to rock and landed on the sandy bottom. Jolie and I followed him across the wash to a wall of eroded sandstone and layers of loose dirt, and we climbed up and onto the floor of the canyon.

A faint purple band outlined the mesa to the east. I announced, "Sunrise in a few minutes."

We were making good time, but not good enough. The deadly rays of the morning sun would burn through our sunscreen and cook us. We needed shelter to survive the dawn.

Coyote quickened our pace. We ran across the desert like our hair was on fire because in a few minutes, it might be. Along with the rest of our bodies.

A glance over my shoulder revealed that the horizon behind us had warmed from purple to a burner-plate red. A bronze light settled across the tops of the hills and mesa to our front and over the summit of Fajada Butte behind us. We had maybe thirty minutes before the dawn sun charred us into undead cinders. My kundalini noir tingled in panic.

"What exactly is your plan?" Jolie asked, her aura bristling with spikes of worry. "Where's the road we used yesterday?"

"Too far." Coyote pointed to a draw up the side of the mesa. "That will take us home."

The light had warmed to yellow and crept down the terrain surrounding us.

"Don't think we're going to make it," I said.

Coyote's aura flashed waves of concern, and he veered suddenly to the right. "There's an old car that way," he noted. "Should give us enough shade to survive."

"Should?" Jolie asked. "I don't like the sound of that."

"At most," Coyote replied, "you'll get a sunburn." Then he mumbled, "Maybe."

We ran past where the draw spilled from the mesa. A rusted '46 De Soto appeared in the creosote and sage about a hundred meters to our front. The derelict hulk looked like it had been plowed into the dirt, the front end and wheels completely buried, its rounded trunk bulging from the ground.

I said, "Doesn't look like much protection."

"Have faith, *ese*."

I spied something to my left inside the draw—my sixth sense pinged a warning—and I slowed to determine what it was. Two round objects were planted on thick wooden shafts midway up the slope, maybe fifty meters away and directly in the path Coyote had been headed for. The morning light seeped down the slope toward the objects, but at the moment they remained in shadow.

"C'mon." Jolie ran back to grab my arm. "We're wasting time."

My sixth sense now rang at full red alert, but I couldn't believe—I didn't want to believe—what my eyes were telling me. My feet halted in mid-stride, my shoulders locked tight, and my hands clutched into trembling hooks.

I recognized the two objects as human heads. Female human heads. Rather, female vampire heads impaled on stakes. One head was caramel brown and topped with dense frizzy hair. The other was pale with angular features and a limp mop of platinum blond tresses. Their mouths gaped open and goo dripped from the severed necks.

The brown head belonged to Phyllis, my minder from the Araneum. The other belonged to her boss, Natacha De Brancovan.

Phaedra had left her calling card.

Chapter Eleven

I stared at the two decapitated heads. Their dead eyes bulged from sockets ringed with sagging skin, their jaws drooping open, fangs protruding.

The world as I knew it turned inside out. Questions crackled through my mind. When had Phaedra done this? Had she brought only the heads or had she dragged Phyllis and Natacha from Denver still alive, and then butchered them close by? If so, how? *How?* How could two badass vampires like Phyllis and Natacha let themselves get murdered?

A small voice whispered through me. *You like my little gift, Felix? I picked these for you.*

Phaedra was watching, leering. But all I could do was put my hands to my ears and shout, "Get out of my head, damn you."

They didn't see it coming, poor things. But you will.

Jolie tugged my arm and brought me back to the moment. She was hollering, "Let's go."

The morning shadow around me turned gray. Light seeped down the mesa, into the draw above me, toward the heads and became a brilliant yellow, the color of molten rock.

Jolie pulled harder on my arm and yelled that we had to get going.

The air grew hotter like I'd stuck my head inside a furnace. Never had I been this exposed to the dawn. As the ground brightened around me, a humming noise began in my ears like I could hear the light growing stronger.

Jolie yelled again, but the humming drowned her words.

The sunlight edged closer to the heads, and my skin tightened, my nerves shriveled. The humming intensified into a shriek.

The instant the light touched the tops of the two decapitated heads, the hair sizzled and smoked. The ray of sunlight traced down their faces, burning whatever it touched. The eyes smoldered, popped, and flames burst from the sockets. Fire jetted out their nostrils, out their mouths. The flaming skin sloughed away, leaving their skulls intact for a moment, before they fractured to pieces and fell in clumps of dust around the stakes. Black smoke twisted up the draw.

Jolie yanked my arm, and I turned to face her. She was yelling, and her mouth formed the words: *Move! MOVE!*

The shriek was now a deafening howl that made my kundalini noir shake. Heated air parched my mouth. Stung my tongue. My nostrils. My eyes.

Jolie kicked the back of my legs. I fell backwards. She grabbed my collar and hauled me beside her. My legs swung around, twisting my body away from the slope.

Coyote was ahead of us, bent over by the rear bumper of the De Soto, struggling to open its trunk. I staggered alongside Jolie, both of us bent over in an awkward duck walk to remain in the sliver of shadow still hugging the canyon's basin. The instant direct sunlight touched us, we'd start to fry. Annihilation was seconds away.

The De Soto was a blur in front of me. The light was blinding, the air thick as hot molasses. Coyote heaved on the trunk lid and the trunk yawned open. He grabbed Jolie's arm. She grabbed mine, and we tumbled in a daisy chain into the De Soto. My sunglasses were knocked away. Coyote climbed on top of me and slammed the trunk closed. A merciful darkness swallowed us.

We wormed deeper into the De Soto. The back wall of the trunk had been removed, and the sedan's interior gutted to form a cocoon-like chamber littered with ratty blankets, clothes, and heaps of fabric. Cardboard and plywood had been fitted into the windows with rags crammed around them to seal out the light and seal in a musky odor.

Coyote pulled a tattered velvet curtain from where it had been discarded on the floor. The curtain rained dirt and ants across us as he spread it over our bodies. We huddled together and waited.

The dawn screamed like a hungry monster. If one ray of light leaked in, our sanctuary would turn into an oven. I clenched my eyes and kept my face down. The howling grew into a hurricane of noise, the beast seeking to devour us. We pressed into each other, squeezing into a frightened ball.

The shriek ebbed into the ringing noise, the ringing into a hum, and the hum faded to silence.

We stayed locked together for several moments until our kundalini noirs stopped quivering. We separated and poked our heads from under the curtain. Coyote and Jolie had removed their sunglasses. He rubbed his eyes.

I fished a tube of sunscreen from my jacket pocket and smeared the soothing lotion on my skin. I passed the tube to Coyote who gooped the sunscreen on and then tossed it to Jolie. She slathered her face, neck, both hands, and tossed the empty tube aside.

I asked Coyote, "How did you know about this place?"

"Me and a girl used to sneak down here for, you know, some hootchie-cootchie," he answered.

"Rainelle?" Jolie asked.

"No. Some *ruca* who worked at Los Alamos. On the bomb. You know." Coyote made the sound of an explosion.

"You dated a nuclear scientist?" Jolie pressed.

"Don't act surprised," Coyote replied in an insulted tone. "Brainy chicas dig me." His voice deepened. "According to the Pythagorean theorem, the square of the hypotenuse is equal to the sum of the squares of the other two sides." His voice returned to normal. "Not sure what that means, *ese*, I was never good at geomagraphy. Besides, she is long gone. *Muchos años*."

We remained quiet, bunched together like dogs in a cage.

Jolie broke the silence, "Coyote, you can teleport on your own, right?"

"If you call it that, *Símon*."

"Then why didn't you teleport us out of danger?"

"Unless there's a portal, each must access the psychic world on their own. I could've teleported myself but I didn't want to leave you behind."

"Fair enough," Jolie said. She scooted under the trunk lid, lay on her back, and cocked a leg. "Everyone ready?"

"Go for it," I replied.

She kicked the trunk open. Sunlight dazzled us. My kundalini noir hitched from so much sudden brightness.

Jolie crawled out, stood, and dusted herself. Coyote emerged next, then it was my turn. A momentary panic whisked over me, a worry that we might have misjudged stepping into the sunlight too soon. But the air was morning cool and fresh. We were safe.

I climbed out of the trunk. "What about Phaedra?"

"She's steps ahead of us," Jolie replied. "She knew we were here and she knew what route we'd take back from Fajada Butte. How?"

We both looked at Coyote.

He said, "There is much that she knows, and much that she doesn't." Spikes of anxiety pistoned in and out from his aura's penumbra.

"What's that mean?" I asked.

Coyote's aura formed a doughnut-shaped halo around his head. Two red beams shot from his eyes through the hole. "Phaedra is using the psychic plane to spy on us. She knows we're going to use the Sun Dagger against her, but she doesn't know how."

"Neither do we." I pointed at Jolie.

"In time, *vatos*." Coyote's eye beams disappeared and the halo melted into his aura.

"And just as worrisome," Jolie offered, "what about your mom and Rainelle?"

His aura started pistoning the spikes again. Jolie and I swiveled our heads as we swept our sixth sense like radar beams across the landscape. Nothing suspicious pinged back.

Coyote slammed the trunk closed and flung handfuls of dirt over the car in a half-hearted attempt to make it look as if we hadn't disturbed the location.

We started up the draw and paused where the vampire heads had been. Nothing much remained, just ash piled around the bases of the stakes.

"Did you know them?" she asked Coyote.

"Only Natacha," he answered. "We weren't friends."

That was no surprise. She was a real ball buster from the Araneum, an icy blonde so cold she could probably chill beer in her cooter, and I couldn't see her chumming up with Coyote.

"She's the one who ran me out of the Araneum." He kicked her ashes into the surrounding dirt and continued up the draw.

Jolie yanked the stakes from the ground and threw them into the desert, where they clattered on rocks and bounced out of sight.

"Why the mind fuck?" she asked. "Why stake Phyllis and Natacha and show her cards? If Phaedra intends to knock us off, why not wait and catch us by surprise?"

"She's toying with us," I answered. "And as far as mind fucks go, I give this one an *A* plus."

"Or maybe Phaedra is waiting," Coyote said. "Maybe she knows about Carmen. Maybe Phaedra needs to make sure she can kill us all at one time."

"That's reassuring," Jolie replied.

"Phaedra has weaknesses." Coyote started walking up the draw.

Jolie and I fell in behind him. "Like what?" I asked.

"Like her fear of you. And Carmen. That fear will make Phaedra overplay her hand."

"How do you know that?"

Coyote stopped and turned to face me, his wrinkled eyes smoldering with feral determination. "*Vato*, have faith. Otherwise lie in the dirt like a turd and wait to be stepped on. Jolie and I will continue. Right, *chica*?"

She nodded.

"*Entonces, sigueme.*" He resumed climbing up the draw.

I felt like Coyote had placed a dunce cap on my head. Jolie and I trailed after him, the three of us hopping from rock to rock until we reached the rim of the mesa. Wisps of smoke twisted from Coyote's home and the neighboring buildings a quarter mile away. Everything peaceful. Everything quiet. Tranquil. A jarring juxtaposition in the wake of our recent brush with the discovery of Phaedra's gruesome souvenirs and our near escape from the murderous dawn.

We trotted across the mesa—Jolie and I panning the seemingly infinite vista—anxious, concerned that a trap or bad news waited.

Maybe Phaedra had also attacked Coyote's mom and Rainelle.

As we got closer to the houses, the dog began to bark. A metal rake skritched the ground. Rainelle's Ford pickup came into view where it was parked on the north side of the doublewide.

Jolie slowed and dropped behind to provide cover—just in case.

Goats bleated. Chickens clucked. The dog barked. A cat meowed from behind the fence. The scene was so homey we should've burst out singing "Old McDonald Had a Farm."

Coyote's posture wilted as if the night's misadventures had at last caught up with him. Lines of fatigue strained Jolie's face, and I was sure I looked just as worn out.

The skritching stopped and Rainelle appeared from behind her home, a rake propped on her shoulder. "Welcome back." She stopped at the fence, stared, and studied our weary faces. "You okay?"

"Why shouldn't I be?" Coyote answered.

That's the dilemma of bringing humans into the circle of the supernatural. How much do you tell them?

She asked, "*Cafe con sangre?*" the question making it obvious that she was used to his evasive replies.

Coyote rewarded her offer with a smile and added, "Have you seen La Llorona?"

"*Your* mother?" Rainelle quirked an eyebrow. "She has a name, you know."

Coyote scoped the area around the house. "But have you seen her?"

"She was around last night."

"Was El Cucuy with her?"

"Don't think so. Why?"

"*Todo está bien?*"

She quirked her eyebrow again. "What are you getting at?"

"*Nada.* Let's go inside. We're hungry."

"Well you can stay hungry," Rainelle replied, "until you tell me what's going on."

Coyote hunched his shoulders and let them drop as he sighed. I could practically hear his thoughts: *viejas, como chingan.*

"There is trouble?" she asked.

He nodded. "I don't want to worry you, *querida.*"

"Anyone comes here for trouble," she brandished the rake like it was a club, "I'll break their heads." She relaxed her stance. "Just tell me what to expect."

She turned to enter the doublewide from the back door. Coyote led Jolie and me through the kitchen entrance. We stowed our sunglasses and our auras were finally calming into a steady orange glow.

Within a few minutes, Rainelle was working an espresso machine that sputtered and spewed steamed blood into our coffee. Breakfast around the living room coffee table: omelets and fry bread, smothered in pig's blood. Afterwards, Jolie and I cleared the table and washed dishes. Rainelle stepped out back and resumed raking the backyard.

Jolie had stripped off her jacket and her pistols hung in their shoulder holsters within easy reach. I took her cue and tucked my Colt into the front of my jeans before I shrugged out of my jacket.

Coyote brought a small cardboard box from the room with all the junk. He set the box on the coffee table and opened it. Nested inside crumpled newspaper was a psychotronic diviner not much bigger than a pack of cigarettes. He set the diviner on the table.

The body of this diviner appeared to be constructed of stainless steel plates welded together. A four-sided pyramid the size of a large olive sat on top. The pyramid was made of sheets of clear quartz, and inside the pyramid stood a pink quartz crystal no bigger than a pinto bean. Coyote flicked a brass switch at one corner of the box. Nothing happened.

He closed his eyes and raised a hand toward the diviner. The pink crystal emitted a faint glow, and the diviner beeped.

"It's working," I told him.

He relaxed his hand and opened his eyes. The glow faded. "This diviner is not very sensitive. But if Phaedra is nearby and she uses her powers, we'll get a warning."

Coyote returned to the kitchen and poured himself a glass of Jameson. He sipped the whisky and studied the diviner.

Jolie took a shower, then it was my turn. As I washed off the grime and scraped away the layers of makeup and sunscreen, my muscles turned to rubber and I looked forward to a nap. Rainelle provided clean clothes she scrounged from the extra room.

Jolie and I slept in the living room, she on the sofa, me on the floor. Late in the afternoon, Coyote woke us. He had set a shoebox filled with papers next to the diviner on the table.

Jolie stretched and got up. She walked into the kitchen and returned to hand out straws and 500 milliliter bags of chilled blood. I fanged a hole in a Type B Positive and inserted my straw. I parked myself next to her on the sofa.

Coyote sorted through the shoebox and withdrew a handful of papers in assorted sizes and types that he smoothed flat on the table. Some of the pages were from motel notepads, others were torn from spiral notebooks, and others were the backs of crumpled receipts or loose sheets of copy paper. All were covered in ink scrawls and sketches. Coyote arranged the papers before him and raised his hands in a proud gesture. "There you have it."

I glanced from scrawl to drawing to scrawl. "Have what?"

Coyote pointed to the confused mess with both hands. "How you're going to bring Carmen Arellano back home from outer space."

Chapter Twelve

Jolie and I studied the papers Coyote had arranged on the coffee table. I tried to decipher the writing. Most were illegible chicken scratches made with a ballpoint pen or a pencil. Plus a black Sharpie. Highlighters. *Crayons!* I recognized a few letters but the words could've been English or Spanish. And some of the writing looked Chinese or Korean or Balanese. Hebrew? Maybe ancient Mixtec. *Perhaps Martian?*

The sketches were just as confounding. Lots of circles and lines and squiggles.

Coyote watched, arms folded, nodding like he was pleased that I understood what he had planned ... which I didn't.

Jolie hunched forward from the sofa and squinted. Her forehead wadded into confused wrinkles. "What exactly are we looking at?"

Coyote fanned his hands. *Isn't it obvious?*

Jolie plucked a drawing of The Sun Dagger and held it up. "Let me guess." She waved her other hand over the table. "All this explains how to use the Sun Dagger?"

He smiled, his thin cracked lips forming an uneven crescent around his crooked, yellow teeth. "Simple, no?"

"Which can only be used during the day?" she asked.

"Why would you ask that?" he replied.

Jolie reached for my knee and squeezed, though I'm sure she would've rather rolled her eyes and screamed in frustration.

Coyote stroked his chin. "I see that I lost you." His voice became very Ivy League, clenched-jaw professorial. The aura over his head formed a mortarboard complete with tassel. "Invoking the Sun Dagger takes one from place to place along the edges of the psychic plane. To do so, we need the rays of the sun, either directly or reflected."

I recalled last night's moon. It shined from the sun's reflected light. Not quite full though certainly bright enough to cast a dagger of light across the petroglyph. I said, "We'll use the light of the moon to orient ourselves on the Sun Dagger."

Coyote's mortarboard morphed into an exclamation mark. "You got it, *vato*. It's transcendental astral physics." His accent returned to barrio Chicano. "In two nights, the Sun Dagger will line up with D-Galtha."

"Which is what?"

"Where you two are going."

Following Coyote's reasoning was like chasing a chicken through a labyrinth. "Is that the planet where Carmen is being held prisoner?"

Coyote rifled through the papers and picked one with a sketch of a circle with an X marked over it. He jabbed at the X. "She's right here."

"D-Galtha? Is that a planet? A spaceship?"

"It is where you'll find Carmen."

Realizing this was all he would share, I pressed forward. "How do you know?"

Coyote put the paper back on the table. "Long ago, and I mean, long, long ago, *un hechicero guajiro*—"

Jolie interrupted, "A who?"

"Medicine man. Shaman," I translated.

"*Sí*," continued Coyote. "He was the one who gave me the name *coyote*, saying that if I was to survive *la conquista*, I had to be as clever and tricky as my animal *tocayo*. Said that I wouldn't be able to get by forever on my good looks."

"Wise man," quipped Jolie.

"He taught me about the world beyond what we can see or touch. He showed me *las puertas*, the portals, into the psychic plane."

Coyote reached into the shoebox and withdrew a large folded paper. He spread it open. It was a charcoal rubbing of the Sun Dagger.

He cleared a space on the table and laid the paper flat. He gestured to me and tapped his finger at a point on the spiral. "Felix, put your hand here. *La derecha.*"

I extended my right hand.

He grasped my wrist and tugged my arm, forcing me to get off the sofa and walk around the table to stand beside him. He said, "Spread your fingers," and adjusted the placement of my hand on the upper left quadrant of the spiral. "You must put your *mano* exactly like this." Reaching behind his ear, he produced the stubby remnant of a pencil that had been crudely whittled to a point and traced around my hand.

Coyote made a whisking motion, indicating that I remove my hand and sit back down. He leafed through the papers until he found one with a list of numbers. He wrote along the bottom of the paper. 12:22:00.

"This is the exact time you must put your hand on the Sun Dagger."

"At night, yes?"

Coyote jotted a.m. beside the time. He frowned suddenly, looked back at the list of numbers, scratched out the number he'd written, and wrote a new time. 11:43:00 p.m.

I stared at the number. "You sure about this?"

He leaned back and crossed his legs and his arms. "*Símon*. It's very technical. You summon the portal at the wrong time, *boom*, you'll find yourself on Jupiter."

Jolie asked, "And you're going to show us how to use the Sun Dagger?"

Coyote sighed. "I'll teach what I can. It took me years of experimenting *con el guajiro* just to find the doors. And many more years to open them. And still more to learn how to enter and navigate the psychic plane."

"Experimenting?"

"With peyote. Much of it." Coyote's eyes crossed, then swiveled in opposite directions, spun a few times, and finally aimed straight. "Fortunately, it didn't affect me at all."

"Of course not," I replied.

Jolie asked, "What if we miss the time?"

"Not good." Coyote grimaced. "It'll be another one hundred and thirteen years before it aligns again."

"How do you know Carmen is on D-Galtha?"

"I was in the middle of one my beautiful peyote dreams," Coyote turned wistful, "when I heard Carmen's voice."

"You know her?"

"No. But I heard this voice and I recognized it as hers."

I asked, "You recognized the voice of someone you didn't know?"

"*Vato*, when you're tripping on peyote, anything is possible."

Fair enough.

"Tonight we'll practice with the Sun Dagger. Nothing fancy. Just a quick spin to Alpha Centauri and back. Dress warm."

"We rescue Carmen and then what? How can she stop Phaedra?"

"Even I have to wait for that answer," Coyote replied. "But once she is back here, then Phaedra must fight the four of us."

"What do you know about D-Galtha?"

Coyote turned glum. "Only that it is a dangerous place guarded by the most dangerous aliens in the galaxy."

"Naturally," noted Jolie.

"What about Cress Tech?" I asked. "We return to Fajada Butte and shoot through the psychic plane again, won't we trip their alarms?"

"I'm sure of it, *ese*. But like I said, tonight we'll go on a quick trip. We'll be on and off that *pinchi* rock before the Cress Tech helicopters and their *pendejo* guards get a clue."

"I'd like to know how close the government is to unlocking the secrets of Fajada Butte." My job as an enforcer for the Araneum was to protect the secrets of the supernatural world. Once humans learned how to enter the psychic plane, then it wouldn't be long before they discovered what shouldn't exist. Vampires. Werewolves. Ghosts. La Llorona. El Cucuy. Fairies. Then humans would do to us what they did to the dodo birds, the passenger pigeon, and most of the Native Americans.

"Carmen first," Coyote replied. "Then we fuck with Cress Tech."

He called for Rainelle. No answer. He got up and looked out back. He returned to the living room, appearing confused. "Her truck is here." He read his Rolex. "Past eight. Time for dinner."

I hadn't been keeping track of Rainelle, and the last time I had seen her was hours ago. Concern nipped at my kundalini noir.

Jolie sensed it too because she got a serious look on her face, reached for her jacket, and slipped it on to prepare for action.

Coyote opened the kitchen door and hollered into the night, "Rainelle."

No answer except for the bleating of goats. He called for Che. Nothing.

A hunch soured my belly, the acid burn telling me to expect bad news. I put on my jacket.

Something beeped. All three of us glanced at the psychotronic diviner on the coffee table.

The crystal emitted a warning glow.

Phaedra was calling.

Chapter Thirteen

Coyote snatched the psychotronic diviner from the table and dashed out the kitchen door. He leapt off the porch, ran the fifty meters to the edge of the mesa and stopped.

Jolie and I sprinted after him.

He held the diviner in both hands like an offering. Its crystal glowed steady. Though it could be detecting any psychic energy burst, no need to fool ourselves about what the clues meant. Rainelle was missing. Phaedra had taken her as bait.

Stars crowded the black velvet sky. The moon hung low over the opposite horizon. Chaco Canyon, Fajada Butte, and the far mesas formed a patchwork of purple and dark gray. More than a mile before us, the dark jagged gash of Chaco Wash ran across the middle of the canyon floor.

Jolie asked, "Why didn't the diviner go off when Phaedra took Rainelle?"

"Phaedra didn't need psychic powers to kidnap her." I answered with conviction even though I was only guessing. "Or she could've sent her human goons. Now that Phaedra has Rainelle, she's letting her presence be known." I looked over both shoulders and lowered my voice to an angry rasp. "And she took Rainelle right from under our noses. That bitch Phaedra could be anywhere."

The crystal dimmed until its light went out. Coyote stashed the diviner in his jacket pocket and stared into the canyon below. "She's there."

"Why didn't she zap us here?" Jolie asked. "If she had attacked just a few minutes ago, she would've caught us with our thumb up our ass."

I recalled Phaedra's debilitating mind blasts. As powerful as they were, they must have range limits. "Maybe she has to trap us."

Jolie tapped the grip of one of her .45s. Her fangs glinted. "Bring it."

Coyote stepped off the mesa and floated down the steep slope. Jolie and I levitated behind him and descended into the gloom, the three of us practically invisible to any human who might have been watching. But to another vampire, our auras glowed like hot irons.

After landing in the canyon basin, we hustled to the wash. The moon climbed high enough to shine like a dim searchlight across the empty landscape.

The psychotronic diviner beeped, and my nerves pulled tight. Coyote fished the diviner out of his pocket, and the light from its crystal cast his face in eerie shadows.

I yanked my magnum from its holster. Jolie had both .45s out and ready.

We kept walking until we reached a ravine branching from the wash. We halted where the bottom was just visible. A hundred meters from us, a human body lay on her back. A woman with her arms folded. Rainelle. A faint aural sheath surrounded her. At least she was alive, though unconscious, maybe comatose.

Coyote squinted, his brow tightening. But he didn't move. None of us did. We knew. Rainelle was bait.

The diviner beeped again, loud.

Its crystal burned with magnesium flare intensity, then exploded like a big firecracker. We jumped back. The report echoed in the night and the blast dazzled my eyes. I blinked them back into focus.

Coyote dropped the diviner and rubbed his eyes. He opened them and grimaced.

A faint white light materialized on the other side of the wash, maybe three hundred meters away. The light glided toward us.

My kundalini noir buzzed in distress, and I whispered, "Phaedra. Get ready for anything." I fought the urge to shoot. Jolie pointed her pistols but like me, held her fire. At this distance our bullets wouldn't nail her spot on. As soon as Phaedra was within pistol range—fifty meters—then we'd drill her with a hail of silver bullets.

Coyote jumped into the ravine. I expected him to scoop Rainelle into his arms but he bounded past her. With every stride, an article of clothing sloughed from his frame. For an instant he was naked and in the next, he had morphed into a coyote. He sprang on all four legs over the ground, his orange aura shimmering with distress. He disappeared down the far end of the ravine to my right, away from danger.

Why did Coyote abandon us? He was no coward. Jolie and I could transmutate into wolves, but the change would take at least a minute. By then, Phaedra would be on top of us.

The light continued to approach, becoming a blur of white and green illumination, coming close enough that I could recognize a human form within the glow. Jolie and I stepped from each other to make two targets instead of just one, and we glanced about in case the light was simply a distraction.

At one hundred meters, the light was a fan of white and green rays. Coming closer, it was clear the form inside the light was definitely female. A bit shorter than Jolie, with a mane of twisting black hair that cascaded past her shoulders, curling around a young woman's face you'd call delicate and girlish if not for the expression of pure hate.

Confirmation: Phaedra.

Her lacy black dress was gathered with a belt from which hung dead crows. Black jewelry clung to her arms like the remnants of chains. Sparks sizzled around her head like she was about to explode. She was an astounding sight, so fantastic and terrifying that Jolie and I stared in disbelief when we should've opened fire.

Phaedra halted at the edge of the ravine on the other side of Rainelle. So far she had not used any of her tricks to probe our minds, confound us with hallucinations, or slam us with blasts of psychic energy.

Felix. Jolie. The ingénue's voice slid into my brain. Out the corner of my eye I saw Jolie flinch. She was hearing Phaedra as well.

Before we get started, let me offer you this chance. Join me. Serve me. Live.

Jolie answered for the two of us. "Fuck you."

I raised my revolver to draw a bead on Phaedra's pretty face.

The ground trembled. To my right, dirt geysered upward. An orange aura shot from the spot. A vampire in a black duster appeared facing me, snarling, talons and fangs extended to combat length.

How was this possible? Had he been planted in the ground, or did Phaedra shoot him from someplace like a dirt torpedo?

More earth spouted upwards. Another vampire. Then another gout of earth. And another. Another. Jolie and I were surrounded by vampires. Eight of them. All in long dark coats like they were dressed for a Goth concert.

Pistols raised, Jolie spread her arms. She alternated firing to the left and right. Her bullets knocked the vampires down like they were bowling pins.

The vampires facing me attacked as one. I aimed the revolver and delivered two quick shots with the speed of a scorpion's tail. Two vampire heads exploded like cantaloupes.

A vampire grasped my right shoulder from behind and aimed his fangs for my neck, an amateurish move against an undead enforcer like myself. I grasped his hair with my left hand and pitched forward. He rolled off my shoulder, and I whipped him flat against the ground. I drove the butt of the Colt Magnum against his forehead and cracked his skull like an egg. Brains and gore spurted out. His aura sparked with pain and began to ebb.

The last vampire, a female, lunged at me. I darted out of her way and sliced her throat with my talons. Her head separated from her shoulders and spun backwards, her aura blinked off, and the blood gushing from both ends of her severed neck turned to flakes.

Score so far ... Phaedra: zero. Jolie and me: eight. The undead bodies lay strewn around us, their auras flickering weakly or already dark. I had four bullets left in my pistol, all for Phaedra.

The ground trembled once more and a fresh volley of vampires sprang from the earth. Another suicide squad. I crouched and got ready to fight them off.

Phaedra had glided closer, maybe thirty meters away. Her aura gathered into a glowing knot in front of her forehead. The knot grew into a plume that extended from her head like a flamethrower. The plume arced over the ravine and swallowed Jolie's aura. My friend froze, her arms dropped to the side, and she levitated.

The sight both stupefied and dismayed me. Phaedra had learned how to focus her mojo into a physical attack.

The plume crackled like fire. Jolie began to tremble.

Rage compressed within me, then exploded. I shot a pair of vampires that advanced between Phaedra and me. The remaining vampires held back, not as fanatical or as stupid as I thought.

The aural plume let go of Jolie and she crumpled to the ground. The plume retracted halfway to Phaedra. She turned her head toward me and aimed the plume like it was a cannon.

My reflexes kicked into supernatural speed, and I cut to the left. But Phaedra was quicker. The plume smacked me hard, like a kick to my solar plexus. Orange light flooded my vision and swirled inside my head. An electric shock slammed down my spine. Spasming in pain, I floated upward.

The orange light dimmed. Through the agony, Phaedra's voice echoed in my skull, a tone both flirtatious and taunting. *It's been awhile, my love. I appreciate that you've grown stronger and more ruthless. But not ruthless enough.*

I wouldn't reply. My mind wrestled to escape the grip of pain.

I could feel her smile turn cruel. My neck began to twist. I resisted but the force contorting my neck wrenched harder.

I was hoping to see you die in a more honorable way. Instead I'll kill you as if you were a chicken for Sunday dinner. So disappointing.

I clenched my teeth and fought against the pain and the grinding of my vertebrae.

Phaedra screamed. The plume and my pain and paralysis vanished. I fell to the ground.

She screamed again. Coyote had clamped his muzzle onto one of her ankles, snarling, jerking his furry head side-to-side, his aura blazing red, orange, and yellow.

I watched, dizzy, my limbs plastic, my kundalini noir limp and weak.

Phaedra turned her head and blasted him with an aural plume. He was thrown back. She stoked the plume until it merged with his aura and glowed with incandescent brilliance. Phaedra lifted him until he was level with her eyes, then slammed him to the ground.

I tried to rise but my legs refused to work. I fought to raise the pistol to shoot but my arm felt like it weighed a thousand pounds.

Phaedra shrieked with anger. The plume retracted into her head. She clenched her right hand and her aura crackled with lightning bolts of pain.

Jolie had staggered to her feet and waved the .45s, firing wildly.

Phaedra faced Jolie, shooting the aural plume, knocking Jolie flat with a punishing blow.

My arm felt mine again and I aimed for a shot.

Two vampires tackled me, and I was smothered under a storm of fangs and talons. I smacked at arms and faces with the butt of the magnum. Claws tightened around my neck. I jerked my pistol arm free and shoved the gun against a torso. Fired once. Felt the body go limp. Grabbed a face with my left hand. Raked my talons through flesh and bone and pushed the screaming, wounded vampire away.

A loud demonic howling echoed across the canyon. *Now what?*

Out the corner of my eye, I spotted a bluish-white light bounding toward us. The light outlined a large gorilla-lizard shape. El Cucuy.

Phaedra retracted her aural plume from Jolie and watched him approach, her aura sizzling in confusion and apprehension.

He raced across the night desert in great leaps, the surface of his metallic segmented body articulating like a mosaic of pewter tile.

I shot one of the vampires in the back. His comrades spun about and sprang at me. The fight disintegrated into a wild brawl, vampires seizing my arms, quick shots at targets of opportunity, and a confusion of fangs, talons, and fists.

I tore free long enough to see El Cucuy get within fifty feet of Phaedra and leap at her. But she was ready and hit him with the aural blast.

He exploded into thousands of shimmering fragments. The fragments bounced across the dirt, but didn't stop. Instead they moved like tiny Cucuys. They leapt at each other, clumping, these clumps sticking to others, all the while the mass approached Phaedra as it reformed the full El Cucuy.

Phaedra hit him with another blast. Again he exploded into pieces. And again, these pieces clumped together and remade El Cucuy.

She gave him another blast, but the plume was weaker. El Cucuy was slammed back, parts of him separating. They jumped back into him, and once whole, he pounced at her.

Another mind blast. This time El Cucuy was knocked to his knees with his head blown off. It tumbled to the ground, grew legs from the stump and jumped back onto his shoulders.

Phaedra retreated from him. Her aura radiated a weak orange light. It pulsed once as if giving a signal. The remaining vampires hopped up and disappeared into the holes they had sprung from.

A fresh aural plume twisted from Phaedra. She raked it across the bodies of her fallen minions. Their corpses burst into flame, flaring like dry tumbleweeds. I covered my face to shield my eyes. The bodies blazed for a moment, crackled, faded to embers, and then to smoke and twists of ash. Phaedra shrank into the distance and faded to nothingness.

Chapter Fourteen

I paused to survey the aftermath. Smoke from Phaedra's incinerated vampires fouled the night air. Dinner-plate-sized divots marked where her undead goons had come out of the ground, the holes now plugged with fresh dirt.

Phaedra was gone but her presence and the mayhem lingered like an echo.

Jolie staggered and sank to her knees. In a weary motion, she shoved both .45s into their shoulder holsters and waved that she was okay.

I turned my attention to Coyote. He remained in the dirt where Phaedra had thrown him. His aura trembled, flickering weakly between yellow, orange, and red. With every shift of color, his body morphed from coyote to human. His bones twisted, his fur dissolved into his skin, and his muzzle shrank against his face until he lay in his previous vampire form, naked.

Rainelle lay in the ravine, still unconscious, and by reading her aura, I could tell she was otherwise unhurt.

El Cucuy threw his shoulders back, his segmented body shimmering in the light of the moon. "It's best that we go."

I saw no reason to stick around. I rose to my feet and trotted into the ravine. Jolie stood and followed me. She scooped Rainelle in her arms while I gathered the clothes Coyote had discarded during his transmutation, including his purloined gold Rolex. His belongings in hand, I continued up the other side of the ravine where I crouched beside him.

Bruises marred the dark skin of his torso and arms. I slipped my hands beneath his shoulders and the back of his thighs. He weighed maybe a hundred pounds. His kundalini noir stirred faintly within him, and I knew he was in bad shape.

Jolie tossed Rainelle onto one shoulder and scurried up the side of the ravine. I hustled behind her with Coyote's bony frame cradled to my chest. He bounced limply in my arms, making me regret not taking the time to stop and tug his pants on so his junk wouldn't be flopping so close to my face.

El Cucuy jogged beside us as we ran to the mesa. I thanked him for his assist.

"Why did you help?" Jolie asked.

"You're my friends, no? Friends help friends, no?"

"Now you're Phaedra's enemy."

"No matter. She wasn't my friend."

"Where's Marina? Aren't you two ... ahem ...?" Jolie cleared her throat.

"She's up north," El Cucuy replied. "Doing her scary magic along Rio Chama." He didn't answer if he and Coyote's mother were friends with benefits. I couldn't imagine getting "friendly" with him—all those metal bits sliding into tight, moist places—and I didn't want a demo.

"I can tell you," he explained, "that she won't be happy about what happened to Coyote. He is her lone surviving child."

"Who's going to tell her?" I asked.

"She probably already knows."

"How?"

El Cucuy's head blew apart. The pieces traveled maybe five feet, held steady in the air for an instant, then smashed back together to reform his head. "Can you explain that?"

"Uh ... no."

"Then don't ask me to explain how Marina knows."

We picked up our pace and hurdled the clumps of prickly pear in our way.

Jolie shifted Rainelle from her shoulder to her arms. "What are you, exactly?"

"I am El Cucuy, the boogieman."

"But what kind of creature are you?"

His arms elongated until they stretched longer than his legs. Then he paddled his arms beneath him and bounded over the ground in kangaroo-like leaps. "*Rey de los espantos.*"

Jolie asked, "Shape-shifter?"

"No," I corrected, "King of the supernatural spooks."

"Shhh," El Cucuy whispered, "Don't say *shape-shifter.*" His arms shrank to their previous "normal" length and he resumed running on his hind lizard legs. "They might hear you."

"They who?"

He pointed to the mesa, now a couple of hundred meters away. Jolie and I slowed to a trot. Bizarre ghostly shapes crawled along the face of the slope. Rectangular shapes that looked like hides stretched over stilts. Skin-walkers?

"Out here, those are shape-shifters. They're very protective of the title. Apparently you have to go to school and learn all kinds of black-magic mumbo-jumbo ceremonies to call yourself a shift-shifter."

Jolie asked, "Who are they?"

"Navajo."

The skin-walkers wandered about the rocky slopes like emaciated horses looking to graze.

"Why do they look so weird?" Jolie persisted. "I thought shape-shifters would turn into animals. Fox. Wolf. Deer."

"This is their in-between form, between human and animal."

"Should we fear them?" Jolie picked up the pace.

"I fear them." El Cucuy chuckled uncomfortably. "To the Navajo, they are the damned. But they are not here to attack. Your fight with Phaedra brought them. This is their turf."

We reached the bottom of the mesa, and El Cucuy led us to an uphill trail. The skin-walkers ambled across the rocks to keep us in view.

Midway up the slope we heard a noise rumbling across the canyon. The ground trembled around us. At first I feared it was the return of Phaedra, but as the noise grew louder I recognized the too-familiar rhythm of helicopter rotor blades.

Three helicopters appeared in Chaco Canyon, flying low and fast, in the direction of our fight with Phaedra. Like I needed these assholes to show up. They cruised without lights and would have blended against the murky background, but thanks to my vampiric night vision, I could easily spot them. The lead chopper was a large CH-53, identical to the one we had seen yesterday with the psychotronic diviners mounted alongside. Its escort was a pair of UH-60 Blackhawks. Cress Tech must have been attracted by the psychic disturbance caused by Phaedra's aural blasts.

The Sea Dragon hovered over the fight area. One of the Blackhawks peeled to the right, away from us, and circled Fajada Butte. The other gained altitude and banked in our direction.

El Cucuy continued up the slope, Jolie and I close behind with our arms full. We couldn't outrun the Blackhawk, and there was no place to hide.

The helicopter slowed above the rim of the mesa. A searchlight beamed from under its nose and raked the ground. The beam swiveled to Coyote's home and reflected off the doublewide with a dazzling glow. The shaft of light swept over the fence, the yard, and in our direction.

Just as the beam was about to wash over us, El Cucuy exploded to thousands of little Cucuys that scattered into the gloom and vanished.

The light fixed on Jolie and me, with Rainelle and Coyote in our arms. The beam held steady for a short moment, then flicked off, leaving me to blink away the spots. The helicopter turned from us and headed into the canyon.

Cress Tech was looking for something and thankfully, we weren't it. Since their system had been triggered by huge pulses of psychic energy, they must've been looking for something more than two people carrying a couple of other people in their arms. To the Cress Tech crew we were probably drunken Navajos wandering the desert. Who else would be out here at this hour?

The Blackhawk joined the other two helicopters. They climbed to altitude and turned on their navigation lights, flashing red, green, and white. Forming a *V*—the Sea Dragon at the lead—they banked to the southeast and shrank into the distance.

"Where are they going?" Jolie asked. "Any military bases close by?"

"Kirkland Air Force Base," I answered. "Just outside Albuquerque."

"Anything special happen there?"

"High-tech black ops stuff."

"I'm not surprised. What about the skin-walkers? Wouldn't the helicopters see them?"

Good point but they hadn't shown signs of having spotted the skin-walkers. Maybe the Navajo spirits had vanished into the night like El Cucuy.

We crossed the last fifty feet from the mesa's rim to Coyote's doublewide. The goats bleated. Coyote's dog stumbled from under the doublewide like he had been sleeping off a bender. Phaedra's minions must've drugged the poor mutt.

Jolie fumbled with the front doorknob and led us in. She turned the lights on, and we entered the master bedroom. I put Coyote on the right side of the queen bed and Jolie placed Rainelle on the left. I grabbed a blanket from the closet and spread it over Coyote's naked body, partly because he needed warmth but more to spare my eyes.

Rainelle's aura was a vivid red, the color of strawberry Kool-Aid. "She's improving," I remarked. "What do you think knocked her out?"

"A potion," Jolie answered. "An injection. Something like that."

Coyote's aura still shimmered like a weak flame. I said, "He doesn't look too good."

Jolie crossed her arms and studied him. "This screws things up. He was supposed to show us how to use the Sun Dagger. Unless he gets better soon, we're fucked if we want to save Carmen."

I tried not to let Jolie's pessimism further sully my already dark mood. "Let's save those worries for later. Maybe his mom has a remedy. Maybe Coyote will get better on his own. Maybe by this time tomorrow, we'll be back from D-Galtha, safe with Carmen."

"Yeah, that's likely," Jolie replied, her voice keen with sarcasm. "And until then, we'll count the bluebirds and rainbows shooting out of my ass."

She grasped a bottle of Presidente brandy from the bureau. She uncapped the bottle and was about to take a sip when I said, "You know Coyote probably drank straight from the bottle."

Wincing, she replaced the cap and set the bottle back down.

We left Rainelle and Coyote in the bedroom. Jolie and I returned to the living room and sat, me slouching on the sofa and she on the armchair. Our eyes settled on Coyote's notes and drawings littering the coffee table. She picked up the charcoal rubbing of the Sun Dagger, squinted and tossed it back down. My sour mood reflected hers. We kept quiet. No need to dwell about the mess we were in. Looming before us was our one chance for the next hundred plus years to rescue Carmen. We'd fought Phaedra and her minions to a draw. Long minutes passed.

Rainelle appeared in the hall. Barefoot. With a bathrobe rumpled over her dress. Her short hair zigzagged in all directions. She wandered into the kitchen. Without asking, she grabbed a couple of blood bags from the fridge, tossed one to Jolie and one to me. Rainelle plugged in the water pot on the kitchen counter. Jolie and I inquired how she was doing.

"Empty headed." She tapped her temple. "Like there's a big hole in my brain and my thoughts are slowly filling up the space. Other than that, just pissed off."

"And Coyote?" I asked.

"Not good. Maybe he'll get better soon."

"We need better than maybes," Jolie said.

"You let me worry about him," Rainelle replied. "If I need to, I'll ask Doña Marina for help. How did he get hurt?"

Jolie and I gave Rainelle a rundown of the fight. When we mentioned how Coyote had been injured, she remained stoic though her eyes did mist.

The water pot boiled. Rainelle fixed herself tea. I got a rag and ran it over my Colt. She leaned across the counter and watched me as I polished the barrel of my magnum.

"Is that all you're going to do?" she asked. "Play with your gun?"

"If we go," rather that *when* we go to Fajada Butte, "I'd like something with a lot more *oomph* than this. Phaedra knows we're packing heat and she's going to up the ante."

Rainelle slurped her tea. "I know someone. He might be of help." She gave me a name—Francisco Yellowhair-Chavez—and an address in Farmington. "He's a local Navajo," she added, like that detail wasn't obvious.

Setting her cup down, she walked around the counter. "It'll be dawn soon." She brought us quilts and padded about the doublewide, securing windows and closing blinds. She clicked off the light switches and the interior became dark as a tomb, which brought a nice comforting feeling. Retreating to the master bedroom, she closed the door.

An hour after sunrise, when the sun was finally at a safe height, Jolie and I crawled from under our quilts. Rainelle made coffee and toasted fry bread to go with scrambled eggs, bacon, and goat's blood. Coyote wasn't doing any better.

Jolie drove Rainelle's pickup to visit Yellowhair-Chavez. I sat next to her, my head on the swivel. Rainelle stayed behind to care after Coyote.

We followed a dirt road to the highway, and my cell phone picked up the network signal. I used the GPS function to guide us to the address—*Yahtahey*—a sporting goods store/game processing/notary public tucked between a Lotaburger and a Church's Chicken, both eateries definitely fine examples of traditional Native American cuisine. The parking lot around Yahtahey was plenty big. In fact, Farmington seemed more dirt parking lot than anything else.

Jolie and I entered Yahtahey. Sporting merchandise—team hoodies, uniforms, footballs, basketballs—on the right, fishing and hunting supplies on the left. We navigated past crowded shelves and spinner racks to a back counter. A short buck-toothed man in thick glasses and a mustache greeted us. When I mentioned Yellowhair-Chavez, the clerk's eyes flared a bit, and he picked up the phone by a cash register. He spoke in a rushed, clipped tone and glanced to the ceiling. I followed his line of sight to a video camera. I sensed a reluctant tone in his voice so I mentioned that Rainelle had sent us.

The clerk relayed the comment, went "Uh-huh" a couple of times, and set the phone back on the cradle. He raised the center portion of the counter to let us pass and pointed to a door along the back wall. A loud buzz sounded from the door, and a dead bolt snapped.

Jolie followed me through. The back room was dimly lit with pools of illumination scattered beneath the ceiling. Rows of gun safes and shelves with boxes of ammo divided the room. The heads of deer, elk, and big horn sheep stared from the walls.

A man rose from behind a wooden desk at the rear of the room. A nameplate on the desk said: Francisco Yellowhair-Chavez. With a name like that I expected a blond Mexican, but his slicked-back hair was raven black with silver threads. He was heavy-set with skin burnished to a mahogany brown. Definitely Navajo.

His huge bovine-like eyes tracked us. A pale-gray cowboy hat with an enormous crown sat on his head. A huge silver and turquoise thunderbird clasped a bolo tie to his meaty throat. A silver and gold belt buckle as big as a saucer peeked beneath the swell of his substantial gut. Silver and turquoise bracelets the size of leg irons hung from both thick wrists. Everything about this man seemed massive and imposing, like he'd been hewn from a boulder.

An open laptop sat on his desk. Flags of the US, New Mexico, and the Navajo Nation hung on staffs behind his chair, and certificates and plaques decorated the wall.

I expected a greeting but he said nothing when Jolie and I halted before his desk. We were close enough that he towered over us, and we stared at each other for an uncomfortable moment. At least, I was uncomfortable. Yellowhair-Chavez could've had squirrels in his pants and I doubt he would've squirmed.

"Ahem," I said, smiling. "Rainelle said you could help us."

It was logical for Frankie here to ask what about. But he kept quiet.

"I need a rifle."

Yellowhair-Chavez just kept looking at me. Didn't blink. Didn't twitch.

"You have something?" I glanced to a row of gun safes.

He stared and stared and finally spoke. "Six hundred dollars." His voice was low and raspy.

"For what?"

"You are a friend of Coyote?"

"I am."

Yellowhair-Chavez walked from behind his desk toward a gun safe. A braid hung down his back. "He owes me six hundred dollars. You have the money? If you do, settle his account. Then we can proceed."

More of Coyote's collateral damage to my wallet. I knew this mission to save Carmen and stop Phaedra would cost me, but I assumed in a purely emotional sense. I counted four Benjamins, Jolie kicked in another two, and we handed the bills to Yellowhair-Chavez. He folded them between his big fingers and stuffed the money into a shirt pocket.

He touched the buttons on the safe's keypad. "I have AR-15, M1A, Kalashnikov, .243, .270. Six point five Grendel. Three-oh-eight. Swiss seven point five. 8mm Mauser. 30-06."

"I need a gun with some balls."

"Not the Swiss? The Mauser? The 30-06?"

"You got a .45-70?"

A smile barely curled his lips. "I thought so. You want serious artillery. I saw you last night. From the mesa."

Jolie started, "You're one of the skin—"

What little smile lingered on his face abruptly vanished. "There are no such things as skin-walkers."

As an undead bloodsucker I'm immune to the creeps. *Usually*.

He opened the safe and plucked a Marlin Guide Gun from a rack of rifles and shotguns. With practiced ease, he worked the lever action. *Click-clack!* A machine oil smell puffed out. He handed the carbine to me. The gun weighed perhaps seven pounds, but its heft implied thunderbolts of destruction and pain.

Without me asking, he reached back into the locker and grasped boxes of ammunition and a cartridge belt with carbine rounds glittering in the loops. The .45-70 cartridges were as long and as thick as a finger. You could drop a T-Rex with a .45-70 and knowing Phaedra, I might have to.

"Silver bullets are problematic," he said. "Silver is lighter than lead, which throws off the ballistics and weakens penetration." After the silent treatment, hearing him talk this much was a surprise. Adding to the surprise was his offer of the silver bullets. This skin-walker-who-didn't-exist knew how to kill vampires.

He gave me the belt and Jolie the boxes of ammo. "These bullets are depleted uranium with a silver jacket and a hollow-point silver core. Fifty rounds for the Marlin. Fifty for your Magnum. Another fifty for her .45s."

Jolie asked, "How do you know about our pistols?"

Yellowhair-Chavez only stared.

I shook the Marlin. "How much?"

"Everything? A thousand dollars."

Who knew saving the supernatural world would be so expensive. "I'm a bit short."

"So-kay. I take credit. I got your Visa on file." His stare didn't waver.

My Visa number on file? How? "Uuh? Isn't there paperwork?"

He blinked once. "Yeah … sure." He scribbled on a Post-It note and gave it to me.

Note in hand, I turned around. Jolie and I started for the door.

"One more thing," Yellowhair-Chavez said. "Some advice."

I halted and faced him.

He tapped his chest. "From the heart of my people."

What valuable Navajo wisdom was he about the share? "What's that?"

"Don't fuck up."

Chapter Fifteen

On the way back to Coyote's house, I sat next to Jolie in the front of the pickup. As I inspected the ammo for the Marlin, I cupped one of the large brass cartridges in my hand, careful not to touch the silver part of the bullet or I'd burn myself.

Where did Yellowhair-Chavez get these silver-tipped/depleted-uranium rounds? They had come disguised in a regular package though I knew he hadn't bought them from a commercial source. And why was a shape-shifter stocking ammunition specifically designed to take out vampires?

Those questions aside, I was grateful that he had sold them to us. With these slugs and the extra range offered by the carbine, I could take Phaedra down as soon as I drew a bead on her evil little face.

I pushed four rounds through the loading gate of the Marlin and worked the lever to chamber a cartridge. Holding the carbine gave the impression I was doing something productive, when in truth, our plans to save Carmen were in chaos, like the scattered pieces of a puzzle.

Jolie drove without saying much. After we'd left the gun shop, she stopped at a 7-Eleven for a pack of American Spirits. She huffed on a cigarette, not looking too pleased that she'd given in to this vice. When I mentioned that I didn't know she smoked, she remarked that there were a lot of things about her that I didn't know and thank you very much for not minding your own goddamn business.

A moment later she tapped my arm in apology. "You must have a plan."

"A couple. The best case is that we return to Coyote's and find him ready to go."

Jolie withdrew the cigarette and worried at something in her mouth. She spit a piece of tobacco. "And the not-so-best-plan?"

"We try using the Sun Dagger on our own."

Jolie glowered at the cigarette butt, then tossed it onto the highway. "Worth a try I suppose. Do you think Phaedra knows about the Sun Dagger?"

"Better to assume that she does."

We reached the turnoff for the mesa and followed the dirt road. After reaching the top of the mesa, Jolie steered through the open gate into the fenced yard behind the doublewide. Marina waited for us on a plastic crate by the door of the large shed. What I thought was a mourning shawl was draped over her head, shoulders, and arms. At the sight of the shawl, my kundalini noir quickened. *Not more bad news.*

Jolie parked close to her. When Marina stood, I saw what she wore was not a shawl but a black hoodie. The front was unzipped and revealed the top of a *low*-cut gown in siren red—a party dress, not a getup for prowling the river's edge and scaring people. Then again, if she intended to lure men into the water, her cleavage was sufficient bait.

I got out of the truck, carbine in hand, gun belt slung over one shoulder. "How is Coyote?"

"The same, unfortunately." Marina strutted on CFM designer pumps as she opened the shed door. The side of her gown split scandalously to mid-thigh.

The inside was gloomy, lit only by narrow blades of sunlight knifing through gaps in the siding. Dust motes swirled in the sunrays.

The shed was large enough for a pickup. Assorted car parts—fenders, tires, bumpers, seats—leaned against one wall. Farm implements—shovels, hoes, rakes, wheelbarrows, pick axes, jumbled coils of hose and rope—rested against the other wall. All the items looked ancient, rusted, or weathered—much like everything else in this part of New Mexico.

At the back of the shed, long wooden planks rested on a pair of saw horses to create a makeshift table. A cheap wooden coffin lay on top.

A faint and troubled aura glowed from the open coffin. Stepping close, I saw that Coyote lay inside, on his back, hands folded over his belly. He was fully clothed. Thankfully. Made sense Marina had put him there. The best place for a vampire to recuperate was in a coffin.

The outside of the coffin was marred with scrape marks and caked with dirt. It smelled of worms and decayed human, confirming it had been recently dug up for reuse. I didn't ask about its former occupant.

I studied Coyote, the deep wrinkles on his face and neck, his sunken eyes in their darkened sockets, the way his bony hands appeared made of crooked brittle sticks. Seeing how death gnawed at my friend made me slide into a depressed funk.

Jolie glanced back to the door. "Where's Rainelle?"

Marina picked up an unlit votive candle from several that stood on a shelf behind her. "She's getting medicine."

Jolie tightened her brow. "What kind of medicine?"

Marina ignited a disposable barbeque lighter and lit the candle. Starting a fire—however small—didn't seem wise in this tinderbox. "Why don't we trust that Rainelle knows what she's doing? My son suffered a gruesome wound to his kundalini noir," Marina explained. "His *chi* is hemorrhaging. If we don't stop his life force from draining, he will die."

She lit all the candles, a total of seven, and arranged them across the shelf. The flickering light dancing across Coyote's face seemed to animate him.

"Is there any significance to seven candles?" Jolie asked.

Marina grasped a ceramic to-go mug labeled *World's Best Mom* and gulped a drink. I smelled scotch. "Certainly," she answered. "That's all I could find at the Dollar Store." She parked herself on a rickety barstool (complete with duct tape) and watched her son.

The reflected candles shone as points in her eyes.

A grim solemnity settled across us, a heavy soulful silence that lasted until Marina slurped from her mug.

Jolie looked at her. "How are *you* doing?"

"Not well." Marina took a sip. "He's the last of my babies."

Coyote as a baby? Well, once, long ago it had been true. Now he appeared decades older than his mother.

"I don't want Coyote to die." Marina teetered on the barstool. "So you know, I never drowned any of my babies."

"I know you didn't," Jolie replied.

"In fact, I never drowned anyone." Marina's words slurred together. "I just have to go through the motions. Forever. And endure. Eternal damnation sucks."

The door creaked. Rainelle entered. She carried a wicker picnic basket. She entered, closed the door behind her, and approached us. She set the basket on the table by the foot of the coffin.

Marina slid off the barstool and wobbled a bit. She placed the mug on the shelf and joined Rainelle behind the table. They each grasped a coffin lid that had been resting against the sawhorses and placed it over the coffin, Rainelle at the feet, Marina at the head.

Rainelle moved the basket to the top of the coffin. She reached inside and withdrew corn cobs still in the husks, assorted flower blossoms, and a bundle of sage and desert weeds. Both women silently arranged the corn and blossoms along the top of the coffin.

Marina handed the lighter to Rainelle who lit the sage and weed bundle. The flame shrank to red embers that unwound curls of pungent herbal smoke. Rainelle closed her eyes and waved the smoldering bundle, chanting softly, and stamping her feet. Her ceremony appeared profoundly sincere and magical in spite of her UNM Lobos jersey.

Eyes still closed, Rainelle placed the bundle on the edge of the coffin. She opened her eyes and gazed at the basket. The twists of smoke angled toward the basket and were sucked in.

Something rustled inside. The lid cracked open and out crawled three Kachina dolls, each about a foot tall. All appeared made of gray suede with outsized heads and were decorated with zigzags and stripes of bright colors. They moved in jerky stop-motion, and I had to blink repeatedly to shed my disbelief.

One had deer antlers and carried a staff. Another had a green face, shook gourd rattles, and wore a skirt. The third had a fan of feathers around its head and feathers trailing from its arms like wings.

Jolie whispered, "More Navajo magic?"

"No," Marina whispered back, "Hopi."

The lid of the basket lifted and dropped. It boomed like a drum. The lid lifted and dropped again to repeat the sound. Again. And again until a pounding beat filled the shed.

The three dolls rocked and bounced to the rhythm. Slowly at first. Then faster to match the quickening cadence of the drum. They danced on the coffin, circling the basket, kicking, skipping, and pumping their arms. The sound of rattles and bells accompanied the drumming. An ethereal green aura trailed behind each dancer. With every lap around the basket, the auras became denser until they formed one continuous translucent hoop that undulated like a halo of emerald smoke.

Marina had draped a brightly colored shawl over her shoulders. She handed an identical shawl to Rainelle, who placed it around her neck. They turned their backs to Jolie and me and clasped hands. Their auras simmered and fused together.

I nudged Jolie that we should go.

Marina turned her head and beckoned Jolie. "Stay. Coyote has a mother and a wife, but he could use the power of a daughter. You can be that daughter."

Jolie brightened and put a hand on her chest. *Me?* Marina handed a new shawl to her. She put it on and walked between the other two women. They joined hands and faced the coffin, their auras blending into a wall of yellow, orange, and red flames.

I stepped forward. "What about a son? That could be me." A force, like a giant invisible hand, stopped me. When I tried to move, it pushed, insistent until I was walking backwards. The shed door opened behind me, I was shoved through, and I found myself in the yard, bathed in bright sunlight and surrounded by curious goats and chickens. Coyote's dog Che stared at me.

The dance music echoed out the open shed door. Then the door closed, muffling the sound.

Stung at being excluded, I blinked at the door, mystified by the Hopi ceremony. Just when I thought I'd seen enough weird, something even weirder happens.

I returned to the doublewide and dropped the gun belt on the kitchen counter. After fishing a bag of Type O Negative from the fridge, I searched the pantry for booze, found a bottle of blue corn Don Quixote vodka, and made a cocktail. Carbine on my lap, I plunked down on the sofa and sorted through Coyote's papers. When my glass was half-empty I topped it off from the bottle. Getting loopy made Coyote's scribblings start to make sense, so if I got good and ripped, I might be able to decipher his notes.

Soon I was hammered, and Coyote's writings still made no sense. Stretching out across the sofa, I let the alcohol dilute my misgivings and I drifted into a hazy slumber.

Someone kicked my foot and I was startled awake.

Jolie stood beside the sofa and tapped her boot against the carbine I'd let fall to the floor. She tossed the gun belt onto the sofa. "Some goddamn guard you are."

I sat up, my head still swimming from the vodka.

She handed me a cup of coffee, which I sipped. It was hot, black, and strong.

"At least you got some shut-eye." She picked up the Don Quixote and guzzled what little remained in the bottle.

"How's Coyote?" I could feel the coffee mercifully rearrange the molecules in my brain.

"Hard to say. Rainelle says that even Hopi magic needs time."

I was getting sober and my fears floated up from my subconscious. I glanced at my watch. 5:22 p.m. "We better get ready to leave soon. At this point, rescuing Carmen is a fool's errand, but we have to try."

"Don't be so glum. Our chances are better than what they were."

"How so?" My head still wobbled.

"Give it a minute."

My mind remained too fuzzy to quiz her.

Marina stepped through the back door and into the living room. She had exchanged her red dress for capris tailored like green military fatigues and her pumps for stylish trail runners. Pink pompoms dangled from the backs of the shoes.

I squinted at her. "Where are you going?"

"If my son can't help, maybe I can."

She plucked the rubbing of the Sun Dagger from the coffee table and eased into the armchair. She squinted at the picture of the petroglyph, and her large brown eyes roamed over Coyote's notes. "I think I can get you to D-Galtha. That might be the easy part."

I might still be boozy but I guessed the hard part. "Don't tell me th—"

Marina cut me off with a smirk. "You got it. The best I can do is a one-way trip across the galaxy."

Chapter Sixteen

Night would provide cover, so we got ready to leave at dusk, which would give us plenty of time to cross Chaco Canyon and reach the Sun Dagger on schedule.

Jolie and I fortified ourselves with blood and coffee. We cleaned our guns and checked our ammunition to the beat of '80s hits blaring from the radio. Marina studied her reflection in the mirror as she touched up her make-up and tied and retied a camouflaged bandana around her head.

Rainelle remained in the shed holding vigil over Coyote. When I mentioned earlier that Phaedra might return, Rainelle replied that the native spirits would protect her. I didn't know what the little dancing Kachinas or the skin-walkers could do, but this was her people's magic so I left it at that.

The rubbing of the Sun Dagger lay on the coffee table. I'd studied the picture so much that its image was practically etched into my retinas. Assuming the best, we'd arrive on D-Galtha—the easy part according to Marina. But she wouldn't accompany us. Couldn't leave Earth, she insisted. A condition of her curse.

Jolie and I would be on our own when it came time to find Carmen on D-Galtha. *How?* Then return home. *How?* And what was D-Galtha like? Would the aliens simply let us take her? How effective would our guns be against the extraterrestrials? Maybe we'd be better off bringing flowers and *pan dulce*.

And then there was Phaedra. Waiting for us now and when we returned. Which raised more questions than what I wanted to mull over.

Marina wore Coyote's gold Rolex on her wrist. "Let's go."

Jolie and I followed her out the back door. Cool night air washed over us. We stared at the shed where Rainelle was with Coyote. I wondered if we should interrupt to say goodbye.

The shed door opened. The ritual dance music spilled forth, the volume low. A green mist rolled over the threshold.

Rainelle walked out, clad in a loose coat and a knit cap. The Kachina with feathers appeared behind her and now it—he?—was as tall as me. He halted at the doorway, watching us, shuffling in place and shaking his arms to the muted rhythm.

Rainelle waded through the green mist to approach us. The door closed, hiding the Kachina and silencing the music. Rainelle looked at me and Jolie. "What's the plan?"

The answer seemed obvious, but I replied anyway, "Go straight to Fajada Butte."

"Knowing that Phaedra might be waiting?"

I stroked the carbine. "We're ready."

"I'm sure Phaedra is thinking the same thing. Why not throw her a curve and go the back way?" Rainelle dug a set of keys from her coat pocket. "We'll take my truck and approach from the south."

That would be on the first road we'd taken to the butte, the one where we'd abandoned the Porsche.

She winged a thumb to the shed. "The Kachinas will take care of Coyote until I return." She walked to her truck to where it was parked by the gate. She opened the driver's door. "Pile in, *comaradas*."

A bird fluttered overhead and landed on the rain gutter of the doublewide. A crow. A red aura swirled around its body. At the far corner, another tell-tale aura from a crow.

Crows are not nocturnal, so I figured these birds were on a mission for the Araneum. But the Araneum was in tatters. Since I became a vampire, I learned to expect bad news anytime a crow shows up. I studied their ankles for a message capsule but saw none.

"What's up with the crows?" Marina asked.

Jolie replied, "Maybe they're wishing us good luck."

I added, "Or *adios*."

Rainelle got in the truck and started the motor. Marina and Jolie squeezed themselves into the passenger's side. I let the truck out through the gate and climbed into the bed. I sat against the back of the cab and watched the crows as they watched us.

We proceeded to the rim of the mesa. Chaco Canyon yawned before us, a forbidding dark expanse. At this distance, Fajada Butte was but a finger-shaped smudge in the faraway gloom.

Stars filled the immense dark bowl of the sky. To the west, a fading band of blue highlighted the horizon. Pinpoints of light crawled along the distant highway to the faraway towns. The moon just started to rise above the eastern hills.

Rainelle turned on the headlamps and drove the Ford along the edge of the mesa. Our lights fell across the narrow, twisting road gouged across the forbidding rocky slope. Along the way down I bounced like a bead in a rattle. The truck's springs groaned when we bottomed out at the base of the mesa. Rainelle muscled the Ford along the road to the highway where we turned south. A sign said: Crownpoint 15 miles. Since this was my second trip through these parts, I should have recognized the surroundings, but we were in the middle of high desert that stretched into more high desert. Thirty miles in any direction and it would look the same.

Tonight was our one shot to rescue Carmen, at least in this century. Then if we got her home, we still had Phaedra to contend with. Coyote had said that only Carmen could defeat her. How? In my first dealings with Phaedra, she hadn't hesitated to use a mind probe to harass me. Now she was quiet. Why?

We turned east on Navajo Service Road 9 and our tires rumbled on the rough pavement. After a few minutes, Rainelle slowed. I peeked around the edge of the cab. A yellow flashing sign blocked the exit toward Fajada Butte. Rainelle flicked the high beams to illuminate the sign.

ROAD CLOSED
Dusk to Dawn
By order Dept of Homeland Security
Area patrolled by Cress Tech Intl.

This was no surprise. We'd tripped their psychotronic alarms twice already so it was about time they sat up and paid attention.

Rainelle drove forward, knocked the sign aside, and followed the road up a shallow incline. A yellow glow flashed on the reverse side of the slope. We topped the crest and saw that the glow came from the hazard lights of a Humvee straddling the road and facing our direction. Search lamps on its roof flicked on, dazzling us. Two silhouetted guards marched into the cone of illumination until they were sandwiched between the search lamps and our headlights. Their red auras burned with irritation.

Rainelle halted fifty feet from the Humvee. She and Jolie climbed out.

Jolie whispered, "Felix, stay down. I'll handle this."

One of the guards cradled an assault rifle. The other shouted, "Turn off your headlights! Stay in your vehicle!"

Rainelle and Jolie walked toward them, slowly, arms relaxed at their sides.

The aura of the guard doing the yelling flared with anger. "Stop right there! Couldn't you read the sign?"

Rainelle answered, "*No hablo ingles.*"

She and Jolie stopped close to the guards. Jolie mumbled something because both guards turned their heads toward her.

The eyes of one guard widened. His aura flashed like a strobe. Jolie turned to the second guard. His eyes widened and his aura also strobed.

Stunned by vampire hypnosis, the guards swayed like reeds. Jolie approached the first guard, clasped him in her arms and fanged his neck. His aura calmed and Jolie pushed him into the cab of the Humvee. She repeated the procedure with the second guard and returned with Rainelle to the pickup.

Jolie wiped her mouth. "Tasty stuff. Nice notes of bourbon."

"Could have asked for my help," I replied.

"Next time."

They climbed into the truck. Rainelle gunned the engine. She drove around the Humvee and up the road. We shimmied over the washboard, the ride just as jarring as I remembered from our abortive try in the Porsche, but the Ford handled the bumps and ruts like a tank.

Rainelle slowed, and I glanced around the cab. A buck mule deer emerged from the dark murk before us, maybe thirty feet away, eyes blazing. Rainelle halted the truck.

The deer's body began to flatten while his legs stretched. His eyes shriveled to points and vanished. He morphed into a hide of skin stretched over a framework that resembled a leather tent on stilts. *Skin-walker!* And probably Yellowhair-Chavez.

His aura shimmered like light reflecting on water. The head was now a simple flap of skin lacking eyes, or mouth, or ears, or anything else. Just a grotesque flap swinging to-and-fro. Behind him, Fajada Butte loomed like a blunt spike.

Rainelle said, "This is far as I can go in the truck," and we all climbed out. She pointed to the right. "There's a path that will take you to a gulley that leads to the butte."

The skin-walker shifted weight and adjusted his long, bony legs. He radiated power like a dynamo.

"Quite a lot of supernatural whoop-ass," Jolie noted. "I'd give good money to see Phaedra take this fucker on."

I turned to Rainelle. "Any chance we can persuade him to follow us to Fajada Butte?"

She shook her head. "That's your fight, not his. He's here to protect me." She glanced at the skin-walker and back at us. "Those guards miss their radio checks and someone will come looking. I better go."

She hugged Marina, then Jolie. I got a wave.

Rainelle got back in her truck. She swung the front end around, tooted the horn, and rumbled south. Van Halen blared from the radio. I looked for the skin-walker and all I saw was a deer sprinting into the night.

Marina said, "There are still miles of desert ahead, but you should get to the Sun Dagger with plenty of time to spare."

"You're not coming with us?" Jolie asked.

"I'll meet you there. You don't need me to slow you down."

"What are you talking about?"

Marina smiled. "I'll see you on top of the butte." Her body began to fade, becoming transparent, then *abracadabra*, she vanished.

Jolie and I stared at the empty space. New Mexico was full of surprises.

We proceeded down the path and picked up the pace to a fast jog. The gulley widened into a ravine with a broad, flat bottom. We passed one of the Cress Tech towers, which meant we were a mile from the butte. As far as I knew, the detectors needed a blast of psychic energy to trip the alarm, so our mere presence shouldn't register. Good. We didn't need any more interference from the government's goons.

A bluish light darted through the shrubs along the side of the ravine. Without breaking stride, I readied the carbine.

"Don't shoot," a voice warned. El Cucuy leapt over the bushes.

I relaxed my grip on the trigger. "How'd you find us?"

"Marina told me to expect you."

I was about to ask when and how and realized these local supernaturals must have their own unearthly Internet.

We climbed out of the ravine and onto flat ground that rose toward the butte. From this vista I could see across the canyon floor. To the west, a quarter of a mile away, a fan of green and white light shimmered.

Jolie pointed. "Phaedra."

If we could see her, she could see us.

The ground trembled. All around Phaedra, spouts of earth showered upward, each revealing an orange aura. Vampires. So many that they appeared like a glowing rash spreading against the landscape. Had we proceeded on our original route, we would've run straight into them. Rainelle's gambit had worked. We had sidestepped Phaedra's trap.

We sped up and continued toward the butte.

"Pity," Jolie's fangs glistened, "I was looking forward to a good brawl."

El Cucuy stopped suddenly. Four vampires emerged from the folds in the ground between us and the butte. Talons and fangs extended, they charged us.

Without hesitation, I blasted one. Levered the Marlin. Blasted another. The silver/depleted-uranium slugs ripped into the vampires like a pickax.

El Cucuy spread his arms and snagged one, scooping and crushing him in his grip. The vampire snarled and snapped at the boogieman but his fangs only skipped across the metallic hide.

Jolie had drawn a .45. She fired, and the remaining vampire's head exploded.

El Cucuy tossed his mangled victim aside. "Keep going. Don't let them bog us down."

These vampires were outliers, put here in case we scored an end run around Phaedra's main force, which we had. They may have been used to intimidating humans but they were fodder against us. No doubt new vampires eager to win Phaedra's approval. Their job was simple. Slow us down until her army could envelop us.

I plucked two rounds from my cartridge belt to top off the Marlin. I aimed at the main force. At this range, I could only hit a big target, but if I fired into a cluster of auras, I was certain to hit at least one vampire. I picked out a group and squeezed off a round. An orange splash from an erupting aura let me know I had hit my mark. I fired again and again. Two more splashes. The group scattered to save themselves.

Phaedra held position behind a phalanx of bloodsuckers, out of range. I tried a shot anyway, hoping for a lucky hit. I missed.

"They've stopped advancing," Jolie announced.

The vampires hadn't just stopped but were retreating. I gave a snort of ridicule. We'd beaten Phaedra without much of a struggle. Maybe this was a good omen for the rest of our adventure.

At this distance, Phaedra was a green and white spot. I tracked her as she moved toward a Cress Tech tower. *WTF?* Her aura brightened like she was stoking a fire. A plume shot from her, splattered against the top of the tower, and shrouded the psychotronic diviner in sparks of psychic energy. She was punching the Cress Tech panic button. If she couldn't stop us, then they could, or at least slow us down. For all their gung-ho bravado and military hardware, there were being played by Phaedra.

My elation sank back into unease. I glanced at my watch. 11:27 p.m. Less than twenty minutes to reach the Sun Dagger. It had taken Cress Tech an hour to respond the first time we'd tripped their alarm. Yesterday, less than thirty minutes. My legs churned with renewed urgency. I could sense the jaws of disaster begin to close.

Jolie and El Cucuy raced ahead, Jolie nimble as a doe, El Cucuy galloping like a two-legged horse. Looking back at Phaedra, I saw that she was gone and that her army of vampires was shrinking.

We sprinted over and around the large rocks on the slope skirting the butte. The tall cylinder of mountain towered before us. Jolie bounded against the face of the butte and scrambled up through a chute between the stone columns. El Cucuy jumped behind her, then it was my turn. The chute narrowed like the neck of a funnel.

Someone at the top called for us. Marina. She greeted each of us as we climbed out of the chute and into the open air. Moonlight painted the summit in muted hues.

A familiar thrumming chewed through the silence and gnawed my kundalini noir. From the south approached the green and red navigation lights of a helicopter.

Marina led us up the terraced summit to the slabs hiding the petroglyph. She reached into a shirt pocket and unfolded the rubbing of the Sun Dagger. She crouched between the slabs and ducked beneath. Jolie went next. Then me. El Cucuy stood guard.

I crowded against Jolie who leaned against Marina. A dagger of moonlight fell between the slabs and across the petroglyph. She placed the rubbing over the carving.

The helicopter grew louder, and I forced my kundalini noir to hold still.

I reached over Jolie's shoulder toward the petroglyph. Marina clasped my wrist and matched it with Coyote's tracing. The dagger of light sliced across my knuckles.

She eased the paper from underneath my hand, careful not to disturb my position on the carving. My kundalini noir quivered again. How precise would we have to be to keep Jolie and me from shooting into oblivion? I swallowed and the more I tried to remain steady, the more my insides trembled. I'd be calmer defusing a bomb.

Jolie placed her hand over mine. La Llorona let go and extended her left wrist to show us the Rolex. 11:43 p.m. *Showtime.* The second hand raced around the dial.

The helicopter's rotors boomed like we were inside a drum. My kundalini noir screamed inside me. My mouth went bone dry.

A glance upward. The moon was a white platter of light. A glance behind. El Cucuy grinned. *Better you than me.* A glance to the Rolex, then to my hand on the petroglyph. *Nada.*

Jolie flexed her fingers against mine.

The second hand swept past the twelve. Nothing.

Outwardly, we were still as statues, but inside the tension was tearing us apart.

Marina whispered, "There must be a blockage."

"What does that mean?" I whispered back. I rested the carbine against the rock and took the rubbing from Marina. As I positioned the paper on the petroglyph the gun belt dug into my back. I unbuckled the belt and handed it to El Cucuy, saying, "Hang on to this for a minute." I placed the rubbing right over the carving.

Marina scooted backwards and got behind me. Out the corner of my eye I saw her raise one boot. Then she kicked me in the ass.

I bumped against Jolie. She bumped against the rock. Something snatched my hand, and we blasted through the petroglyph.

Chapter Seventeen

I had the sensation of being caught between being awake and asleep. No sound. Just the impression I was moving.

Then came a howl, growing louder, and in the next instant, all was again silent and I was surrounded by light.

I blinked and found myself standing upright. I faced a landscape of rolling hills covered in what looked like grass and a pattern of dense green shrubs. The sky was an immense yellow bowl bisected by a thin black line. I studied the thin black line as it looped over me from horizon to horizon. Then I figured out what it was—the planet's ring. A band of blue rimmed the horizon. A quarter of a mile away stood a collection of tall structures covered in shiny facets like they'd been sculpted out of quartz.

D-Galtha?

The air was cool, temperate. No smells. I flexed my knees and measured the pull of gravity. Seemed earth-like. I still wore my clothes. But the carbine and my gun belt remained back on earth. *Shit.*

When Coyote had first demonstrated the power of the petroglyph, we had been whisked across the U.S. in a blink. This trip took much longer. Maybe traversing the galaxy takes time.

Where was Jolie?

I sensed movement to my right.

Jolie stood beside me, her eyes the size of eggs. She blinked in supreme astonishment. Her eyebrows inched upward as she gaped at our surroundings.

"You okay?" I asked. My voice sounded normal so the atmosphere was similar to Earth's.

Slowly, her mouth closed. She kept blinking and her eyes shrank to normal size.

But she had no aura. I raised one hand. Neither did I. Without the ability to see auras then we had probably lost night vision as well.

Jolie surveyed the area about our feet. We stood on a path made of red hexagonal bricks that curved across a lawn of dense grass. Other than the weird-ass sky and the funky buildings we could've been on Earth.

She patted her arms and chest as if to prove to herself she was here. "Can't speak for you, but this is some fucked-up bullshit."

"Could be worse," I replied. "I mean what are the chances? The atmosphere could've been corrosive high-pressure methane." I breathed deep and exhaled dramatically. "Air seems fine."

Jolie hopped upward and levitated to a height of twenty feet and then sank back down.

I did the same. At the top of my jump, I got a better view of the odd buildings in the distance. When my feet returned to the ground, I said, "At least we have that power. When we get a chance, let's test our strength." I swept an arm across the vista. "If nothing else, this planet looks like a bizarre theme park."

"Now what?" she asked, her tone panicked and angry. "So we're on D-Galtha? How do we find Carmen? This is like landing in Moscow when the person we're looking for could be in Los Angeles."

"Why don't we think positive?" I replied. "How many earth vampires could be here? I'll bet only one ... besides us."

"That's fucking brilliant, Felix." She cupped her hands around her mouth and shouted, "Carmen! Carmen! Where are you?" Jolie placed a hand behind her ear, waited for an answer that never came, then smirked. "*Nada*. Am I not surprised?"

"Then we go looking for her." I began down the path toward the glassy structures. Jolie fell in step beside me.

My kundalini noir remained at a steady vibrato of alarm. I had to assume we were on D-Galtha but there were other possibilities. Maybe we had landed on the wrong planet. Maybe we were in a computer simulation. Maybe I was dreaming.

The path beneath us wound between two shallow hills. As we approached the structures I could see they were high-rise buildings some sixty stories tall, each of a golden or silver hue, and covered in rows of dimpled windows. Rounding a bend, we slowed our steps and proceeded hesitantly toward the closest building, a glassy structure with golden highlights that stood on our side of a broad plaza paved with large red tiles.

Some kind of erect creatures ... walked? ... slid? ... across the plaza. The creatures had yellow heads and shoulders, red upper torsos, and a lower torso of red and yellow horizontal bands. Noodle-like dreads hung from the backs of their heads. A red cone or skirt covered their feet, if they had feet. Long spindly arms dangled from their shoulders. Many carried flat rectangular objects. Books? Briefcases? Laptops?

I counted perhaps fifty creatures crisscrossing the plaza, gliding in and out through arches along the base of the golden building. Other similar creatures traversed at a higher speed on bridges connected to the other buildings. I figured these were high-speed walkways like in an airport terminal. Everyone moved with a purpose, as if they had business on their mind.

On one hand, the scene was remarkably pedestrian. Literally. It appeared to mimic the commercial bustle of any Earth city. But on the other hand, the bizarre creatures, the fantastic buildings, and the garish primary hues—*red! blue! yellow!*—reminded me of a Frank R. Paul cover from a vintage science-fiction magazine.

Jolie asked, "Do we just go up to these guys and ask for directions?"

How to answer? I wished I was dreaming. Assuming we were on D-Galtha, our predicament was simply too overwhelming to comprehend.

Jolie grasped my wrist and pulled me off the path to shortcut across the lawn. As soon as we stepped on the grass, or whatever it was, blue rings began to emanate from the bottoms of our feet. The rings floated across the grass and faded away. We must've trigged an alarm.

The heads of the creatures closest to us rippled in our direction. A few slowed to watch. None acted too concerned.

Jolie and I gingerly stepped back onto the path but the blue rings kept growing from under our feet.

"If they wanted us to keep off the grass," she groused, "they should've put up a sign."

The creatures in the middle of the plaza parted to make way for a pair of their kind. These two each rode a contraption that resembled a hover Segway.

A voice in my head yelled: *Run!*

Another voice yelled back: *Where to?*

Jolie clasped my fingers and squeezed. I squeezed back, afraid ... make that *terrified*. My right hand tightened, ready to snatch the revolver from inside my jacket.

The two creatures halted their hover Segways in front of us, levitating about a foot off the ground. Up close, these creatures were at least ten feet tall, and appeared taller on their floating machines. The one on the right was a bit leaner. Both creatures wore a blue pillbox hat, which cinched the notion they were cops. Or mall security. They stared at us with white eyes inside deep black sockets. A horizontal slit of a mouth cracked open across the bottom half of an otherwise featureless face.

The creatures tilted their heads as they studied us. Their dreadlocks began to undulate. I couldn't read anything in their eyes. I couldn't hear them communicate. I saw nothing on their bodies like a belt or a weapon.

I raised my left hand. "Hi."

The skinnier creature touched the steering bar of his (her?) vehicle. The rings quit growing from under our feet.

So far, they hadn't threatened us, but that didn't soothe me.

The creature on the left tossed something small and shiny toward Jolie and me. The object stopped above us and rotated like a spinning coin. Then it extended into a rod, which in turn sprouted ribs like an umbrella. The umbrella grew and fell over us like a cage.

My kundalini noir rang in panic, and I wanted to tear at the cage, but I started to tremble uncontrollably. Then my jacket melted off my torso and fluttered to the ground. Followed by my shirt. My pants. My underwear. My socks and boots vibrated right off my feet. Within a moment, Jolie and I stood naked, helpless in a trembling palsy, our clothes and possessions piled around our feet.

The umbrella clamped tight around us, forming a missile shape. The metal was cold and unyielding. Squeezing. Mashing Jolie and me together like sausages. In other circumstances, pressed against a naked Jolie in an S&M cage might have brought me to the money shot, but now, my kundalini noir had my mind screaming in horror.

The creature on the right touched the handlebar again. The umbrella cage shot from the ground and carried Jolie and me into the sky.

Chapter Eighteen

Imprisoned in our flying cage, Jolie and I raced through the sky above D-Galtha, my fear meter pegged deep into the freak-out zone. Then my brain said, "Screw it," and embraced a Zen-like calm. *Hunker down, wait, and hope for the best.*

The wind blasted through the metal ribs of the streamlined capsule locked around us. My naked flesh felt cool, and Jolie's hair whipped against the back of my neck. I couldn't hear anything. Couldn't smell anything, either. I couldn't do much except watch. With this paralysis I was little more than a pair of eyeballs.

The landscape scrolled below. Without a scale of reference, I couldn't tell how high we were but I guessed a couple of thousand feet.

A jade carpet of vegetation covered the planet, the landscape dotted with small clusters of crystal buildings connected by roads and narrow winding paths. Everything seemed uniformly spread out and orderly like we were flying over a well-groomed, never-ending campus.

The paralysis ebbed. I could blink, then swivel my eyes. I was able to move my face ... a little. Enough to grimace.

Where were we headed? I had assumed the locals who had captured us were cops, but they could have been custodians. Maybe

Jolie and I were on the way to a landfill.

Or an incinerator.

Something flashed at our side, then disappeared from view.

I spied movement on the roads. From this height, the vehicles looked tiny as specks but they could've been the size of eighteen wheelers.

Another flash caught my attention and I managed to lock on it. Light reflected from a circular object of a dull pewter color and with a diameter of a hundred feet. The object crossed a few hundred feet below us, made an abrupt flat turn to fly parallel to our course, then made another abrupt turn and began to descend. As it receded, I could tell it was disk shaped with a spherical center: a flying saucer.

The saucer approached one of the crystal buildings, which had flying saucers stuck to its sides like gigantic petals. The one I was tracking docked in a gap between two others. A moment later, another saucer uncoupled from the building, backed away, and lifted straight up, accelerating into a blur that disappeared high into the atmosphere.

The saucer port scrolled out of view. We passed over more crystal towers and roads and acres of green rolling hills.

Our missile-cage tipped downward, and fear poked its ugly head from the box I'd shoved it into. I rolled my eyes to see where we were going. Our trajectory aimed us at an orange crystal structure, only this one was long and horizontal, with a rounded roof like a Quonset hut. The far end of the building faced a copse of earth-like trees that surrounded a large blue pond, the first evidence of water.

We dove straight toward the building. I hoped we weren't going to smash into it, but we weren't slowing down. I tried to make my fingers touch Jolie, to reassure her that we'd survive—or that we'd perish together—but nothing but my eyes seemed to work.

The ground rushed to meet us. The individual clumps of vegetation fused together into an emerald smear. My kundalini noir vibrated like a tuning fork, pulsating ever faster the closer we approached.

I strained to rotate my eyeballs as far up as they could to track our point of impact. The side of the building filled my field of view, and my kundalini noir compressed in anticipation of the crash.

A square window opened and we sailed through. We were bathed in brilliant white light. The cage abruptly stopped and snapped open. Jolie and I tumbled forward, to spin on our bellies across a hard floor.

The paralysis gone, I extended my arms to halt my rotation, and once I had stopped, I lay with my face against the cool tile floor. Everything remained out of focus; my eyeballs still quivering in their orbits.

Jolie lay sprawled beside me.

My vision slowly clearing, I lifted my head to take in our surroundings. We were in a gigantic atrium made of translucent orange material. A matrix of white lamps hung from the curved ceiling. Rows of balconies terraced the walls. Everything seemed made of the orange stuff.

Jolie sat up, her parts jiggling. She blinked, no doubt as dazed and astounded as I was.

A rapid, slapping noise drew our attention, and we turned to face it.

Someone sprinted toward us ... a woman as far as I could tell, dressed in a white tunic, the soles of her bare feet swatting the glossy floor. Her legs pumped between folds in the tunic. She shrieked, her voice very much human.

I rose to a crouch. She lunged at me, snagging my neck and knocking me over. She hooked Jolie's neck and fell on top of us, pulling us close until our heads bumped. Her shriek softened into sobs of joy and then into laughter. Smooth, firm hands caressed my torso and neck. Moist kisses slid over my face. Curls of black hair tickled my skin. Fangs raked across my shoulders and throat. Her red vampire eyes glistened with elation and darted from me to Jolie. My kundalini noir melted with a welcome and familiar warmth.

Our vampire host sat back and squashed Jolie and me to her breast with a superhuman hug. "What took you so fucking long to get here?"

We had found Carmen.

Chapter Nineteen

Carmen Arellano held us close, and I surrendered to gratitude. Despite the odds, Jolie and I had found her. The years of guilt over losing Carmen evaporated, and I soaked in the heat and cheer of the moment.

Carmen let go and sat back. Her dark eyes pulled at us, shiny and irresistible as polished magnets. Her cheeks were flush, steaming with happiness. The white gown clinging to the curves of her physique did nothing to stifle her provocative vibe. Except that her hair was shorter—her tresses barely raked her shoulders—she looked the same as I remembered her. Sleek. Sexy. Seductive.

She helped Jolie and me get to our feet. "How did you guys get here?" Her voice was giddy.

Jolie and I took turns telling her about Coyote and the psychic portal.

"Coyote?" Carmen asked, brow furrowed, her eyebrows tilting. "Never heard of him. And how did he know I was here?"

"He knew the aliens had taken you, plus he can access the psychic plane," I answered. "Have you had a dream or a feeling that someone was reaching out to you?"

"I wish I had, but no. I spent many days and nights praying someone would find me. Maybe that's what Coyote heard, though

I don't understand how." Her eyes turned from me to Jolie. "This portal that brought you here, is that how we get home?" she asked, her voice hopeful.

Jolie and I glanced at each other.

"Not sure," I answered, trying to keep an optimistic tone. "Getting here was a one-shot deal, and we had to leave before Coyote could explain how to return using a portal."

"Had to leave?" Carmen deadpanned. "I'm getting the impression there's trouble back home."

I went on to tell her about Phaedra, the vampire civil war, Coyote's injuries, and Cress Tech. At the mention of Cress Tech, Carmen's lips pursed angrily and her eyes slit. They were the reason why she was here. Jolie finished bringing her up to speed on events back home. Carmen winced and blinked as she took in this synopsis of our bad news.

She shook her head. "Phaedra? You mean a sixteen-year-old has the Araneum on the ropes?"

"Not just any sixteen-year-old." I described her powers.

Carmen wrinkled her nose like she needed more convincing.

Jolie added. "Remember Phyllis and Natacha De Brancovan?" She drew a finger across her throat. "Both of them. Phaedra's doing."

Carmen's eyebrows nicked upward.

"And that's the other reason we're here," Jolie added. "To bring you back so you can help us defeat her."

"How?"

Jolie shrugged. She pointed at me. "Ask genius over there."

I also shrugged. "Coyote only said you were needed."

"I don't understand," Carmen replied. "But that doesn't matter unless we can get back to Earth."

I studied the atrium. The immaculate floor was as large as a football field. The window we had flown through was about fifty feet up on the wall and was now covered by a pane of the orange crystal material. Dozens of doors stood equally spaced behind the balconies.

"Are we on D-Galtha?" I asked.

"You are," Carmen said. "How did you know the name?" Before I could answer, she replied, "I know ... Coyote." She spread her arms. "Welcome to D-Galtha, which means in the local language: Planet Pleasure."

Our surroundings gave me the creeps. "Planet Pleasure? Then why am I not feeling amorous?"

"Is this a prison?" Jolie asked, adding her heebie-jeebies to mine.

"Technically, Facility Two-Four," Carmen said. "But in reality, yes it's a prison."

"Run by who?" Jolie pressed.

"The Nancharm." Carmen cocked her head toward the distance. "Have you seen those red-and-yellow creatures outside? They run D-Galtha."

I gave Carmen the once-over. "Planet Pleasure and you. I'm not surprised, but what's the connection?"

Carmen replied with an uneasy smile. "There will be plenty of time to answer that question. But for now ..." Her gaze ranged over our naked bodies. "Oh my, I never dreamt that you guys would arrive so perfectly—undressed."

"It was unintentional," I explained.

"Don't be modest," Carmen said. "To be fair." She lifted her tunic and flashed us her toned body, the choice parts deliciously firm or delicately coiffed. She dropped the hem and started walking toward a door at the far wall. "Both of you look fantastic."

"As do you," Jolie replied, grinning.

"How much of our superpowers do we have?" I asked. "We can't see auras but we can levitate. How about you?"

"We retain our speed and strength," Carmen replied, "but don't use them unless you have to. Let's not tip off the Nancharm about what we can do."

A door slid open in front of Carmen. We passed over the threshold and into a hall. The walls were painted in pastel hues, a blue carpet covered the floor, and bright flowers (at least I thought they were flowers) stood in vases on console tables. The colors were a welcome relief from all the orange in the atrium.

"These are my private quarters." Carmen continued through another doorway and into what resembled a luxury hotel suite. A young woman in a silken robe lay asleep on a chaise longue.

I raised an eyebrow.

"That's Juanita," Carmen said. "My chalice."

"One of the women you were kidnapped with?" I asked.

"No. None of them are on D-Galtha." Carmen's expression took a sad cast. "Truth is, abducted women seldom survive, wherever they are sent. They might live in opulence but they go mad with loneliness and either waste away or kill themselves."

"There's another alien home besides D-Galtha?"

"Hundreds," Carmen replied.

"And Juanita?" I asked.

Carmen gave her a sanguine look. "I didn't ask for chalices, but the Nancharm brought them to me anyway, knowing that I need the sustenance."

"There are more?"

"The other three are in their rooms."

"And you? What's kept you from losing it?"

"Two things. One is the hope that I will be rescued, and here you are. And two, I have an important job."

"Job?"

A chime interrupted.

Carmen said, "This way," and ushered us back to the atrium.

One of the Nancharm waited for us, large white eyes glaring from its cylindrical head, with a small gray box sitting on top like a cap. A hover scooter floated behind the creature, and on the back end rested a wire crate with our clothes and belongings ... including our pistols.

The creature's dreadlocks began to undulate and a moment later, a surprisingly dainty voice emitted from the box. "Carmen, I trust your friends are doing well?"

Carmen slapped my naked butt. "Go on," she whispered, "pretend you have manners."

I acted like I was tipping a hat, as coyly as I could considering my junk was on display. "Thank you for the hospitality."

Jolie did a little bow.

"This is Doctor Moots." Carmen spread her arms to encompass the building. "This is her research laboratory."

Her? I studied Moots the way I would an exotic zoo creature. Her torso looked smooth and hard, and her body articulated in sections like an exoskeleton. Her thin arms and hands were coarsely textured and swayed in graceful sinuous movements. But I saw no evidence of female parts. She seemed to communicate through her dreadlocks and used the gray box on her head as a translator.

She crooked a finger, and the scooter drifted around her and toward us. "I brought your ornamental coverings and toys."

"You mean our clothes?" Jolie asked.

"The Nancharm don't understand human modesty." Carmen glanced at me and pointed to the crate.

I took the crate and placed it on the floor. "Isn't she curious about why we're here?"

Moots' cluster of dreadlocks spread like the tentacles of a sea anemone, and after a short delay, her voice emitted from the gray box. "You are guests of Carmen, no? To help with our research, no?"

"Of course," Carmen answered.

Planet Pleasure research?

Moots waved her spaghetti arms. "I do wish someone would tell me when new specimens arrive."

Specimens? That didn't sound good.

"Next time," she continued, her voice cross, "please advise your friends not to wander off the Path of Conformity. I get charged by the Safety and Aesthetics Patrol every time they return a specimen, and my anal chute is already taking enough of a pounding from the Budget Oversight Committee."

The hover scooter lowered to the floor, and Moots glided onboard. "We've dawdled enough for one day." The scooter lifted and floated to a door that scrolled open on the side of the atrium. "We'll get a fresh start tomorrow. Be ready."

Chapter Twenty

Moots drove her hover scooter out the building and onto the paved apron outside. A door on the ground swung upward, and she floated down the opening. The door closed after her.

Carmen stared blankly at where Moots had disappeared.

"What's going on?" I asked. "Moots mentioned something about research and specimens. What research?—"

"... And what specimens?" Jolie pointed at herself. "Us?"

Suddenly glum, Carmen's let her shoulders droop. Witnessing her spirit sag caused a sharp pit in my gut.

"It will probably be best for me to start at the beginning." She gestured to the crate with our belongings. "Get dressed if you want."

Jolie and I plucked our clothes and began to put them on. Carmen gazed in our direction, but the distracted look in her eyes revealed her mind was elsewhere.

I pulled on my pants, feeling more at ease because I was no longer naked. "I know the aliens had trapped you in suspended animation and teleported you off Earth."

Jolie had her panties and tank top on and was slipping into her jeans. "And you've been here since?"

Carmen shook her head. "First I was sent to a processing center with all kinds of weird creatures—both in and out of cages. Then I was pinballed from planet to planet until I got here a few months ago." She named the places she'd been, using awkward sounds like grunts, whistles, and clucks.

I asked, "Weren't you considered contraband?"

"As if that made a difference. The penalties against interplanetary smuggling are a joke. Smuggling contraband out of a quarantine zone like Earth is illegal. But once contraband is in circulation, trafficking in it is not against their law. Figure that out."

I buttoned my shirt. "I thought the Galactic Union put Earth under quarantine because humans were too warlike and a threat to the rest of the galaxy."

"True." Carmen pointed a finger in emphasis. "The quarantine was put in place to keep advanced technology away from humans. Compared to the rest of the galaxy, humans are still in the Stone Age, and the Union aims to keep it that way."

Jolie smirked. "So we're a danger?"

"Don't get carried away by that thought," Carmen replied. "The Nancharm are the bad asses of the Union. They want something, they take it. This planet used to belong to another species, a rather advanced one. The Nancharm offered a deal, which the inhabitants refused." She turned her eyes toward the door and the sky beyond. "You noticed the planet's ring. That's what is left of them. After demolishing their cities, the Nancharm blasted the debris into space as a monument to the victory and as warning to everyone else. *Don't fuck with us.* And in a touch of irony, renamed this planet D-Galtha: Planet Pleasure."

I slipped on my boots and reached for the magnum revolver. It lay in the crate beside Jolie's pistols and our ammo. I swung open the cylinder and checked that the cartridges remained chambered. I snapped the cylinder closed and tucked the revolver back into my jacket. "Trusting souls, our hosts."

"Moots called the guns, 'your toys,'" Carmen reminded. "For good reason. Shoot one of the Nancharm, and they'll reassemble your molecules into dung worms."

"Thanks for the notice," I replied. "I'm already in deep shit."

"Why are you here?" Jolie was dressed except for her cross trainers, holster harness, and jacket. "You couldn't be a pet. Not if you're helping Moots with research."

The building's door scrolled closed. When it thumped against the threshold, the noise echoed in the cavernous interior of the building, sounding exactly like a cell door slamming shut in a prison. Carmen extended her arms and took Jolie and me by the hand. I felt the longing in her touch. Here we were, the three of us, so far from home with no idea how to save ourselves.

Carmen kept quiet, and I waited for the familiar, mischievous twinkle to appear in her eyes. It didn't. She let us go and exhaled, her expression heavy with melancholy and anxiety. "I'm here as the Nancharm's last hope."

"What?" I asked.

"Two centuries ago, the Nancharm faced a rebellion from within the Galactic Union. They barely beat the rebels, and the slim victory shook them up. As a result, the Nancharm males altered their genome to hone their warrior characteristics. Speed. Intelligence. Sensory acuity. Strength. Ruthlessness."

"I take it things didn't go right," Jolie said. Like me, she didn't get into her jacket. She carried her holster harness draped over an arm.

Carmen nodded. "They had made a deal with the devil, a devil they didn't know even existed. It took three generations for the unintended consequences to become apparent."

"Which are?" I asked.

"The Nancharm men lost their mojo."

Their predicament sounded so ridiculous I snorted. "Seems like an easy fix to me. A trip to the drug store for the right meds."

Carmen started back to her quarters. "Exactly, but it's not an issue with faulty plumbing. The problem is here." She tapped her head. "Or with the Nancharm …" She touched a spot below her neck. "This is where their brains are."

"Basically," I replied, "the Nancharm men can't get it up, whatever 'it' is?"

"That's correct."

When we passed through the threshold, I estimated the size of the door, human-sized and too small for the Nancharm, and commented, "At least you get privacy."

Carmen frowned. "They can come and go as they please. You'll see."

We entered her suite. Juanita was gone. At the moment, my guns seemed useless. I hung my jacket, with my revolver still inside, over the back of the loveseat.

Jolie followed my example and dropped her jacket and her holster harness close to mine. "You still haven't told us why you're here."

"Apparently, I put off some kind of a sexual vibe." Carmen at last grinned. "The aliens really get off on us Earth women. You know how dogs and cats can pacify people, somehow read your mood? Earth women have the same gift, only more so, which makes us quite valuable. And me? Apparently, I have the extra-special touch."

She led us through another door and into a kitchen with a sink and cabinets on one end and a bar on the other. The counters and ceiling hooks glittered with shiny utensils like a display at Williams-Sonoma. My gaze ranged to the bar and its rows of bottles: scotch, rye whiskey, bourbon, vodka, gin, and tequila. All in my favorite brands. The possibility of a good cocktail smoothed my worried edges.

Jolie ran her fingers along pots and pans hanging from the ceiling and made them clatter. "What do you cook?"

"The Nancharm import all sorts of grains, fruits and vegetables, meats, fish. We grind our own flour to make bread, tortillas, and pasta. Keeps us occupied and breaks up the monotony."

She proceeded through yet another door and into a dining room with a massive wooden table and five matching chairs. The interior was decorated in Tudor-style: lush carpets, dark paneling, heavy wooden beams, and wrought iron fixtures. Still no sign of Juanita. A man's sport coat rested over one of the chairs. Carmen had mentioned she had other chalices and perhaps the coat belonged to one of them. If so, who? And why a sport coat?

Before I had a chance to ask, Carmen said, "Owning an Earth woman is a big status symbol. My first owners—"

Owners! Carmen as property? Reduced to chattel? I suspected that of course, but I hated to hear it. My stomach churned, and I wished for a martini to wash down the rising bile.

"—were the Wah-zhim," she continued. "They look like pygmy elephants, only with a trunk on either end. One is a nose, the other prehensile junk—"

"Even the females?" I tried to form a mental picture.

"Yes. Imagine the possibilities." A long-absent gleam finally sparked in Carmen's eyes. "The Wah-zhim love to play with both ends during sex."

"And you helped?" Jolie's voice trembled with disgust.

"No big deal." Carmen shrugged, still amused. "It was like being a large-animal vet. Quite fascinating. These guys were really into daisy-chain orgies. After I showed them positions from the Kama Sutra, modified of course, I about went deaf when they trumpeted with pleasure. The Wah-zhim thought they knew everything about sex until I came along."

"Your contribution to cosmic harmony," I added.

Carmen didn't linger in the dining room and we followed her to yet another door, this one larger than the other and made of smoked, faceted glass. "But the Wah-zhim aren't only about sex, they are also gifted inventors. You noticed the flying saucers?"

Jolie and I nodded.

"The Wah-zhim make those."

"Where do the Nancharm fit in?"

"They heard about my reputation as an 'arousal facilitator,'" Carmen made air quotes, "and were so desperate for a solution, they confiscated me. My Wah-zhim owners weren't too happy, but what could they do? If they complained, the Nancharm would use megaton particle slammers to smash them into cytoplasm jelly."

I couldn't imagine the Nancharm kicking anyone's ass. They looked harmless as Doctor Seuss characters. Then again, they had paralyzed Jolie and me and blasted us here in that flying umbrella cage.

I studied the room and keyed in on what was missing. Monitor screens. Televisions. Any kind of a computer, clock, or communication device. I was certain there was no cell phone service here; the roaming charges would be a killer.

Carmen stood with her back to the door. "The Nancharm reengineered the planet into a gigantic combination laboratory and resort. A romantic getaway to try and kindle some Nancharm whoopie. Planet Pleasure, remember? Among the men, I need to emphasize. Their women don't have a problem. They're the ones who brought me here."

"In the hopes of a good boning?" I asked.

"That we all need from time to time."

"Other than frustration, what's the problem?"

"The problem is, no Nancharm babies. The youngest are adolescents. They are a dying species."

"Can't they harvest eggs and sperm?" Jolie asked. "In vitro fertilization would be an easy fix."

"Nancharm 'ootz'—their word for spooge—doesn't activate until it's been primed by an orgasm. Unless the release of ootz is accompanied by bells and whistles, their men are just shooting blanks."

"Why don't men," Jolie pumped one hand, "just watch porn and beat off into a cup?"

"First of all, the Nancharm don't have or understand porn. But more importantly, their men have lost the urge."

"Let me get this straight." The explanation baffled me. "The Nancharm men don't want to get their nut off? The whole point of progress and technology is to make it easier to get some tail."

"It's been bred out of their genetic code. They inadvertently made themselves warrior eunuchs."

"Can't they reverse the process?" Jolie cinched her eyebrows. "Monkey again with their DNA and reset the chromosomes?"

"They've tried. Only made things worse."

"What can *you* do?"

Carmen stuck out a finger. "Figure something to make the Nancharm men go *boing*."

"Do they even have penises?" I asked. "Not that I'm curious."

"Oh, Felix," Carmen replied, "you and your hang ups."

"And after we put lead in their pencils? Will they return us to earth?"

Carmen turned somber. "I've asked Moots, but she doesn't give an answer."

"You save them from extinction," Jolie replied sharply, "they should at least give you a cab ride home. It's only simple courtesy."

"You think? My one-night stands have ended with more civility."

"Where are the Nancharm men?" I asked.

"All over. Why do you ask?"

"Right after we landed, we stumbled across buildings with Nancharm going back-and-forth. None of them looked like soldiers. In fact, they looked like bureaucrats. And I can't tell the men and women apart."

"Outwardly, they appear the same."

"That might another part of the problem," I said. "I wouldn't want to hit on anyone who looks like me. They might want to go for cosmetic surgery. Moots could get implants."

Carmen rolled her eyes. She reached for the brass door handle and pushed. The door opened onto a patio cluttered with furniture. The vista overlooked the pond and trees I'd seen from above when Jolie and I flew at this place. The pond was about the size of a baseball diamond with a waterfall cascading over rocks at the far end. A horseshoe of lush trees enclosed the pond and patio. Plants of all shapes grew along the bottom of the trees and to the edge of the pond, forming a tapestry of verdant greens, decorated with swaths of flower blossoms in a rainbow of colors.

Splashing and voices drew us. We walked to the edge of the patio and looked down on marble steps that led into the pond.

Four humans—Juanita, two men, and another woman—frolicked at the water's edge, splashing and laughing. Their sleek, handsome bodies glistened invitingly. Curiously, they wore swimsuits. *Tiny* swimsuits, but large enough to cover their private carnival rides.

"Your chalices?" Jolie cocked an eyebrow.

"Yes."

I scoped out the view. "Rather nice back yard ... and decorations."

"Absolutely idyllic," Jolie added. "Your personal Garden of Eden."

"Don't be too impressed," Carmen replied. "A gilded cage is still a cage. A cage for lab rats." She sighed. "Us."

Chapter Twenty-One

Jolie studied the chalices swimming in the pond. "I could use a snack."

"No problem," Carmen replied. She put two fingers into her mouth, puffed her cheeks, and let loose an ear-splitting whistle.

The chalices in the water froze, turned their faces toward us, and swam to the marble steps. Carmen proceeded down the steps to the edge of the pond. Jolie and I followed.

None of the chalices acted surprised that they had guests. Maybe they were so used to being watched and probed that another pair of visitors was no big deal.

The female chalices emerged first. Water filled the cups of their bikini tops, stretching them open, and I craned my neck for a better view. Juanita's postage-stamp yellow bikini glowed against her olive skin. The other woman, a slender blonde with a pink complexion, wore a floral print swimsuit that was equally abbreviated and revealing.

Carmen introduced Jolie and me to Juanita—Juanita Pacheco from Rivas, Nicaragua—and the other woman, Cassie Tait, from Arnhem, the Netherlands. Both women smiled politely, but their eyes expressed dampened curiosity.

The two men climbed out of the pond. Water dripped from the bulges in their banana hammocks. One of the men had a compact build, and his black hair lay in thick, shiny strands down the sides of his head. A knobby chin punctuated his square-shaped face. His name was Irsan Hirari, and he mentioned that he was from Semarang, Indonesia.

The other man—Toby Huxley, a long-limbed blond from Melbourne, Australia—replied to our introductions with a hearty, "G'day."

All the chalices looked to be in their mid-twenties, with radiant skin and well-toned physiques. They reminded me of Olympic athletes, the healthiest examples of humans anyone could possibly find. Even after Carmen explained that Jolie and I were also from Earth, the chalices remained reserved and cool.

I glanced at Jolie to gauge her reaction. Her gaze roved over the chalices and while her mouth held a pleasant smile, I could sense the gears and switches in her head working to figure out the deeper meaning of what was going on.

"Convenient that everyone speaks English," she commented.

Carmen replied, "The Nancharm made that a requirement when they placed the order."

"An order for what?" Jolie asked.

"Not what," Carmen answered, "who. The chalices."

My turn. "An order with who?"

"The alien gangsters," she explained. "Clayborn's people." Of course, the same bunch of intergalactic criminals that had engineered Carmen's kidnapping.

Ignoring that we were talking about them, the chalices picked up towels from a stack on the steps and began blotting themselves dry, stretching their lean legs and twisting from side to side, their muscles flexing deliciously beneath taut skin.

Toby turned away to dry the back of his legs and I noticed a thin scar that ran down his spine. The scar started from under the hair at the back of his head and continued down to his trunks. I squinted at the scar and saw four more, short parallel lines just visible at the base of his skull. The scars were precise and straight—surgical, not souvenirs from an accident. I couldn't think of a medical reason for such incisions and when I looked to Carmen, her guarded expression told me to hold my questions for another time.

She told Toby and Cassie to gather the towels and go inside. Irsan and Juanita were instructed to lie on the table.

We climbed the steps back to the patio. Carmen asked Jolie and me to join her at the table. Irsan and Juanita stretched on top of the table and laid down on their backs, Irsan with his head in front of Jolie, Juanita rested her head in front of me.

Irsan smiled eagerly at Jolie, and then at Carmen. He presented his wrist, which she grasped in one hand the way one might a martini glass. Juanita kept her lips tight as she offered her neck. I guess she didn't want me to feed off her but too bad. I was a vampire, she was a chalice, and them's the rules.

Fangs extended, we vampires pressed our mouths to the inviting skin, Jolie and me to the chalice's throats, Carmen to Irsan's wrist. Blood spurted onto my tongue, the liquid warm and delicious, resplendent with notes of chocolate and ripe peppers—what you'd expect from a good Type O Positive. Full-bodied with no fast-food chemical aftertaste. I lapped healing enzymes and for her troubles, gave Juanita a good dose of endorphins. She gasped and released a tiny moan. I held her trim middle and appreciated her firm flesh. Mr. Happy was getting a blood rush, and I wondered if I should propose a free-for-all, in the interest of Nancharm science, of course.

Carmen cleared her throat and snagged my attention. She narrowed her eyes and shook her head.

Another time then. I relaxed my grip on Juanita and let her catch her breath. She took one of my hands and kissed it in gratitude.

She and Irsan slid off the table and left tracks from their wet bathing suits. Carmen dismissed them. Juanita departed first. Irsan stared pleasantly at me before he left her side. He didn't go so far as wink, but I knew he had sword fighting in mind.

A vampire mentor once explained that in view of our immortality, I would eventually let go of any inhibitions I had about indulging in homosexuality. For one, he explained I was a vampire, one of the Damned, an undead bloodsucking killer, so playing catcher or pitcher with another man wouldn't even register in my list of pervy extracurricular activities. Given that I could live forever, shagging vaginas might get a little monotonous, so why not smoke a pole on occasion?

But I had plenty of time to switch teams and I was still curious about plumbing the depths—so to speak—regarding the pleasures of female company.

I watched Juanita as she walked away and appreciated how the wet bikini clung to her curvy bottom. "I don't understand the need for bathing suits. You said the Nancharm don't understand modesty. Seems like the pond makes for a great opportunity to skinny dip."

"Moots explained that they prefer to see us wear clothes," Carmen replied. "That way, when we do 'show-and-tell,' it signals them we're about to have sex."

"I thought they'd be monitoring your brain waves or something like that."

"They do." Carmen pointed to ferns growing beside the patio. "These are sensors."

I reached down and touched the leaves. They were delicate and very life-like. I broke a stem and the milky sap that oozed from it seemed authentic.

"It's a mutant," Carmen explained.

"Seems with all their DNA problems," Jolie said, "the Nancharm would've learned their lesson about screwing around with chromosomes. Theirs and everything else's."

Carmen shrugged. "That's their business. But back to the question about why the Nancharm make us wear clothes. They're astonished how much sex we humans have on the brain."

"They can read our minds?" I asked.

"No. They monitor brain-wave activity and chemical levels and correlate those to our behavior. To them, we're obsessed with sex, and their instruments have a tough time distinguishing between when we're merely fantasizing and when we're committed to the deed. When we drop trou in one another's company, that signals 'Blast Off!' and the Nancharm scramble to pay attention. I've seen their monitoring room. It looks like mission control at NASA."

I imagined the scenario. Carmen and her chalices expose their junk and start playing. An alarm goes off. Nancharm men in skinny ties and nerdy glasses hustle to their desks and put on headsets.

They stare at banks of monitors to study their human prisoners performing the pelvic boogie and maybe even cheer a cream pie.

"And you don't mind the show?"

"You learn not to care. They have cameras all over." Carmen waved a hand. "Tiny and practically invisible."

"Next question," Jolie said. "What's the deal with Toby's scars?"

Carmen replied. "Aside from being stranded billions of miles from Earth, there's an even darker side to our cozy, little paradise. The Nancharm dig into Toby on occasion to learn how he works."

"Works?"

"His erections."

"What about Irsan?" Jolie continued.

"He's the control specimen," Carmen replied. "But my boy-toy Toby has got so many sensors and scanners implanted inside him he's practically bionic." She pinned me with a stare. "And I fear the Nancharm will do the same to you."

Chapter Twenty-Two

Carmen's gaze turned icy cold. I was certain the climate-controlled air around the patio hadn't dropped a degree in temperature, but my skin still goose bumped.

The Nancharm might slice me open and stuff me with wires like they'd done to Toby. I looked across the table at Carmen. "Why don't you tell Moots that since I'm a vampire, I can't be monkeyed with."

"If the topic comes up, I'll give it try," she replied. "In the meantime, I suggest you keep your dick limp and corralled in your pants. You start sporting wood, and you could find yourself as the new Exhibit A."

Great. I mean, really fucking great! The one bennie of this outer-space escapade was the chance to score some leg from Cassie and Juanita—Carmen and Jolie were welcome to join in—but if I did, I was sure to find myself pinned and splayed against an examination table.

"What about Jolie?" My gaze slid to her.

She fought a grin. "The issue is not with the women, which means I'm free to party." The grin deepened. "Must suck to be you."

"It's the lack of suck that's pissing me off."

Carmen tapped my hand. "Poor Felix. But look at the bright side. Without the distractions, you'll have plenty of time to figure a way home."

The chill gave way to a warm flush of resentment. "If that means I'm getting a rain check on the sex, expect me to cash it in when we get home."

She grasped my hand and planted it on one of her boobs. Her breast was exquisitely firm and delectable. "That's the spirit. Set goals and think positive."

I glanced between my legs. "You're not helping matters."

Her eyes twinkled. "I know, and don't you hate me for it?"

Reluctantly, I withdrew my hand so I didn't set off an alarm and have the Nancharm rush in with nerve connectors and laser scalpels.

Jolie chuckled, and since I didn't see the humor in my situation, she was definitely laughing at and not with me. After a moment, she grew quiet and pensive and looked back to the building. "Why are the chalices so uptight? The arrival of friendly company should brighten their day. Plus, they seem a little slow on the uptake. Are they drugged?"

Carmen shook her head. "Actually, they're quite sharp. Their lack of cheer is that they're not happy to meet new prisoners. Several other chalices have cycled through this laboratory, and we've learned that for us, there's only one way off D-Galtha."

"Not alive, I take it?" I replied.

Carmen nodded.

Our prospects curdled what remained of our satisfied mood from the blood meal. We took in our surroundings and brooded. The garden, once so perfect and comforting, now seemed cartoonish and diabolical.

The blossoms around the patio began to pulse with light and go *Bing! Bing! Bing!*

Carmen's eyes crinkled with displeasure. She obediently stood and faced the door. Jolie and I pushed away from the table and rose to our feet.

The door swung open. The doorframe amazingly widened and grew taller. The flower blossoms dimmed and went silent.

Moots glided through the doorway and once she had passed, it shrank to its previous dimensions. She waved her skinny arms and slid toward us. Her head tendrils fluttered, and her translator/cap said, "Well ..."

"Well, what?" Carmen asked.

Moots pointed at Jolie and me. "We're waiting."

None of us moved.

"Oh, reeeallyy ..." Moots said, the translator/cap doing a good job of relaying her sarcasm. "You humans can be so difficult. Too difficult for your own good." She stabbed her fingers in all directions. "The committee is watching."

"What committee?" I asked.

"The Erection Analysis Committee. In the control room, which you know all about, thanks to Carmen." Moots pointed at my crotch. "We're waiting for the boom, boom."

"I'm flattered by the attention, but I'm not in the mood."

Moots dropped her arms and approached close to tower over me. "Not in the mood? Not in the mood!" Her tendrils shook like tree branches in a wind, and the translator blared so loud the air trembled around me. "*Not in the fuckin' mood!*" She twisted her torso to face Carmen. Her voice softened. "How was that?"

Carmen nodded. "Good."

"Thanks. I have been paying attention to your human mannerisms." Moots faced me again. "Then Felix, what is the problem?" She touched her chest and waved her hand. The glowing outline of a human female materialized before me. "Explain something. As a sexual anthropologist specializing in the most bizarre of extraterrestrial forms," she tipped her head toward me, "I've learned that the human females here fall into the ninety-eighth percentile of what you human males find desirable. What I named the Booty-Call Index." A full-body image of a naked Cassie rotated inside the outline. The number 98.45% flashed above. That image was replaced by one of Juanita. 98.72% Jolie. 99.05% Carmen. 99.99% "Unless ..." Moots wiggled her finger. The outline broadened to depict a rather plump, busty woman. "Maybe you prefer BMWs?"

"That's BBWs," corrected Carmen.

"No? Yes?" Moots asked, waiting for me.

Actually, I liked most women, and a chunky gal could smother you with warm, sweaty love. But I thought it best to keep quiet because I didn't want the Nancharm to kidnap yet another chalice. Besides the lack of shag-worthy women wasn't the problem.

"Oh!" Moots exclaimed. "You are gay."

"No," I protested. "I'm just not in the mood."

Moots' tendrils fell limp, and I could feel the pressure of her glare through those cold, blank eyes. Her tendrils puffed once, and she sighed, "Men."

She slid over the patio back toward the door. I watched how the bottom segment of her body skirted against the ground, hiding her feet or whatever it was that propelled her so smoothly.

"Carmen," she said, "he is your responsibility. I want to see a Felix erection, and I want to see it go pop."

Normally, not a problem.

Moots spun in place and looked at me. "If you're going to make me wait this long, it had better be good."

"I'll try."

"Do better than try."

Jolie elbowed me and whispered, "How's that for pressure?"

I whispered back, "Thanks for your support."

Moots continued for the building. "Carmen, I brought supplies for your kitchen. In my study of human-mating rituals, a good meal helps set the right mood." Moots twisted to stare at me again. "And we want the right mood, don't we?"

"Absolutely."

"Otherwise," Moots said, "well ..." Her tendrils dropped, and her voice trailed off. "Carmen can explain."

Carmen shook her head. "It's not a good thing. You'd be mulched for the plants."

My dilemma pinched like the jaws of a vice. If I performed, they'd open me up for study. If I didn't perform, I'd be turned into fertilizer.

When Moots drew close to the door, it opened, and the doorframe grew to let her pass. Carmen, Jolie, and I followed her through. I glanced warily at the frame, not convinced it wouldn't snap tight around us. But it returned to its safe, human size. Moots led us through the salon, the dining room, and to the kitchen. At each threshold, the doors stretched open to let Moots pass, and I wondered why the doors hadn't been made large enough to begin with.

The chalices were all in the kitchen. They were dressed in jeans and t-shirts and were busy picking through metal containers stacked on a hover platform. Juanita was giving orders, and Cassie and the two men sorted through sacks, packages, and small boxes they'd retrieved from the containers. Everything was decorated with pictures of food. Most were labeled in languages I didn't understand, but a few were in English, complete with bar codes. Baking soda. Salt. Sugar.

Moots motioned to the door that led back to the main room. "Carmen, I need to speak with you alone."

Carmen's eyes flashed *now what?*

She and Moots left through the door and it shut behind them. Juanita put Jolie and me to work. She asked Jolie to help her and the two men store the packages in the cupboards and to replenish the cabinet bins with tea, coffee beans, and grain from the sacks. I was to help Cassie make bread. We washed our hands in the counter sink, then scooped flour from a bin and into a large ceramic bowl. She added salt, yeast, and water and folded the ingredients with a big spoon.

"I'm surprised the Nancharm don't provide ready-to-eat food," I said.

"They prefer not to," Cassie answered, her voice thick with a Dutch accent. "Boredom can be a problem. Having us make our own food is busy work, but it is a good busy." She pushed the bowl across the counter toward me. "Now, you knead the dough."

I jammed my fingers into the damp lump and began to squeeze. "You guys make everything?"

"What we can. We once tried cheese and chocolate, but they were terrible." She grimaced. "The Nancharm import the food." Cassie opened one of the refrigerators. The shelves were stacked with meats and fish in vacuum-packed wrapping.

"Import from where?" I imagined a farm of octo-cows or an aquarium of wooly fish.

"Earth ... mostly," her voice trailed off. "But it's all tasty and nutritious."

I studied a package of meaty rings. Might have been calamari, or alien bung sliced into imitation calamari.

Cassie kicked the refrigerator door closed.

I kept kneading the dough. "How did you get here?"

"Much like the others. One foggy night I was minding my business, riding my bicycle along the Rhine near Schuytgraaf-Noord." Cassie raised her head and stared at the wall. "There was a bright light." Her eyes widened. "And a blink later." She blinked. "I was awakened and sliding from a silver tube far, far from earth."

"That was how long ago?"

She shrugged. "Many, many months. A year. Perhaps two. I had no calendar. Then I was brought here to help Carmen." She nudged me aside and plunged her hands into the dough. Her fingers dug angrily as if she wanted to strangle the lump.

I asked, "You miss home?"

"That's a stupid question." Cassie pressed down hard and the dough pushed between her fingers. "Of course I miss home. I'm grateful that Carmen tries as best as she can to make life here tolerable and—"

I glanced at our sumptuous five-star surroundings. "Seems more than tolerable."

"A prison is still a prison." Cassie lifted a shoulder and blotted a teary eye. "I have children. Two boys, and I miss them very much."

"And your husband?"

She gave a brittle chuckle. "You don't need a husband to have children." She kept her face down to hide her despair.

I looked to see what the others were doing. Juanita and Jolie pulled fresh produce from another container on the hover platform. They inspected cauliflower and heads of lettuce that they placed in the sink. Irsan and Toby were busy chopping tomatoes and bell peppers.

Cassie pressed against me, and her cheek brushed my ear. She whispered, "You're expecting to return home?"

I whispered back, "That's my plan."

"How?"

"That's still a little unclear."

She leaned back so that her eyes locked with mine. I realized that my gaze had no effect on her. Not only could I no longer see auras, I had apparently lost my powers of hypnosis.

Cassie grasped handfuls of my t-shirt and pulled close. "Take me with you."

We were close enough to kiss, but her expression was far from amorous. Her blue eyes were pools of cold hate. "The Nancharm have good reason to fear us humans. Sooner or later we'll adopt their technology, and when we do, we'll return and grind them into dust."

"Provided they're still around."

"If they all dropped dead this instant, it wouldn't be too soon."

I whispered, "Aren't you afraid they can hear you?"

"I hope they can. And *fuck them!*" Cassie's bitterness unsettled me, and I pulled loose from her grip. Did the other chalices feel the same way? How much were they willing to sacrifice to escape?

I had to sort through my thoughts, so I excused myself and went outside to the pond.

I stood on the patio and looked up. I could detect the spinning motion of the ring circling the planet. The sky darkened directly above, and the veil of twilight seeped evenly toward the horizons, instead of moving from east to west like on earth. Stars glittered faintly in the gathering darkness. One of the tiny ones might be the earth's sun.

I had to avoid the Nancharm's experiments, but my priority had to be fleeing this planet with Carmen and Jolie. And with the chalices.

Then how to escape? I had no idea how to find a portal.

A silvery craft cruised along the lower sky. One of the Nancharm's flying saucers.

I watched it glide past when an idea blossomed.

Our ticket home.

Chapter Twenty-three

The flying saucer disappeared behind the trees.

I stared at the spot where I'd last seen the ship, my imagination racing ahead to where I saw myself sitting at the saucer's controls as it raced to earth: Carmen, Jolie and the chalices safely onboard. I was missing a lot of the details in this plan, but at least it was a plan.

I went back inside and returned to the kitchen. Jolie and the chalices were at the counter making dinner, chopping cuts of beef and vegetables before dropping them into a stockpot. Cassie threw a glance over her shoulder at me and scooted over.

I wasn't in the mood to help. My mind tingled with excitement as it sorted through the question of how to steal a flying saucer. First, how to get one? Next, how to fly it? Could it make the journey to Earth? Wouldn't the Nancharm try to stop me?

The missing details piled on top of each other like pieces of a 3-D puzzle too enormous and intricate to fit together. An impossible task. I might as well be wishing for a pair of magic ruby slippers.

But I was a vampire, which meant my existence alone was an example that the impossible was quite possible. Plus we had arrived on D-Galtha. The New Agey transcendental astral physics and quantum mechanics sleight-of-hand we used would make any rocket scientist bang his head on the floor in a conniption of disbelief.

I wandered to the other end of the kitchen, toward the bar, and decided on a vodka martini. Reaching for the Belvedere, I noticed the seal on the bottle hadn't been broken. A cursory appraisal of the other bottles told me most of them hadn't been opened either. Couldn't understand why. I hadn't been here longer than a few hours and already I needed a stiff drink to cope. If I'd been stuck here as long as the chalices, I probably would've crippled myself with liver failure.

Thankfully, the bar was stocked with the other necessities for civilization: ice, olives, and a cocktail shaker. I cracked open the vodka, poured a measure into the shaker, added ice and a splash of vermouth. The rhythmic sound of ice sloshing in the shaker prompted the chalices to turn and look at me, eyebrows lifted in surprise.

I emptied the drink into a martini glass and dropped in an olive. Cupping the glass, I raised it to salute my fellow prisoners. I sipped, and the alcohol made the idea of stealing a flying saucer more plausible.

I leaned on the bar and meditated, confident that little by little the details of commandeering a flying saucer would present themselves. It was a matter of time. If I could stall the Nancharm from Nurse-Ratcheting my brain, then eventually, we could escape.

The door into the kitchen opened. The doorway stretched to accommodate Moots as she glided through. Carmen trailed behind, her face pinched with what I was sure had to be troubling news.

The Carmen I preferred was the upbeat snarky bloodsucker with a reputation for gaming any situation to her pervy advantage. Here, she carried herself like the captain of a doomed ship striving to save her crew.

Moots entered the kitchen and swiveled her head to take in the busy work. "Excellent. I love to see you all gainfully occupied and happy. Happy! Happy! Perhaps, we should sing!"

Carmen groaned. Her eyes rolled in my direction. *Have mercy.*

Moots reached up and touched the side of her translator/cap. It emitted a single tone that played steady for a moment. Carmen and the chalices hummed to match the note. The cap next produced a cacophony of chirps and grunts that barely followed a melody. A metallic crashing, like garbage can lids used as cymbals, accompanied the noise. Carmen and the chalices joined Moots in a chorus of atonal confusion. Jolie winced.

Thank goodness for the alcohol. Everything—even this din—sounded better when filtered through booze.

Moots waved her hands. "Aren't we all happy!" She hesitated and her head jerked from side to side. The song kept blaring from her cap, and Carmen and the chalices kept making noises. Moots faced me and shot across the floor to within an inch of my nose. "What are you doing?"

"Getting happy."

Her arm lashed out and smacked the glass from my hand. What was left of an acceptable cocktail spattered on the bar. The glass bounced off the counter and shattered against the floor.

"No drinking for you," Moots exclaimed. She reached up to her hat again, touched the side, and the music stopped. Carmen and the rest closed their eyes and sighed in gratitude.

Moots aimed one long slender finger at me. "You already said that you haven't been in the mood. I'm not going to let you come down with a case of whiskey dick."

"I was drinking vodka."

She extended an arm and her fingers grasped my face. Her touch was firm, warm and leathery. "You want to drink?" Her other hand pointed at my crotch. "Then first some magic from your wand." She let go and glared.

Carmen stepped around her. "I'll handle this."

It looked as if Moots had drooped her shoulders in resignation. She turned, patted Carmen on the head, and glided out of the kitchen.

I grasped a towel from the bar and began to clean up the spilled booze. The martini dripped from the edge of the counter like tears.

"You'll have to cut Moots some slack," Carmen said.

Little chance of that. Besides ruining my impromptu happy hour, I saw Moots as my number-one obstacle in escaping.

"She's under a lot of pressure," Carmen explained, her voice low. "Her boss expected a breakthrough by now. She's getting a lot of heat from their higher-ups. Even among the Nancharm, shit rolls downhill."

She continued, "Moots is disappointed in you. She was excited to have a male vampire to study. Convinced that surely, you'd deliver the macho goods."

"Wouldn't be my first time to disappoint a woman." I blotted the last of the spilled cocktail from my shirt and dropped the towel in the bar sink. "Tell Moots that if she guarantees I won't be sliced open, then I'll do my best to put on a good show." I slid my arm around Carmen's waist to signal I could be coaxed into performing.

She pulled away. A surprise because her libido was always spring-loaded into the *sex-me-now* position. But I didn't take her rejection personally. She had priorities slamming her from all directions.

"Moots has been given a deadline," Carmen said. "Either produce results—and soon—or the project is done."

Jolie stepped between us and asked, "What does that mean?"

"Nothing good," Carmen replied. "No matter the results, the Nancharm will auction us to recoup the expense of the research."

"Then we better hurry," I said.

"With our experiments?" Carmen asked.

"No," I replied. "With an escape."

Jolie blinked. Carmen's head rocked back in surprise. Her eyes slid back and forth and then fixed on me. I waited for her to smile in approval and ask for more details, but instead she whispered, "Later."

The chalices resumed chopping at their cutting boards.

Carmen whispered to Jolie, and I leaned in to listen. "I need you to distract the Nancharm. Get frisky with the chalices."

"Which one?"

"Take your pick. Any or all of them. Dealer's choice." Carmen grasped my arm. "Meanwhile, Felix is going to explain how he intends for us to make a break for it."

Jolie saluted. "Aye, aye, captain. I'm prepared to shiver some timbers." She spun on her heels and retreated to the kitchen counter. She swatted Irsan and Toby on their butts and pulled them close.

Carmen led me from the kitchen to the bedroom. She slipped out of her cloak and gathered it in her hands. Naked—and I mean NAKED! If you had only one woman to see in the buff, it had to be Carmen—she opened the dresser, stuffed in the cloak and unfolded blue yoga pants and a yellow tank top. She slithered into the pants and top, and the image of her choice bits—and the way they were packaged—lingered in my retinas.

I lowered my gaze and cleared my throat.

Carmen chuckled and when I brought my head up, she was smiling mischievously, quite aware of the effect she had on me. Her eyes slid from a second door to the bed as if teasing me with the choice. She started for the door, and I stepped beside her, promising myself that when the time was right, I'd show Carmen who was boss in the sack. We entered a hall.

"The problem is that I'm fighting a lot of obstacles," she said, turning the conversation back to business. "Physiologically, the Nancharm aren't that easy to figure out—"

No argument from me. I had yet to tell the difference between the Nancharm men and women.

"—and their erogenous zones are elusive as butterflies in a tornado. It took me a while to find out what excited the women, and *they* were willing. The men?" Carmen shook her head. "Even as they face annihilation, they have a tough time accepting advice from an extraterrestrial. Culturally, the Nancharm remain convinced they are superior. Plus, in spite of the certain danger of self-extinction, the Nancharm fear that if they divert too many resources to this process, the other planets may seize upon that distraction and attack."

"How likely is that?"

"I don't know, but you can imagine they have plenty of enemies waiting to settle scores."

"And you've had no success hooking up with the Nancharm?"

"I never said that. Like I said, the Nancharm women are willing."

"And …?" I drew out the question. "Have you had sex with Moots?" I couldn't help chuckling.

"Not with her. She's very professional in that regard. Feels that her participation in the studies might taint her judgment."

"How was it?"

"Sex with a Nancharm?" Carmen chuffed softly. "The experiment was very clinical. Most of the time, the women need a lot to prime the pump. Conversation, touching, foreplay."

"Most of the time?" I asked.

"Once in a while, the subject demands a quickie. When things get going, they really dig the Kama Sutra, modified of course. Their favorite is position 42. Goat Climbs Tree."

I pictured a goat bleating high in a tree and couldn't see the analogy.

"The Nancharm women are surprisingly flexible and it's easier than you think to get under their carapace." Carmen tipped her head and raised one hand like she was holding up a car hood to inspect the engine.

"What did you do?"

"I used a tool." She rocked her hand. "A heated vibrator-thingy. The Nancharm women are into sex toys. That's what kept them smiling while they waited for their men to come around."

We turned the corner and approached a spiral staircase.

"What about companionship?" I said. "There's more to a relationship than sex."

"Did *you* just say that?" Carmen exploded with laughter. "They made do. Apparently, Nancharm men are a real pain in the ass to live with. Not having sex with them didn't become an issue until the population problem."

I still couldn't see their men completely dismissing sex. I'm a vampire and though making babies was out of my equation, giving up sex would be like giving up drinking. Thankfully, we are sterile and procreate by fanging and turning victims.

"And you've had no success with the men?"

"None."

I supposed I needed an explanation of Nancharm physiology, although I didn't really care. However, some Nancharm boners might buy us time, time enough for me to steal a flying saucer.

Carmen climbed on the first step of the staircase and made room for me. When I stood beside her, the stairs automatically ascended like a corkscrewing escalator. But the process didn't seem mechanical like the turning of rigid components but more like the metal changed shape to lift us.

"Are the chalices practicing safe sex?" I asked. "A successful experiment would mean that Cassie and Juanita get pregnant."

"When conception happens, the Nancharm use sonic waves to coax the fertilized egg through the uterus in a way so it won't implant. Definitely not pro-life."

We arrived on a mezzanine overlooking the gigantic main room, where Jolie and I had landed earlier in the day.

Carmen proceeded toward a narrow slit in the wall. It widened to let us pass and we emerged onto an outdoor balcony to face a twilight landscape. The air smelled fragrant. The green rolling hills faded to gray. Lights twinkled in the distance. A band of greenish yellow rimmed the horizon. The planet's ring shined bright as gold wire against the jewel-like stars and an iridescent nebula of shimmering purples and blues.

"Hate to admit this, but D-Galtha can be quite beautiful," I said. "This planet could be a great tourist destination."

Together we stood against the balcony wall.

She wrapped her arm in mine. "Tell me about your plan."

"If you could call it that. At this stage, it's more like wishful thinking." I glanced around us. "Aren't you afraid of the Nancharm listening in?"

"The only thing they care about is sex. Besides, what chance do they think we have of pulling off an escape?"

An alarm rang. Carmen let go my arm, and I looked about in unease.

A spectral shape floated in the air and Juanita's face materialized before us. "Carmen," she exclaimed, her eyes wide with distress, "come to the kitchen."

"What's happened?"

"Toby tried to kill himself."

Chapter Twenty-four

The walls blinked in cadence with the alarm. Carmen and I rushed back to the stairway and bounded down the steps to the ground floor.

Juanita waited for us at the door to the kitchen. My mind pinged at the smell of fresh human blood, and my fangs instinctively snapped into place.

Toby lay on the floor, his head resting in Jolie's lap. His wrists were wrapped in blood-soaked towels. Two streaks of blood trailed from the dining room to his body.

Cassie and Irsan stood beside him, both holding clean towels. I suppressed my thirst for blood and withdrew my fangs.

Carmen ordered, "Alarm off."

The walls quit pulsing, and the alarm fell mercifully silent.

Jolie said, "I heard Toby fall in the next room, and when he didn't answer, I checked on him and found this." She opened her free hand showed us a bloodied paring knife.

Toby's eyes seemed to spin in their moist, red-rimmed sockets. Sweat on his face mingled with tears cascading down his cheeks. "I'm so sorry," he repeated between sobs.

Carmen knelt beside him and cupped the back of his head. He grasped her wrist, pulled himself from Jolie and pressed his head against Carmen's thigh. She ran her fingers through his moist hair.

"I didn't want to do it," he wept. "I knew if I offed myself then Irsan would be the next one to be cut open." Toby's crazy eyes swept the kitchen and locked on Irsan. "But I can't stand this misery anymore. Take me home. Take me home, please." His gaze broke from Irsan and speared me. "You, tough guy, find a way. Save us from this hell." He raked the air with his bloody crooked fingers. "Take us home!"

His despair pressed against me, and I had to take a step back. My responsibilities weighed heavily on my shoulders, but I felt dumb as a trapped beast.

Carmen and Jolie replaced the towels on Toby's wrists with makeshift bandages, then helped him to his feet. His knees buckled, but they held him steady. Irsan and Cassie began wiping the blood-spattered counter.

The kitchen door stretched open. Moots and another Nancharm, this one shorter and stockier, rode side-by-side on one hover scooter. Moots and her partner slid off the scooter and floated to the floor.

The tendrils on the shorter Nancharm flailed about, and a baritone voice boomed from the translator/cap, "You assured me this was not going to happen again."

Again. I remembered that Carmen mentioned that human captives had a limited shelf life—they tended to kill themselves.

Moots' face was a hard, featureless mask, and her eyes opaque as alabaster stones. Yet I sensed her distress. She pointed at the other Nancharm. "This is Doctor Fastid ... my boss."

I assumed from his deeper voice that he was male. The last time I had seen two of the Nancharm together, one was tall and lean like Moots. The other was shorter and stout like this guy so I supposed this size difference was the easiest way to distinguish between their men and women. His face was more square then hers, and his eyes almond-shaped. His mouth was wider. His speaking tendrils were thicker, which may have accounted for his deeper voice ... or not.

Though he was shorter than Moots, Fastid was still close to ten feet tall. He slid across the floor and stared at Toby. "You have no idea what this does to our budget."

Toby dipped his head in shame.

Carmen motioned toward his injured wrists. "He's going to need medical attention."

"The iatric team is on the way," Moots said.

Fastid turned to Moots. "Explain to me how this happened? We ..." he stabbed a finger in her direction. "*You* are supposed to be in complete control of this research. Self-destruction by a specimen is completely outside the test protocols." Toby's spilled blood seeped across the floor toward the doctor and he retreated out of the way.

Moots kept quiet. She leaned ever so slightly from side to side and drummed her fingers against the side of her carapace.

"Maybe, we should confine them in pens," Fastid said. "Take away a few of their amenities so they can focus on the task at hand."

"That won't work, and you know it," Moots replied defiantly. "Humans are complex."

"Yeah, yeah, I know." Fastid waved his hands. "The humans are complex. The Dacheen are complex. The Ekwistas are complex. Every species we're studying on D-Galtha is complex."

"And so are we," Moots noted. "The men especially."

Fastid's tendrils puffed but nothing came out of his translator/cap.

Fastid glided back to the hover scooter. "I want a report on how and why this happened."

"I can tell you why," she replied. "He's unhappy."

Fastid's tendrils shook, and his translator/cap bellowed, "He's unhappy? We're all unhappy! Tell me who isn't unhappy on this miserable rock? Planet Pleasure my ass."

Fastid levitated and slid onto the hover scooter. His head swiveled to pan the kitchen, and I caught his disgust with us. The scooter rotated and disappeared out the doorway. The doorframe shrank back to normal size, and the door slammed shut.

"Asshole," Moots muttered. She approached Toby, Carmen, and Jolie. "How close are you to expiring?" she asked of Toby.

He raised his bandaged wrists. "Not close, not anymore."

"Fastid and the Erection Analysis Committee were hoping for plenty of sex, but I'm going to tell them you'll need time to let this trauma pass."

"How much time?" Carmen asked.

"How much time do you need?"

Carmen looked past Moots and at me. Her eyes asked *A week? A month? A year?*

I had no clue. It all depended on getting my hands on a flying saucer. I shrugged.

Carmen wrinkled her nose in displeasure and answered Moots, "I don't know."

"Figures," Moots replied. "Our motto should be, 'We don't know what the fuck we're doing.'" She paused as if distracted, then thumped the center of her chest. Her tendrils wiggled and odd, squeaking sounds came out of her cap. She kept quiet for a short moment, replied in more squeaking sounds, and tapped her chest. "That was the iatric team. They can't make it here, which means I have to transport Toby to the infirmary."

"How?" Jolie asked.

"In one of our shuttles."

"The flying saucers?" I asked.

"Flying saucers?" Moots chuckled, sounding surprised. "I guess if that's what you want to call them, sure. We'll be going in a"—she made air quotes—"*flying* saucer."

"Then let me help you with Toby," I replied.

Chapter Twenty-Five

Carmen narrowed her eyes. I could sense her mind echo with the question: *Why?*

As in why did I want to accompany Toby to the infirmary?

Jolie added to the pressure by giving me the fish eye.

I nudged her out of the way and took my place at Toby's side. "Moral support."

Carmen's lips curved into a wry grin. "Then I'm also going." She tipped her head at Jolie. "I'm leaving you in charge. We should be back soon."

Jolie saluted. "Roger, dodger."

A soft ticking sound from the dining room drew my gaze. A dinner plate-sized device—imagine a Roomba with spindly legs—crawled over the threshold like a spider. It advanced head down to vacuum Toby's spilled blood.

Moots glided toward the door to the main room. It swung open and stretched to let her pass. Toby sagged against me. His already wan face faded to a grayish pallor, and his eyes became hooded. Carmen and I half carried, half dragged him behind Moots.

Cassie and Irsan continued wiping up Toby's blood from the counter but their attention was on us. Jolie gave an anxious wave goodbye.

We caught up with Moots in the main room. Tall as she was, Moots looked tiny against the scale of the spacious interior. The big door scrolled open and revealed the star-filled night.

A glint in the sky snagged our attention. The glint turned into a crescent outlining the edge of an approaching disk. The hemispherical bottom of the flying saucer materialized beneath the disk. The saucer slowed and descended, accompanied by a hum that steadily increased in volume.

An hour ago, my dilemma was how to get close to, and hopefully inside, a flying saucer. Then Toby tried to commit suicide, and tragic as that was, his misfortune had created this opportunity.

The saucer halted and hovered maybe twenty feet above the edge of the paved apron surrounding the building. Three landing struts unfolded from its lower hemisphere. The saucer sank to the ground, and the struts flexed to absorb its weight. The humming noise softened to a murmur. Up close, the saucer rim was about a hundred feet across with the spherical body maybe fifty feet in diameter.

A rectangular door levered downward to become a ramp. Moots proceeded forward. Toby winced and gulped hard. I paused to let Moots put distance between us, then asked in a low voice, "Why is he afraid of the flying saucer?"

"It's not the flying saucer, per se," Carmen replied. "It's that bad things happen to those who leave the facility."

"But you've left. To visit the control room."

"I'm not worried," she explained. "I am a vampire."

"How does that protect you? Do the Nancharm even care about vampires?"

"I doubt it matters to them, but they do consider me higher on the food chain. And you and Jolie, too. But what gives me confidence is that if they fuck with me, I'll take a whole bunch of them out before I'm incinerated." Carmen extended her free arm and talons telescoped from her fingertips. She smiled, revealing her fangs, and then retracted the talons and teeth.

Moots glided up the ramp. Carmen and I nursed Toby along. A bright, hazy light spilled through the door, making it difficult to see the interior details. The surface of the ramp was smooth but as we put our weight on it, I felt it grip the bottom of my shoes.

The top of the ramp was level with a round floor the bluish-gray color of steel. The white walls curved outward to the circular ceiling. The space was illuminated with a glow that seemed to come from everywhere.

A round hatch opened above Moots. The spot on the floor where she stood rose to piston her through the open hatch. The piston withdrew and the hatch snicked closed.

The boarding ramp retracted with a hiss. The edges of the door melted with the surrounding wall and the doorframe became invisible. A long segment of the ceiling lowered and unfolded into a mechanical arm with hooped jaws. The arm swung toward Toby, the jaws spread and caught him by his waist. The arm tugged gently. Carmen let go and I followed her lead.

A tube wide as a bowling ball emerged from the floor and swallowed one of Toby's hands past the wrist. He moaned in discomfort. I moved to help him but Carmen held me back.

Toby's arm slipped from the tube. The bloody bandage was gone, and a gauzy cocoon covered his lower forearm, wrist, and hand. The mechanism repeated the procedure with his other arm so that both of Toby's hands and wrists were gloved to resemble the heads of Q-Tips. His eyes dilated into a hollow stare, and his mouth broke into a rictus of goofy pleasure. Whatever alien drug he was given spun his mind in supersonic circles.

A panel on the wall slid open and revealed a green mattress like a folded Murphy bed. The mechanical arm pressed Toby against the mattress, which molded around him, leaving his face and the front of his body exposed. The arm released him and snatched me by the waist. I resented its grip and grabbed the jaws to break them apart.

"No," Carmen cautioned. "We'll be okay."

I relaxed and let the arm position me against another mattress that appeared beside Toby. The mattress flowed around me like warm dough and solidified. The arm retracted and left me fro⁻ in place.

The arm collected Carmen and stuck her into a mattress on the other side of Toby. The arm folded upward and its contours blended with the ceiling. The light dimmed. My insides shifted as if we were in a moving elevator. The saucer swayed but without a viewing port, I had no idea where we were headed or at what speed.

"Carmen, you do this often?" I asked.

"Usually I fly topside."

"That was my plan," I replied. "Instead we're in the trunk."

"Maybe on the way back you'll see what you need." After a moment of silence, she added, "I appreciate that you and Jolie came for me. Regardless of the outcome."

"I'm trying to undo a lot of guilt for what I let happen to you."

"Felix," she snapped, "get over yourself already. You're not everyone's goddamn hero. Being here is my fault. I let that bastard Clayborn and his human goons get the drop on me."

The saucer swung ever so slightly, making minor adjustments in flight. After thirty minutes, maybe an hour and a half—I couldn't tell—the saucer shifted abruptly, its movements smoothed, and we stopped.

The lights brightened and the circular hatch opened above. The floor pistoned upward and lowered Moots. She slid to the opposite side of the compartment and faced us. I expected the mechanical arm to extend from the ceiling and extract us from the mattresses. Instead, my mattress squeezed like pursed lips, spit me loose, and I tumbled to the floor. Carmen was also spit loose and landed beside me. Then Toby.

The door opened and the boarding ramp lowered. Moots said, "Follow me," and glided down the ramp. Outside, a hover scooter waited for her.

Carmen and I helped a rubber-limbed Toby to his feet. We hobbled down the ramp, wary of our surroundings, then halted to take in the magnificence of what we saw. A gigantic yellow orb dominated a sky blacker than I'd ever seen. A ring of gold surrounded the orb.

Toby broke free enough from his drug-induced euphoria to crane his neck back and gape at the orb. "D-Galtha."

Carmen explained, "We're on one of its moons."

Shiny curves of light reflected inside an enormous bubble that encased us. Another flying saucer approached the bubble. The ship passed through the bubble's walls like a platter slipping through soapy film and then landed on the other side of our saucer.

The immediate landscape was dusty gray, littered with rocks and pockmarked with craters. An igloo-shaped structure, the same gray color as the dirt and maybe two stories tall, stood before us. A glass and metal tube connected the landing pad to a door of the igloo.

Moots levitated onto the scooter and swung the back end toward us. "Put Toby onboard."

Carmen and I helped him up and into the wire basket behind Moots. Toby sat down cross-legged and rested his Q-Tip hands on his knees. Moots wiggled forward against the scooter's controls to make room. "Get on."

Carmen and I climbed behind her and stood side-by-side. We wrapped our arms around Moots' middle, which was hard and smooth like fiberglass. She tooted the scooter's horn, and we zipped forward. I glanced back at the flying saucer and suspected it might be harder that I thought to steal one. I looked up at D-Galtha. "Long way to the nurse's office, don't you think? I'd figure you guys, being the smart ones, would have more convenient medical facilities."

"I just work here," Moots replied.

The igloo door opened. Moots steered the hover scooter inside. As soon as we stopped, the floor sank, and we descended a deep shaft. That god-awful Nancharm music played through an unseen speaker.

"Catchy tune, don't you agree?" Moots asked, her back to us.

Carmen put an extra-sarcastic spin to her eye roll. "Quite lovely."

"It's a sad song," Moots explained. "About a great Nancharm hero who ran out of ammunition and had to let some of the enemy escape." She sighed. "Such heartbreak."

"Don't you have any love songs?" I asked.

"We have many songs about love," Moots replied enthusiastically. "Songs about a Nancharm's love for victory. Songs about the love of watching your vanquished enemy tremble in terror."

Her head swiveled around. "The love of a good blaster."

The sight of her head rotating like this freaked me out. "But what about songs of love for one another?" I muttered, trying to act nonplussed by her backwards-facing head. "Romance. Desire. Get you in the mood."

Moots turned her head back around. "Mood for wha—" She interrupted herself with a chuckle. "Oh that. Sex. Of course."

"The Nancharm have different courting rituals," Carmen said, emphasizing a flat tone that told me to drop the subject.

The elevator slowed and stopped. The wall in front of us parted, and we rode the scooter out of the shaft and into a corridor. Unlike the other Nancharm structures, these walls weren't smooth but undulated with translucent white bumps. The bumps might have been ice or crystal buildup, but as we passed, I picked out bones beneath the surface. "Those fossils?"

"Hardly," Moots chimed. "Those are the remains from various other species. The Zupatz. The Gleeglee. The Hi-Pa'an ... all guests."

"Guests?" I replied.

"They *were* guests. Then they became prisoners of war. They objected to the conditions of the mining camp here, rioted, and our guards were forced to contain the troubles. Rather than atomize the corpses, someone decided to decorate the walls with their remains. Quite attractive and inventive, don't you think?"

I answered yes, though my kundalini noir quivered in horror. Maybe at the end of the research, the chalices and us vampires would be turned into wall art. And I wondered why they hadn't yet added Earth dwellers to their trophies.

We cruised past open doors and through several intersections. In the other corridors, clusters of Nancharm glided past on their "feet" or on hover scooters. On occasion, some of them tooted their horns and Moots tooted back. The ambiance was like being in a busy office complex, a hamster cage of constant motion.

Moots drove around a corner and into an atrium filled with a dazzling white light. Glass cabinets and rows of pipes and cables lined the walls. Bizarre instruments jutted from pedestals.

She halted by two other Nancharm standing beside a padded table that looked very much like one in a doctor's examination room. Neither of these Nancharm wore a translator/cap and when their tendrils waved and puffed in animated conversation. Naturally I couldn't understand a thing.

A hologram materialized between them and us. One of the other Nancharm touched a button on the hologram. A pedestal slid toward Toby. The instrument on top looked like a combination giant microscope and metal cockroach. The "legs" quivered. The carapace opened and revealed a glassy cylinder that pulsed with a green light.

Toby levitated from the scooter and floated toward the table where he was laid flat on its long cushion. Metal straps scrolled out from the sides of the table, extended across his lower legs, thighs, torso, arms, neck, and tightened like tentacles.

The cockroach closed upon one of Toby's gauzy mitten hands. The legs extended and seized his wrist. Its mandibles opened and closed. The vacant haze on Toby's face evaporated. His skin flushed crimson, and the pupils of his eyes sharpened to points that locked on the cockroach's jaws.

I didn't appreciate the Nancharm's bedside manner and clenched my fists to prevent my talons from sprouting. Carmen clasped my arm to keep me calm. I turned toward Moots and saw those inert white eyes of hers staring at me.

"Something the matter?" she asked.

"Why?"

"You seem bothered by this," she insisted.

"Should I be? I'm sure it's a routine medical procedure."

"There is nothing routine about what we do." Moots rested her hand on my shoulder. She drummed her long, ropy fingers and they each tapped me with a menacing heft, like individual leather saps. "If you think this is disturbing, imagine what happens to subjects who don't behave themselves." Her fingers snaked around my neck and she said, "Especially to those who try to escape."

Chapter Twenty-six

I fixed my stare directly into Moots' white, bottomless eyes. How did she know I was planning to escape?

Moots returned my gaze with laser-like intensity. But good luck to her if she wanted to win a staring contest with a vampire.

Everything in the room seemed to rotate on the axis of our glare. After a long, dramatic moment, she broke focus and withdrew her hand from around my neck.

"Very well," she said. "So you're not planning to escape?"

"How could I?"

"I don't know. I still haven't figured how you and Jolie got here. There's no record of you two being processed through inventory control or alien-species quarantine."

"Is that my fault?"

A loud huffing distracted us. One of the other Nancharm—head tendrils fluffing in agitation—stared at Moots and pointed at Toby as if asking *Are you done? Can we get back to work?*

Moots emitted an irritated chuff through her translator-cap. She turned to Carmen. "I'm holding you responsible."

Carmen crossed herself. "Felix will behave himself. Scout's honor."

One of the other two Nancharm got busy with the menu on the holographic control panel. The cockroach device on the pedestal chewed and swallowed the gauzy wrapping on Toby's hand. His fingers splayed apart. A red gash ran up his wrist, a wound maybe four inches long. The exposed flesh was red and raw but didn't bleed. The cockroach's mandibles oozed yellow goop into the wound, then began to ratchet along the gash, stitching it closed.

The straps holding Toby popped loose and retracted into the table. His body stiffened and elongated as if in rigor mortis, but his eyes still shined with life. An arm swung up from the foot of the table. The end of the arm had a leathery three-fingered claw. A similar arm extended from the head of the table. Both sets of claws clamped on him, one on his feet, the other around his skull. He was lifted and rotated like a pig on a spit until he faced the table. His other hand was now closer to the cockroach device. It repeated the first-aid procedure, and the wounds on both of Toby's wrists were mended.

"All done?" I asked.

"Not yet," Moots replied.

The cockroach device folded its legs tight to its body and scooted away from the table. Another device slid forward. This one looked like a praying mantis. The Nancharm must really be into bugs.

The triangular head of this device swiveled, its antennae twitched, and the two bulging eyes opened to reveal binocular lenses that zoomed in on the scars down Toby's spine and at the back of his neck. The mantis' arms stretched forward, and a multitude of blades unfolded from the ends, Edward Scissorhands-style. Toby's shirt was cut to ribbons and the shredded cloth was sucked up a tube to expose his naked torso.

As the blades approached the back of Toby's neck, *my* skin started to crawl. Two blades extended past the others, glowed red, and touched his neck scars. The tips of the blades sank into his skin. Toby gulped and spit drooled from his lips. I glanced at Carmen for her reaction. She watched the blades, but her face remained free of emotion.

The blades proceeded to slice open Toby's scars. The wounds on his neck resembled little crimson mouths, mute and yet screaming obscenities. The skin along his backbone was peeled open, revealing a wiring harness braided into his vertebrae. The Nancharm watched an image of his brain and spinal column on their hologram.

If their intent was to give me the big freak-out, it was working. "Are you cutting him open for my benefit?" I asked solemnly.

"Of course not." Moots laughed. "Honestly Felix, you're not that important. The Erection Analysis Committee needs his diagnosis implants replaced. Toby's attempt at self-destruction pushed the sending units off their calibration scale."

The mantis device replaced grain-sized implants from his neck and spinal wiring harness. It lowered its head to upchuck goop over his incisions and sew them shut. The mantis head moved to his shoulder. A needle-like tongue shot from between its jaws and pierced his skin. The praying mantis retracted all of its blades and tongue and pulled away from Toby.

The claws holding his feet and head let go simultaneously and he plopped face-first on the table. Barnyard animals got treated with more dignity.

His skin began to glow a rosy pink. Head wobbling, he blinked himself back to alertness and pushed up from the table.

Moots and the other Nancharm exchanged displays of puffed tendrils. She slid toward the hover scooter. "Back to work. We've wasted enough time for one day."

Carmen and I helped Toby slide off the table. Red welts marked his fresh scars.

"You have another shirt for him?" Carmen asked.

"Let's see what's in Lost-and-Found." Moots opened a drawer in a wall cabinet and pulled out a white shirt. "Try this."

I helped Carmen slide the shirt over Toby's arms and shoulders and button the front. Surprisingly, the shirt fit fine except that it had four sleeves.

Toby smiled at Carmen and his gaze roved hungrily over her breasts.

"He's looking horny," I noted.

"It's a side effect of the drug," she replied.

"Seemed potent. Why don't the Nancharm use it on themselves?"

"The men have tried, but their DNA is too screwed up."

Toby brushed us away and stood tall. His muscles flexed with renewed vigor. "Carmen, have I ever said that I love you?"

She clasped his hand. "And I love you too." She said this the way you might to a dog.

"I mean, I really, really love you." He pointed to the bulge in his pants. "I mean like right now."

She smiled at him, then at me. I didn't understand what she meant by the look, other than to expect something. She clasped his upper arms, stood on tiptoe, and stretched up toward his neck. Her fangs snapped out and she put her open mouth to the side of his throat.

Toby went, *Uggh*, his eyes rolled back, and he fell toward me.

I caught him. Carmen spit out his blood, saying, "Whatever shit they put in him, I don't need." She motioned to the wire basket on the back of the scooter. I lowered him in, legs dangling over one end, head over the other. Blood dotted his fang marks. Carmen and I climbed behind Moots, and she drove us out of the lab.

We wended through the corridors and up the elevator. A different flying saucer waited for us outside. This one was Frisbee-shaped with no spherical central body. It hovered on pillars of faint green light. A ramp beckoned.

We ascended the ramp and entered a small room cramped with boxes and large tube containers. Moots directed Carmen and me to stuff Toby feet first into a clear tube that swung up against the wall. She dismounted the scooter and it disappeared on its own down the ramp.

"For the flight back you two might want to get comfortable." Moots panned the compartment. "But not here. Come with me."

She turned toward the wall. A panel swooshed open to let us pass. We followed Moots down a tall, narrow corridor that curved around and around. Another door opened and we entered what had to be the flying saucer's command bridge.

I was not sure what the crew were, but they looked like a couple of pint-sized elephants resting on their bellies on top of side-by-side cradle-like couches. They faced a wide screen. Lights blinked along a console below. Levers protruded from the floor around the couches.

One of the elephants turned toward us. Its enormous brown eyes peeled open. The trunk curled over its head and let out an eye-splitting trumpeting. The other elephant also looked and trumpeted. The first elephant sat up and used the large hands on its forelegs to unbuckle straps clipped to a body harness. Myriad gold rings pierced its ears, and bejeweled golden hoops decorated its thick wrists and fingers. A tasseled skirt of satiny burgundy and gold draped its hindquarters.

The creature slid from the couch and scrambled toward us on all fours, its metallic jewelry clicking and clacking. I waited, wary, but Carmen beamed a welcome. The creature reached up with its trunk and snatched the translator-cap from Moots' head. Moots tried to grab the cap but the creature hip checked her with its broad caboose.

"Who is this?" I asked.

"Blossom," Carmen answered. "One of the Wah-zhim. She was my first owner among the aliens."

Other than the trunks, I remembered Carmen informing me that the Wah-zhim had ginormous prehensile pudenda, which was thankfully covered by Blossom's voluminous skirt.

She wiggled her big can to keep Moots at bay. Moots' tendrils shook in silent fury as she groped for the cap. Blossom chuffed through her trunk. Moots retreated and dropped her arms. Blossom must've told her in Nancharm to back the fuck off.

Blossom placed the translator-cap on her head. She traced the tip of her trunk across Carmen's face, the touch tender as kisses. "Carmen, Carmen, I missed you so much." Her voice bleated out the cap.

"And I missed you." Carmen clasped the trunk to her face.

Blossom slithered her trunk from Carmen and pointed it at me. "Who are you?"

"Felix Gomez," Carmen answered. "A long-time friend."

"Well, you're not as pretty as Carmen." Blossom's trunk wrapped around my neck—it was heavy and very strong—and pulled me off balance. "But you look like fun. Lots of fun."

Shuffling my feet to stay upright, I gulped nervously. I wasn't as open-minded about these matters as Carmen.

Blossom withdrew her trunk but kept her big, soft eyes on me.

"What are you doing here?" Carmen asked.

"Gotta make a living. Build the ship. Fly the ship. Rinse and repeat." Blossom raised her out-sized hands, set them on Carmen's and my shoulders and gently pulled us close. Her translator-cap whispered. "Actually, I've been looking for you, Carmen. It wasn't right that the Nancharm took you away from me."

"If you think I'm returning to Wah-zhim, think again."

Blossom's eyes saddened.

"But it good to see you again," Carmen said. She grasped Blossom's trunk and brought the tip to her face. Blossom hunched forward until the translator cap brushed Carmen's ear. It looked like Blossom was whispering something to Carmen, but I wasn't sure. Carmen kissed around the end of the trunk and let go.

Blossom caressed Carmen's face. If Blossom had passed along a message I couldn't tell. The trunk then whipped to me and pinched my butt. "We'll see you later, big boy." She turned around, and hips swaying, sashayed toward Moots. Blossom plucked the translator-cap from her head and offered it to Moots, who took the cap and stuck it to the top of her head.

Moots asked, "Are we ready?"

"As soon as we find a place to sit," Carmen replied.

Blossom's co-pilot hooted through her trunk. Two panels opened in the floor beside Carmen and me and a pair of stout columns rose. An overhead spotlight bathed us for a short moment. The light went out and the columns melted into beanbag-like Barcaloungers, compete with cup holders.

A large, open-sided basket pushed up from the floor between us and the Wah-zhim. Moots backed into the basket and stood facing the instrument screen with her back to Carmen and me. She and I screwed our butts into our newly formed seats. Safety belts snaked across our hips and down our shoulders to cinch low on our waists.

Blossom climbed into her couch and strapped in. Her hands grasped controls and her trunk raked across the front console, pushing buttons. Strange symbols flashed on the screen. The saucer lifted.

This close-up study of flying saucer controls made me realize how naive my idea had been to steal one of these spaceships. I'd be like a monkey trying to pilot a 747.

A plastic bottle sprang up in one of my cup holders. A thick drinking straw wobbled from the top. Carmen received a similar bottle, and without hesitating, she lifted the bottle and sucked from the straw.

I followed her example. The drink was sweet, pulpy, and carried a welcome kick—a wheatgrass Mojito would be a good description.

Unshelled, salted peanuts filled my second cup holder. Music wafted from my seat's headrest. I couldn't recognize the words, but the tune was soothing and melodic, unlike that tin-can-in-a-washing-machine-noise the Nancharm were so proud of.

A square hologram appeared before Moots. Her tendrils swaying in silent conversation, she tapped at the virtual screen, appearing much like a human road warrior clicking earnestly at a laptop while on a commuter flight.

I relaxed in the seat, munching on peanuts, tossing the shells, getting buzzed on my cocktail, and enjoying this unexpected interlude. Carmen barely sipped at her drink and didn't touch her stash of peanuts. Her eyes glazed over with faraway concerns.

Maybe she was considering the same thing I was thinking. It was no coincidence that Blossom was piloting this ship. I sensed that the opportunity for an escape was brewing. Carmen and I had better be ready.

Chapter Twenty-Seven

Blossom and her co-pilot touched switches and adjusted the control levers along the instrument console. A bell chimed inside the bridge. The interior lights dimmed.

Moots' hologram vanished. My bottle and the peanuts disappeared into the cup holders. The commotion alerted me that we were about to land, and I expected a flight attendant to announce: *Please make sure your seat backs and folding trays are locked in their full upright position.*

We swayed left and right. My stomach rose in my throat and then settled back down. The saucer cushioned to a halt. The lights brightened. Blossom unsnapped her safety harness and sauntered on all fours toward Carmen and me. Moots' basket chair sank back into the floor, and she scooted free.

My safety belts released and retracted. My chair pushed me up and forward until I stood upright. Peanut shells crunched beneath my feet.

Blossom stared at the mess around my seat. She snorted.

"What did she say?" I asked.

Moots translated. "*Men.*"

Blossom opened a cabinet in the bulkhead and withdrew a whiskbroom and a dustpan that she pushed into my hands. I figured the ship had one of those spider Roombas to tidy up, but apparently not. Under the glare of three women from different home planets, I dropped to my knees and swept up the shells.

Minutes later, I trailed after Moots and Carmen. Blossom and her co-pilot remained on the bridge. We returned to the central hold. The tube holding Toby tipped from the wall, and he was puffed free with a gust of air. He spilled onto the floor, and Carmen and I helped him to his feet. His horn-dog jitters for Carmen had worn off, and he stood slump-shouldered and dull-eyed. Moots pointed to the ramp.

The saucer had landed outside Facility Two-Four. It was still night. Carmen, Toby, and I started for the ramp and the instant we set foot on the incline, it collapsed and sent us tumbling. We fell three feet and landed in a heap on the hard red pavement.

Moots floated beside us on a hover scooter. With a goodbye wave, she zipped down a door that opened in the apron.

Above us, the ramp closed. A wave of static electricity fluffed our hair, and tiny sparks crackled in our clothing. The saucer lifted from us and *whooshed* toward the sky.

Carmen and I had to lift Toby again, and we started back to the facility. The main bay door was closed so we headed toward a smaller door at the far end, near the living quarters. She flattened her hand against the door. A blue outline glowed around her fingers. A lock snapped and the door slid into a recess. She called out in jest, "Honey, I'm home."

We didn't expect an answer and proceeded inside. The interior was gloomy as a cave, and I regretted not having vampire vision. A single light flickered on above us, hovering like Tinker Bell, and followed us to the first bedroom. Carmen touched the wall beside the door. The ceiling began to glow and our fairy light disappeared. Toby staggered to the bed and toppled onto the mattress.

"Seems too quiet," I noted. "Where is everybody?"

Carmen shrugged and continued past the bedroom. The kitchen was empty, as was the dining room.

We entered the den. Jolie and the rest of the chalices were sitting on the floor, looking worried and dejected. Jolie rose to her feet. "How is Toby?"

Carmen answered, "He's in the front bedroom, resting. He'll be okay."

"Just okay?" Cassie asked, her eyes red.

"Considering what the Nancharm put him through, I'd say that's the best we can expect." Carmen winged a thumb to the dining room. Jolie and I trailed after her and when she gestured at the table, we took seats.

Carmen rummaged through a hutch drawer and retrieved a notepad and a pen. She sat between Jolie and me and said, "Jolie, I need you to help Moots with her research. Tonight was a good start." But as she spoke, Carmen wrote:

distract the nancharm. Felix and I have to work on an escape plan.

Even if the Nancharm weren't eavesdropping for anything except for sex, I appreciated Carmen's regard for secrecy. I reflected to the moment back on the space ship when Blossom seemed to have whispered something to Carmen. I took the pen and wrote:

Blossom?

Carmen nodded once. Jolie squinted at the note and looked at Carmen, then me.

Carmen added, "It's important that we cooperate with Moots and Fastid."

Jolie replied, "I'll do what I can." She took the pen and scribbled:

what's the plan?

Carmen drew a flying saucer.

Jolie kept a poker face and wrote:

how?

Carmen circled Blossom's name. She wrote:

just be ready.

Jolie drew a smiley face.

Carmen scooped the note, crumpling it. "Jolie, go mind the kids. Felix and I need time alone."

Jolie returned to the den. Carmen and I walked to the kitchen. Once there, she fed the note through a slot in a cabinet beneath the sink. A red bar on the cabinet lit up. *Incinerator activated.* The bar turned green. *Incineration Complete.*

Carmen hooked her arm into mine. "Remember how Toby got all randy after his surgery?" Her body pressed against mine, and my blood rushed to all the right places.

I wrapped my arms around her taut waist. "Is this what you meant by time alone?"

"Not quite." She pushed me away. "But hold that thought. And save your strength."

"For what?"

"For Moots."

Chapter Twenty-eight

Carmen led me out of the living quarters to an abandoned fabrication shop off the main bay. She explained that most of the original equipment had been left in place when this facility was hastily converted to a sex research lab.

Once in the shop, Carmen began rummaging through boxes and shelves and when she couldn't find what she wanted, she asked me to make a soldering gun. She didn't explain why.

Jolie's part in our plan was more straightforward. She had to misdirect the Nancharm's attention from Carmen and me by orchestrating an orgy with the chalices. Taking the long view in this arrangement, Jolie was getting the shaft (two of them, if Toby came around), but she was having more fun and I'd trade places—on the giving end, of course.

Everything in the shop was sized for the Nancharm so Carmen and I had to improvise step stools to plunder the upper cabinets and shelves. After an hour, we managed to scrounge a heap of tools and parts. While a lot of the gizmos were undecipherable in their function, surprisingly, many weren't. Though we were billions of miles from Earth, a hammer still looked like a hammer.

I constructed a soldering gun by taking apart several devices and fitting the parts into what I hoped would work without blowing up. Who knew, but what I thought was a heating element might actually be an Illudium Pu-36 detonator.

The busy work kept me distracted from what Carmen had said last night: *That I was to save my strength for sex with Moots.*

The idea was as appealing as sliding my johnson into a toaster. I remembered my earlier thoughts about Doña Marina getting it on with El Cucuy. But if this was my sacrifice to assure our escape, then so be it. *Close your eyes and do it for God and country.*

Carmen and I were soon surrounded by gutted and disassembled appliances. She collected batteries, the Nancharm equivalent of the D-cell. I hooked up a pair of wires from the soldering gun to a battery. The gun's tip heated and glowed. "How's this?"

Carmen hitched her shoulders. *Good enough.* She was handling a combo power tool and had just finished boring holes into a flat plastic bar the length of her forearm. She twisted the bar onto a pole so the two sections formed a *T*. After fitting identical thumb-sized doohickeys through the holes, she used the soldering gun to connect wires from each doohickey to a battery pack.

She tore a length from a roll of Nancharm duct tape and secured the wires and the battery pack to the pole. With a twist of the switch on the battery pack, the doohickeys vibrated. She rotated the switch to its stop and the bar about shook to pieces. "W-w-we shouldn't n-need th-this s-s-setting," the trembling made her stutter, "b-b-but just in c-c-case." She turned the power off.

With a proud flourish, she raised the pole like a battle standard. "This is what a Nancharm penis looks like."

So we were making a sex toy. I was amused rather than impressed. It looked like a cross between a short-tined pitchfork and a rake. "Seems complicated."

Carmen's smirk reflected my skepticism. "The Nancharm *are* complicated. The women have six vaginas, all of which must be stimulated simultaneously to induce ovulation."

"Six vaginas? Their monthly cycles must be murder."

"Actually, they don't menstruate. Ovulation doesn't occur until the men deposit ootz in all six of the women's hoo-hahs."

I realized the Nancharm's dilemma. "If their men don't perform to task, the women can't even provide eggs for artificial insemination."

Carmen elaborated on the thought. "They've tried to harvest eggs using synthetic hormones, but the results didn't produce healthy babies."

"How am I supposed to 'do' Moots?"

"You'll see that the Nancharm vagina is very accommodating."

"*The* vagina," I replied. "As in one. You're not balancing the equation."

"Work with me, okay? When it's time for the nitty-gritty, go with the flow." She gave the toy a spin. "A perv like you will figure it out."

I watched the six units go round and round. "The Nancharm men walk around with junk like that in their pants?"

Carmen measured the pole about three inches from the bar. "It's this long."

Nancharm coitus sounded bizarre and outlandish and was even more unsettling because soon I'd be putting Mister Mushroom Head where no man has gone before.

We searched for material to coat the "business" end of the toy. We opened cans and jars and tested the liquids inside. Soon we had left spatter and graffiti all over the lab and settled on a purple rubbery paint. When the bar and doohickeys were painted a uniform color, the device looked like something you'd buy at a fetish store.

I cast a paranoid look about the lab. "Is it safe to talk?"

"Trust me." Carmen smirked. "If Jolie is doing what I asked her to, every Nancharm eyeball and sensor is glued to the sexual shindig she's orchestrating."

"How is doing the nasty with Moots going to help us?"

"Up until now, she's has maintained a clinical distance from me." Carmen spun the toy. "I aim to change that. With a three way. You, me and her."

"Why me?"

"To spice the offer. None of the Nancharm have had sex with a human male. You'll be the first."

I tried to imagine the scenario. To access Moots' matched set of vaginas, we had to get under her carapace. "The first man to have sex with a Nancharm." I gulped. "That's an honor I'd rather not have. Why not Irsan or Toby?"

"They might be a little too delicate."

My penis turtled tight into my crotch. "What exactly is Moots going to do?"

"She might start by giving you a hummer."

I didn't need that visual. Sticking my fingers in my ears, I began to sing, "La, la, la."

Carman jabbed me in the belly with the end of the toy. "Now you have standards. I've seen some of the skanks you've porked. Moots would be a step up."

I needed a tall, stiff drink of ninety-proof to cleanse my mind.

Carmen twirled the toy overhead like a baton. "Don't know when or how, but something is going to happen," She added, "When it does we have to be ready. To do that we need to play head games with the Nancharm. Make them drop their guard until you-know-who makes her move." Carmen wagged her hand in front of her nose like a trunk in case I didn't get that she was referring to Blossom.

"Seems you're counting on a lot of chickens before you even get eggs in your basket."

Carmen jabbed the toy toward my crotch. "You got a better idea, Mr. I-prefer-to-keep-my-dick-in-my-pants?"

Sadly, I didn't.

Chapter Twenty-nine

Carmen and I returned to the living quarters through a back way that took us first to the pond. Discarded clothes, dildos, vibrators, and empty bottles of lube and wine lay strewn about.

"Looks like we missed a hell of a party," I said.

Carmen stashed the Nancharm sex toy by the patio table. We entered the den. Wall sconces illuminated the room with a faint, amber light. Jolie and crew sat cross-legged on the floor. They wore fluffy robes and their hair remained wet, no doubt from a group shower that followed their orgy. They smelled of soap, shampoo, and satisfaction.

Cassie brushed Juanita's hair. Irsan sipped languidly from a glass of wine and appeared as if he needed a cigarette to polish his aura of contentment. Toby leaned against Jolie, one arm draped across her shoulders.

A pair of panties and rumpled towels lay across the coffee table. *Who had been the main course in that exchange?*

Carmen and I were still in our paint-spattered jeans and t-shirts. I felt like a nerd pressing his snotty nose against the window of the cool kids' playhouse. For me, this place wasn't Planet Pleasure but Planet Frustration.

Jolie raised her head, blinked, and offered a sleepy, "Welcome back."

Carmen toed a pair of swimming trunks. "When did the clothes come off?"

"Sometime between the second and third bottle." Jolie stood and padded about, the ambient light outlining the robe where it hugged her sleek body. "By the way, positions 17 through 34 of the Kama Sutra leave your lady parts really sore."

Carmen allowed a smile. "In a good way, for sure."

A wall chime announced that Moots was on the way and we gathered in the dining room.

She arrived, oblivious to our scheme to seduce her. *When? Soon,* I imagined. *And then what?*

A translucent wall panel projected a life-sized hologram of Dr. Fastid into the middle of the room. He clapped his hands. "Bravo. Bravo. Finally you're back on the ball. On the ball." He pointed at Toby. "Subject 39172 ..."

Toby hitched his shoulders and touched his chest. "Me?"

"Yes, you," replied Fastid. "Is there another 39172 on the premises? You have really thrown yourself into this research. Perhaps you should try to kill yourself more often!"

Toby lowered his head. He pressed his wrists, wound-side down, against his lap. Jolie gave him a side hug and shot a dirty look at Fastid. Moots' tendrils shivered and she pointed a scolding finger at him.

"Moots, I'm just kidding," Fastid exclaimed with a laugh. "I'm well aware that our overhead doesn't cover attempted suicides."

Carmen poked me in the ribs. I knew what she was thinking. Toby tried to kill himself and what irked Fastid was the impact to his budget.

"Keep up the good work," Fastid continued. "While the information we're getting is a little marginal, my staff and I are enjoying the show. Enjoying the show." He paused, then asked, "Subject 41866?"

We looked at each other to see who he referred to and gave a collective shrug.

"Jolie," Moots said.

She let go of Toby and pushed from the floor.

Fastid gestured that she remained seated. "We especially appreciate your enthusiasm, 41866. You choreographed some exceptionally intriguing positions."

"It's a gift," Jolie demurred.

He looped his arms and rested his balled fists against his middle carapace. "Keep up the good work. Make me proud."

The wall panel pulsed. His hologram fuzzed over and vanished. We looked at each other and then at Moots.

Her tendrils puffed. "What?"

"This is good, no?" I asked.

"For him."

"It's your project."

"Your sudden outburst of activity attracted the attention of the Most High Research Council," Moots explained. "Dr. Fastid is making sure he gets the credit."

"That's not fair," Cassie blurted.

"Tell me what's fair about anything." Moots cocked her head and seemed to have squared her shoulders. "But that's my problem."

Carmen stood and clapped her hands. "Recess is over. Jolie, have these kiddos tidy up and get started with dinner."

Jolie rose to her feet, and in a drill sergeant's voice, barked orders to the chalices.

Carmen grasped my arm and led me to the den. "Moots," she added, "join us. We need to discuss something."

Carmen had more than talk in mind, and my kundalini noir cringed as we approached the starting line for interspecies hide-the-salami.

The three of us continued through the den and to the back patio where we halted by the table. Carmen's sex toy lay on the paving stones, the business end tucked inside a beach blanket, the long handle sticking out. If Moots noticed, she made no comment.

"What you've done for us is appreciated," Carmen said to Moots.

"I execute my duties in accordance to my responsibilities, not to please you."

With an attitude that gruff, getting Moots to drop her guard—and her "pants"—was going to take buckets of emotional bullshit.

Carmen smiled at her. "That doesn't change what I just said."

"*Meh.*" Moots shrugged. "Is that why you asked me out here?"

"Tell us how we can help you succeed. Even if Fastid grabs the credit, I want you to know—"

"Help me succeed?" Moots interrupted. "It's not like you have a choice, is it? Besides, success here depends on the effect you have on our men. And that, so far, has been one big zip."

We stayed quiet, me glancing at Carmen and Moots, Carmen glancing at Moots and me, Moots staring into whatever with her blank alabaster eyes. Outwardly, I was as calm as the mirror-like waters of the pond. Inside, I roiled with dread.

I have to screw Moots!

I wondered about the mechanics of boning her. Did the Nancharm copulate standing up? How was I supposed to get in the saddle? Did Moots even have a saddle? She was ten feet tall. Plus she had six vaginas. Suppose I did find them, how was I to choose? *Eenie, meeny, miney, mo?*

And once I did the deed, how was that going to coincide with Blossom arriving right on time with a space ship?

The questions made my stomach churn. Any other chance to slap skin, my lust would stew in a pressure cooker of anticipation. Now, getting excited about Moots was like trying to light a match underwater. I was one soggy noodle.

Carmen broke the meditative spell by walking to the grassy rise overlooking the pond. She stripped out of her t-shirt, unbuttoned the jeans and wiggled out of them. Naked, she took running steps to build up speed—the choice parts of her jiggled invitingly—and dove into the water.

Moots glided to the edge of the pond. Carmen broke the surface in a swirl of bubbles and swam parallel to the shore. Her body stretched and twisted beneath the undulating water.

I noticed how Moots studied Carmen. "What are you looking at?"

"In my youth, I was a champion swimmer." Moots sounded wistful. But wistful for swimming, her youth, or for Carmen?

"Felix," Carmen yelled. "Jump in."

With me joining her for a skinny dip, our raw bodies would tell Moots to expect a sex show. Fine by me as long as my partner was

Carmen, but I knew this was the kick-off for our bizarro ménage à trois.

I peeled off my shirt and pants and trotted toward the water. Moots glanced once and then fixed her stare back on Carmen. Good choice, I'd rather look at her as well.

I dove in. The pond swallowed me with a cool, pleasant embrace. As a vampire, I don't need to breathe and can stay underwater almost indefinitely, but we do suffer from shrinkage.

Carmen scissored her legs and I paddled toward her. When I was about to grab her, she sank beneath the surface and swam away. I chased after her, and her playing hard-to-get pumped my juices. This was no accident. Carmen was getting me in the mood. We rubbed our slick bodies against one another and frolicked like horny otters.

Moots followed our antics. She could've gone back inside, but she didn't. Despite her inscrutable face, I sensed a melancholia radiating from her, as real as her bright yellow and red colors. If I was to guess, I'd say that Moots wanted to join us.

Carmen waded to the shallow end and climbed the steps toward the patio. Water sheeted down her sleek, muscular back and round, perfect ass. She scooped a towel from the patio table and patted herself dry. I followed her lead and stood beside her.

Moots glided close and towered over us. She held still and stared at Carmen.

"I have something for you," Carmen said.

Moots didn't react.

Carmen pushed a chair against her and climbed on it. Even so, she had to look up at Moots.

Something gelled between them as if the pheromones circulating in their bodies congealed into a solid invisible mass. Carmen stood on tiptoe and reached for Moot's translator-cap.

Moots seized her hand.

"Trust me," Carmen said.

Chapter Thirty

Moots slowly let go of Carmen's fingers. Carmen eased the translator-cap off Moots' head and placed the cap on the patio table. She again stood on tiptoe and faced Moots. She raised her right hand, spread her fingers, and slowly, carefully—as if handling a precious treasure—slid her fingers into Moots' tendrils.

Moots began to quiver.

Carmen whispered, "Aside from their genitalia, this is their most sensitive erogenous zone."

"Why did you take off the translator-cap?" I whispered back.

Carmen stared at Moots. "Words will only get in the way."

Moots' arms undulated like reeds in water. I stared into her blank, white eyes and wanted to believe that I saw a blossoming of emotions. Anticipation. Desire. Vulnerability.

Moots' lower-middle carapace, the yellow one, the one about even with my chest, expanded in girth, then it split along vertical seams. Each segment tilted downward like flower petals, revealing a trunk of lime-green flesh.

And there it was.

Her vagina.

Or should I say, her six vaginas? A row of vertical slits, each maybe three inches tall and three inches apart. They opened and closed like gills.

"Now what?" I thought about the mating habits of the praying mantis, especially when after copulation the female bites the head off the male.

Moots raised one arm and beckoned me.

Carmen made room on the chair. "It's show time."

"What about the toy?"

"That's for later."

I guess that made me the hors d'oeuvres. I tried to move but my legs wouldn't budge.

"Quit stalling." Carmen scolded. "You're about to make history. Don't be a pussy. Man up before we lose the moment."

"Cut me slack, okay. I'm still trying to find the moment." I climbed on the chair.

Her eyes cut to my flaccid junk and she frowned in disapproval. "Geez Felix, show a little enthusiasm."

"I'm not feeling the love."

"You will now." Carmen slid a hand from Moots' tendrils to draw me close. She pressed her mouth against the side of my neck. I closed my eyes as her fangs stabbed my throat. Her sex enzymes flooded through me, an electric pulse exploding from the bite and zapping down my spine and straight to my groin. My kundalini noir rang like it had been kicked by a horse. Waves of glorious heat channeled to my crotch, and I got so hard I could've hammered nails into concrete.

Carmen withdrew and cooed, "Much better."

My head swam in a delicious stew of super-charged endorphins. The narcotic buzz filled my mind with all kinds of pleasurable images, episodes of sexual bliss. I locked on one. With Carmen. Back in South Carolina before she was kidnapped. A fast-n-furious lunchtime quickie in the parlor of a mortuary.

Something warm and leathery snaked up my leg. I pushed aside the creepy realization it was Moots and forced myself to try and enjoy the touch. Her fingers fondled my parts, gripped the shaft and began a steady stroking motion. Maybe this was all Moots wanted to do: give me an alien hand job.

Carmen pressed on my shoulders, forcing me toward Moots' battery of cooters.

So laying pipe was still the plan. I wasn't sure about the mechanics. Was I supposed to wrap my legs around Moots and ride her? Or lean against her cylindrical torso like I was screwing an oil drum?

Carmen kissed the back of my neck and worked her way down my spine. Moots guided me toward her orifice of choice until labia puckered around the end of my crank.

My inner wingman hollered, *Eject! Eject!*

But we were too committed to turn back so I squelched his microphone. Carmen pushed against my buttocks, sliding me into Moots like an artillery shell loading into a breech. I plunged into a moist and heated envelope. Nancharm men might have only been three inches long but I managed to sink all the way in. Her flesh was warm against my belly like I was leaning across an oven.

Moots' vagina tightened around me with a firm and pleasant grip. She had extraordinary kegel muscles and started an expert massage. With six penises, the Nancharm men must have six times this fun. I couldn't believe they had so fucked up their DNA that they'd given up such a pussy ride. And if this thrill ride wasn't enough, Carmen crouched behind me for some appreciated teabag action.

Usually I like to draw out the ceremonies, but I decided that *slam, bam, thank you ma'am* would do. I was certain the Nancharm erection committee was watching, but this was my limited engagement performance. I relaxed into the sensation and let myself get milked to release. My nerves compressed around my groin, and my hips tightened as I plunged through orgasm.

I shuddered in ecstasy. A tingling followed the delicious climax, my mind cleared and I opened my eyes. The world slowly came into focus. I was staring at the center of Moots' red torso. This close it looked like the hood of a car.

"Whoa there, Hercules," Carmen exclaimed. "You're not supposed to drown Moots. Where the hell have you been keeping all that?"

"It's been a while."

Moots' hand slithered across her "crotch" and wiped the mess. In a classy move, she flicked gobs of spunk from her fingers.

I hopped off the chair and stumbled over the grass, weary and quite spent. A gigantic *EWWWW!* plowed through me. I could bathe in hot Clorox and not feel clean, but for now the best I could do was pat myself dry with a towel. Carmen had gone back to stroking Moots' tendrils. "She took care of you, now we take care of her." She gestured to the sex toy by the table.

I was hoping to bail but apparently an intergalactic gigolo's work is never done. I withdrew the toy from between the folds of its towel. A bottle of lube rolled free.

Carmen asked me to trade places. She cautioned me to be very gentle with Moots' tendrils. They floated around my fingers and felt like strands of spongy yarn.

Carmen slathered lube on the six vibrators of the sex toy. She aligned the vibrators with Moots' slits and slowly worked them in. She flicked the battery switch, and the end of sex toy vibrated with an aggressive hum.

Moots tentacled her arms around my torso.

Carmen adjusted the angle of the sex toy. It was a truly bizarre sight. Naked Carmen—her muscles tensing, her boobs and butt wiggling to-and-fro, her eyebrows pinched in concentration—as she pumped the toy into Moots' vaginas. Green froth bubbled around the vibrators.

Moots squeezed me.

Carmen quickened the tempo.

Moots squeezed tighter.

Carmen brushed a lock of hair from her forehead and kept pistoning the sex toy. Green foam spurted from Moots and onto Carmen's hands and forearms. "I'm getting her close. Keep playing with her tendrils."

Moots' arms coiled vice-tight around me. If Carmen didn't finish her soon, Moots was going to break my ribs. Her tendrils puffed straight in a silent Nancharm scream. She looked like a black dandelion. Her arms clenched and then eased the pressure.

Carmen slowed her stroking and shut off the power. She withdrew the sex toy and the vibrators slurped free.

Moots' tendrils relaxed and her arms uncoiled. Carmen dropped the sex toy and asked me to again switch places. She placed the translator-cap on Moots and stroked her face.

Moots huffed gently like she was trying to find her breath. "Sorry about the mess." Her fingers traced across Carmen's face. "I'm a bit of a squirter."

Carmen kissed Moots' cheek. "That's okay. So am I."

The exchange was loaded with blissful tenderness and I felt like an intruder. "Uh … h …" I stammered, not sure of my part in this post-coital snuggle.

Carmen didn't look at me when she said, "Clean up as best you can."

So now I had been demoted to jizz mopper. I used a towel to blot the green foam from Moots' "crotch." Her carapace petals folded shut, and I backed away.

Carmen and Moots hugged. Carmen said, "If you don't mind, we need time alone."

Fair enough. I started for my clothes when Moots snapped her fingers and pointed to the sex toy, the bottle of lube, and the stained towels. I collected everything and headed across the patio for the back door. Just as I touched the doorknob, Carmen called me.

I faced her.

She winked. "Good job. Thanks."

I entered the den, acknowledging that despite my misgivings I had pressed ahead like a trooper. In fact, I felt a little proud after performing like a mighty, mighty man even though Moots and her kung-fu grip vagina had done the work. Jolie and the chalices stood in a semi-circle and stared.

I expected applause. I knew I was unclothed but that wasn't why they were gawking. I hitched my shoulders. *What?*

Juanita shook her head. "Now you've done it."

"And quite well," I replied. "Let any of the Nancharm men try and match me."

"That's exactly the problem." She pointed to a wall panel that glowed with this message: *Specimen 92712 is scheduled for therapeutic intervention.*

"Therapeutic intervention, what the hell is that?"

"Electronic implants. What the Nancharm put in Toby."

"And who is Specimen 92712?"

The chalices looked away. Jolie's eyes canted into sad angles. "You."

Chapter Thirty-One

Carmen and I sat at the dining room table. Moots was beside us, but I wasn't sure if she was relaxing or standing because the sections of her carapace had telescoped into one another. Even so, she loomed above us.

Like Carmen, I was sipping coffee—laced with Cassie's blood. The caffeine and hemoglobin washed through me and scrubbed away most of the lingering heebie-jeebies of doing the nasty with Moots and my fear of being reengineered into a sexual cyborg.

But doubts remained, as in, what had happened to Blossom? I had done my part, where was she?

I'd thought that after our ménage a trois, Moots would get clingy with either Carmen or me, maybe us both. After all, according to Carmen, it had been awhile since our Nancharm minder had gotten her rocks off. But while Moots remained her usual stoic self, the way she stayed close made me suspect she was waiting to segue into something. What exactly? Who knew? Not even Carmen with her intuitive juju had any luck reading that porcelain-like face of hers.

Moots suddenly extended her carapace and rose to full height. Her tendrils fluffed and she faced the doorway between the dining room and the kitchen.

The door stretched open. Dr. Fastid entered, leading a mob of Nancharm on a small fleet of hover scooters. They halted and floated off their rides. He clapped his leathery hands as his translator-cap boomed, "Bravo. Brav-OH!"

Their tendrils puffed in silent, animated conversation. His crew looked at each other, back at Fastid, then each other, and began to clap half-heartedly.

"Most wonderful progress," Fastid gushed. "Let me offer my personal congratulations, specimen 92712." Fastid slid to my side. "You sir, are the hero of the day. The hero of the day."

He draped one hand around my arm and winched me to my feet. An odd device that looked like a toilet plunger resting on the bell part disconnected from a hover scooter and zipped our way. The device halted and the tip flashed a soft orange color.

Fastid's crew formed a semicircle around us and faced the device. Moots started to join us when Fastid held up his hand to tell her to not bother. She retreated against the table. Carmen stroked her arm.

He wrapped his fingers around my neck and aimed my head at the device. His minions crowded against us and held still for a group selfie. The device's tip flashed and dazzled my eyes. The minions relaxed, then crowded once more for another group photo. The device flashed again.

Fastid scooted from me. I was left blinking the spots from my vision. He perched his clenched fists on his hips and leaned left and right. "Finally, some progress. You sir, deserve a commendation. I know I do."

"Commendation for what?"

"For this." He snapped his fingers. The toilet plunger device beamed a hologram into the middle of the room. Charts and odd writing scrolled across the image.

I studied the hologram, then glanced at Carmen. She shrugged. I turned back to Fastid. "What am I looking at?"

He huffed in exasperation. "Let me dumb it down for you." He snapped his fingers. The image refreshed. The figures were different but still indecipherable.

I tried to grasp a little understanding, but the effort made me tilt my head like a confused dog. "Uhhh ... I'm not good at math."

"This is not math!" Fastid exclaimed. "This is middle-grade biology. No wonder Earth is such a backwards planet." He faced his coterie and puffed his tendrils. The Nancharm began to shake and wave their arms. I worried what was going on until he guffawed out his translator-cap. Then the others joined in. Even Moots. The pompous bastard probably mocked us. *How many humans does it take to screw in a luminescent triode emitter?*

"I wasn't too good at biology either," I said. "You'll have to enlighten me."

"Not good at biology?" Fastid replied. "Why 92712, you're a natural."

Again, I exchanged bemused looks with Carmen.

Fastid waved his hand through the hologram. "We're talking major progress."

"Progress?" I asked.

"Tumescence!"

"You mean wood?"

He scratched his head and commenced a tendril exchange with Moots. "Ah," he said, "a hard-on. Not yet. But we're closer than ever." He pointed to one of the charts. "This is you." He pointed to an adjacent chart. "This is the Nancharm subject we hooked up to replicate your effort. Previously, our best results were minor undulations in the levels of Type Z1 lutropin and Type Beta-3 androgen. Mostly attributable to statistical variation. But because of you …" Fastid snapped his fingers. The hologram changed to show what appeared to be a row of six prunes protruding from a Nancharm belly. They quivered and became swollen, but only enough to smooth a few of the wrinkles. I chuckled when I realized it was Nancharm man junk.

"What about Moots and Carmen?" I asked. "They did most of the work. I only supplied a little help."

Fastid's tendrils trembled. The other Nancharm's tendrils shook. They pivoted and slapped one another on the shoulders in masculine bonhomie.

"A little help? 92712, you are much too modest. Your little help is exactly what is going to save us from extinction."

"I brought back your mojo?"

"Well ..." Fastid wiggled his fingers and the hologram disappeared. "Not exactly. But the physiological telemetry looks promising. First, we have to wire you up. You see—"

"Wire up?" Carmen interrupted. "Like Toby?"

"Who?" Fastid asked.

Moots fluffed her tendrils to answer.

"Ah, yes. Him," Fastid said. "92712, your implants will be much more sophisticated. Imagine your pride knowing how you've contributed to my success."

None of this sounded good. "And when we're done?"

"Why, you'll be recycled to recover the precious metals and components. We can't let that expensive material go to waste." Fastid paused and stared like he expected me to leap for joy.

When I didn't, he and Moots began an animated tendril conversation, during which she must have explained that I would object to being recycled.

Fastid draped his hand on my shoulder in avuncular fashion. "92712, you look like a member of an intelligent species. You know about money? Credits? Debits? Balance sheets? The bottom line?"

I knew all about this bottom line, as in my bottom on the line. I nodded.

"Good. Better. Excellent. I know you won't disappoint me." Fastid drummed the hard shell of his torso carapace. "92712, I like you. And if you're worried about not getting any recognition from this, I promise that you'll be mentioned in a footnote when my report is circulated during the peer review. For a foreign species, there is no higher honor." He grasped and shook my hand. "Congratulations."

The toilet plunger device skimmed close and flashed.

Spots careened through my vision like bumper cars. I tried to pull my head away but Fastid held tight. "One more," he muttered. The device took another photo. "Wait, my little alien friend, that is not all." Fastid gestured to the toilet plunger device. The tip beamed a ray that materialized into a hologram of a Nancharm. "After your splendid performance with Moots, you've earned the right to practice your technique with my daughter."

My guts melted into a slimy, queasy ball.

He snapped his fingers and the hologram cycled through images of more Nancharms. "The rest of my team has also volunteered the services of their female staff and kin. 92712, you are a lucky, lucky man."

No way was I being forced into a Nancharm stud farm. Disgust filled me until it seeped out my pores. "There's no point," I protested. "You've seen how it was done."

"Absolutely. I've reviewed the holographic video many times. You're quite the performer," Fastid elbowed my shoulder. "If you know what I mean. *Heh, heh, heh.*"

His laughter dripped buckets of creepiness. Carmen looked at me and shuddered.

"I've already scheduled your surgery for the implants," he continued. "Unfortunately, the iatric modules are still being calibrated. But patience, my extraterrestrial Lothario, patience. In two days, you'll be a new man. Parts of you at least." Fastid started back to his hover scooter. "And once we get the data we need, then it's off you go to the materials recovery and recycling center. Again, congratulations."

Fastid and his team levitated back onto their hover scooters. They started out the door like a pack of Shriners in go-karts. "And Moots," he said over his shoulder, "I need a draft of my commendation first thing. Make it sing my praise." The door shrank after they had passed.

Two days. My knees weakened under the weight.

Now that the Nancharm had designated me as their prime specimen, what were the chances that once Blossom arrived I could get away?

Carmen took my hand and led me back to a chair. She pushed my cup toward me, but even if the blood-coffee mix was warm, anything that I drank now would be unpleasantly bitter.

Moots had her eyes leveled on us but I couldn't tell what she was looking at or thinking. Maybe she stewed in indignation because Fastid treated her like a kitchen wench.

"You got anything to say?" Carmen asked.

"Plenty," Moots shot back. She reached to the table, grasped our coffee cups, and crushed them. Blood-coffee and shards of crockery shot from between her fingers.

Carmen and I shrank back in surprise. My talons strained inside my fingertips, ready to spring out.

"What is the problem?" Carmen spoke slowly.

"I know your game," Moots replied.

Carmen shot me a look of bewilderment. I shrugged nonchalantly though my kundalini noir quivered in alarm.

"Sex with me was only a distraction," Moots declared. "You and Blossom are scheming something. An escape?"

Carmen reached under the table and touched my knee. I clasped her fingers.

"Escape? With Blossom?" Carmen's voice cracked with feigned hurt. "I'm shocked you would think such a thing."

Moots pointed to the ceiling. Blood-coffee dripped down her wrist. "Don't take me for a fool. Blossom never left D-Galtha. She's in orbit right now."

She was? This was news.

"So? She's a pilot." Carmen's reply sounded perfectly sincere.

Moots' voice turned into a growl. "She's been trying to access the Erection Committee communications network. The only reason she would do that is to contact you."

If Blossom was trying to contact us, she was doing so in a damn clumsy way.

"Suppose this is true. Dr. Fastid doesn't know, does he?" Carmen asked. "Why haven't you told him?"

"Don't tell me my job." Moots slammed her fists on the table. "Both of you, listen and listen well. You will complete your sexual protocols as required. You will then be disposed of as Dr. Fastid so orders. And you will never, under any circumstances, ever leave Planet Pleasure."

Chapter Thirty-two

I paced inside the dining room, flipping out about my dismal future. In two days I was to be sliced open, reconfigured into a sex machine, and forced to stoke a train of Nancharm señoritas. In the end, regardless of whether I helped the Nancharm figure out their boner problem, I'd be scrapped and recycled.

The fate for the rest of the crew wasn't any rosier. Carmen and the chalices would be sold at auction. Jolie's fate hadn't been discussed but I was sure it involved wearing a collar and a leash and eating extraterrestrial kibble.

But there was a grain of hope. Carmen's former master, Blossom the Wah-zhim pilot, circled the planet with undefined plans to get us out of here. The flip side was that Moots knew about Blossom and had warned Carmen and me to give up trying to escape.

Jolie entered the room, the chalices trailing after her. She wore her pistol harness with the .45s snug in the holsters and carried my leather jacket. "Here." She tossed me the jacket.

"What's this for?"

"We need to shake this funk we're in," she replied. "Putting our gear on might put us in a more receptive frame of mind. You know, channel the universe for possibilities, yada, yada."

I slid my arms into the jacket and enjoyed the feel of leather and the weight of the big revolver against my chest. Already I could feel my thoughts shifting into kick-ass mode.

The chalices huddled side-by-side and gazed at me with tense expressions like they were sheep and I was the shepherd who would lead them to salvation. Too bad my neck was numero uno on the chopping block.

Jolie reminded. "We can't forget what's at stake."

"No chance of that." I tapped the butt of the revolver. If we had to shoot our way out, Moots would be the first to interfere and if so, these bullets were meant for her. I could see her shudder under the impact of repeated .357 magnum slugs. I'd already drilled her once, and I didn't relish drilling her again. Then again, the Nancharm hadn't shown any concern over our guns. The weapons technology was probably so ridiculously simple that our pistols didn't even register as dangerous. That might be a fatal oversight on their part. Or a laughable mistake on ours. When the time came for violence, we might be better off hitting the Nancharm with spit balls.

Jolie glared. "There's more at stake than our skins. I mean when we get home."

"Home?" the chalices repeated in chorus.

Cassie asked, "Why do you need guns at home?"

"There's a welcoming committee waiting for us who is not very welcoming," I answered. How much had happened back in New Mexico since Jolie and I had left? Had Coyote recovered? Had Phaedra and her minions harmed him? What about Marina? And his girlfriend, Rainelle? Did the Navajo skinwalkers still protect her? I was already wound plenty tight over our problems here; thinking about Phaedra took up the remaining slack and my anxiety squeezed into a chokehold.

Toby stepped away from the others and approached me. Juanita and Cassie clasped each other's hands. "Whatever you have planned, we're in," Cassie said, her voice quaking.

I panned their faces. Juanita. Cassie. Toby. Irsan. They each looked so desperate for escape that I'd bet any one of them would throw their bodies on barbed wire if it meant the rest of us could run across their backs to freedom.

I noticed Carmen was missing and asked where she was.

"The main bedroom," Juanita answered.

I left the dining room and found Carmen sitting in an armchair, her eyebrows and face pinched in deep, sullen meditation. If I ever brooded this hard, I'm certain smoke would shoot out my ears. Two carafes, one for coffee and the other for blood, rested beside her cup on the table. Jolie and the chalices crowded into the room, but Carmen made no notice of our presence. None of us dared disturb her, and we waited for her to ease out of the trance.

With a faraway look in her eyes, she announced, "Remember you told me that I would sense mind probes?"

The floor seemed to shift beneath me. Our dilemma had just gotten worse. "You felt them?"

Carmen nodded. "She knows we're here." Her expression darkened and her gaze cut to our guns. "You're going to need those. The Nancharm won't be able to protect us."

"From who?" Cassie asked.

My nerves tightened. I knew the answer though I wish I didn't.

The alarm exploded with a loud wail. Ceiling panels flashed red. The hologram reappeared, blaring the message: Intruder Alert. Priority One Lockdown.

Carmen said, "Phaedra."

Chapter Thirty-three

Phaedra. The name sent questions ricocheting through my head. How did she get here? Doubt it was a spaceship. Had to be a portal through the psychic plane. But how?

Coyote had said our access to D-Galtha came only after a hundred and more years. Something was very wrong. I retrieved my revolver. Jolie already had one of her .45s in hand.

The alarm's blare echoed through the building, so loud it hurt our ears. The hologram kept flashing: *Intruder alert! Intruder alert!*

"Phaedra's on D-Galtha?" Jolie yelled the question.

I asked Carmen, "How can you tell it's her?"

She stood, moving slowly as if fighting a trance. "I just know."

I remembered that creepy feeling. Years before, when Phaedra's thoughts had wormed into my mind like clammy tentacles.

The chalices gawked at Carmen and asked all at once. "Who is Phaedra?"

I looked back at them. *Where to begin?*

The alarm faded and the hologram warning disappeared, replaced by an image of Moots. "Stay in the building. A guard force is on the way." Her image blinked off.

Phaedra's arrival had triggered a massive alarm from the Nancharm. Now they dispatched guards to protect us. Meaning Phaedra was on the move. If they knew where she was, why didn't they stop her? The Nancharm could demolish planets, obliterate civilizations, yet I feared their weapons and defenses were no match for this maniacal ingénue and her psychic superpowers. We were in deep trouble.

A worried grimace spread from chalice to chalice. Cassie said, "Whoever this Phaedra is, she must be bad news."

"In the worst possible way," I replied.

"What's she doing here?" Juanita asked.

Carmen blinked as if shaking off the last of the spell. "Phaedra has come here to kill Felix, Jolie, and me."

Toby and Irsan's expressions warped into frowns. Cassie and Juanita asked in chorus, "Why?"

I replied, "Because she knows that only Carmen can stop her."

Cassie looked at me. "What about you?"

I tightened my grip on the revolver. "The last time Phaedra and I met one-on-one, it didn't end well for me. She intends to end what she had started."

The chalices volleyed questions. "Who is this Phaedra? Why can't the Nancharm protect us? Stop her from what? What can Carmen do?"

Carmen managed a grin that tempered our doubts. "Now I understand why Phaedra fears me. Every time she tries to get into my mind, I can read hers. The intuition the aliens prize in me has that unexpected benefit. Jolie, watch the chalices. Felix and I are going upstairs for a look see."

Carmen and I left the dining room, went through the kitchen, and entered the hall on our way to the escalator. The door from the bedroom stretched open. A Nancharm guard wearing an oversized suit rode through on a hover scooter. The suit shimmered as if it was made of mercury. Thick sleeves encased the arms, and a cylindrical helmet with a dark face-shield covered the head. A small dish antenna jutted from the top of the helmet. One arm had a spatula-like device fixed to the wrist and the other had a trident. A second Nancharm guard with similar arm attachments waited behind on another scooter.

"The perimeter around the building is secured," the first Nancharm announced through a translator box attached to his helmet. "Our priority is to stop the intruder. Stay out of the line of fire."

"No problem." I backed away. I wasn't going to let myself become collateral damage. But if these guards were here, they must have assumed Phaedra might breach their other defenses.

The two guards turned about and returned to the main bay. The door between us shrank until it was barely large enough for a Yorkie.

"They don't stand a chance," Carmen said.

"How do you know?"

"Because I saw into her mind. She knows how to beat the Nancharm."

Minutes ago, I was in a funk because I had two days before Dr. Fastid put his alien mitts on me and sliced me open. Now I was on a shorter countdown to a bigger disaster, and my mind clicked like a revolver cycling through empty cylinders as it searched for a solution to our worsening troubles.

Carmen and I climbed the escalator to the second floor. That Phaedra feared Carmen was the key to an answer. "What's this connection between you two?" I asked.

She gave a weak shrug. "It's not like I can open the top of her head and rummage around. But her thoughts come to me."

"How does that help us?"

"At the very least, she loses the element of surprise. Down the line, there might be more that I can do."

The door onto the balcony opened and we stepped onto the balcony overlooking the paved apron around our building. A dusky twilight muted the evening's colors. The landscape scrolled toward a yellow horizon that blended into an indigo sky dotted with stars. D-Galtha's pale moon floated beside the planet's ring. Other buildings glimmered around us, and flying saucers zipped through the air like schools of silvery minnows.

A fireball rose in the distance, and though it was but a yellow and orange smudge, I sensed the danger it promised. Phaedra was doing a Godzilla rampage across the Nancharm's turf.

The fireball faded into a cloud of smoke. A faint green light passed through the base of the smoke and moved in our direction. The light was a tiny glowing dot like a colored lamp on a faraway porch.

A thought clanged through my head, Phaedra announcing herself. *I'm here!*

A hatch opened in the apron below us, and two more guards on hover scooters popped into view. They glided across the apron, dismounted the scooters and turned to face the light.

Two Nancharm saucers zoomed overhead, powerful and menacing, racing like a pair of fighter jets to obliterate the enemy. A crimson beam shot from one saucer toward the light. The beam missed and set the ground on fire. The beam flicked off, then flicked on again, this time aiming at the second disk, its wingman. It exploded with a sickening boom and showered the ground with burning debris.

The first disk continued on its path toward the green light. Unable to control his weapons, the pilot must've decided on a kamikaze run. A cheer in appreciation of his ballsy self-sacrifice tingled through my kundalini noir. But the disk abruptly veered away, knifed the ground, shattered, and exploded.

My congratulatory cheer congealed into a sinking, dismal feeling. Phaedra was using her mental powers to seriously mind fuck the Nancharm. Of what I knew about the aliens, at least the ones who had visited Earth, they were aware of the psychic dimension. They had invented the psychotronic projector, in fact the mission of the Roswell UFO was to test it on humans. As for what they knew about psychic powers, they were still at the trying-to-light-a-fire-by-rubbing-two-sticks-together stage while Phaedra was well into its laser inferno capabilities.

I expected more fleets of Nancharm flying saucers, but none arrived. Explosions lit far up in the sky. What was going on?

The light kept approaching and was now a half-mile away. The emerald bubble floated over the rolling, vegetated terrain. Our two Nancharm guards skated to the edge of the apron and raised their arms to point the attachments at the light. I had the impression of two squirrels baring their teeth at an oncoming freight train.

"If the Nancharm are dead meat," I said, "we are screwed."

"Let's not underestimate ourselves," Carmen replied in a flat tone. "We'll let Phaedra do that." She glowered and squinted at the light. "She's going to blast her way in."

"How?"

"Her minions. She's going to use them as suicide bombers."

I had to consider that a moment before it sank in. Phaedra was even more diabolical and depraved than what I thought was possible.

The light was now close enough that I could recognize her glowing figure in the center of the green bubble. She stood on a platform on an alien tricycle tractor, an elephant-like creature at the controls. The bubble must be a force shield. Six more figures crowded beside Phaedra and the driver inside the bubble. Was the driver Wah-zhim? A hunch told me that it wasn't Blossom. If it was Wah-zhim, why help Phaedra? What was going on? I thought Blossom was going to help us escape.

Giant electric arcs cracked from the Nancharms' tridents. The arcs dazzled my eyes and their heat spanked my face. They zigzagged toward the bubble and splattered clouds of sparks where they made contact. Phaedra and her crew kept approaching. The arcs looked strong enough to slice through an aircraft carrier and here they had no effect.

I waited for the Nancharm to let loose another volley but they kept quiet. Their armor suits began to vibrate, then shook like stockpots boiling over. The Nancharm flicked their arms and their weapons clattered to the pavement. They desperately twisted their helmets to yank them off.

Yellow froth seeped from the helmet collars, the shoulder sockets, their wrists, and pooled underneath their bodies. The shiny armor panels turned blue like the chrome of overheated exhaust pipes. Smoke vented from between the panels. Sections popped loose and clanged to the ground. Clouds of smoke roiled from inside. Phaedra had found a way to cook the Nancharm within their armor. Drifting smoke brought the sweet, sickly smell of charred cotton candy.

A tremor of panic wiggled down my spine. I hoped Moots wasn't one of the guards.

The bubble rolled closer. Phaedra shimmered like she was a celestial being in a religious painting. The six vampires waited with her, three men and three women, all dressed in black with bulky leather jackets.

A sleek, tapered object fell from the sky and landed on the apron between the two incinerated guards. I thought it was an artillery shell until it broke apart to release dozens of hand-sized winged robots. They flocked together and swirled in front of the bubble.

The bubble stopped a hundred meters from us. One of the female vampires pushed through the bubble's membrane and once clear, sprinted directly into the flying robots. They swarmed over her, clumping to her arms, head, and shoulders. She staggered under their weight and dropped to the pavement.

An explosion engulfed the robots. Carmen and I ducked to avoid the cascade of debris.

Smoke wafted from a crater in the pavement where the vampire had been. Had the robots blown her up? Or had the vampire blown them up?

Phaedra's forward progress answered that question. Just as Carmen had announced, Phaedra's macabre arsenal did include vampire suicide bombers.

The bubble tractor rolled over the blasted section of pavement and halted again, less than fifty meters away. I raised the magnum and drew a bead on Phaedra. One quick shot and the battle ended here. If my bullet penetrated the force shield.

Waves and waves of anguish flooded my mind. Blinded with pain, I crumpled to the balcony.

Carmen hugged me and propped me upright. The pain lifted. She quivered as if in the grip of a fever.

As I groped at the railing I asked, "What's happening?"

"Phaedra's using her mind powers on me."

My vision cleared enough to see a second vampire, this one male, push out of the bubble. I was too woozy for a shot at him or Phaedra. He sprinted toward the building and from our vantage on the balcony, disappeared from view.

A loud blast shook the building. When the smoke cleared, the bubble advanced through a fan of scattered rubble.

I shouted, "She's blown a hole in the wall."

Carmen sighed, and the strain eased from her face. Phaedra must've shifted her attention to control another of her minions. Now it was my turn to prop Carmen.

I scooped the revolver from where I had dropped it on the balcony. We raced downstairs as best we could with Carmen hobbling beside me. Smoke from the second suicide bomber fouled the hallway. Electric arcs crackled in the main bay where the Nancharm guards were in futile combat against Phaedra.

Jolie beckoned us to the kitchen. The chalices waited behind her. Juanita brandished a chef's knife and Irsan a pair of Molotov cocktails made from emptied bottles of olive oil. Had to admire their spunk.

The sound of the electric arcs died, replaced by the clanging of armor plates falling apart. Carmen's eyes cut toward the bay, and I read the message in them. *Phaedra was moving in for the kill.*

We were on a gangplank that kept shrinking beneath our feet. Though my kundalini noir sputtered in anxiety overload, for the sake of our morale I put on a mask of determination and defiance.

Jolie drew a .45 and flicked off the safety. "What do you think, Felix?"

I surveyed our merry little band of forsaken humans, four mortals and three vampires. The only plan that came to mind was, "Fall back to the pond. We'll have clearer fields of fire."

"Make our stand there?" Toby asked. "Like the Texans at your Alamo?"

"I hope not," I replied. "The Texans lost."

Chapter Thirty-four

Toby stayed by my side, his face fixed into a scowl that looked defiant enough for the both of us. Jolie herded the other chalices out of the kitchen and into the dining room.

A hum echoed in my brain. Phaedra was trying to put the whammy on me.

Carmen staggered against the sink counter. Her complexion curdled into a sickly green pallor, and her eyes dimmed behind a nauseous haze. She and Phaedra were in a knock-down psychic brawl, invisible to the rest of us, and my friend looked to be getting the worst of it.

I started to wrap my arm around Carmen's waist until she raised a hand to reassure me. Her fingers and lips trembled. Her eyes were red with strain. She swallowed again, held her belly as if tortured by cramps, and took baby steps toward the dining room.

Another blast shook the building. The explosion reverberated through my feet and up my legs. Pots and pans clanged and clattered to the kitchen floor. Wine bottles tumbled out of the rack and shattered against the floor, spraying glass fragments and vino.

That had been the third suicide-bomber vampire. Three remained. How far had Phaedra and crew advanced into the facility? Were they in the bedroom or had they already made it to the hallway?

I heard something scramble against the wall between the kitchen and the hall. *Question answered.*

Toby shouted, "A bomber! A bomber!"

I fired twice at the sound and punched two bullet holes through the wall.

Someone dropped to the floor with a loud thump.

I was about to congratulate Toby for his quick action when another thunderclap shook the world into a blur. A wave of smoke clotted my throat and pricked my eyes. Debris whipped against our bodies and ricocheted off the ceiling and walls. Smoke twisted through a ragged hole about a foot square at the bottom of the wall.

My ears ringing from the blast, I ordered, "Fall back before the next bomber strikes."

We had to retreat past the dining room, through the den and to the patio. That would put three walls and their locked doors between us and Phaedra, which was one more than the two bombers she had left. Hopefully this meant that her plan was unraveling, and that we might have a chance of surviving.

I nudged Toby to stay behind me, and we shuffled backwards to the threshold, my pistol trained in the direction of the attack. Light from the overhead panels diffused through the twisting fumes, and shadows comingled in the smelly murk. A shape darkened the bomb hole, and it could only be another vampire crawling through.

"Back, back," I shouted. We crowded against Carmen.

"No time for that, mate," Toby replied. He stepped around me and lunged forward.

I had a split-second to decide: grab him or push Carmen back.

I straight-armed her into the den and was reaching for Toby just as he rushed at the vampire.

Who exploded.

The air flashed hot as dragon's breath. One moment I was in the kitchen and the next, I found myself in the dining room, heaped on top of Carmen. Smoke wafted from our clothes. My skull rang like a bronze bell smacked by a wrecking ball.

Jolie hurdled over us, a .45 in each hand, and emptied her magazines into the sooty vapor, screaming, pistols blazing. Spent cartridges rained on me, the hot brass prickled my skin. No sounds got past the numbing static in my ears.

Pain filled the moment, the hurt surging over me, then diminishing, surging again, then diminishing, every cycle weakening like waves retreating at ebb tide.

I rolled to my feet and helped Carmen up. Toby was gone, blasted to bits of gore. His sacrifice had saved us.

The door to the kitchen closed behind us and shrank. Carmen tore loose from my grip. Her eyes crinkled with hate. She mouthed a command to the others and gestured that we continue to the patio.

Pistols reloaded, Jolie covered our withdrawal. I staggered behind Carmen. Juanita waited outside.

After I had set foot on the patio, I took a moment to gather myself and let my hearing come back. I took stock of the patio, the pond, the garden, and the surrounding walls, seeing it not as landscape but as military terrain. We could take positions in the garden at the left and right of the pond and catch Phaedra and her surviving minions in a crossfire.

But what if we were playing into her hands? Her attack had methodically pushed us farther and farther back, so maybe it was her plan to corner us by the pond.

I scanned upward in the hopes that Blossom was coming to our rescue, but the sky was clear of spaceships.

We were trapped. If we scaled the walls and made it to open ground, Phaedra would pick us off one by one. With no good choices, our predicament made my chest tighten until it ached.

Carmen plopped into a patio chair. Her normal color had returned and her face appeared relieved. Phaedra must've backed off the psychic attack. She, like us, needed to regroup after this last skirmish.

Carmen's eyes lifted to me and she offered a haggard smile. "You okay?" Her voice sounded like it came from the far end of a long tunnel.

"I've been better."

I thought about Toby. I supposed this was the second time he wanted to die here. But this time he was a hero, and for that, I was grateful.

I let the sadness wash though me. A eulogy would have to wait. Our best memorial to him would be to kill Phaedra.

Jolie stared at the door leading into the patio. "Phaedra came here for a fight, let's push it back in her face." Jolie glanced at Carmen. "Are you up for a counter attack?"

Carmen rose from her chair. "I'll do what I can."

Jolie and I faced the patio door. I topped off the revolver with the speed loader in my other pocket. Guns ready, we both advanced, one resolute step at a time. All we needed were jangling spurs and a soundtrack from a Sergio Leone spaghetti western.

The plan wasn't sophisticated. Carmen would run interference with a mind shield while Jolie and I moved into firing position.

Once through the door and into the den, Jolie and I separated to advance in alternating bounds toward the dining room. Our fangs and talons extended to combat length. I had my pistol up, finger on the trigger. Jolie held both pistols before her like the pincers of a scorpion.

Foreign thoughts pierced my mind. Phaedra trying to harpoon our psyches.

Hold her off, Carmen.

I covered Jolie when she proceeded through the door into the dining room. Then it was her turn to cover me. A strange quiet filled the space. The *scritch* of our shoes on the floor and the rustle of our clothes sounded loud as a garbage truck emptying a dumpster.

A deafening crackle ripped the silence. My arm hairs tingled from a rush of static electricity, and my nostrils twitched at the acrid smell of ozone.

We halted at the threshold to the kitchen and the door opened to let us see inside. The crackling noise grated my ears.

A white flame, bright as the sun, waggled along the wall beside the far door, gushing smoke and leaving a smoldering gap snaking behind it. The flame circumscribed a rough semi-circle around the hole the suicide bomber had made earlier. The flame reached the floor and the section of wall fell toward us with a *smash* and a cascade of smoke.

A vampire marched through the opening and into the kitchen, a female holding one of the Nancharm's lightning bolt tridents. Her hands smoldered where she clasped the weapon, sparks crackling around her fingers from the intense electrical discharge that charred her flesh. Jaw clenched, she strained to keep from dropping the trident. Phaedra must've had a vice-grip on her will. Phaedra didn't need suicide bombers to smash through the walls. She was saving her last pair of explosive-laden stooges to use as two-legged precision-guided artillery.

A green glow suffused the kitchen's smoky pall. Phaedra's bubble tractor rolled behind this vampire. The second vampire waited inside the bubble.

I stared, transfixed by this spectacle of both nightmarish and supernatural beauty. My kundalini noir quivered like the tail of a rattlesnake. My fangs pushed to such lengths they pinched my gums. I slipped into a feral, murderous trance. I would empty the Colt magnum at Phaedra and charge forward to shred with tooth and claw.

A keening sound echoed in my head and I couldn't pull the trigger.

Give it up, Felix. There's only one way this will end. Me ... using your skull for a soup bowl.

Jolie knocked me aside and trained her .45 at Phaedra. But the vampire with the trident leaned into the bullet.

I ducked behind the doorway and covered my ears. The vampire exploded and I bounced on the floor. Dust choked the air. Jolie lay sprawled on the debris-covered carpet. She blinked, coughed smoke, and shouted, "Take the shot. Take the motherfucking shot!"

I rose to a knee and aimed the revolver. The circumference of Phaedra's bubble sharpened in the clearing dust. I aligned the pistol at its center, but the keening sound returned to lash my nerves, becoming louder, louder, louder until I fought to keep from tossing the gun aside and grabbing my ears and screaming in pain.

Someone bounded over me, heading toward Phaedra.

It was Irsan, a lit Molotov cocktail in each hand. He cocked one back. It arced from his hand and splattered against the green bubble, exploding. He was drawing his other hand back to hurl when the tractor lurched forward. At the instant the bubble force field touched Irsan, he screamed and his body sizzled, crumbling into burning pieces.

His death had bought time for Jolie to seize my collar and yank me to my feet. Her tortured grimace mirrored mine as Phaedra flayed us with a bullwhip of psychic juju.

We stumbled back through the den and emerged onto the back patio, smoke and dust sloughing from our bodies.

Juanita and Cassie had Carmen's arms hoisted across their shoulders. She stood weak-kneed between them. A sheen of sweat glistened on her brow. Her normally full lips had thinned to a pale rind around her mouth. Veins pulsed on her temple and neck. I feared that Phaedra would make Carmen's head blow apart like a watermelon stuffed with TNT.

With the Nancharm all but vanquished, Toby and Irsan dead and Carmen on the ropes, we were riding the express elevator to hell.

Chapter Thirty-Five

I surveyed our tiny perimeter and calculated our odds.
Not good.
I reflected on all the soldiers sent to fight on faraway lands never to return. Fallen souls swept into the gutter of history. Spartan hoplites. Roman legionnaires. Viking raiders. French Foreign Legion paratroopers. My army comrades who died in ones and twos in the tumbled, back alleys of Iraq.

The sky above D-Galtha receded to infinity, reminding me that I was so very far from home. Should Phaedra win and I find myself at the veterans' reunion in Valhalla, when the toastmaster asks who came the longest distance, I was sure I'd win that prize.

A wash of bitter bile soured my mouth. I ground my teeth to fight the rancid taste.

The battle wasn't over yet. I still hadn't fallen. If I had to die, I'd perish gloating over Phaedra's corpse. Somehow. Some way. I clenched the revolver. To paraphrase Charlton Heston: *From my cold, undead hands.*

Though my mind was free of psychic probing, I knew it was because Phaedra was biding her time, husbanding her strength, studying the angles, honing her scheme. She had one suicide-bomber vampire left. And she could manipulate him to use whatever Nancharm weapons remained handy before ordering him to charge and blow himself up.

Juanita and Cassie huddled together like chickens waiting to get quartered and shrink wrapped. Jolie's eyes scrunched in bitter defiance. Carmen ...

Carmen ... I wasn't sure what I saw in her expression. Confusion? Anger?

A surge of bubbles in the pond tore my attention from Carmen. The water agitated and a yellow metallic cylinder wide enough to park a VW Beetle broke through the rippling surface. The cylinder was sheathed with rectangular windows and it extended to a height of thirty feet. Our sanity had been so mangled by Phaedra's manic assault that none of us acted surprised.

A door in the cylinder swung open and a flat beam of light connected the threshold to the edge of the pond. Moots appeared, and she slid from the cylinder across the bridge of light. She carried a brassy contraption that looked like a cross between a pistol and a bugle. If it was a weapon, I hoped it was at least the Nancharm version of a Desert Eagle .50 caliber. Then again, Phaedra had wiped out their flying saucers so Moots' gun may have been nothing more than a lucky rabbit's foot.

When she reached solid ground she panned the bell-shaped muzzle of the pistol across us vampires. We appeared to be outgunned so Jolie and I lowered our weapons.

Carmen glowered at Moots. "What's this about?"

Moots pointed to the cylinder. "Inside."

"Sounds like a damn good idea," I said. "And about time."

"Quickly," Moots added. "Before you escape."

I was about to summon the chalices when I froze in mid-cue. "Before we escape? I thought we were escaping."

"I mean escape off the planet," Moots replied.

The hairs on my arms tingled again, and my shoulders clenched for another psychic attack. Inexplicably, the air darkened, then turned into a deepening shadow, and I sensed a new threat, from something huge looming above. All of us, Moots included, tilted our heads back to see.

A flying saucer descended toward us, a wide flat circle a hundred meters wide that seemed to fill the sky. My bewilderment congealed into one big *Huh?*

Phaedra interrupted our gawking by unleashing a psychic attack. The keening noise returned and it lanced through my head from ear to ear. My mind wobbled and my knees buckled, but I managed to keep from falling. Jolie and Carmen staggered in place. Moots let her pistol drop and clang on the patio pavement. It rolled into the pond and sank. She put both hands on her chest—where her brain was—and pressed against the carapace. Her head tendrils writhed like the tentacles of a spastic octopus.

The saucer kept descending, slowly until it touched the top of the yellow cylinder. The disk continued to lower and the cylinder crunched and crumpled beneath its great weight.

Fearing the saucer would squash me, I tried to run for cover but the keening had short-circuited my legs. The chalices, unaffected by the psychic barrage, rushed to drag us vampires out of the way.

Carmen brushed them aside. She tightened her jaw to keep her face set and rigid, then stood proud. The keening softened to a dull hum, and my body managed to relax. Moots' tendrils settled around the back of her head.

The disk was right over us, as close as the ceiling in a house. A long rectangle glowed on the disk's belly, outlining a ramp that lowered to the patio. None of us were certain who the ship belonged to—Blossom?—but it represented our only chance to escape. We hustled toward the ramp.

"Don't do this," Moots shrieked at Carmen. "You were our last hope. Leave and you doom us ... me ... to extinction." Our Nancharm minder had recovered her pistol and aimed it at us. She hollered, "Don't do this!" I could hear tears in her voice. "Please. Don't leave us." She glided toward Carmen.

Jolie was first up the ramp and I tried to shepherd the chalices between us. But they stumbled from me, looking overcome with fright and confusion. Tears staining her eyes, Juanita dropped to her hands and knees and crawled beside Moots like a helpless puppy. Cassie waited on the edge of the ramp, trembling.

Carmen turned and faced Moots. "You kidnapped us. Kept us prisoners. You offered other chalices no relief from their misery so they had to kill themselves. And when you were done with us, we would've been exterminated."

"Recycled," corrected Moots.

Carmen motioned us to continue up the ramp.

Moots steadied her pistol. "I'll kill you. Stop. Now."

Cassie leapt and hooked her hands around Moot's gun, angling it down. Juanita screamed, "Get up the ramp, Carmen! Get away." She palmed the chef's knife and jammed it into a gap of Moot's segmented carapace.

Moots backed away, her tendrils quaking in a silent shriek. She knocked Cassie aside and brought the pistol up. Its muzzle strobed and a brilliant light dazzled my eyes.

"No. No," I heard Carmen shout.

I smelled burnt meat. As I blinked my eyes back into focus, I saw swirls of sooty dust where the chalices used to be. Juanita and Cassie were gone.

"What have you done?" Carmen screamed.

Moots seemed taken aback by Carmen's reaction. Moots waved her pistol erratically, like she wasn't sure of what to do next.

But I was.

I aimed and fired once. The bullet knocked a neat hole in the upper center of her chest carapace. She quivered for a moment and then steadied the pistol.

Jolie pushed me aside. "Let's finish this." She blasted Moots with a barrage of .45 slugs. Moots staggered backwards and fell into the pond, splashing, a puss-yellow stain spreading from her many wounds.

Carmen tried to lunge past us. Jolie and I held her back. She shrieked, "Moots. Moots. Why did this have to happen?" She collapsed into our arms as if she'd taken one punch too many.

A light flashed in the distant sky, the light so bright it momentarily blanched everything to a dazzling white. My face felt a flare of heat. The light faded into an orange ball that corkscrewed upward into a mushroom cloud of fire and smoke. Had Phaedra gotten her hands on a nuke? The obscene growl of the explosion echoed to us. A gust of turbulence mussed our hair, made us wince, and rocked the saucer perched overhead.

Jolie and I dragged Carmen up the ramp. No time for reflecting on what had just happened. We had to get out of here now.

Once at the top of the ramp, we entered into a compartment similar to the one in the saucer Blossom had piloted from D-Galtha's moon.

The ramp lifted, closing the opening, compressing the outside world into a narrowing slice. Moots floated face up in the pond. Her blank white eyes revealed nothing. The opening kept shrinking until she disappeared from view. The ramp closed with a hiss, and a hatch slid across the top to seal the floor. Overhead panels provided illumination.

Jolie and I rested for a moment, unsure of what to expect or that we weren't in a bigger mess. I was still processing the loss of the four chalices. We were the badass vampires and yet they had saved us. Carmen sagged between us, limp, drained.

The light in the compartment dimmed, the saucer swayed and a lifting sensation pushed up through my guts. A door to our right opened. Green lights blinked along the floor, forming a trail that snaked out from the compartment.

Carmen found her strength, pulled loose from Jolie and me, and squared her shoulders "I'm all right." She studied the trail of green lights. "Someone's laid out the welcome mat."

"Blossom?" I asked.

"Let's hope so." Carmen led us out the compartment, through a winding corridor lined with conduits and consoles until we reached another wide door. This door split down the middle and opened with an old-school *Star Trek*-like *shoosh*.

No surprise that Blossom waited on the other side, standing on all fours and beaming with enthusiastic cheer like a big, fat retriever. She wore a shiny, crinkly helmet. With her trunk curled to one side, she presented a toothy grin. "Welcome, welcome, dear friends." She spoke through a translator box attached to the front of her harness. She shifted her weight onto her haunches to stand and crane her big head above ours. She beckoned with thick, bejeweled fingers that we enter the bridge. The door *shooshed* closed behind us. She acted oblivious to our guns.

Two other Wah-zhim crewmembers straddled the couches facing the controls. An animated display of D-Galtha, its moon and the crisscrossing orbits of numerous spaceships filled the forward control panel. The two Wah-zhim were busy adjusting levers, twisting knobs, and swiping small panels, and their frenzied motions mirrored the chaos engulfing the planet. All that was Phaedra's doing?

Blossom clapped her hands. Our host's sunny mood was the opposite of our gloomy wariness and the loss of the chalices. "It's a great day in the Wah-zhim continuum," she said. "The Nancharm are done. Finished. Dead as desiccated bung worms." She twisted a heel against the deck. "Your Earth friend has done the impossible. She so dis—"

"Earth friend?" I interrupted.

"Yes. Phaedra," Blossom replied, sounding surprised by my question. "She so disrupted the Nancharm defenses on D-Galtha that they panicked and diverted forces to contain her attack. And then we struck." Blossom pounded a fist into her other hand, jangling her many bracelets. "No mercy was ever shown by them. And no mercy given. We caught them bare assed with their skirts up. Like this ..." She reached for the hem of her skirt and started to lift when I grasped her wrist.

No way did I want to see her voluminous junk. "That's fine. I get the idea."

"Wait a minute," Carmen said. "What's this scheme with Phaedra?"

Blossom became quiet, sullen. She then squeaked out her trunk. One of her co-pilots glanced at her and squeaked back.

"Uh ... well ... uh." Blossom brought her hands together and tapped the fingertips. "She contacted me and we made a deal."

"Contacted you how? What deal?" Carmen asked.

I slyly cocked back the hammer of my revolver. Our escape from D-Galtha might not be an escape at all.

"She didn't contact me exactly." Blossom caressed her foil cap. "It was a scientist working in our psychotronic intelligence unit. Phaedra used her mind connection or whatever you call it. Since I knew you best, I was ordered to find you and ..."

"Narc our location to Phaedra," I said.

Blossom wrung her hands, her bracelets ringing like jingle bells. "Something like that."

Jolie tensed, ready to shoot. I glanced about the cockpit to decide how to unload my magnum.

Carmen sensed our tension. She put her hands on ours, gesturing that we remain calm. "Phaedra had us cornered. Why did you rescue us? What's this deal that you made?"

"Even if Phaedra found you, she couldn't get to you without help," Blossom said. "She used a wormhole to travel to Star B-43, where another Wah-zhim ship picked her and her minions up, and then she used another wormhole to arrive on D-Galtha."

"And you guys provided the bubble tractor?" I asked.

"Bubble tractor?" Blossom replied, bewildered. "Ah yes, the Iron Fist Assault Penetrator. She needed that to breach the Nancharm defenses."

"You haven't told us about the deal," Carmen reminded.

Blossom cleared her throat. "Yes, that. In exchange for Phaedra helping us beat the Nancharm, we would let her kill you."

Jolie and I brought our pistols up. Carmen tightened her hold on our wrists to keep us from shooting. She continued, "Is that what you're doing?"

"That *was* the plan." Blossom glanced at our guns and blew a dismissive snort out her trunk. "Put those away before you shoot yourselves."

Carmen nodded, signaling that Jolie and I stow our pistols.

"But we've changed our minds. You three are headed to Wah-zhim."

"For what purpose?" I asked.

Blossom laughed. "For making whoopie, what else? Oh Felix, you have so much to learn."

My butt clenched and my pecker shriveled. I wanted no part of Wah-zhim whoopie.

She waddled to a couch mounted on a dais between us and the other two crewmembers. A control panel on a console stood at the front of the dais. She pivoted to face us and then planted her wide can on the couch.

"Is Moots dead?" Carmen asked.

"You tell me," Blossom replied, a shrug evident in her tone, "you guys are the ones who shot her." She reached for a tall cup resting in a holder attached to the console. She slipped the thick straw from the drink between her lips and slurped.

She touched buttons on the console. "Everything is under control." A hologram appeared in a sizzle of lights in front of Carmen and me. The image sharpened and showed a green bubble rolling over a landscape dotted with wrecked buildings and burning saucers, an overhead view of a battle between Phaedra and the Nancharm on D-Galtha's surface, the details rendered in small scale. Saucers in tight formations unleashed more destruction on the planet's surface. "We'll let your friend run amok for a bit to keep the Nancharm disorganized. In the centuries we lived under their lash, never did we imagine that our freedom would come from a young girl from such a backwater planet. I mean, really, *Earth*?"

We three vampires cleared our throats in unison.

"And then?" I asked.

Blossom made a loud *ka-blew-wee* sound, complete with hand choreography, followed by, "Adios, *muchacha*. Phaedra and the Nancharm are history. I won't need this anymore." She skinned the foil cap off her head and balled it up, dropping it on the floor. "Pretty good double-cross, don't you think?"

"All of the Nancharm?" Carmen asked.

"Eventually. Of course they're scattered all over the galaxy so it'll take a while to hunt them all down. Statistically, it's highly improbable that we'll get each and every one of them." Blossom heaved her shoulders for a long sigh. "The cost-benefit algorithm will argue against a prolonged campaign of extermination. But no worries, since Nancharm can no longer reproduce, the survivors will eventually die out on their own."

"Rather cold-blooded," I said.

Blossom shrugged. "Like I'm going to lose sleep over it. All the planets in the Galactic Union kept a standing military force, ostensibly under the command of the Nancharm. But the union was a simmering keg ready to explode. The moment the Nancharm got distracted, we turned our weapons around and *bang*."

The back of the couch swung up and Blossom leaned against it, reclining like a smug princess. She crossed her ankles. Her bejeweled anklets and many toe rings sparkled.

"Look," Carmen exclaimed. She gestured to the hologram. Phaedra's emerald bubble started to shrink, becoming a pinpoint of light, then disappeared.

Blossom's bulging eyes searched the miniature landscape. "Where did she go?"

"A portal," Carmen answered.

"And went where?" Blossom drew close to the display and squinted.

"On her way to Earth, I'm sure," Jolie replied.

A hearty guffaw exploded from me.

"What the hell is so goddamn funny?" Blossom looked up and groused.

I rubbed my stomach, the laugh cramps ached but I managed to say, "Blossom, Phaedra has forced your hand."

Blossom curled her trunk and frowned. The wrinkles on her elephantine face deepened into craggy features. "I am not amused. Explain yourself."

"It means you are fucked unless you cooperate with us."

Chapter Thirty-Six

Blossom repeatedly uncurled and curled her trunk as she stalled for time while deciding if I was bluffing.

Which I wasn't.

"In my culture," she said, "when one is told they're about to be fucked, that's a very good thing. We Wah-zhim spend most of our time anticipating getting fucked. But I know among you humans, that getting fucked is a euphemism for finding yourself in a difficult situation." She tapped the translator box dangling in front of her throat. "I do not believe I am in a difficult situation. So tell me, little human, how am I about to get fucked unless I cooperate with you?"

I hustled to the hologram and raked my finger through the ghostly image of the destruction on D-Galtha. "See what Phaedra did to the Nancharm? Cracked them wide open so their enemies could attack. What makes you think she can't do this to you?"

"Why should she?" Blossom asked, sounding worried.

"Because you tried to kill her and now she's escaped," I explained. "She learned the Nancharm's weakness, she'll learn yours."

Blossom leaned forward and her trunk groped for the ball of metal foil she had discarded earlier. "You're exaggerating her abilities." She scooped the foil from the floor and began to unwad it. "You have no proof that we're vulnerable."

I fought back a grin. "Fine, if you want to be the one who brought Phaedra to Wah-zhim, then be prepared to suffer the consequences."

Worry deepened the already substantial wrinkles that crosshatched Blossom's face. She smoothed the crinkled foil over her head to reform the aluminum cap. She snapped her fingers, the hologram clicked off, and she wrung her hands. The bangles on her wrists clinked together. "If I take you to Earth, you'll stop her there?"

"That's what we intend," Carmen answered.

"Or we'll die trying," Jolie added.

"That goes without saying," Blossom snapped. "If I return you to Earth, Phaedra won't follow me to Wah-zhim?"

My thoughts rambled over unpleasant ideas that I decided to keep to myself. The Wah-zhim weren't completely safe. Phaedra might well raid the Galactic Union to extort help or confiscate weapons. "I can't promise that. But this fight is between Phaedra and us. Your best bet is to head to Earth and let us fight her there."

Blossom steepled her fingers. Her trunk swung back and forth like a windsock searching for the prevailing wind. "How will you defeat Phaedra? If the Nancharm didn't have a chance with their weapons, what can you hope to accomplish with your puny earthling weapons?"

"The difference," I replied, "is that we know what we're up against."

Blossom returned to swinging her trunk, unconvinced.

Carmen said, "We'll be fighting her on our home turf."

Blossom caressed her chin with her trunk. "I could drop you guys off, fly into orbit, and when Phaedra shows up, nuke Earth with a volley of thousand-megaton planet wreckers."

"Wouldn't work," I said. "You just nuked D-Galtha and Phaedra got away."

She stamped one foot on the dais and uttered a string of commands in her language. The two pilots danced their fingers across the forward controls. The saucer swung around. A new panorama of space with constellations and gas formations panned across the view screen.

I asked, "Where are we going?"

"Earth. Via the 3 Kiloparsec Arm Highway."

The view screen aligned on a cluster of blurry glowing objects.

"Wormholes," Blossom explained, anticipating our question. "Shortcuts through the galaxy."

"How long to Earth?" Jolie asked.

"Depends on traffic," Blossom said. "We haven't scheduled a trip through the Central Wormhole Transportation Authority, so we'll have to take our place in the access lane."

The image on the screen magnified, showing three wormholes. Each were faint clouds of gas pinwheeling into voids that looked like holes punched in the fabric of space. A grid appeared on the screen and dotted flashing lights funneled into and out of the wormholes. An arrow pointed to a light that joined one line arcing toward the wormhole at our upper left. Symbols lit up above the light, and I assumed one of them was our ship joining the queue.

"Seems pretty orderly considering the war against the Nancharm," Jolie noted.

"Commerce has to keep churning," Blossom replied. "Cold fusion powers our ships but it's money that makes everything run."

Blossom's eyes followed the symbols scrolling across the screen, left to right. "According to the traffic report, they've rerouted the trans-galactic turnpike because of construction in the 47 U Majoris Bypass."

The screen switched to a forward view of saucers approaching a wormhole, our lane of traffic spiraling toward the black center. I didn't know much about wormholes or quantum physics. The best I could remember was a show on the Discovery Channel talking about stuff getting zapped to another dimension as sub-sub-atomic particles. My gut lurched in dread. To hold myself steady, my hand grasped the edge of a wall panel and my toes clutched the insides of my shoes.

"We'll have to detour through the Denebola Sector." Blossom kept reading. "That will delay our arrival at 43 Zeta Twelve."

"What's that?" I asked, trying to sound curious instead of anxious as hell.

"You know it as Earth."

The ships in line zipped into the wormhole.

"How much of a delay?"

"Considerable. Maybe as long as two minutes."

The saucer in front of us elongated into the wormhole and disappeared. It was our turn.

Next stop ... home.

And Phaedra.

Chapter Thirty-Seven

The view screen remained fixed on the center of the wormhole, a whirlpool of gray mist that receded into a distant black dot. Symbols flashed staccato-like all over the screen. The two Wah-zhim pilots made final adjustments on their controls, then paused, their bejeweled fingers hovering above the buttons. Blossom sat upright, appearing just a bit tense.

Carmen and Jolie swung their gazes at me, and I tried to act all ghetto-cool behind a taut smile.

Our saucer sped to the wormhole. Points of light streaked past us, like fireflies sucked into a vacuum cleaner. The wormhole filled the view screen and though the saucer made no change in attitude, I felt a *whoa!* top-of-the-roller-coaster moment. My throat clamped tight, my guts somersaulted, all followed by a *whoosh!* And we dropped.

Or so it felt.

The view screen showed us zipping through a tunnel of blurry lights. The pilots toggled buttons and nudged the control levers. The symbols on the screen slowed their flickering. A collective *whew* washed through the bridge. Blossom drummed her fingers on the dais console. Jolie crossed her arms and stared at the screen.

Carmen leaned against the bulkhead beside the dais.

The tunnel forked ahead. One of the pilots tripped a short lever and a yellow arrow on the left side of the screen blinked. We followed the left fork and the pilot flicked off the signal. But the ship held rock-steady. The wormhole rushing by made the whole experience seem fake, like we were watching an IMAX movie.

"How fast are we going?" Jolie asked.

"Just a tad over the posted limit," Blossom answered.

"The galaxy is huge," I noted. "Getting to Earth will take time even at this speed."

"We're in the HOV lane," she replied.

I thought about the little of my science classes that I remembered. Time should slow inside the ship as we approached the speed of light, though it would continue at its normal rate in the world outside, which should play hell on everyone's calendars. But that didn't concern the Wah-zhim. Plus we were hauling ass way past the speed of light. An impossibility according to Einstein. Maybe as smart as Albert was, he hadn't gotten past remedial extraterrestrial physics.

I watched the Wah-zhim at work and wondered what it would be like to command this saucer. Put that on my business card. *Felix Gomez. Detective vampire. Starship captain.*

We blasted through another wormhole interchange. After a while, accelerating to warp factor whatever lost its novelty and the sensation was like standing in the crosstown bus waiting for the next stop.

A new set of symbols lit on the screen. The pilots became more alert and adjusted their controls. Up ahead, the sides of the tunnel unraveled and *Presto!* We were cruising past a planet the color of red dirt.

Blossom said, "Mars."

Back in the hood, baby.

An orange aura blossomed around my hands and arms. I glanced at my torso, legs and feet. The aura shimmered around me bright as a flame. I looked at Carmen and Jolie, and similar auras sheathed their bodies, head to toe.

They gawked at me, eyes shining red as burning rubies. Our supernatural powers were back. My kundalini noir spiked with joy.

I had no clue why we had our powers here and not on D-Galtha. But no matter. We pumped our fists and shouted, "Yes!"

Blossom reacted to our outburst with a bemused smirk, though she had no idea what had just happened to us vampires. A yellow aura only we vampires could see shined around her. The color was typical for an alien, and it sparked with puzzlement.

Jolie clasped her hands like she was holding a pistol and aimed it at me. "Once we corner Phaedra, I got dibs on the last double-tap."

"Let's not get ahead of ourselves," I said. "Whoever gets the first chance at the killing blow, go for it."

"How far to Earth?" Jolie asked. It was a simple question but one loaded with anticipation and vengeance.

"Thirty-million miles, give or take," Blossom answered. "We've had to slow to sub-light speed so it should take about five minutes."

The view screen shifted toward a very bright star. Our sun. The white ball of light looked so friendly, and to be honest, I missed its gaseous smiling face.

The screen shifted again and aligned on a planet surrounded with a faint glow. The screen reset and the planet got bigger in stuttering increments until it appeared as a blue marble bathed in clouds.

Our beautiful Earth. No place like home.

This close to our turf, my thoughts turned to Coyote. I hoped he was okay. What loomed ahead, though, was the upcoming battle with Phaedra. As long as we could avoid her psychic mind grip and dodge whatever tricks she pulled out of her wicked little ass, we should be able to beat her. Somehow.

"Are you going to beam us down?" I asked.

"Say what?" Blossom asked.

I explained what I meant. Blossom tried to keep a straight face, then cracked up. She said something to her pilots and they guffawed out loud.

Blossom wiped her eyes. "No, I'm not going to"—she made air quotes—"'beam you down.' We're going to land."

"What about the quarantine?" I asked. "You're not supposed to land on Earth."

Blossom tossed a dismissive wave. "The Galactic Union is in disarray. At the moment they have bigger *gogzams* to fry than watching what goes on in this corner of the Milky Way." She pressed buttons on her console and the hologram reappeared in front of the dais.

The hologram projected snapshots of tropical landscapes. I guessed the Amazon, Africa, Southern India. The snapshots disappeared into a fuzz of light and reformed into a hemisphere of the earth's surface.

Blossom leaned from her couch to study the view. "Where do you live?"

Carmen spun the hologram like a globe. "Take us here." She centered the 3D image on New Mexico and wagged her fingers to magnify the scene. Necklaces of tiny lights snaked over the darkened landscape, headlamps from lines of cars cruising the night highways.

Blossom touched a button. A filter of bright daylight bathed the landscape. She frowned. "A desert? You live in a desert when you could live in a jungle paradise?" She shook her head in bemusement. The hologram map resumed its nighttime shade and zoomed in until we could see individual cars moving on the roads. They crawled along like roly-polies, cones of light beaming from their heads.

Carmen turned the map until we were above the basin. The spire of Fajada Butte was on the left, the mesa on the right. The trough of Chaco Canyon lay in between. I studied the features to get my bearings and searched the edge of the mesa until I spotted a mobile home the size of a matchbox. Coyote's casa.

Yellow light flicked through the tiny windows. I leaned close to the hologram for a Peeping Tom glimpse of my ancient undead friend.

The ship rocked beneath us.

"Earth's atmosphere," Blossom explained.

"Won't the saucer glow from the heat?" I asked.

She chuckled. "If you're worried that we'll be spotted, forget it. We've got our cloaking shield activated. Where do you want to land?"

I spun the hologram and pointed to a spot on the mesa behind Coyote's mobile home. "How far are we now?"

Blossom pressed a switch. The forward screen showed a map of New Mexico. We were north of Gallup headed east. "Hundred miles."

My kundalini noir hummed with pleasure. A last-ditch battle with Phaedra notwithstanding, I was eager to plant my feet on terra firma.

A window at the right side of the main screen showed a cartoon depiction of the saucer in overhead view. Rays pulsed over the ship. "Radar," Blossom noted.

The radar beams converged on us. She jabbed at buttons. "Hmm."

I didn't like the sound of that "What's going on?"

"For such a primitive species," she answered, "you humans sure catch on quick. Now I understand the need for the quarantine. Your electromagnetic locator technology is now sophisticated enough to detect us up to Level Four mode." Blossom stroked her chin.

"What does that mean?"

Blossom trumpeted a command. The chief pilot flicked a switch.

"It means we're going to Level Five jamming. *Duh?*"

A fan of pink sparkles swept over the picture of our saucer.

"What's that?" Blossom asked, her unease obvious.

Carmen touched her temples. "Psychic energy sweep."

"Phaedra?" Blossom asked, her anxiety pumping up.

"No," Carmen replied worriedly. "It's electronic in origin."

The two pilots bleated excitedly. The front screen showed the fan collapsing into a line of sparks headed right at us.

"They've locked onto us," Blossom shouted.

"How can that be?" It was my turn to sound as nervous as our captain.

Blossom zoomed in and pinpointed the energy emitter, a tower mounted on a large truck parked at the base of Fajada Butte. A fleet of Humvees surrounded the truck.

"Zoom in," I ordered.

The hologram magnified until I recognized the markings on the truck. Unfortunately it was the one wild card I'd forgotten in this escapade.

Goons working for the federal government. Cress Tech International.

Our welcoming committee.

Chapter Thirty-eight

Blossom shouted commands to her pilots. They frantically manipulated controls to react to the surge of radar and psychic energy signals. They managed to break the radar lock, but the psychic energy ray remained pinned to us.

One of the pilots turned toward Blossom and yelled. All of the Wah-zhims' auras sparked with panic. Blossom scrambled from the dais, waddled across the bridge, and stared at the view screen and the forward console. Red and yellow lights flashed across the instruments.

Alarms screamed. Blossom and her pilots shouted back-and-forth. The pilots punched buttons and frantically adjusted their controls. The deck leveled. The alarms died out, and most of the warning lights dimmed.

"Any ideas where to set down?" Blossom asked. The screen refreshed with a map of New Mexico and it showed us heading to Fajada Butte. "I've shifted maximum power to our cloaking device. That should keep the radar from tracking us."

Carmen replied, "But they'll lock on again when they sync the radar with the psychic energy ray."

"We'll be low to the ground. Below the radar as it were."

Carmen shook her head. "Wouldn't do any good. Psychic energy isn't affected by ground clutter."

I didn't have to think much about what this meant. "They'll be able to pinpoint our landing spot."

On the front screen, the green radar beams swept blindly for us, but the trail of pink sparkles remained fixed to our ship like a tether. The radar aligned on the sparkles, then drifted away on account of the Wah-zhim jamming. But the psychic energy ray could track us to touchdown, after which the Cress Tech guards would be on us like bloodhounds.

The pink sparkles stopped.

"The hell ..." Jolie said.

"Maybe they had a malfunction," Carmen explained. "Or someone is interfering."

"Who?" Blossom asked.

"Does it matter?" I rushed to the front screen and pointed at the map, to a spot close to Coyote's home. "Put us here. On this mesa."

"Better not," Blossom replied. "Too high on the terrain." She selected a point west of Farmington and gave orders.

The saucer wheeled to the left in a turn so steep that we almost tumbled over one another. The screen switched to a panoramic night view of the topography zooming beneath us. Yellow lines outlined terrain features, and orange symbols danced over the screen. The saucer leveled off in a flat glide over the open, uneven ground.

"Phaedra is not your only worry," I said. "Cress Tech and the government are obviously interested in the potential of psychic energy. Your ship is an unexpected dividend. They're going to pull out all the stops to find you."

Blossom waddled back to the dais and climbed to her couch. "Shit. The bad news just keeps coming, doesn't it?" She touched buttons on her console. A panel in the floor opened. Jolie and I had to step aside when a totem pole-like cylinder pushed up. It extended to a height just above my head. Tiny lights glowed beneath its darkly-tinted surface and gave the device was a sinister *don't fuck with me* appearance.

"If it looks like the ship or any of us are going to get captured," Blossom gestured to the device, "I have to self-destruct."

Chapter Thirty-Nine

The self-destruct device loomed in the center of the bridge, its lights blinking in homicidal-suicidal fury.

"If that thing goes boom," I pointed to the device, "how big a blast are we talking about?"

"Ever hear of the Tunguska event?" Blossom replied.

Jolie and Carmen smirked at her.

"Of course," I answered. "Hang out long enough with vampires and you become a walking encyclopedia about the weird and bizarre. The Tunguska event was an explosion that flattened a Siberian forest in 1908 and—"

Carmen interrupted. "Supposedly it was a huge exploding meteor."

"Right ..." Blossom rejoined in a sarcastic drawl. "Like the way this ship is not here."

"One urban legend says it was a malfunctioning flying saucer," Carmen added.

"Oh, it malfunctioned all right," Blossom explained. "When that ship's gravity redirector failed, it tripped their self-destruct device. And *ka-blooie*. Forty kilotons worth. What happened to them is taught in interstellar flight safety 101."

"Who was on the ship?" I asked.

Blossom shrugged. "Someone who wasn't supposed to be here."

By now our saucer was skimming low over the desert, rocking like a subway car during rush hour. Jolie, Carmen, and I jostled against one another with every jarring bump. We watched the vista scroll past on the forward view screen, mesas on our right, mountains on our left.

On Blossom's command, the pilots slowed the ship. We braced ourselves for a tight turn. The saucer slipped to the right and eased over a hummock separating two gullies. A herd of deer looked up, twitched their ears, and bounded out of sight.

"I thought we were invisible," Jolie noted.

"We are," Blossom replied, "but animals of all species can be remarkably aware."

She directed the pilots to land in an arroyo beside a large mesa. The saucer settled into a hover. I heard servos whine and the clunk of what had to be landing struts locking into place. We descended into a cushioned stop.

Blossom hacked into a nearby cellular tower, got on the Internet, and within seconds had found a US government topographic map of the area. She overlaid that map on the one already posted on her forward screen. We were tucked against Piñon Mesa, eight miles northwest of Farmington and about two and half miles west of state highway 170.

Blossom slid from her couch and stepped from the dais to the cockpit door. It opened and the green lights on the floor showed us the way out. Carmen, Jolie, and I got ready to file out. Our auras brightened in anticipation of at last setting foot on planet Earth.

Blossom braced an arm across the doorway to block our exit. Her wrist bangles clacked together. "So this is it, Carmen?"

To get this exchange in perspective, Blossom weighed maybe a ton. When on her hind legs, she stood over eight feet tall. She had a trunk, ears the size of hubcaps, and legs and arms as big around as telephone poles. She wore a voluminous pleated skirt that presumably hid equally voluminous pudenda. Yet at the moment her voice quaked with heartbreak. I should've been drawn into the moment, but the juxtaposition between Wah-zhim and human as lovers was too damn strange even considering that I had boinked Moots.

"I guess so." Carmen sounded wistful.

Blossom wiped a tear.

Arms open, Carmen stepped forward. Blossom crouched and they hugged. Blossom stroked Carmen's head with delicate pats of her immense hands. Their auras fused like big swirls of glowing jelly.

"I'll miss you so much." Blossom wept as they separated. "Too bad it had to end this way. You were the best ever. The next time I rub one out, it'll be for you."

I winced and blinked hard to get that image out of my head.

"I won't forget you either," Carmen replied. She started out. "*Adios.*"

Blossom stood aside. "*Au revoir.*"

We entered the passageway. The door behind us closed. We followed the lights to the cargo compartment. At our approach, the ramp lowered.

Fresh air and the aroma of sage washed over us. We proceeded down the ramp.

My kundalini noir grew warm from a comforting flush of energy. My aura sizzled, my fangs extended, and my arms flexed from the surge of rejuvenated power. Carmen and Jolie's auras burned bright as mine, and I caught them examining their hands as they clenched and unclenched their fists. Felt good to be home.

At the bottom of the ramp and when we stepped outside the saucer's cloaking shield and onto terra firma, the saucer disappeared from view as quick as the snap of my fingers. I slowed my steps, cognizant of the sand crunching beneath my boots. My kundalini noir melted a bit, the way my heart did (before I was undead) when first returning home from my army training—basic, advanced, and airborne. After months of suffering through heat, humidity, cold, fatigue, and the nonstop attentions of inventively cruel NCOs, I had welcomed the familiar embrace of home. Jolie and I had survived an odyssey through a world as fantastic as anything from the Land of Oz.

I pulled my cell phone and my watch from my jacket pockets. The phone was dead, but the second hand on my watch jumped to life. It read nine twenty-three, which I knew was way off. I jammed the phone and watch back into a pocket.

The hairs on my arms suddenly rose on end. Carmen and Jolie's hair fluffed. A hum started behind us, and we halted and turned in place to watch the saucer leave.

But of course, it remained invisible. Regardless, we all waved—seemed the appropriate thing to do. The saucer beeped back.

Another wave of static electricity prickled our skin. The air gusted as the saucer passed unseen overhead. Then my hair flattened and my skin and muscles relaxed.

"Now what?" Jolie asked.

"We head to Coyote's," I answered.

We continued to the top of the rise. Carmen stopped suddenly. She remained still. I wanted to ask what was the matter but I got the sense she didn't want to talk so I kept quiet and waited for her lead.

From the apex of the hill and looking south we could see the chaotic glow of Farmington, brilliant under an umbrella of stars. Random lights from scattered farmhouses punctuated the gloomy landscape. Closer in, tiny red auras quivered in the scattered weeds, then darted away; rabbits and mice scampering for safety.

Carmen shot a glance in their direction. She inhaled deeply, closed her eyes and rubbed her face. Her aura faded to a dull orange, spotted with red. "I've been gone so long and so many terrible things have happened to me. I was kidnapped by the aliens and held as a slave. I've seen so many chalices commit suicide or murdered. Moots, poor thing, was only trying to save her people."

"But she had to die," Jolie said, "or we wouldn't have escaped."

"I know," Carmen replied. "Our survival depended on so much treachery." Her voice trailed off. Second by second her aura brightened until it became a fiery orange. She started walking down the hill. "But the show must go on."

We broke into a fast walk, then a trot. We traversed the rising and falling ground until we reached a second rise overlooking the state highway. Pairs of headlights shuttled along the lonely north-south road. Though none of us said it, we all had the same idea. No way we were walking back to Coyote's place, not when we could ride.

After cresting the rise, we followed the low ground to the highway. We paused in a gully. Jolie shed her jacket and pistol harness and handed them to me. She kept one of her .45s and tucked it into the back of her jeans.

She and Carmen climbed out from the gully and onto the highway shoulder. When headlights approached from the north, the two tossed their hair. Carmen arched her back to emphasize her chest while Jolie cocked her hip to show off her world-class *nalgas*.

I stayed in shadow, my revolver at the ready.

The vehicle slowed and parked on the shoulder. The headlamps of an older model pickup dazzled around the curvy silhouettes of two hot vampires.

If the driver thought he was about to score, he was in for a surprise.

Chapter Forty

Carmen and Jolie greeted the driver of the truck with their most syrupy *we-luv-you-long-time* voices. They advanced toward him and got lost in the dazzle of the headlights.

A red halo rippled from the cab. They had zapped the driver good. A door clicked open, springs creaked, the bed gate clanked, then was slammed closed. A door shut. After that I didn't hear anything except for the rattle of the idling truck engine.

The horn blared and Jolie yelled, "Felix, get your lazy ass over here."

I scrambled out of the gully. The passenger door of the 70's model Jimmy was propped open. Jolie was behind the steering wheel, Carmen in the middle of the bench seat, the long gearshift bouncing from side-to-side and knocking against her knees. I slid onto the threadbare blanket covering the seat. A pine tree air freshener dangled and danced beneath the rearview mirror.

"Where's the driver?" I asked.

Carmen wiped droplets of blood from her lips and winged a thumb out the back window to the bed. "After a steady diet of the same four chalices, he was a nice change. Been a long time since I've had Southwestern."

Her victim lay heaped under a tarp. His aura stewed on a low burn of post-orgasmic contentment, courtesy of her endorphins.

I crowded against Carmen and rested Jolie's jacket and pistol harness on my lap. Jolie had tucked her .45 between her legs. I was reaching for the door when she released the clutch and stomped on the gas. The Jimmy lurched forward and gained speed, shaking the entire time like it was held together with duct tape and wire. We drove with the windows open because the interior smelled like the musty bed in a cheap motel. Riding in this junker brought a sense of déjà vu. The first time I had met Coyote he drove a similar jalopy pickup so it was fitting that I was heading to see him in this beater.

Carmen turned on the radio and twisted the tuning dial to sample the slim pickings this early morning: *¡Canción Mexicana!*, evangelists hyperventilating about the End Times, back-to-back infomercials promising a fortune in no-money-down real estate. She settled on a forgotten favorite, *Coast-to-Coast AM*. I was hoping this would be a broadcast about alien abductions, vampires— something suitably paranormal and known to me. The guest was instead some weirdo yapping about time travel and his involvement in a secret government project (naturally) where he had been teleported back to Ancient Egypt. He sounded convincing enough until he argued that the pyramids were actually built using robots from Atlantis. When he mentioned that "fact," Jolie and Carmen exchanged a look that said *could be*.

The truck clattered and clacked through Farmington. We needed gas and stopped at an all-night convenience store south of town. After all we'd gone through—the psychic jump to D-Galtha, surviving the Nancharm, escaping in Blossom's flying saucer—the experience of using a credit card to pay for gas jolted me with its mundaneness, like I'd never left. I topped off the tank in gratitude to the driver. Not that he cared, as he floated somewhere in happy land.

Jolie coaxed the truck to the highway.

Now that we were on Earth, we had our superpowers back ... and our vulnerabilities. I checked the time stamp on the gas receipt—3:28 a.m.—and set my watch. None of us wore sunblock, and if we were caught in the open at dawn, we'd fry like chiles rellenos. I mentioned this and added my reassurance. "Worst case scenario aside, we should be at Coyote's place well before sun up."

Red and blue lights flashed ahead. A tremor of worry radiated through the cab.

"You were saying something about worst case scenario?" Jolie quipped.

"Let's not wet our pants," I replied. "The lights could be a police cruiser pulling someone over—"

"Or something else," Jolie shot back. "Phaedra?"

Carmen remained still and closed her eyes. "Not her."

The closer we got, the pulsing glow grew and grew to reveal not one set of emergency lights, but several.

Jolie took her foot off the gas and engaged the clutch. "I don't like this. Should I turn around?"

They would've seen our headlights approaching for miles. "Too late now," I answered. "If we turn around, we'll draw more attention to ourselves."

Things had been going so smoothly. Our auras sizzled with increasing apprehension.

Carmen turned the radio off. She placed her hand on the dashboard and stared at the lights.

"What about the guy in the back?" I gestured to the truck bed.

"We'll wing it," Carmen answered.

A pair of SUVs with Border Patrol markings blocked the highway. Traffic cones funneled the road into a single lane between the cruisers. Two military-style Humvees were parked parallel on the shoulder. Four men stood outside the funnel of cones, their bodies shimmering from the red and blue lights. Our headlamps blazed off the reflective stripes on their safety vests.

Jolie doused our lights. We slowed to a crawl. My kundalini noir thumped to the frantic, menacing beat of the flashing emergency lights.

The vests on two of the men said Border Patrol. The other two wore generic tactical uniforms: cargo pants tucked into suede boots, Kevlar helmets with night-vision goggles attached to the brims, reflective vests stretched over equipment ammo magazines and radios. All of the men cradled either M4 carbines or MP submachine guns. If my nose wasn't detecting Cress Tech pork, it needed recalibrating.

Their red auras simmered in boredom. These guys had no clue about our true identities. Hopefully, if we didn't get close enough for them to see our eyes, we could creep through the roadblock using hypnosis.

Then a third Border Patrol agent walked from behind a Humvee. Her aura glowed orange. *Vampire!*

My anxiety heated up several notches. Vampires were everywhere. Rather we were everywhere before Phaedra's insur-rection. Why was this vampire here? Her aura shined cool, like running into us was no big deal.

But it was a big deal. Other than us three in the truck, and Coyote, the only vampires we've seen lately belonged to Phaedra. I studied this vampire's aura and couldn't get a read. Was she foe? Friend? Neither? Did the other Border Patrol agents and the Cress Tech guards know she was a vampire?

Jolie reached between her thighs and adjusted the .45. I swept the harness from my lap and let it fall out-of-sight to the floor. My jacket was unzipped and my arm tensed to snatch the .357 magnum. Even moving at vampiric speed, a gunfight against all this firepower wouldn't end well.

The vampire said something to her human counterparts. They took positions to block us and let her advance alone to the driver's side of the truck.

"What do I do?" Jolie whispered.

"Smile," Carmen advised. "Let your inner light show."

"What the hell does that mean?" Jolie groused out the corner of her mouth. She crooked her right arm and rested it inside the open window.

The vampire Border Patrol agent bent down to look at us. Our naked vampire eyes let our tapetum lucidum burn like road flares, but hers remained dark in comparison, meaning she was wearing contacts. Conversely, we could read her aura but she couldn't read ours.

She wore gold oak leaves on her collar and was certainly the senior officer of this little roadside fiesta. "Are you all American citizens?" The question seemed ridiculous considering our circumstances.

Jolie, Carmen, and I replied in unison, "American citizen."

The vampire continued with the Border Patrol drill. "Anything to declare?"

"Nope," Jolie answered.

"What's with the roadblock?" I asked.

The vampire replied with a very noncommittal, "Homeland Security." She tipped her head toward the truck bed. "Who's your friend?"

"Another American citizen," Jolie explained. "We're giving him a lift home. The three of us are his designated drivers."

The vampire laughed, stepped back, and waved to the other agents. "Have a safe trip."

They stepped aside to let us pass. Jolie turned the headlamps back on and away we drove.

When the emergency lights shrank to embers in our rearview I finally let myself relax. "I got a ten dollar bill for the one with the best explanation of what just happened."

Jolie was also watching in the rearview. "Fuck if I know."

"Carmen," I asked, "any ideas?"

"Only that she let us go when she could've given the order to shoot," Carmen said. "That puts her in the plus column. Here's my guess—something new has stirred up the pot."

With what? Neither Jolie nor I could follow up. We traveled south on the highway, beneath a canopy of stars even more numerous than my questions about our future.

After another ten miles, Jolie pulled against the steering wheel and panned her head from side to side. "How close are we to Coyote's?"

I scanned the desolate landscape. "Beats me." We had approached Coyote's home only once from this highway and that was during daylight. Even using vampiric night vision I wasn't able to spot any familiar landmarks.

I glanced worriedly at my watch. A quarter after 4:00 a.m. If we didn't get to Coyote's soon we'd have to get creative about finding shelter from the morning sun.

The night exploded with wings and feathers. I shouted in surprise. Crows swarmed in front of us, shining in our headlights like twirls of black metal.

Jolie slammed on the brakes, and the truck rocked to a stop. The flock of crows teemed around us.

"What the hell are they doing?" I asked, nervous. Me and these birds never got along.

The crows began to circle the truck. The entire flock peeled away and headed straight down the highway. The line of flapping wings glistened in the bright fan of our headlamps. At the point where our lights faded, the stream of birds hooked left and disappeared into the gloom.

Jolie and Carmen stared wide eyed. One of them gasped, "What the hell was that about?"

Crazy-ass birds. Messengers and spies of the Araneum. Phaedra had made it a point to massacre any that ventured close.

The engine's rumble echoed in the stillness. Jolie put the truck in gear and started forward. My nerves had sharpened to needles and my eyes took in every detail.

The crows returned. The three of us shrank from the windows, unsure of what the birds were up to. They orbited the truck, skimming close before peeling off again to follow the road. They made another left turn at the exact spot they had before.

Jolie drove until we reached a gap in a fence at the left where a dirt road intersected the highway. "They're showing us the way to Coyote's."

I chuckled. "Didn't think those feathered pests had the smarts."

Something pinched my right arm, hard, right through the leather sleeve. A crow bolted from the window, and it cawed, the corvus equivalent of a derisive laugh. I rubbed where it had bit me. *Fucker.*

Jolie veered onto the narrow, bumpy road. Dust churned in the glow from our headlamps. A crow stood in the dirt before us. When we approached, it flew off.

"Keep going," I said.

We continued far enough to see another crow waiting in the road.

"Cut the lights."

Jolie switched off the lights. Without the truck's headlamps interfering with my night vision, the terrain ahead sharpened into greater detail. A row of red lights followed the road. Like all living creatures, the crows had auras, and they were usually dim red. But they had somehow boosted their psychic energy so their auras shined in the murk like a string of red Christmas lights. I didn't know the crows had that ability but I've learned never to underestimate the tricky winged bastards.

Jolie continued down the line of crows and drove fast enough to keep us bouncing in the cab while the Jimmy made noises like rocks tumbling in a steel drum. Our human passenger thumped and rolled in the bed but remained asleep.

The line of crows climbed up the side of a mesa.

"Now I recognize the road." Jolie craned her neck to look upward. "Coyote's house is on top." She halted the truck and turned off the engine. "No way can this bucket of junk make it."

Pistol in hand, she climbed out. Carmen and I slid out from my side.

"What about him?" Carmen pointed to the human.

Jolie said, "He'll wake up in the morning and wonder how the hell he got here. I'll bet it won't be the first time."

She asked for her jacket and pistol harness. She shrugged them both on, cocked her head—*let's go*—and started up the road. The three of us broke into a fast trot.

The crows acted as if they didn't notice us, but when we got within fifty feet they'd leap upward and their auras would fade until they were practically invisible.

We made good time climbing the roller coaster of a road. When the crest of the mesa came into view, I caught the scent of coffee. Jolie and Carmen smelled it too, and we slowed to a walk.

Carmen sniffed. "Is that AB Negative?"

"Fresh, arterial AB Negative?" Jolie added hungrily.

The fragrance filled my nose. My mouth watered.

"Hey, *vatos*!" The voice hailed from behind us.

We spun about.

Coyote grinned from inside the ball of a bright orange aura. He leaned on a wooden crutch and a crow sat on his shoulder. He said, "Arrgh," and shook an open Thermos, the source of the coffee-blood aroma. He shifted weight to his good leg and waved his crutch at us. "I was getting old waiting for you guys, and look at me, I'm already older than this *pinchi* mesa." He capped the

Thermos and shoved it into my hands. "Make yourself useful, *cabron*." He shrugged the shoulder with the crow and it flew off. Coyote lowered the cane and hobbled toward us. Jolie and Carmen made way.

"C'mon," he said. "We got a war to fight."

Chapter Forty-One

I followed Coyote as he levered up the trail on his crutch—step, crutch, step, crutch. Jolie and Carmen joined ranks with me and then gave the same curious look. *No welcome back? No pleased to meet you, Carmen?*

I shrugged. *Welcome to Coyote's world.* For the last few days our worried thoughts kept circling back to him, and I had hoped for a more enthusiastic reunion.

"It was good to see you, too," I said.

Coyote acted oblivious to my comment—step, crutch, step, crutch. His shirt and jeans were a baggy fit around his skinny arms and legs. A white bandage covered his left leg from knee to foot. Graying hair curled from under a greasy ball cap. He looked like a convalescing scarecrow. Step, crutch.

His aura plumed around him, a megawatt flame of yellow and orange. Phaedra or Carmen would've been able to spot him from the moon.

"Carmen," I said, "with your new psychic powers, how could you let him sneak up behind us?"

She furrowed her brow and confusion streaked through her aura. "I was wondering the same thing."

We hustled to catch Coyote as he continued—step, crutch, step, crutch. I cradled the Thermos in the crook of one arm. His aura began to dim and shrink. By the time he'd gone ten paces, it had faded to nothing. I mean completely gone, as in zilch, as in what you'd expect from a week-old cadaver. The crows had muted their auras in a similar fashion.

Coyote gimped over the ruts and rocks in the mesa trail. With every new step, his aura returned until it was as bright as before.

I stifled an amazed chuckle. His trick answered my question about how he had managed to get the drop on us. I thought back to our arrival in Blossom's flying saucer and the moment when the psychic ray had quit tracking us. "Coyote, it was you who interfered with the psychic ray, wasn't it?"

His aura sprouted dozens of bulbs that flashed like the frenzied lights on a slot machine when it hit the jackpot.

"Okay, so it was you," I said. "How did you stop the tracker? What did it look like? Where were they?" Coyote could give us plenty of details about Cress Tech's equipment and tactics.

The bulbs morphed into words that scrolled around the perimeter his aura. *LATER VATO* The letters reached the bottom of his aura and vanished.

"Is he always this ... weird?" Carmen asked.

"This is nothing," I cautioned. "In a world where everyone wants black-and-white answers, Coyote finger paints in Technicolor."

She gave him an appreciative look. "That's not so bad."

"Don't encourage him."

Jolie asked, "Where's Rainelle?"

"*En el chante.*" Coyote hobbled off. Step, crutch.

"What?" Jolie asked.

"His home," I translated.

"Did Rainelle nurse you back?" Jolie asked.

"No." His aura darkened. "My mother did."

"Did she conjure some fancy juju to fix your leg?" Carmen asked.

"It's not fixed yet."

"But you're up and around."

"*Es verdad.*"

"Then what?" Carmen persisted.

Coyote paused and his shoulders sagged. "She did help, but in a way true to her character."

Carmen started, "What do you—"

He cut her off. "Once La Malinche, always La Malinche."

"I don't follow."

Coyote tilted his neck back and stared at the night sky. "She cut a deal to save me. A very bad deal."

My thoughts raced ahead to what he meant. My kundalini noir chilled and before I could manage a word, he said, "My mother betrayed you three like she had betrayed the Aztecs and the Toltecs. The Zapotecs. The Mayans. If you know my mom, she'll eventually double-cross you." His aura formed a peak that separated into a knife. It flew over his head and plunged into his back.

"What was the deal?" Jolie asked.

"If Phaedra kept me from dying, my mother would show her how to use the Sun Dagger."

"That's how Phaedra first reached Blossom and then us," I said. "Now that she's learned how to navigate the psychic plane, she can run amok throughout the galaxy."

"The deal cut both ways," Carmen noted. "Phaedra actually helped us out. It was her attack on D-Galtha that led to our escape. Don't forget that until Phaedra attacked, the Nancharm were going to fillet you." Carmen pointed at me.

Coyote shook his head as if her explanation didn't matter. Then he walked away—step, crutch, step, crutch.

"So where is she?" I asked.

"Who?" he replied.

Carmen said, "Doña Marina," while I answered, "Phaedra."

"My mother, *quién sabe?* Phaedra, on the way here. Which is why we must hurry. Less talking. More walking." Step, crutch, step, crutch.

A million questions remained, but if Coyote was done talking, no point in asking. I uncapped the Thermos and took a swallow of the warm coffee-blood mix. Carmen snagged the Thermos from my hand and gulped heartily. Jolie was next and she returned the Thermos to me, empty.

Coyote reached the crest of the mesa and disappeared from view. Jolie, Carmen, and I marched after him. When we topped the summit, all three of us abruptly stopped.

Coyote ambled between two skin-walkers. The hides on their bizarre sawhorse frames rippled as if from a breeze the rest of us couldn't feel. Their long, angular heads dipped to track our approach.

"Skin-walkers," I explained.

"I know what they are," Carmen snapped.

"They seem calm enough," Jolie offered. "The only reason they would be here is to guard Rainelle and in that case, I'm guessing she's okay."

Coyote step-crutched to his doublewide. Light glowed from a porch light and through the curtains and blinds.

The skin-walkers pawed the ground with their club-like front feet. They projected a vibe that said they could stomp us to pieces.

A crow fluttered overhead and joined a line of others on the roof of the doublewide.

"What's with the crows?" I asked.

"It's their fight too, *ese*," Coyote replied.

By that I figured they would help by scouting for Phaedra and her minions. Beyond that, I didn't know what else the crows could do other than shit on her head.

Che trotted out from under the doublewide. Coyote halted momentarily to scratch the dog's head.

Backpacks and camping gear lay in piles around the front porch. I had no idea where this stuff had come from but guessed that Coyote had probably raided a Boy Scout camp.

His crutch rapped against the wooden porch steps. The kitchen door clicked and was pushed open.

Rainelle stepped out, barefoot, her short hair spiked up. She wiped her hands on an apron and held the door ajar with an ankle. Her round face beamed. "Jolie, Felix, you're back. Hope you're hungry." She said this as if we had just returned from a trip into town.

Coyote step-crutched past her and into the doublewide.

Carmen climbed onto the porch. Rainelle tilted her head and arched an eyebrow. "You must be ..." She extended a hand and exclaimed, "Caramella."

"Actually it's Carmen."

"I was close." She clasped Carmen's waist and drew her in for a bear hug. "Coyote told me all about you."

Carmen pulled free. "He did, did he? And what did he say?"

Rainelle rolled her eyes. "That you are *bien caliente. Muy pecosa.*" Rainelle tapped her temple. "And smart, too."

Carmen grinned. "I'll take that."

Rainelle pressed her meaty hip against the door. "Come in. We have a treat for you."

Jolie and I followed Carmen and we sauntered through a rich aroma of young pheromones.

Jolie sniffed the air. "What's on the menu?"

Rainelle blushed. "It was Coyote's idea."

We were in trouble.

We turned the corner into the hall and toward the living room. An assortment of teenage boys lay stacked on each other like harvested timbers. Bony legs jutted from green cargo shorts. Hiking boots covered the feet. Socks sagged around their ankles. Pimply faces rested cheek-to-jowl. Most wore khaki shirts decorated with cloth badges. Coyote *had* raided a Boy Scout camp and not for the gear.

I groaned in despair.

"Don't give me that," Coyote said. "They came out here for communing with nature and all that. We're nature. Let the communing begin." He tapped his crutch against the sole of a boot. Rainelle stepped forward, grabbed that boy's ankles and yanked him out of the pile. He thumped against the carpet and laid still, a blissful expression pasted on his peach-fuzz mug.

So we dined on the necks of the free range, catch-and-release Boy Scouts until our auras simmered in contentment.

Rainelle brought me the Marlin carbine and the cartridge belt. "El Cucuy left this for you."

I checked the carbine to make sure it was loaded. It was. This extra firepower would've been handy on D-Galtha when Phaedra had attacked.

Jolie and I dragged the boys out and loaded them in Rainelle's pickup. I asked Coyote how he had collected the scouts considering his lame leg.

"It's the land of enchantment, *ese*," he answered cryptically.

We heaped the backpacks and gear on top of the scouts. Jolie climbed in the cab with Rainelle and drove off to dump the troop a safe distance away.

I returned inside the doublewide. Coyote and Carmen studied a map stretched flat on the coffee table. She rested on her knees with her elbows anchored on the table. Coyote sat in the armchair. He grimaced and massaged the calf of his injured leg.

I took a knee beside Carmen. "We need to hash out a strategy for Phaedra."

Carmen nodded without looking up. "We should let Phaedra come to us." She tapped a finger in Chaco Canyon. "This way."

"What's to keep her from using a portal and popping up on top of the mesa? Catch us from behind."

"The skin-walkers."

I chuckled derisively. "She beat the Nancharm."

"Difference is, the skin-walkers have home-field supernatural advantage."

"*Vato*," Coyote interrupted, "you have doubts about their powers, why don't you fuck with them?"

I raised my hands. *That won't be necessary.* "Why would the skin-walkers help us?"

"They won't. They'll be protecting Rainelle."

"So our back is covered."

Carmen nodded.

I looked at Coyote. "Maybe now you can tell us how you stopped Cress Tech and their psychic ray?"

He smiled. "It was as easy as taking a piss."

"I don't understand."

"Would the guards care about a coyote? That is, until he peed on their generator. Had to make it real quick or I would've fried my *chilito lindo*."

"How did you manage that with your bad leg?" I asked.

"You've never seen a three-legged dog?" he answered. "Try catching one of those fuckers."

I leaned across the table. "What did the psychic ray look like? Who was there? It is important to know if there were government agencies present with Cress Tech. CIA. NSA. DOD. Homeland Security."

"Good point. Which brings me to ..." Carmen planted a fingertip on the highway we had taken here and lifted her gaze to Coyote. "We ran into a vampire at a Border Patrol check point."

The penumbra of Coyote's aura formed question marks. He leaned from the chair and stared at the location under Carmen's finger. "*Que?*"

I explained what had happened. "Do you have any idea who that vampire was? Or who she is with?"

Coyote frowned and the question marks morphed into exclamation marks that dissolved like smoke.

"Hold that thought," Carmen announced. She sat straight and her aura brightened. "We have visitors."

I readied the carbine. My fangs dropped into attack position. What a time for Jolie to be gone.

Carmen tiptoed to the window and parted the blinds. Carbine at the ready, I peeked over her shoulder. The porch light shined on a Ford Sport Trac parked out front. Two vampires, a male and a female, stood beside the SUV, their bodies swaddled in orange auras. They were looking to their left. Footfalls brushed against the porch. I counted two sets, another pair of vampires I was certain but from this angle I couldn't see who.

Carmen's aura relaxed. She whispered, "Stay cool."

Someone knocked on the kitchen door. Coyote rose to his feet and step-crutched toward the kitchen. He motioned with a nod that Carmen should answer.

I kept enough distance from her to use the Marlin. She opened the door.

Two vampires waited just beyond the threshold, auras burning not with menace but with anxiety. Both were tall, but the shorter and more muscular of the two stood closest. And both were black.

And I knew them.

The beefier guy was Antoine Speight, who I had last seen in a South Carolina swamp after we lost Carmen to the aliens. He'd run off when a flying saucer landed to arrest the alien gangster who was in on the plot to kidnap Carmen. The lanky vampire was King Gullah, the head of the nidus in Charleston. He had sold me out to the werewolves in order to keep a supernatural war from breaking out.

Antoine gave a measured smile. "May we come in?"

Chapter Forty-Two

I hadn't seen Antoine Speight or King Gullah in years and in both cases, their parting remarks to me should have been, *So long, sucka*. But that was long ago, and the way the glint of their auras slipped from unsettled to hopeful told me to get ready for a three-way bro-hug.

Though they were both dressed in denim, Antoine looked ready for action in his faded jeans, a matching shirt that bunched around his muscles, a Chicago Cubs ball cap, and suede work boots. Gullah wore a trim designer jacket, the cuffs turned back and the front unbuttoned to show off a gold-lamé shirt. A heavy gold chain glistened below his throat. Sharp creases ran down the front of his jeans, tailored so they broke just right across the tops of his shiny cowboy boots, gold-tipped of course. A short-brimmed fedora sat on his head. He looked in prime ghetto-player mode except that he was missing the crystal-knobbed cane he always carried back in Charleston.

I stepped around Carmen. "Antoine. King Gullah. Get your asses in here." I beckoned them inside and scanned the night beyond them. The two vampire guards by the Sport Trac waved. I didn't see the skin-walkers and guessed they had left to watch over Rainelle.

But neither Antoine nor Gullah moved. They remained rooted in place, and their auras dimmed to a simmer of worry.

Antoine said, "We can't stay."

His reply surprised me. I had so many questions volley through my mind that I couldn't pick one. *Why can't you stay? Why are you here? Where have you been? What are you doing in this war?* And most ominously, *whose side are you on?* My finger curled around the trigger of the Marlin.

Carmen crowded against me in the doorway.

Antoine's gaze shifted to her. "I'm glad you're back." His remark revealed that he knew about her recent history. I had met him through Carmen and figured the two must've been business partners with benefits. Her lips twitched with a slight, hesitant smile. The last time they'd seen each other was just before her abduction by the aliens, so I was sure Antoine's presence brought a lot of memories, pleasant and painful. Their auras prickled until each of their penumbras got fuzzy and rippled with misgivings. The moment stretched awkwardly.

Coyote step-crutched behind Carmen and me. "*A la madre*, close the door already. The welfare barely pays for food. You think I got money to air-condition the goddamn atmosphere?"

"That ancient wreck of a bloodsucker is Coyote?" Gullah asked, amused.

"So you've heard of him?" Carmen replied. "Then you should be aware that he knows more about the supernatural than the four of us put together. I suggest you show some respect."

Antoine introduced himself and Gullah. Coyote replied with an unimpressed snort.

Gullah said to Carmen, "Antoine's told me about you."

Carmen folded her arms. "While I know shit about you."

"An oversight that will be corrected in due time. But I'm not here on a social call." He tapped Antoine on the shoulder. "We're with the Blood Force."

"Blood Force?" I asked.

"The vampires united against Phaedra," he explained. "At least those of us willing to fight."

"Which aren't many," Antoine said, "Most vampires are lying low, waiting to see who wins. They'll pledge allegiance to the victor."

"I pledge allegiance ..." Coyote began. We turned toward him. He stood erect, the crutch tight against his leg like a rifle, his right hand over his heart. He continued, "to that *desgraciada hija del demonio....*" The top of his aura flattened into a rectangle that fluttered like Old Glory in a breeze. He lowered his hand and relaxed against the crutch. The flag dissolved. "What *pendejo* would ever serve Phaedra?"

"You'd be surprised," Gullah replied. "Plenty of undead bloodsuckers weren't happy with the Araneum."

"You included?" I glanced to his left hand, specifically to the stub of his pinkie. As the head of the Charleston nidus, Gullah had gotten lax about his duties. To keep his post, the Araneum demanded that he reaffirm his pledge of loyalty by asking that he cut off his little finger *yakuza-style* and send it via messenger crow. He had plenty of reasons to buck loose of their undead reins.

"Me included," Gullah admitted. He clenched his fist to hide the missing digit. "And it was a mistake. Phaedra is one psychotic and paranoid bitch. She culled through the older vampires and killed the ones who didn't toe the line. She turned vampire against vampire and has even enlisted the blunt tooths into her army."

I raised my hand to stop him from continuing. He wasn't sharing anything we didn't already know. Jolie and I had already dealt with Phaedra's renegade vampires and their human minions. "What's your business here?"

"Thought it was obvious," he replied testily. "Beating Phaedra. Keeping the peace."

When Gullah had sold me out to the werewolves, and I asked him why, his answer had been: *Keeping the peace. Saving my ass. It's all the same thing.*

"I've heard that before." I gripped the carbine with both hands and raised the barrel. "And you expect me to trust you now?"

Anger swirled in his aura.

The two vampire guards by the SUV perked up. Their talons extended and the porch light glinted from their growing fangs.

Antoine put his hand over the muzzle of my carbine. "Hear us out. We came as friends. Allies."

I pulled the carbine free. "How did you find us?"

Antoine looked past my shoulder to Coyote. "Your mother, La Malinche."

Coyote pounded his crutch against the floor. "Doña Marina, to you."

"She found us," Antoine said. "Told us you were here."

"So you're close by?" My gaze tripped from him to Gullah and to their guards. "This is your Blood Force? Just you four?"

"There are others. You've already met one."

"The chief at the Border Patrol checkpoint," Carmen offered.

"She told us that you had passed through," Antoine acknowledged. He tossed a nervous glance toward the east. "With the sun coming up, we don't have time to fill in all the blanks."

Carmen stepped from the doublewide and onto the porch. She held the door open. "Then come inside. Hide from the dawn with us."

Antoine shook his head. "Other plans need tending to. Gullah and I came here to let you know that we've got your back in this fight."

I pointed the Marlin at Gullah. "Still not sure I can trust you."

He flipped the front of his jacket back to reveal a nickel-plated automatic tucked inside his waistline. "You wanna play games, bring it."

Carmen put her hand on my chest and nudged me back. "Save the dick measuring for another time."

Antoine and Gullah needed my help against Phaedra, and I needed theirs. I lowered the carbine.

Gullah draped his jacket over the pistol and smirked. "Let's put the past aside. We have your back. I have to know that you have ours as well."

She said, "We got your back."

He glared at me. "I want to hear it from him."

"*I* said it and that's all you need to hear," Carmen snapped. "We clear about that?"

His lips flattened into a tight, angry line, and he answered sarcastically, "Yes, ma'am." Gullah wasn't stupid. You don't fuck with Carmen.

Anxiety coursed through Antoine's aura. "Everyone keep a cool head. We've got to stay focused on Phaedra."

"Where is she?" I asked.

Antoine shrugged. "Haven't seen her for several days. We tracked her here, and poof, she disappeared."

Carmen said, "That's because she was attacking us."

"Impossible. We would've seen her."

"I didn't say here." She pointed to the sky. "We were on a planet on the far side of the galaxy."

Antoine and Gullah followed the direction of her finger to the stars and gaped. Antoine asked, "How did she get there?"

Coyote step-crutched to the doorway of the doublewide. Flames roiled from his aura. "*Que chingados preguntan?* She got there the same way she's coming back. She's going to pop from place to place like a *pinchi* genie."

Gullah grimaced. "What's he talking about?"

Carmen said, "Phaedra has learned how to use psychic portals."

Antoine and Gullah blinked and blinked, which only drew attention to the blossoming comprehension in their eyes. Finally Gullah said, "We know about psychic portals. Which explains a lot about why Cress Tech is here."

"So they're a wild card in this fight?"

Which was bad news. They had plenty of guns and equipment. Armed Humvees. Helicopters. And I was sure heavy ordnance on call from the military.

"They know about Phaedra?" Carmen asked.

He shook his head. "Not yet."

"But they will."

"Probably," Antoine continued, "but by then, it won't make a difference. Remember, our government had cut deals with the aliens before so expecting our elected leaders to watch out for the common good is ridiculous. I don't know what Phaedra would offer, but I'm sure it will be on her terms and by the time the government figures that out, it will be too late."

"Aren't you worried about getting caught?" I asked.

"Cress Tech has no idea about us supernatural creatures," Gullah said. "If we register on their psychotronic diviners, they figure we're aliens."

"How do you know?"

Gullah let his lips pucker around a tight grin then said, "Thought that should be obvious. We have family on the inside." He elbowed Antoine and both of them backtracked off the porch. "Our fight is against Phaedra. We came here to tell you that we're with you."

Gullah and the other vampires climbed into the Sport Trac. The engine cranked over. The Sport Trac turned in a circle and headed to the trail that led down the mesa. The brake lights flashed like red comets, and the SUV disappeared over the crest.

Chapter Forty-three

Carmen and I stepped back inside Coyote's doublewide. She pulled the curtain over the window and used binder clips to seal out the impending morning sun.

Antoine and Gullah's visit should've comforted me with the news that we weren't alone in the showdown against Phaedra. But her powers seemed to grow whenever we were unlucky enough to run against her. Besides mental mojo, she had suicide bombers and psychotronic disrupters in her arsenal. What could Antoine, Gullah and their mysterious Blood Force do that Carmen, Jolie, and I hadn't already tried? Plus we couldn't discount whatever mischief Cress Tech might add to the fray.

Coyote step-crutched from his bedroom, a comforter gathered under his free arm. "Hey *vato*, why the long face? If you wanna look like a horse, choose a more impressive part of his anatomy."

He dumped the comforter at my feet. "Cover up, *ese*. You get roasted, and Rainelle will compost your ash. That's not a good end for a hero."

Coyote retreated to his bedroom and closed the door. Carmen and I finished securing the curtains and blinds around the living room. We spread the comforter on the floor and slithered underneath to lie face-to-face. Her aura was an orange blob surrounding her head. For the next few hours we couldn't do much except hide from the morning sun and worry. Hunkered down like this, we were at our most vulnerable. Coyote's watchdog should be reassuring, but he could be silenced like he had been once before. I turned up my vampire sixth sense to maximum gain.

Carmen asked, "Do you think that Phaedra has to hide from the sun like this?"

"Good question. I don't know. Maybe her enhanced psychic powers have made her more vulnerable."

"Or less."

"Either way, she could still send her human goons. And if they show up ..." I flashed my fangs.

"I hope Jolie is okay," Carmen said.

"I'm sure she is. She's with Rainelle, and the skin-walkers are looking after her."

"I want to think our situation isn't hopeless." Carmen's aura darkened a shade, then brightened again. "When we've gone fang-to-mano against Phaedra and her lackeys, we've held our own."

I smiled to encourage her optimism. But the fights weren't entirely one-sided. A wounded Coyote and the dead chalices on D-Galtha testified to that. Her aura undulated with the rhythm of her concerns. Without prompting from me, she said, "Coyote's mom can find Phaedra. She did it before. When she ratted on us to save him."

"Maybe the deal's still on."

"What do you mean?" Carmen asked.

"We're still around. Marina could make another offer, us for Coyote."

"I hope not," Carmen replied, sounding conflicted. She closed her eyes and tilted her head to rest one cheek against the backs of her hands. She looked like a thirty-something taking a break after a hike instead of a vampire who had only recently escaped from years of alien imprisonment.

Dawn arrived. The gloomy air beneath the comforter grew heavy from the incandescent pressure of the sun beating against the doublewide. My kundalini noir tensed. I imagined the rays of light as poisonous tentacles searching for our skin. The weight of the air increased and slowly rolled over me and then lifted as the sun rose above its deadliest zone.

My watch read 8:30 a.m. Carmen and I threw the comforter back. The glow of sunlight outlining the blinds and curtains stung my eyes. While Carmen made blood-infused coffee, Coyote returned to the living room with a vintage makeup case banging against his crutch. He set the case on the coffee table.

Carmen and I watched from our perch beside the counter and drank our blood-infused java. Coyote said nothing, just step-crutched to the kitchen to pour himself coffee and blood. Curiosity got the better of Carmen, and she eased off her stool. She popped the brass latch on the case.

Plastic cases rattled in the tray that swiveled beneath the lid. The case contained dozens of tubes and jars of cosmetics. She picked through the items and read labels. Vampiric contact lenses. Ezee-On makeup especially formulated for the undead complexion, now with SPF 110+ sunblock.

I had gotten so used to seeing Carmen and Jolie au natural that our anemic flesh and red vampiric eyes looked normal. We needed the makeup and contact lenses to circulate in public and the sunblock to protect our skin.

She opened several of the jars to peruse the skin colors. She found one she liked and dipped her fingers into the cream. She smeared lines of beige across her cheeks and neck and covered the blue veins throbbing beneath her translucent skin. I pushed away from the counter to join her. We removed our shirts, Carmen her bra, and smoothed the makeup over one another's backs and arms. She gooped makeup into her hands, cupped those magnificent breasts of hers and massaged each perfect mound.

"You expecting to go topless?" I kept my voice even to hide my arousal.

Carmen pinched a teasing glance through her narrowed eyes. "If duty calls."

"What about your legs and the rest?"

She slapped her ass. "When it comes time to show this, I expect to be under cover."

Coyote stood beside the counter and leered, his fangs extended. The penumbra of his aura formed curled branches that straightened—*sproing*—into a mantle of boners.

"Careful, you might kill him." I tipped my head in his direction.

"*Vato*," he panted, "mind your own *pinchi* business. There are worse ways to go."

Carmen folded the cuffs of her jeans. She balanced on one foot while she rubbed makeup on the other, ankle to toes. Her breasts jiggled invitingly in an R-rated show. She paused to consider the old vampire. "What would Rainelle say if she caught you looking at me like that?"

"She would say that I am *bien macho*."

"Are you sure?"

"No," Coyote whimpered. He lowered his eyes and the protuberances on his penumbra shriveled, broke free, and fell like withered fruit. They bounced on the floor and disappeared in puffs of supernatural vapor.

Carmen slathered makeup over her other foot and straightened the cuffs of her jeans. She put her bra and blouse back on.

I finished applying the makeup and yanked on my t-shirt and shirt. I opened a contact case and put one contact in and then the other. I blinked to mold them against my corneas. Auras vanished and Carmen and Coyote appeared to be ordinary, boring humans. I pocketed a tube of makeup and a handful of contact cases.

Outside, Che barked, no growls, just friendly *woofs*. If it was Rainelle, I should've heard her rattle bucket of a truck. So who was here? Coyote hobbled to the back wall of the living room and peered out the window. His pained expression alerted me to uncomfortable news that he didn't bother to explain. Steps tapped up the back porch. The door opened and Doña Marina emerged from the brilliant splash of sunlight. Coyote greeted her with a scowl.

She wore a colorful sundress with a matching bow on her wide-brimmed straw hat like she was on her way to a Derby Day party. She halted between the door and the counter and panned a glossy smile at Carmen and me. "You made it back!"

I wanted to pounce on Marina and wring her neck for betraying us and revealing the psychic portals to Phaedra. But she was Coyote's mom so I kept my claws retracted.

Carmen leveled a stare so cold it could freeze nitrogen. "Doña Marina," she said curtly.

Coyote's mom removed her hat and frisbee tossed it onto the sofa. "Don't you want to say, La Malinche?"

"Where have you been?" Carmen's question frosted the air.

"Adding to my reputation ... like it's any of your business. Where are Rainelle and your friend, the redhead?" She raised her hands to the ceiling and announced, "Everyone, please save your shame and blame for someone else. I'm quite used to *el ojo malo*. People want something from Doña Marina, they get all kissy-face...." she pursed her lips and repeatedly smacked the air. "But when I act to protect my own," she looked at Coyote, "then I'm La Malinche."

"Mom, leave me out of this," he said.

"Where's Phaedra?" Carmen's gaze lost its chill but there was still no friendly warmth.

"I don't know," Coyote's mom answered.

"How did you find her before?"

Marina batted her large brown eyes. "When Coyote was laid up, about to die, and I was going to lose another one of my children, I only did what Fate has condemned me to do. Wander the wilderness and cry for my lost babies."

"So you didn't find her, she found you?" asked Carmen.

Coyote winced and hung his head.

"Yes, Phaedra found me and offered a deal."

I started, "That doesn't—"

Marina glared at me. "Do you have children?"

"That doesn't make a difference."

"You say that because you've never been a mother."

I felt my face wrinkle as if my skin wrestled to keep anger from seeping out my spores. I pressed the issue. "Whose side are you on?"

Marina replied, "Coyote's. And mine."

"You sound like King Gullah."

"Then he must be a smart man."

"Mom!" Coyote yelled. "It was a simple *pinchi* question."

She rotated her head toward him like it was a gun turret and her eyes twin laser cannons. "*Desgraciado*, is that how you talk to your mother? In front of guests? The woman who suffered to give birth to you and—"

He placed both hands against his head and squeezed. "Just answer the question. Are you with us or Phaedra?"

Marina walked to the coffee pot and poured herself a cup. "I already told you. I'm with you, *mijo*." She said "mijo" like our five-hundred year-old vampire trickster was barely out of diapers.

Coyote sputtered like he was about to explode. Before he did, I said, "That's fine, Doña Marina," to end the argument.

Carmen, Coyote, and his mom quieted and their thoughts turned inward. With this welcome break in the drama I could focus my attention to our mission.

Che barked again, another chorus of friendly yaps. A truck clattered and wheezed to a halt. Its doors creaked open and slammed shut. Footsteps climbed the back porch. Two sets, light and quick, joined by a third set, heavy and deliberate. A man. A big man. Wearing boots.

The door opened and Rainelle stepped in first. Jolie followed. She removed a battered cowboy hat, and then large sunglasses and a bandana from her face. Without makeup, those had been her protection from the sun. Appearing next was Francisco Yellowhair-Chavez, the super-sized Navajo skin-walker who had sold me the Marlin. He dipped his head to keep the crown of his Stetson from scraping the top of the doorway. The glint from massive gold rings drew my attention to his huge, dark fingers resting on Jolie's shoulder.

Her step hitched when she recognized Marina and then hitched again when she realized that Carmen and I wore makeup. Against her milky skin and its network of veins, Jolie's red hair shined like crimson wire, though it was matted into a tangled brush like she'd just dragged herself out of bed. Yellowhair-Chavez gave her a tender squeeze before dropping his hand.

"What's going on?" I asked.

Rainelle closed the door behind him. His right hand gripped the handle of a battered army surplus .50 caliber ammo can. She invited him to the living room. "Coyote," she scolded, "where are your manners? Say hello to our guest."

"Don't you start," he snapped. "I'm getting enough shit from my mom."

Yellowhair-Chavez reacted to the exchange with as much emotion as a rock to the rain.

His visit puzzled me. The skin-walkers had stated they would stay clear of the fight between Phaedra and us vampires as long as Rainelle was left alone. "What can I do for you?"

He entered the living room and set the ammo can on top of the map. "Bloodsucker, you got the question backwards. I'm here to help you, specifically her"—he pointed a sausage-like finger at Carmen—"find the devil-woman, Phaedra."

A grin just barely creased Jolie's lips, and I knew that Yellowhair-Chavez was here to return a favor. While Carmen and I hid from the sun beneath a comforter, Jolie must've been playing Indian bride in his hogan.

Chapter Forty-four

Jolie regarded Marina with suspicion. When she and Carmen had first met Coyote's mom, they felt empathy with her plight. Now that we had been burned by Marina's double-sided deals, we weren't so eager to have her in our camp.

Marina acknowledged Jolie's glare with a hard look of her own. She walked out of the kitchen and disappeared into Coyote's bedroom.

I didn't ask Yellowhair-Chavez what was in the ammo can, figuring he'd let me know when he wanted to. Rainelle offered him coffee but he declined, asking instead for a hatchet and rope, an odd request but I wasn't from around here so I didn't judge. Coyote said he'd get the items and step-crutched out the back door. Yellowhair-Chavez picked up the ammo can and lumbered after him. He asked Carmen to join them. Her eyebrows did a little cha-cha as she pondered his offer. She put on her sunglasses and followed.

Jolie peeled off her jacket and pistol harness and dumped them on the sofa. She asked about a bath and Rainelle pointed to the hall. Jolie snatched the makeup case and took it with her to the bathroom. Faucets squeaked and water splashed in the shower.

I heard a chopping sound outside and opened the door to see what was going on in the backyard. Yellowhair-Chavez whacked the hatchet at the middle of a pine tree log about as thick as my calf and maybe ten feet long. Carmen unfolded a small blue tarp in the middle of the yard. Coyote stood behind them and was busy untangling a rope. The three of them were discussing something in hushed voices and became quiet, turning as one toward me as if I had interrupted them.

"You need help?" I asked.

Yellowhair-Chavez returned to chopping. Hens pecked around his feet, oblivious that one day, that hatchet would come for them.

"You know anything about magic?" Coyote asked.

"I know enough," I replied.

Coyote sneered. "How about you don't know *caca*. Now get back inside and leave this to us professionals."

"So you don't need my help," I replied, crossly. "What's this for?"

"To locate Phaedra," Carmen answered. "According to Francisco, this will let me use the psychic plane to find her no matter where she is."

Yellowhair-Chavez didn't add anything but only kept chopping the log.

"Leave this to us," Carmen said. "Why don't you get the guns ready?"

Her words were a pat on my head, but there was no point staying out here if I was getting in their way. So I returned inside. Rainelle must've overheard Carmen because she waited with my backpack. I'd left it here the night Jolie and I had left for D-Galtha. I pulled out a gun-cleaning kit and the boxes with the remaining silver-tipped, depleted-uranium ammo. I emptied my magnum revolver, swabbed the barrel, wiped the dust and fingerprints with a flannel rag, and worked the action. After feeding fresh rounds into the cylinder, I set the magnum aside and started on the carbine.

The shower squeaked off, and Jolie rustled in the bathroom.

I loaded the Marlin and replenished the ammo cuff on its butt stock. Jolie emerged from the bathroom, a large towel wrapped her torso and moist hair matted to her scalp. She brought the aroma of soap and shampoo and freshly scrubbed vampire. What I could see of her body was expertly covered with makeup. I was hoping she would ask me to help touchup her hard-to-reach areas, then remembered Jolie didn't have any considering she was as flexible as Gumby.

The chopping sound outside was replaced by digging. She nodded at the door. "What's going on?"

"Some secret magical bullshit," I answered and repeated what Carmen had told me.

Rainelle brought clean clothes. Jolie shucked the towel and before the thought, *hello momma!* had even formed in my mind, she had whisked on pink panties with a skull-and-crossbones on the butt, then jeans, and a red t-shirt. She pulled a chair to the coffee table, took a seat, and field stripped and cleaned her one of .45s. She kept the other loaded and within reach on the table. Meanwhile I emptied her spare magazines to relieve the springs and then topped them off again. Jolie and I were really into gun porn.

The digging stopped. She and I quirked our eyebrows as we waited for noise from outside. When nothing sounded, we turned our attention back to our guns. I polished one of the anti-vampire cartridges. "This is the best all-purpose magic against Phaedra and her minions."

Jolie fit her pistol back together. "I was thinking of trading these 1911s for newer handguns. FN makes a .45 with double the magazine capacity." She inserted the clip and racked the slide. "But something about these old-school heaters speaks to me." She aimed the pistol at the wall. "Once we pinpoint Phaedra, we strike. End this once and for all. She won't have a chance. To paraphrase Jesus from *The Big Lebowski*, 'I'm going to shove this gun up her ass and pull the trigger until it goes *click*.'"

Good thing Jolie was on our side. I put on my sunglasses and stepped out to measure progress of the secret project.

Coyote sat on the bottom step of the porch. He slouched against a banister and appeared ready for a siesta. Yellowhair-Chavez had cut the logs into four poles that were now planted upright in freshly dug holes. A rusted post-hole digger lay nearby. The tarp had been tied with rope to the tops of the poles to form a canopy. Carmen sat in the rectangle of shade beneath, cross-legged on a folded blanket. She faced northwest and remained in a serene yet expectant pose, hands resting on her knees.

Corn-husk dolls, vintage toy cars, clippings from ocatillo and cholla, old vacuum tubes, and bundles of sage and wild flowers circumscribed a circle around her. With the open ammo can cradled in one arm, Yellowhair-Chavez paced the circle, his attention fixed on the objects. Sweat stained the armpits and the front of his white shirt. His bolo tie was gone and his collar undone. He stopped and crouched to adjust one object, then rose to continue along the circle, adjusting the objects, occasionally swapping one for another from the can. The entire time he gave the impression that everything had to be arranged with great precision.

The skin-walker completed the circle one more time, nodding as if finally pleased with his handiwork. Closing the ammo can, he joined me in the shade slanting from the doublewide. He faced Carmen, lowered himself onto a stack of adobe bricks, and placed the can next to his boots.

This was definitely a mysterious ritual. I asked, "You've done this before?"

Yellowhair-Chavez kept his attention on Carmen. A minute later, as if my question had negotiated a labyrinth into his brain, he answered, "No."

"Then how do you expect—"

His reply was quick. "Never had the chance to work the magic with a vampire like her."

Good answer. "What do we do now?"

"Isn't it obvious?"

Now it was my turn to let his question negotiate the labyrinth in my mind, and before it found the cream-filled center, he said, "We wait."

So I sat on a step of the porch and waited. Coyote's dog Che crawled beneath the fence and trotted to Rainelle's pickup to plop down in the shade beside her front tire. Crows landed on the gutter of the doublewide and the roof of the barn.

The sun climbed above us. The shade narrowed to a sliver against the doublewide, and the sun beat across my shoulders and the back of my neck. Yellowhair-Chavez removed his Stetson to wipe his brow with a handkerchief. Coyote bent forward as if he was melting. But the tarp's shadow stayed centered on Carmen despite the sun's shifting arc. The chickens pecked along the outside of the circle of magic trinkets but never ventured inside its perimeter. Flies buzzed around us but none bothered Carmen.

I asked Yellowhair-Chavez, "I thought you skin-walkers weren't supposed to help us."

"We're not, but the rules are not written in stone."

"Are they written anywhere?"

"Beats me."

"Then what changed your mind?"

Another pause. His thoughts must've been channeled back to the labyrinth. "Two things."

More waiting.

"Phaedra might not have designs on us now," he said, "or so she says. We Native Americans have heard that before."

More silence.

"That's one thing. The second?"

"It's amazing what a man, even a skin-walker, will do for pussy." He tipped his head back toward the doublewide.

Jolie deserved a gold star.

Che piqued his ears and rose to his feet. Our audience of crows squawked. The hens lifted their heads and cackled excitedly. The goats bleated from their pen. A rooster fluttered to a fence post and crowed. Che lay in the shade beside the doublewide and watched.

A dust devil whirled through the yard and brought an unexpected chill. Bits of dried grass and grains of dirt pelted my face and sunglasses. Loose panels on the doublewide rattled. The tarp buffeted against the tops of the poles. The wind ruffled Carmen's hair and clothes but she remained still.

Che backed into a corner of the yard and barked. The hens flocked into the barn. The rooster hopped from the fence and crouched between the hens and Carmen. It stretched its neck and spread its wings and crowed a warning as it backed into the barn. The crows hunkered in place and cawed nervously.

The door from the doublewide swung open. Jolie and Rainelle emerged onto the porch. Rainelle clung to the door and crossed herself. Jolie cupped a .45. Both women slit their eyes and grimaced at the dirt flung against their faces.

The dust devil swirled around Carmen. The corn-husk dolls and the bundles of sage and flowers rustled in place. The filaments in the vacuum tubes began to glow. All the objects fell over and rolled in herky-jerky movements. I thought it was because of the whirling wind, but the objects were migrating to group in front of Carmen.

The tarp tore loose from one anchor. Another anchor gave way, then a third, and the tarp twisted and beat the air. Amazingly, the square of shadow remained on Carmen. Two poles clattered to the ground. The objects formed a line pointing north.

With so much supernatural energy at play, I wondered what I could see. I plucked off my sunglasses and dipped my head to remove my contacts. The sunlight lashed my eyes and I squinted painfully at Carmen.

Waves of silver light cascaded from the yellow aura that flamed around her and formed a trail across the objects. The auras belonging to Coyote, the crows, and the dog inflated and deflated like the throats of croaking frogs. Yellowhair-Chavez's aura strobed in bizarre rectangular flashes. In spite of the sting to my eyes, I watched, fascinated. This was powerful magic and hopefully spelled doom for Phaedra. My kundalini noir began to stir. In awe and excitement at first until the tingling became an ominous twitch.

A spot in the air between the fence and the edge of the mesa began to shiver. My kundalini noir rang the alarm: *Phaedra.*

The spot *blinked* and there was Phaedra, standing on the edge of the mesa. A halo of psychic fire crowned her head. Carmen's magic hadn't just found Phaedra, it had brought her to us.

A ray of white light shot from her halo of fire. A deafening howl pummeled my mind. I lurched in panic. My feet slipped off the steps and I tumbled off the porch. When I looked up, I saw the ray had splattered against Carmen, blasting her flat. Phaedra shifted the ray to Coyote. He was overcome with spasms and he fell on me, twitching like he'd been tasered.

The back door to the doublewide flew open. Marina bounded down the porch steps. She threw herself on Coyote, squashing me underneath him as she screamed, "We had a deal."

I crawled free, the sun burning my eyes, the howl echoing in my skull. Remembering that Jolie had her pistol, I screamed, "Shoot! Shoot!"

The ray whooshed toward me and hammered my brain. My arms and legs jolted from under me and I writhed in the dirt. The ray lifted and I lay still for a moment. Teeth clenched in rage, I raised my head to appraise the chaos through the blur in my eyes.

Jolie lay on the porch, squirming helplessly like I had done. Rainelle stood against the doublewide.

The crows remained paralyzed until the ray flicked them to the ground like Phaedra was plinking tin cans. The ray next washed over Yellowhair-Chavez but to no effect. He was on his feet and advancing toward her.

The ray vanished. As had the hurricane of noise. Phaedra waited menacingly.

The air beside her shimmered and a figure appeared in the spot. A vampire. She had used her psychic portal to bring him here. He flung himself from her side and dove toward us. Suicide bomber. I pressed against the ground to launch myself at him but my arms and legs quivered like splintered wood about to break.

Yellowhair-Chavez bolted toward the vampire, scrambling so fast that his hat tumbled off. Rainelle bounded from the porch and chased after the skin-walker. The suicide bomber hurdled the fence into the yard.

Yellowhair-Chavez dashed between Carmen and the vampire. The skin-walker scooped the suicide bomber in both arms and raised him high to hurl him back at Phaedra. But he put too much force behind the throw and the vampire sailed into the empty air over her, past the lip of the mesa. He dropped out of sight and exploded with an earthshaking thunderclap. A ball of smoke rolled upward.

Rainelle aimed Jolie's pistol at Phaedra and shrieked like an avenging banshee. She jerked the shots. *Pop. Pop. Pop.*

A second vampire—a female—materialized, took a couple of long steps, and jumped over the fence.

Rainelle hit her once on the shoulder but the vampire kept running, fangs and claws extended.

Che lunged at the vampire and snagged her leg. She stumbled and fell. He renewed his attack, launching himself into her side. She was on all fours when he struck. The impact pushed her under the far end of the doublewide.

Yellowhair-Chavez grabbed Rainelle's arm and flung her to the ground.

I covered my ears and flattened myself against the dirt.

The vampire exploded. The end of the doublewide bucked upward. The blast slammed the ground and the earth punched against me. The wave of over-pressure slapped my skin. A ball of flame and smoke tore through the walls of the doublewide. The windows blew out in a shower of broken glass. The pickup truck was kicked sideways and rolled onto its side. Debris rained over us. My eyes were clenched tight and yet a brilliant yellow light flooded my vision.

The light faded. The darkness returned. I opened my eyes to gather my senses. The world looked blurry and with every blink came a little more into focus. Broken glass and torn pieces of siding from the doublewide littered the ground. Embers and ash swirled in the air.

My ears still ringing from the explosion, I had to peel myself from the ground. I forced myself to fight through the confusion and pain. My fingers extended as if on remote control and clasped my revolver. I looked up and saw Phaedra.

She took a step back, the air shimmered around her, and she was gone.

Chapter Forty-Five

I rose to my feet and staggered away from the burning hulk of Coyote's home. One half of the doublewide had buckled on itself, the roof and walls blown out and shredded. The rest sagged like a ruined accordion. Most of the fires had died out, but the air stank of charred wood and burned plastic. The truck lay on its side like a dead hippo. Fence posts lay strewn about. Smoke lifted from the walls of the barn that had faced the explosion. Dead crows rolled off the roof and plopped to the ground beside the corpses of their comrades.

I mouthed a prayer for Che. If it hadn't been for his selfless bravery, we'd be flat in the dirt like those dead crows, and Phaedra would've won. Though we had survived, we were still fucked. Backwards. Forwards. Inside and out.

The ringing in my ears turned into a keening wail. I shambled in a circle to find its source. The noise came from two people.

Marina was on her knees, hands raised, one hand clenching Coyote's greasy ball cap, her mouth ratcheting open as she cried out, "Phaedra, you monster, what have you done with my son? We had a deal! We had a deal!"

Rainelle ran toward the doublewide, screaming, "My house! My house!" She bounded up the porch toward the door, the entrance having crumpled to half its size. Smoke plumed through the cracks.

Yellowhair-Chavez was at her heels. He seized her arm and pulled her back down the steps. She collapsed in the dirt, hands tearing at her hair.

My gaze widened from them to take in the rest of the yard. I didn't see Coyote. He *was* gone. Once again Phaedra had almost kicked our ass for good. Now she had Coyote hostage, which meant another showdown on her terms. My kundalini noir drooped under the weight of so much gloom.

I counted noses to make sure the rest of us were still here. Jolie, looking pissed, wiped dust from her pistol. Carmen was sitting up, appearing as dazed as I felt.

The skin-walker crouched beside Rainelle. She leaned into him, sobbing and cursing. She stared at Marina, then shrieked, "Coyote?"

I'd forgotten that as his girlfriend, she would be as concerned about his fate as was Marina. Rainelle swiveled her head in all directions and hollered his name. The desolation swallowed her voice and the enormous quiet, contrasted against the ruin of her home, highlighted our desperate straits.

Yellowhair-Chavez enveloped her in his massive arms and gave a hug. She wiped her tear-soaked eyes and nudged him away. She remained on her knees and appraised the scorched wreck of her home. "Che," she cried out. "Poor, brave dog. You died proving you were the best of us."

I helped Jolie hoist Carmen upright.

Marina pressed Coyote's cap to her face and cried out again.

"Maybe Coyote escaped through a portal," I offered. "He's done that before."

She lowered the cap and skewered me with a glare. "I know what happened. He was right under me when I felt her snatch him away."

"Are you sure?" I replied. "He could've—"

"Tell me what you know about portals," she said.

"Doña Marina," I began, "we need to stay posi—"

Jolie put two fingers against my lips. *Give it a rest.*

Coyote's mom walked to the fence—this portion was still intact—and leaned against a post. She rubbed her forehead, murmuring and sobbing.

Carmen slipped loose from Jolie and me. She raked fingers though her hair and grimaced. Her aura roiled in anger and pain. The sunlight grated my eyes. I covered them with a fresh set of contacts that I retrieved from my pocket.

Rainelle had composed herself and rose to her feet. She climbed back up the porch steps, tore loose what remained of the door, and ducked inside. Marina followed.

Yellowhair-Chavez scooped his Stetson from the ground and whisked dust from the brim and crown. He set the hat on his head and retrieved the ammo can. He gathered the charms from where they lay scattered in the dirt. Most were either broken or torn apart.

Crows circled overhead and cawed softly.

Jolie and I climbed up the porch and stooped through the door into the doublewide. It looked like … well … a bomb had gone off inside. Pictures, knickknacks, the remnants of furniture, broken dishes and bottles had tossed all over. Vinyl paneling curled from the interior walls like peeling skin. Scabs of burned, melted polyester spotted the carpet. Pockets of smoke lingered in the nooks and crannies. I found the Marlin carbine and my backpack in what was left of the living room, buried under the smoldering couch.

We gathered back outside. Jolie carried a cooler filled with bags of blood she had salvaged from the refrigerator. Rainelle stoically hefted a couple of Pullman suitcases and made a beeline to the barn. Her flip-flops slapped the bottoms of her feet.

We watched Marina climb out a window of the master bedroom and float to the ground. She wore a denim barn coat and carried a cigar box. She set the box on top of a fence post and lovingly plucked items from the box and dropped them into a coat pocket. I was curious about what she was doing but could tell she wanted to be left alone. I guessed that the items were mementoes of Coyote.

I levered the carbine and made sure it was fully loaded. Jolie racked her pistols. The mechanical sounds comforted us. We might have been vampires but cold steel and high-velocity ammo was as soothing to us as warm human necks. And right now we needed plenty of soothing.

Marlin in hand, I walked past Rainelle's pickup and the blackened fence posts where the fight had gone down. I halted at the rim of the canyon and gazed down the slope of the mesa. The smoke from the suicide-bomber had vanished and I was sure nothing remained of him but shredded clothing. The minced parts of his flesh would've been incinerated by the sun.

With my contacts in, the supernatural dimension of our world was invisible. I wondered how much of this battle would've been seen by humans. As an enforcer for the Araneum, my job had been to keep the existence of the supernatural world—and us vampires specifically—secret from humans. But Phaedra was reckless in her tactics—or worse—letting humans know about us might be part of her agenda.

Carmen sat on a stack of cinder blocks. Eyes closed, she massaged her side.

"Are you going to be okay?" I asked.

She kept her eyes closed and gave her head a tiny, pained shake. "Phaedra did to me what she did to Coyote. It feels like a hole has been punched through me and my life force is draining out."

Jolie knelt behind her. She draped her arms across Carmen's shoulders and pulled her tight. She kissed Carmen's cheek. As close as I was to both of these women, I could never match their sisterly bond.

"Maybe Marina can help you," I said, grasping for ideas. When I looked up, she was gone. I asked Yellowhair-Chavez if he'd seen her. He panned to the left and to the right, then shook his head once. I wasn't surprised she'd ditched us.

"Maybe she went to look for Coyote," Jolie said.

Maybe. She could access the portals but I suspected traveling across the psychic world involved a lot of voodoo rigmarole so getting to Coyote might not be a straightforward process. And I suspected she was up to something else.

Crows fluttered about and landed in the yard. They pecked at the feet and tail feathers of their fallen comrades and began to tug them into the middle of the yard. Other crows pushed the remaining dead off the barn roof and the gutters of the doublewide and then glided to the ground. They joined the others in dragging the bodies into a pile.

I reached for a dead crow with the intention of tossing it into the heap. The crows and I never got along but they could've used my help.

A pair of crows lunged between the dead one and me. They spread their wings and cawed angrily. The rest of the crows joined their pissed-off chorus.

I backed away. The two crows that had instigated the protest became quiet and eyed me warily. All the birds became silent and returned to their funereal labors. I guessed fifty dead. About twenty surviving crows arranged the feathered corpses into a heap five deep in the center. Once they were done, the live crows hopped into a circle around the pile and faced the center.

A yellow flame flickered inside the heap. The flame licked around the bodies, growing into a fire. Each dead bird burst to flame, the wings and body writhing into a gnarled piece of glowing coal. A sheet of fire beat the air. One by one, the burning crows crumpled into ash. The heap collapsed, and the fire shrank into a trembling flame and then went out. The remaining crows kept their silent vigil around the smoking pile of ash.

A small dust devil whisked through the yard. Dust blasted me, and I shielded my face. The mini-tornado brushed over the crows and churned the air with the smoke and gray soot of their dead compatriots. The ash twisted into a column that corkscrewed upward and blossomed into a smudge that faded away.

The crows ruffled their feathers and shook ash from their bodies. In ones and twos, they sprang from the ground and flew over the mesa, soaring and cawing.

What brought the crows in the first place? Yesterday they had pointed the way here to Coyote's home. But what was their purpose today? Did the skin-walker's magic summon them? What was the point of them showing up only to have Phaedra kill them in droves?

The last of the crows disappeared. For a moment, the yard and the mesa grew so eerily quiet that I could hear my watch tick. The rooster emerged from the shadow inside the barn. He strutted to where the crows' funeral pyre had been. Tipping his head side-to-side, he scratched at the dirt and cinders. He crowed what had to be the all-clear because the hens meandered out of the barn. Their clucking brought a semblance of peace and normalcy.

Rainelle emerged from the barn, wearing hiking boots, a tattered straw hat, and an army fatigue shirt over her sundress. She and Yellowhair-Chavez stood side-by-side and appeared ready to leave.

I asked, "Where are you going?"

The skin-walker rattled the ammo can. "You're going to need more help than this."

"Against Phaedra?"

"You got more enemies I don't know about?"

Plenty, and fortunately they're not here.

He and Rainelle started walking down the road and off the mesa. Her truck was wrecked and the nearest anything was miles away. I had to repeat. "Where are you going?"

Yellowhair-Chavez gestured with the ammo box and grunted. *That way*. Which from my vantage was hundreds of square miles of empty desert. He and Rainelle hiked down the road, over the crest, and disappeared out of sight.

Jolie said to Carmen, "Better get you out of the sun."

Carmen raised her arms. Jolie and I grasped a wrist and yanked her upright. We were heading to the barn when a drumming noise echoed up the canyon. The chickens clucked raucously and scattered for cover. A loud whine blared across the mesa.

I knew the sound. A helicopter. A big one. We cringed, waiting for Cress Tech to arrive.

The helicopter lifted above the rim of the mesa. I was right, it was a big one. The bus-sized CH-53 we had seen days before. Lattice outriggers reached from both sides of the broad fuselage. Psychotronic diviners rotated at the ends of the outriggers. The giant helicopter roared toward us.

Our battle with Phaedra had surely blasted out gobs of psychic energy, and now Cress Tech had dispatched this airborne mechanical beast to pinpoint the source. The sensor turret below its nose twitched back-and-forth and fixed on us.

Chapter Forty-six

The gigantic CH-53 roared loud and low over the doublewide. The air and ground shook. The windows rattled. The chickens retreated to the barn in a panicked rush.

I craned my neck to get a good look at the helicopter as it passed overhead. The sensor turret swiveled over Coyote's ruined home like the eye of a flying cyclops. A crewman tipped his helmeted head out an open cabin window and panned the yard. Heat waves blurred the fuselage behind the massive engines. The rotor wash blasted an eddy of dust and debris across the backyard.

The CH-53 flew between the sun and me. For an instant the big machine became a black silhouette outlined by a dazzling lace of sunlight, then it dipped below the sun to continue its noisy trek down the canyon.

Jolie squinted and raised a hand to drop a shadow over her eyes. "Are they on to us?"

"You think it's a coincidence that a helicopter flew over the house so soon after Phaedra was here?"

"So what do we do?"

I didn't know how to answer. We couldn't hide. Where would we? We had to find Phaedra. Our business here wasn't done until we killed her.

Carmen wasn't paying attention. She pinched her eyes shut like she was in a lot of pain.

I nodded toward the barn. "Let's get her inside."

Jolie and I held Carmen upright and led her into the barn. Inside its gloomy interior, sunlight lanced through the cracks in the wall and ceiling. Dust motes swirled like tiny, agitated flies. The coffin Coyote had been lying in earlier was gone, but the table it was propped on remained. Before we let Carmen rest on top we had to find bedding so she'd rest comfortably.

I stood my carbine against the table and rummaged through the shelves. I found cardboard boxes marked FEMA: Property of the United States Government. For Official Emergency Use Only!

Well, this was an emergency. Our emergency, and I was declaring it official.

I extended a talon and sliced open a box to discover several woolen blankets. Carmen leaned against a shelf while Jolie and I spread blankets over the table and folded one to serve as a pillow. We then tucked Carmen into this makeshift bed. I went back outside and retrieved the cooler with blood.

Jolie rummaged through the suitcases Rainelle had dropped here earlier, finding clothes, some toiletries, a bag of mini-Snickers, and a large can of Folger's coffee. She dumped the can on a bare shelf. Out rattled a small glass bottle with dark liquid, metal cups, plus small cloth and paper bags. She opened the bags and said, "Felix, see if you can find a camping stove, I need to boil water."

"What have you got?"

"Something that might help Carmen."

None of the other FEMA boxes had a stove, Sterno, or heat tablets. I did find matches. From a box of discarded electric coffee urns and teapots, I pulled out a vintage one-burner portable stove. I gave it a shake and heard a slosh inside its sausage-shaped fuel tank. Five minutes later the barn was filled with the odor of burning kerosene. Blue flames danced around the burner until it glowed cherry red. In the murky darkness its warm radiant light shined like a humble beacon of hope.

Jolie squatted beside the stove, set a cup on the burner, and emptied the bottle into it. She tapped the contents of the bags into the cup and stirred. I smelled elderberry wine, pumpkin and watermelon seeds, juniper berries, honeysuckle, clove, and crushed rose petals.

"That some kind of a potion?" I asked.

"It will be." Steam curled from the cup. "But it needs fresh lamb's blood."

I didn't recall any sheep in the yard. "We have goats. Chickens."

Jolie shook her head. "Come here and stir this." She let the spoon rest and started to roll back one of her sleeves.

"No, you stir." I crouched beside her and extended my arm. "Use my blood."

"Goddamn it, don't argue. Do what I tell you before the potion boils over and gets ruined."

I stuck my arm in front of her and skinned back the sleeve. Lips pruning into a tight frown, she extended an index finger. Her talon sprang out like a switchblade. I rotated my wrist to give her a good angle. She sliced into my flesh and gave the claw a hearty, sadistic twist. Though pain whiplashed my nerves, I rewarded her with a smile. My blood seeping into the cup should've dried into flakes to form a crust, but the concoction kept it liquid.

When Jolie had enough of my blood, she nudged my arm away. I clamped my free hand over the wound. Blood oozed around my fingers and dripped to the dirt floor where it spattered into reddish-brown dust.

Carmen shifted. Her aura lit up a notch. At least she was still lucid enough to appreciate the aroma of fresh blood, even tainted ichor such as mine.

Jolie stirred the cup for another minute, then grasped it with a rag to lift it off the burner. She stood and offered the cup to Carmen who strained to lift her head. Her nostrils quivered at the fragrance and her lips parted to accept the drink. The scintilla around Carmen's aura quivered with a burst of fresh energy, then calmed as the rush passed. Sip by sip, she emptied the cup.

"This helps for now," Jolie set the cup aside, "but I'm afraid as long as Phaedra lives, she will continue to drain your kundalini noir."

Carmen rested her head and swallowed, her neck cording from the effort. She whispered, "Then we better hurry up and kill her."

Jolie laid a palm on her forehead. My wound had scabbed over and I smoothed my sleeve over my wrist. "Where did you learn about this potion? Vampire home ec?"

"At least one of us knows what to do."

My nerves jittered from inaction. We ... I had to do something. "How far is the skin-walker's home from here?"

"Why?" Jolie replied.

"We can't wait for Phaedra to show her cards. Maybe Yellowhair-Chavez knows a way to find her."

"We tried his magic once," Jolie waved a hand over Carmen, "and look what it got us. Besides, it took us forty-five minutes each way, by truck."

"It's what, four, five miles to the next paved road? I'm bound to find a set of wheels between here and there."

Carmen began to cough. She wiped her face and turned onto one side, pulling her body into a semi-fetal position. I smoothed the blanket over her form. If I had a heart, it would've sank against the bottom of my belly like a ball of cold mud. My kundalini noir creaked like a branch in a windstorm.

She opened one eye and caught my look of pity. "The way you two are carrying on it's like someone is dying." Her hand emerged from under the blanket and reached for mine. We clasped fingers. She smiled and closed her eye. She was gravely wounded and it was me who drew strength from her. She managed a weak laugh that pumped life back into her expression. "What would Coyote say if he was here?" She patted my hand, her touch light as a cat's. "I can't believe the fate of us *vampiros* rests on your dumb ass, *ese*."

"Something like that, for sure," I said.

"Give me a bit to feel better. Then we'll all go together." Carmen gave another squeeze and withdrew her hand under the blanket.

Jolie walked from the table toward the door. She turned an old metal bucket over, set it in the shadow away from any sunbeams, and sat on it. Pulling the cooler by her feet, she opened it and fished out a bag of blood. She fanged a hole in the foil wrapper, inserted a straw, and drained the bag.

I stepped from the table and leaned against a shelf covered in dust and a jumbled assortment of tin cans and glass jars. Jolie tossed me a bag and I fed and thought.

Phaedra was going to use Coyote as bait, that was obvious. Afterwards, she would kill Coyote as well. I wondered if Phaedra knew about Antoine and King Gullah. Surely she had to. Maybe that was where she was now—taking care of them. But she had double-crossed Marina, and who knew what Coyote's mom plotted. The skin-walkers were another wild card that could spoil Phaedra's plans.

Outside, the rooster crowed, and we perked up. I glanced at my watch. It was late in the afternoon and it could be Rainelle coming back. About time. Carmen propped up on her elbows and considered what was outside. "The bird sounds pissed. He doesn't like who's here."

So it wasn't Rainelle. Jolie stood and drew a pistol. I palmed the receiver of the carbine and rested my finger over the trigger guard. "Phaedra?"

Carmen shook her head. She sat up and swung her legs to the floor.

Jolie stood and opened the door. Brilliant light washed over her as she stepped outside. I hefted the Marlin and followed her across the yard to the fence by the wrecked doublewide.

The hens clucked nervously. The rooster had flown to a corner fencepost, and feathers ruffled, stared down the eastern slope of the mesa. Jolie and I stopped against the fence. Below us, a plume of dust billowed behind a Humvee in desert tan camouflage. Cress Tech. The vehicle scrambled up the narrow, twisting road toward us. The helicopter must've relayed our location.

Jolie followed the Humvee's progress. "Like we need these idiots. Any ideas?"

One came to mind. My kundalini noir tingled with anticipation. I handed the carbine to Jolie. "Get back inside the barn."

"What?"

"Stay out of sight but keep tabs on me. I'm going to lure them close." I put my contacts back in.

"And ...?"

The road hugged the mesa and from my angle, the Humvee momentarily disappeared from view. "You'll know when the time comes. Hurry, hide before they spot you."

Jolie jogged back into the barn. She closed the door but left it cracked a bit so she could watch.

The Humvee grunted over the lip of the mesa. It crunched over the broken glass and debris and halted by the doublewide, next to the scorched remains of the front porch. Three men dismounted, one from the front passenger's door, the other two from the rear. The driver stayed inside the Humvee and rolled his window down. Like the other Cress Tech vehicles, this one had no badges or lettering besides numbers stenciled on the bumper.

The men were dressed in drab tactical overalls with matching helmets, vests, and magazine pouches. Plus sunglasses and matching frowns. They each carried an M4 carbine with a grenade launcher attached under the barrel. They halted and studied the blasted heap that had been Coyote's home.

I took a step toward them, my hands in plain sight, claws itching to spring free. "Have you come here to help us?"

The three men traded looks and chuckled. One of them said, "Yeah, right, we're here to help."

"We had an accident. A gas leak, I think."

"Or a meth lab gone boom," another muttered.

"S'cuse me?" I asked, all innocent like.

The guy who had climbed from the front passenger's seat replied, "Mind if we look around?"

I took a step backward. "Who the hell are you?"

They sensed my fear, an act on my part, and advanced like dogs sniffing their prey. Their arms flexed around their carbines. "We're with a federal task force."

"So you say. You guys could've bought those guns and gorilla suits at Surplus City."

The boss man advanced to the fence. He cradled his carbine and flipped a tag velcroed to the front of his armor vest. It read in yellow letters: DHS. He pulled a badge from a pocket on the vest, let it hang on a lanyard. He was close enough for me to read his badge: Bart Devane, Special Operations Division, Department of Homeland Security, along with his headshot, was a picture of a police-type shield and a jumble of barcodes, abbreviations, and numbers.

I looked from the headshot to his face. "This badge yours? Can't be sure until you remove your sunglasses."

"You might want to back off on the attitude, wise ass." He tucked the badge back into its pocket.

"Why are you here?" I asked.

Devane raked a dismissive glare over the remains of the doublewide. "We need to search your home, or what's left of it." He pointed to the barn. "What's in there?"

"Barn stuff."

"Then we'll need to take a look."

"What for?"

"That's classified."

"You got a warrant?"

The three agents shifted like they were ready to start an ass kicking. "We don't need a warrant," Devane replied. "We're acting on a presidential security directive. Besides, whatever blew up your home gives us probable cause."

"You guys fire investigators?"

Devane's jaw hardened. His men began fingering the triggers of their carbines.

I crossed my arms. "Sorry, but no dice. This might be nowhere New Mexico, but we're still in the United States of America."

"We can do this the hard way if you want to take it to the next level. But let me advise you. If you resist, you'll be arrested for interfering with federal law enforcement and abetting terrorism."

I shook my head at the government bullshit spewing out his overpaid pie hole.

His two goons flicked off the safeties to their grenade launchers. Appreciative grins wrinkled their mouths. They were probably going to hit me with rubber bullets or pepper bombs. What a bunch of fools, brandishing all this firepower and *Soldier of Fortune* accessories to stroke their macho egos. If they started trouble, Jolie and I would go full-monster and eat these *pendejos* like tamales.

"Easy guys," I said, apologetically. "Come inside and look around."

One-by-one, they climbed through the fence and crossed the yard. I backtracked to the barn door. Devane and company closed in on me and lost visual with the Humvee on the other side of the doublewide. My back bumped against the barn door. Jolie whispered from inside, "The fuck you doing?"

"Don't we need a ride?" I whispered back. "Because here it is."

Chapter Forty-seven

Devane and his two goon sidekicks stepped close to the barn door. I dipped my head and popped out my contacts.

"Anything the matter?" Devane asked suspiciously.

I said, "Not anymore," and looked up. Right on cue, Jolie pushed the door open. We gave the Cress Tech men a full-bore vampire stare. They froze in place, auras pulsing like emergency lights. I fanged Devane—damn he tasted good. Jolie took care of the other two. She then sauntered around the doublewide toward the Humvee to finish off the driver.

Ten minutes later Jolie and I had dumped Devane into the back seat of the Humvee. Carmen followed our lead and climbed in with him. She tapped his jugular and feeling better, said she could baby-sit him. Jolie and I dragged the three other Cress Tech guards to the shed inside the goat pen. We stripped them of their gear and left them in a heap next to bags of feed and old, rusted tools. With all the vampire enzymes pumped into them, they would be dead to the world until tomorrow. Jolie stashed their carbines and ammo pouches in the Humvee.

We checked out the Humvee to see what could be of use. The urgency to rescue Coyote hovered above us like a storm cloud. My fear was that we'd find him in the same condition we had discovered Phyllis and De Brancovan. As decapitated heads impaled on stakes.

Jolie climbed into the driver's side, I got into the front passenger's seat. A psychotronic diviner and a radio buzzing with radio traffic were mounted on the front dash.

The first diviner I had ever seen was built by the Araneum, and this example was similar. A metal box the size and shape of a large dictionary. A fist-sized, transparent pyramid protruded from the top, a crystal fixed inside the pyramid. But the diviners fabricated by the Araneum were of an ornate, baroque construction. Filigreed polished steel, gemstones on the rivet heads, gold seams, an on-off switch fashioned from a ruby. This diviner was a plain box made of spot-welded sheet metal and a generic, hardware-store toggle switch. A USB cable connected the box to a vertically-mounted compass fastened to the middle of the dash.

"Bastards," I said, "they've figured a way to get a directional fix from the diviner." The previous examples could only detect a physic energy burst, not its location. Humans were remarkably adaptive, and that was why they were so dangerous.

The radio interrupted. "Stallion Five Seven." The call kept repeating until someone shouted, "Stallion Five Seven, this is Pitbull Two Six. Acknowledge, over!"

Pitbull 26 had to be the bossman and Stallion better answer before Pitbull shit his pants. Then I noticed that S-57 had been scrawled on masking tape stuck to the radio.

"They're calling us." I plucked the handset from the radio and offered it to Carmen. "Get Devane to answer."

He was sitting next to her on the back seat. His dilated eyes seemed to spin in crazy cartoony circles. Blood trickled from the fang marks on his throat. Carmen had his hands on her lap and massaged the webs of the flesh between his thumbs and index fingers to deepen her hypnotic control.

"Devane," she ordered while kneading the skin, "Answer the radio. Act as if all is okay." She let go of one hand and took the handset from me. She held it in front of Devane and pressed the transmit button.

He stared cross-eyed at the handset, blinked once, and the crazy spin in his eyes slowed. "This is Stallion Five Seven," he replied in a clear, calm voice. "Go ahead, Pitbull."

"Why the hell have you not been answering?" Pitbull was clear but not calm.

"We're here, Pitbull. Status Delta One. All okay."

"GPS shows you on the mesa in grid Alpha Tango."

Devane blinked slowly and the crazy spin returned to his eyes. Carmen massaged him with her free hand. He gulped and answered, "That's correct."

"From now on, make sure you answer ASAP. Understood?"

"Roger that. Stallion Five Seven out." Devane closed his eyes and settled against the seat as he muttered, "Douchebag."

I took the handset and clipped it back on the radio. Carmen sighed and relaxed. Lines of fatigue etched her haggard face. Sweat beaded her hairline. I would trade places with her if possible, but there was nothing I could do now but watch her suffer.

Jolie's brow furrowed. Distress darkened her eyes and she turned away from Carmen.

The low afternoon sun cast long shadows across the mesa and the canyon below. Crows landed on the barn roof, the fence, and the nearby junipers. The rustle of their wings and the Humvee's radio murmured through the cool, quiet air.

We finally had wheels, so I said, "Let's get going." I rolled my window down and cradled the Marlin in my arms.

Jolie nodded and started the engine. The V8 diesel gave a reassuring rumble. She steered around the doublewide and followed the path that lead down the mesa.

More crows fluttered into the nearby shrub. A cool snap tightened the air. Stars blossomed in the darkening night. Traffic lights on the highway and the lamps from random dwellings burned tiny dots across the blanket of dusky earth.

Midway down the mesa, crows sprang from a stand of junipers and dispersed silent as a cloud of smoke. Curiously they gave no warning about what startled them.

The crystal on the diviner began to glow. The pointer on the compass illuminated and swung to the left. Jolie halted and rested an M4 on her lap. Carmen opened her eyes and leaned forward.

My kundalini noir tingled, and I readied the Marlin. "Phaedra?"

"No, not her."

The junipers at our left rustled. Jolie and I pointed our guns.

"*Calmanse*," a voice shouted. El Cucuy bulled through the junipers. His mosaic of pewter-colored skin glittered in the twilight. He brought a fist to his brow in an internationalist salute. "*Hola camaradas.*"

I never pictured him as a Marxist. I waved a greeting. Jolie relaxed her grip on the M4.

He lumbered close, an automaton of magical presence and equally important, a powerful ally. "Heard you got your asses kicked good."

"You heard that from who?" Jolie asked.

"Rainelle."

"Where is she?"

"Yellowhair-Chavez is watching over her."

"Are you here to help us rescue Coyote?" I asked.

"For sure, unless you just want me to stand around and look pretty. Which I can do." He vogued a pose.

But El Cucuy did present an unexpected problem. With the diviner locked on him, it wouldn't detect Phaedra.

"Where's Doña Marina?" I asked.

The boogieman mugged unconvincingly. I was about to quiz him about what she and him were cooking up when the crystal in the diviner flared brighter. The compass pointer swung to the right, away from him and to the east, down the canyon, drawn by a stronger signal.

Carmen sat up and stared out a window, in the direction the compass indicated. She didn't have to say it, for we knew who it had to be.

Jolie stared into the distance. "What's there?"

El Cucuy replied, "The Chaco Canyon ruins."

I stepped to the edge of the mesa. The ruins were tucked into the folds of the ground and almost invisible. "What's there exactly?"

"Mostly debris left by the Anasazi centuries ago. A few adobe walls. Some underground chambers."

Bingo. "Chambers? How big?"

"Big enough to hide someone if that's what you're thinking," El Cucuy with growing comprehension.

"That's exactly what I'm thinking." I cradled the Marlin. "In the words of the Thing from the Fantastic Four, it's clobbering time."

Chapter Forty-eight

Our Humvee rumbled over the edge of the mesa and down the road into Chaco Canyon while Jolie followed the compass heading to Phaedra. Carmen sat up front next to her. Devane remained in the back seat, comatose with vampire enzymes. I stood in the open roof hatch like I was commanding a tank.

El Cucuy refused a ride. Anyway, it wasn't like we had a seat that would accommodate his super-sized, supernatural ass. He trotted alongside us and adroitly hopped from outcropping to outcropping.

I kept the Marlin tucked under my arm. Both my revolver and the carbine were loaded with depleted uranium-silver cartridges. The speed-loaders for the revolver, the carbine's ammo cuff, and my pistol belt were fully stocked. My pockets bulged with the remaining rounds. When Phaedra showed herself, I was going to fill her with so much metal she could be used for ballast.

So far, all of our battles had resulted in a draw. Whenever she tried to kill us, we managed to hold her off. When we counter-attacked, she'd squirm free only to later reappear and cause more mayhem. The war continued to unfold into a deadly chess game. Move. Counter-move.

Until tonight, our tactics had been defensive, basic survival ploys improvised on the spot. Now we'd take the offensive and press forward to destroy her.

But she wasn't stupid. She had announced herself with a telltale flare of physic energy and now we advanced her way.

I wondered if she was keeping Coyote prisoner at the ruins. Considering her ability to transport through the psychic portals, she could've stashed him someplace far away—an ice cave in Antarctica, a mountain hideaway in Nepal, a dumpster in deep space.

Then again, Phaedra needed Coyote as a pawn. So that meant she had to keep him close by to use him in her gambit to destroy us. The subterranean chambers beneath the ruins were perfect.

Move. Counter-move.

The moon rose above the horizon and washed the landscape with a silvery tint. Our destination, the Chaco ruins, remained hidden from view behind the low rolling terrain to my right.

Crows glided past the Humvee. A few at first. Then dozens.

At the bottom of the mesa, hundreds more had landed and waited. They turned and strutted parallel in our line of travel, a feathered mass of red auras so numerous they flowed like lava around the bigger rocks. Then one by one, their auras faded until they became a black undulating carpet creeping over the ground.

"Are you watching this?" I asked.

"What are they up to?" Jolie replied.

"Carmen," I asked, "what's your take?"

I hoped she would chime in. Not that I expected an explanation, but her silence meant she might have relapsed. Maybe I should've insisted on leaving her behind at Coyote's home under El Cucuy's protection.

Which brought to mind. Where was he? I swiveled in the hatch to look around. "Where's El Cucuy?"

Jolie let the Humvee coast to a halt. "Why are you asking me?"

I thought he had joined us for the fight. But he had skipped out, and that made me wonder if he was scheming with Marina.

"I'm guessing that Marina must've sent him."

"Why?"

"Maybe she knew all along that Phaedra was going to appear. Marina had El Cucuy make sure that we would start after her."

"Is Marina setting us up?" Jolie snapped.

Before I could answer, a dim flicker approached over the gloomy landscape to my left. I studied the glinting light until I determined it was moonlight reflecting off rotorblades. A helicopter cruised straight for us. A Cress Tech aircraft for sure.

"Carmen, get Devane ready in case we get hailed over the radio."

Far behind the helicopter, headlights spilled from the highway. They formed a line and convoyed along the bottom of the canyon in our direction.

The timing couldn't be coincidental. Phaedra's psychic burst had not only caught our attention but Cress Tech's as well. Maybe this was her plan. Have us cross paths with them. Let the government's goons do the heavy lifting for her. Then she could swoop in and bayonet the wounded.

We couldn't retreat up the mesa without getting spotted. The helicopter was now close enough that we could recognize it as the massive CH-53 Sea Dragon, the one mounting psychotronic diviners. More helicopters appeared behind it. Probably Blackhawks and Apaches. The CH-53 was leading a Cress Tech posse right to the ruins ... and us.

Maybe this was the true reason El Cucuy had bugged out, and if so, a little warning would have been appreciated.

I was flipping through our options when Jolie gunned the engine. We bounced to the right, away from the road and into a draw deep enough to mask the Humvee. Crows scooted out of our way.

Under the best of circumstances my Marlin and its .45-70 ammo would need a miracle to bring down the Sea Dragon. And even if we could, the other helicopters would pounce with mini-guns, 30mm cannon, and Hellfire missiles. If we abandoned the Humvee and scattered, then Phaedra could finish us off one-by-one.

Move. Counter-move.

I expected the huge CH-53 to roar over us at any second. The chatter of its blades built to a crescendo. The seconds ticked past. Still no helicopter.

More anxious seconds passed. Still no helicopter, only the staccato echo of rotorblades that rose and faded, rose and faded.

Jolie called out. "Felix, listen to this." She turned up the volume of the radio. A chaotic jumble of frantic voices shouted over one another.

I couldn't make sense of the chaos. "Climb the slope on our right," I yelled.

The Humvee crawled out of the ravine. I stood as tall as I could in the hatch and craned my neck for a view to the canyon.

More than a mile from us, a fireball painted the landscape with splashes of yellow and orange light. A burning helicopter fuselage tumbled down the mesa cliff, breaking to pieces and shredding its rotors. Along the canyon floor, more fireballs mushroomed into glowing clouds of smoke. Tracer bullets, rockets, and flaming debris streaked through the air. The muffled booms of the distant explosions growled through the darkness.

The Humvee lurched to a stop. Jolie yelled, "What the hell is going on?"

"It's a firefight," I offered.

"No shit," she replied. "But who is fighting? Phaedra versus Cress Tech?"

Another helicopter thundered over the top of the mesa right behind our heads. Its tadpole shape gave it away as a UH-60 Blackhawk. Jolie and I panned the ghostly form with our carbines to shoot, but then the helicopter's navigation lights blinked on. The searchlight on its belly projected a glimmering saber of light toward the earth.

I shouted, "Hold your fire. They're lighting up to identify themselves."

Jolie dipped the muzzle of her carbine. "Who the hell are they?"

The helicopter slowed and circled back toward us, the searchlight sweeping over the sage and dirt. It stopped in a high hover and seemed balanced on the rod of light protruding from its belly. The helicopter slid downward until dust billowed beneath.

Two orange auras appeared in the cargo door. *Vampires.* They dropped and arrested their fall by levitating the last few feet into the cloud of dust. They emerged running toward us.

One vampire was short and female. The other taller and male. The closer he approached, the more he adopted a familiar gait like his hip bothered him. A slight limp complete with cane. King Gullah. I climbed from the Humvee to greet them. Carmen slipped behind me and braced herself against a fender. Despite her weakened condition, she glared at the two strangers.

The woman wore the green fatigues of the Border Patrol. I recognized her as the one in charge at the highway checkpoint, the officer who had mysteriously let us pass.

The helicopter doused its lights and accelerated into a wide orbit above us.

"You owe us a loud and sincere thank you." King Gullah swung the cane toward the bedlam in the canyon. "If it wasn't for Antoine, me, and the rest of my undead team, you and your merry band would be ass deep in bad trouble."

"Thanks then," I replied. "But you could've clued us in."

"Not while Phaedra has you as target *numero uno*. Consider our silence as operational security."

"How did you know the convoy was on its way here?" Jolie asked.

The border patrol officer tugged at her shirt collar to show off the insignia. "We have family on the inside. We got these guys shooting at each other. That fight you see is fratricide gone amok."

"So Cress Tech is off our back for now," I said. "I can't imagine the load of reinforcements that's going to follow this shitstorm."

The agent sneered. "You're giving the federal government too much credit. Cress Tech's operation was buried beneath layers of deniability from the get-go. Ain't no one copping to this disaster."

"Which gives us till morning," Gullah noted. "Cress Tech located Phaedra in the Chaco ruins. Once we got a fix on her," he said, pointing his cane at the circling helicopter, "we'll shoot so many Hellfire missiles up her ass she'll explode like a piñata."

"As much as I enjoy the visuals, you can't do that," I countered. "She's taken Coyote hostage."

Gullah set his lips into a hard line. He looked at the border patrol agent and she looked back at him. "Considering all that we've sacrificed," he said, "and all the vampires Phaedra has killed, we have to take advantage of our firepower while we have the opportunity."

Carmen's aura flushed with anger and erased any sign of her impaired condition. "If you mean writing off Coyote as collateral damage, *that* is not going to happen."

Gullah raised a finger. "Sacrifice one to end this calamity, I say that's a bargain. If that bothers you, I'll feel guilty enough for the both of us."

Carmen started toward him, but I held her back. As distasteful as Gullah's proposal was, I had to consider it. If Phaedra was betting the last of her chips and using my friend as a shield, then we had better be ready to double-down and live with the consequences.

The border patrol agent grasped the radio mike attached to her shoulder and barked an order. The Blackhawk banked and descended. She and Gullah backed away toward where they had been dropped off.

Carmen broke free of my grasp. For a vampire in such a debilitated state, she remained surprisingly strong. "We won't do Phaedra's dirty work. I'll rescue Coyote on my own."

Gullah and the agent kept backing away. Carmen kept after them. "Promise me that you won't harm Coyote. I need your word."

"You have my word that I'll do what needs to be done," Gullah said. "While you were in outer space, she was annihilating the Araneum. She tortured vampires in ways that would've made Vlad the Impaler cringe. When this is long past, feel free to look me up and give me hell."

The Blackhawk slowed and swooped low. Gullah and the agent turned and sprinted toward the helicopter. They leapt and glided to the open cargo door. The Blackhawk continued in its swooping arc and climbed. The lights clicked on once, then off as if to say goodbye.

Carmen's aura roiled in distress. "You don't agree with them, do you?"

I didn't answer. Jolie averted her eyes and returned to the Humvee. She understood the weight of difficult choices. Years ago she had been sent to execute me. Duty was a heavy burden. Carmen knew that, too.

Let Carmen forever condemn me, but if Phaedra thought she could hide behind Coyote, she was mistaken. If necessary, we would have to sacrifice one pawn to get the queen.

Carmen brought a hand to her head and knees buckling, she reached for the Humvee to keep from falling. She whispered, "Phaedra."

From inside the Humvee, Jolie exclaimed, "The diviner's really lighting up." The glow from its crystal lit up her face.

What was Phaedra doing?

The turbines in Gullah's helicopter hiccupped and that answered my questions. I sprang from the Humvee and looked up. The Blackhawk rocked and yawed violently. I imagined Antoine and Gullah and the others inside writhing as Phaedra's mental ray hammered their brains. She could only use her psychic powers on one vampire at a time, but she could whip the ray from mind to mind, scrambling their thoughts into pudding.

The Blackhawk bucked like a gaffed fish and rolled onto its back. The helicopter nosed straight down and smashed into the ground, disintegrating and exploding into a monstrous shower of flame and sparks.

We stared slack-jawed at the fiery deaths of our doomed friends. Just like that, Phaedra had evened the odds.

Move. Counter-move.

The burning wreck settled against the ground and pointed down the canyon. Crows emerged from the darkness and flowed toward the ruins like pools of oil.

A glowing light with swirls of red, yellow, and green, materialized between us and the ruins.

Phaedra.

Waiting.

Chapter Forty-nine

My neurons fired at super speed as I calculated how to put a bullet through Phaedra.

Air ... calm. No need to adjust for windage.

Range to target ... five hundred meters, give-or-take. The .45-70 wasn't a long-distance cartridge. Compensate for the bullet drop by aiming way over her head.

Jolie bolted from the driver's seat, M4 at the ready.

I was pulling the carbine to my shoulder when Phaedra's psychic blast thundered into my head. Clenching my teeth, I tensed to withstand the attack.

To no avail. The blast crashed against my kundalini noir and ricocheted down my spinal column. Megawatt jolts of pain charged through my arms and legs. My mind flipped left, right, upside down, and all went black.

I woke face down in the dirt. My consciousness swam through a cesspool of nausea and pain. Round one of this battle and Phaedra had kicked my ass. Even with supernatural strength I'd need a minute to recover. As my thoughts cleared and I regained control of my limbs, I pushed up from the ground to see what more damage that witch Phaedra had inflicted on us.

Jolie lay beside me, on her back, squirming like a poisoned bug. Second by second, her aura morphed from red to orange. She rolled onto her belly, and the string of curses coming out her mouth assured me that she would survive.

Carmen had advanced a few steps and stood, fists against her sides, her posture rigid as she absorbed the full brunt of Phaedra's barrage. Carmen's posture eased, and I figured Phaedra had backed off from her attack.

An image projected into my brain. Coyote lay heaped on the ground inside a cramped enclosure, a small underground room.

I have him. Phaedra's voice echoed in my skull. *And he's going boo hoo hoo. Oh woe is me.*

The image dissolved into a gray noise of dull pain. Queasy and weak, I reached for the Marlin from where I had dropped it. I brought my knees under me and leaned on the carbine to rise to my feet.

Phaedra retreated down a trail to where tumbled adobe walls marked the edge of the Chaco ruins. My brain was still stuck in neutral and by the time I raised the Marlin for a shot, she had disappeared into the zigzag maze of the ruins.

Jolie hadn't fired either, and we used this intermission to collect our marbles.

She, Carmen, and I occupied a draw in the sloped escarpment of the southern mesa. The escarpment flattened into the sandy wash at the bottom of the canyon. A dry creek meandered down the middle of the wash.

The Humvee idled fifty meters behind us. To the north and beyond the smoldering wreck of Gullah's helicopter, smoke from the Cress Tech ambush rose over the ridge and unspooled across the stars in a crimson film. Gullah and Antoine hadn't attacked alone, but I had no way of communicating with the rest of their forces. Even if I tried the radio in the Humvee, who would I contact?

Behind Phaedra, the canyon opened around Chaco ruins. Crumbling adobe structures filled the space between the cliffs of the northern mesa and the remains of the circular kivas. The tumbled walls were lined up like rows of weathered tombstones. Coyote could be locked up anywhere down there.

Along the creek bed and the trail, red auras burst among the shrubs and rocks. Eight, nine, ten humans formed a line two hundred meters away, between Phaedra and us. She had used this recess to deploy her human minions through psychic portals. Up until now, Phaedra had only used vampires. And these humans had come armed. Moonlight glinted off their pyschotronic disruptors.

Shaking from Phaedra's mind blast, Jolie fired out her magazine as she fell. Tracers blasted from the gun's muzzle and streaked through the air.

Psychic waves hammered my brain, punching from different directions like I'd been jumped in a barroom brawl. I dropped, but the pain halted because I had landed behind cover and out of the line of fire from the disruptors.

Carmen remained in the open. Flames of agony enveloped her aura. Not only was she absorbing the focus of Phaedra's power, she stood in the intersecting blasts from the disruptors.

Helpless against the disruptors and Phaedra's psychic mojo, I kept my body flat on the ground. I'd felt like this before in Iraq when the enemy rained mortar shells on my position. Like then, my mind clawed for a way out. But I couldn't jump up and run or crawl out of this escarpment without getting mowed down.

I knew what was next. If Phaedra used the psychic portals to deploy the humans, then she'd soon dispatch her vampires. I drew my carbine close and waited. My reflexes, normally quick enough to steal cheese from a mousetrap, now creaked at rusty, blunt-tooth speed.

Carmen's knees weakened. The crossfire of psychic blasts was beating her down. The final attack was about to commence. When the vampires appeared, the humans would advance behind them and give covering fire with the disruptors. Phaedra's weapon of choice was undead suicide bombers, and she'd probably groomed her most devoted martyrs for this knockout blow.

Death was so close its icy fingers caressed my kundalini noir. If Phaedra won, all of our heroics had amounted to nothing. I would die. Jolie would die. Carmen. Coyote. All of us undead would be vanquished.

Our only option was to die fighting. Nothing glorious about our situation. The enemy would storm us until they wiped us out.

The ground stirred as if it were coming alive. Crows darted between the clumps of grass and sage. They moved like drips of inky black syrup, practically invisible in the gloom even to my vampire eyes. I saw them collect in twos and threes, then assemble in larger groups as they oozed over the ground in mass toward the humans. They walked around me. Over me.

I raised my head just enough to see what they intended. The humans had no idea the crows were marching on their position, and apparently, neither did Phaedra.

On some secret signal, the crows lit their auras and sprang upward in gouts of flaming red and orange. They swarmed over Phaedra's minions, cawing and pecking. The humans screamed, dropped their disruptors and tried to fight them off.

I took my chance. I raised my carbine and hunted for Phaedra. But she was gone. So I drew a bead on a human covered in crows and sent him to minion Valhalla.

Jolie slammed a fresh magazine into her M4 and dropped two more humans.

Orange blobs of light erupted from the ground between us and the humans. Phaedra's vampires had at last arrived. They wore suicide bomb vests and rushed us.

Another wave of crows roiled from the ground, a fountain of auras melding into a fiery smear. Raucous cawing blared through the night air. The crows descended on the vampires, enveloping them in a tsunami of feathers and beaks.

A vampire blew himself up. Pieces of crow spun past me. A second vampire exploded. More shredded crow. And a third vampire went boom. I levered the Marlin and fired, triggering another vampire explosion. Jolie and I panned our guns from vampire to human to vampire to human until we had run out of targets. The growl of explosions faded up the canyon. The air stank of spent ammo and burnt meat. Smoke corkscrewed from the muzzle of my carbine. The barrel of Jolie's M4 glowed cherry red. I fished cartridges from my pocket and fed them into the Marlin.

Smoldering craters marked where the vampires last stood. The few surviving humans dragged themselves along the ground, whimpering and bleeding. Flocks of crows glided to the earth, darkened their auras, and retreated into the gloomy crevasses of the canyon floor.

Nerves primed, my vampire senses swept the darkness for more enemy. I headed toward Carmen and stepped over the smoking remnants of crows. As much as I disliked the feathered bastards, I had to acknowledge that they had saved our butts. The crows joined our attack because they had suffered as much as vampires under Phaedra's hand, and apparently, they were just as eager to settle the score.

When I propped up Carmen, I felt the trembling of her maimed kundalini noir. I brushed a curl of sweat-matted hair off her forehead. She grimaced, then clasped my wrist and held my hand against her face. Sobbing quietly, she leaned into me. I couldn't imagine the ordeal she had endured. If it had been me, I would've broken and we'd all be toast.

Jolie tossed her carbine aside and drew her .45s. "Let's finish that bitch."

Carmen let go of my hand, straightened and whispered, "Pity party over."

"Maybe you should stay here," I suggested.

Her aura bristled. "Fuck you."

Jolie handed her one of the .45s. Carmen brushed it away. "When it comes time for me to kill Phaedra, it's gonna be done old school." Her fangs shined bright as polished daggers, and the talons sprang from her fingertips, menacing as straight razors.

I took the pistol and again offered it to Carmen. "Let's not let pride get in the—"

"What did I just say?" she snapped.

"Fine, you win." I slapped the .45 back in Jolie's hand. "Let's do this."

We advanced down the center of the draw, Carmen in the middle, Jolie to her left, me to the right. Out the corners of my eyes, I saw columns of crows snaking along the ground toward the ruins.

Phaedra could appear behind us, but then who was left to guard Coyote? I doubted she kept a force in reserve. Once she thought she had us trapped, she would've thrown everything in her arsenal at us. Thanks to the crows, we had kicked the props from under her plan.

A green light dazzled my eyes and a fresh wave of psychic pain knocked me back a step. I gathered my strength to stand fast. But fighting against the mind blast was like trying to stay on your feet while getting smashed by a Mack truck.

The pain eased and it was Jolie's turn to stagger backwards, then Carmen's. I brought the Marlin up for a quick shot at Phaedra but her psychic wave whipped me once more.

When my vision cleared, I saw at the far end of the ruins, two auras rushing from the creek and darting behind the walls. Doña Marina and El Cucuy. As reinforcements.

"Watch your fire," I warned Jolie. "Doña Marina and El Cucuy are here."

"I'm glad they got off their asses to do something," Jolie replied. "Phaedra can't defend herself against all of us at once."

That and El Cucuy could absorb her blasts and wear her out. That would let Jolie and me maneuver close for one quick shot.

The crows rose from the ground and lit their auras. They formed two orange, twisting pillars, one on Phaedra's left, another to her right. The scream of the birds echoed against the mesa walls with immense fury, announcing their savage desire for revenge. They arced toward Phaedra like the jaws of giant pincers and clamped around her.

Her aura pulsed and the envelope of crows burst into a cloud of torn feathers and dust. The debris sloughed around her feet.

Another wave of crows poured over Phaedra. And again she pulsed her aura and hundreds of the birds vanished in clots of feathers and dust.

The auras reappeared from behind the ruins and sprinted back to the creek. Doña Marina and El Cucuy, who carried Coyote in his arms. Doña Marina hadn't arrived to help us. No wonder she had agreed to my demand that she remain behind. She had conspired with El Cucuy to use our attack as a diversion to rescue Coyote. While I was willing to sacrifice Coyote to destroy Phaedra, Doña Marina was willing to sacrifice us to save her son. With centuries of practice, she was the master of playing one side against the other.

If Phaedra had figured out what Doña Marina had just done, she didn't get the chance to act on it because another wave of crows attacked. They shrieked in hatred, rising and descending in a tsunami of wings and beaks and claws.

I yelled to Jolie, "Here's our chance."

I aimed the Marlin at the middle of the boiling mass of birds—certain that I could've drilled Phaedra—when crows swooped low to knock the Marlin aside. They fluttered around my head and Jolie's, cawing angrily.

Carmen shouted, "They're claiming dibs on Phaedra."

And again, Phaedra pulsed her aura and dozens more crows died. She raked us with another psychic ray. When we recovered, she was retreating into the ruins, running away like a cowardly thief instead of the once mighty and self-proclaimed Queen of the Vampires.

Dazed crows limped on the ground, heads down, wings and tails drooping. One glanced up at me as if to say, *Okay vampire, your turn.*

Having lost Coyote as a hostage, I was certain Phaedra might try to escape through a psychic portal. Yet I saw her dash through the ruins as if she were searching for a place to hide.

Mule deer appeared around the perimeter of the ruins.

Jolie shifted weight from foot to foot and flexed her grip on the .45s. "What gives?"

A buck circled behind us. It dissolved into a blur that stretched into the weird ungainly shape of a skin-walker.

We are blocking Phaedra's escape. The familiar voice unraveled in my mind. Yellowhair-Chavez. He advanced toward us, slender legs pivoting like stilts, preternatural hide shimmering like metallic gauze. He pointed his elongated, sightless head at me. *We cannot kill her but we can deny her entry access to the psychic portals.*

I replied, "I thought you couldn't interfere."

Technically, no. But I'm bending the rules. Capiche?

I nodded. "Capiche."

You have until daybreak.

"That's plenty of time." Jolie hustled to the ruins. "You guys cover me."

Chapter Fifty

Jolie ran ahead of Carmen and me. She hurtled a wall and dropped out of sight. Didn't she know our chances were better if we attacked as one?

I wanted to chase after her, but I couldn't leave Carmen, who wasn't in any shape to go leaping through these ruins. The best Carmen could do was amble forward, and she winced in pain with every step. My nerves were still frazzled from the repeated psychic blasts. Jolie's must have been as well. But she smelled prey, and like an injured shark, ignored her wounds and dashed impulsively for the kill.

The skin-walkers wandered closer to the ruins. I didn't know how their magic worked but they had boxed in Phaedra so we vampires could finish her off. For now, her dreams for domination of the undead world were in tatters, but she remained as dangerous as a viper.

Alone, Carmen and I wended through the maze of broken adobe walls, worn smooth by centuries of erosion. The crisp night air magnified the crunch of our footfalls on the sand. My fangs and claws were extended, and my finger curved over the trigger of my Marlin. I wanted to call out for Jolie, but then I'd give away my location.

A gunshot rang out. Then another. Then a woman's muffled cry of pain.

Carmen and I froze, hoping to hear Jolie shout that she had gunned down Phaedra.

Nothing but silence.

We had stopped in a narrow corridor between two walls that stood taller than our heads. I peeked through a gap in the wall at my right and saw yet another wall. Too bad the crows weren't around. I could use their scouting skills.

Another cry shattered the quiet. Carmen and I traded anxious glances. It was Jolie. This scream was louder, more brittle, and very close.

Jolie needed help, *now!* I whispered to Carmen, "Catch up when you can."

I gathered my strength and sprang upward. I cleared the first wall, landed on the dirt, then flung myself over top of a second wall, ready to shoot.

A psychic blast knocked me blind. I came to as I tumbled across the ground and landed on my belly. The Marlin clattered just out of reach.

Felix, look at me.

A giant invisible hand clamped onto my skull and lifted my head from the dirt.

Phaedra had pinned Jolie to a wall. Their auras had melded in a boiling swirl of red, orange, yellow, and green. Jolie's legs thrashed beneath her and it was Phaedra's hold on her neck that kept her from sliding to the ground. Jolie's arms hung to her sides and the .45s lay by her feet. Her eyes were bugged out, and her mouth opened to let loose another cry, a humiliating, frail sound that reminded me how impotent we could be against this evil cunt.

Phaedra stared hungrily at Jolie, the same way a serial killer studies a victim, searching for the best way to feed on the agony. She wore a denim jacket over a black lacey skirt and a matching waist sash decorated with glass vials, human bones, and dead crows. Clusters of herbs and dried flower blossoms clung to her tangled tresses. Phaedra looked like a teenage hippie chick who had given up granola and patchouli for torture and murder.

I groped for my carbine. Another mind blast slapped my brain. A dull ache replaced the receding pain. I blinked my eyes back into focus.

Adobe walls enclosed us on three sides. A rectangular hole had been recently dug in the center of the enclosure. Wooden surveyor's stakes marked the corners of the hole. A small metal trailer rested close to the hole. The side of the trailer bore the markings: University of New Mexico, Native American Studies. The lock on the rear door had been torn off and the trailer gaped open. Shovels, a pick ax, and brooms lay scattered about.

I pushed from the ground to sit up. The world wobbled around me, and it took all my resolve just to keep from toppling over.

Phaedra pulled Jolie close.

Now for a taste of victory.

Phaedra opened her mouth and clamped her fangs to Jolie's throat. A ring of white light burned where her lips touched. She released Jolie, who fell gasping and clutching at her neck. Her fading aura resembled the hesitant flames over a dying bed of coals.

Wiping her lips, Phaedra stepped back and licked blood from her fingers. Another blast kept me dizzy. An electric tingling itched my skin and paralyzed my limbs.

This war is far from over. Once I kill you three pests, I'll regroup and start over. You have taught me much, and in gratitude, you will all get a quick death.

She bent down and picked up a shovel.

Watch.

Phaedra kicked Jolie onto her back. She planted her bare foot on Jolie's chest and gripped the shovel with both hands, lifting it to use the blade as a guillotine. I struggled to move my hands and legs, but nothing worked.

An outburst of cawing thundered like a blast of artillery. A wave of crows surged over the walls and plunged down on Phaedra. They tore at her face and hair while she swatted at them with the shovel.

Her aura condensed and an intense keening drilled my ears. She pulsed her aura and its energy splashed like heat. Smoking bits of crow pelted me.

Weakened by the effort to create the pulse, Phaedra let her shoulders droop for a moment, then took her place over Jolie.

I drew from a reserve deep inside of me. Her spell fought back and tightened its chokehold on my kundalini noir. Trembling from the strain, I managed to slide my hand inside my jacket for the Colt magnum.

Phaedra lowered the shovel, turned her head and glowered. Her spell loosened from my kundalini noir and wormed into my right arm. My fingers closed around the grip of the pistol and slid it out of my jacket. My arm moved robotically, horrifically, and my wrist twisted until the pistol swung toward my face. The depleted uranium-silver bullets glistened in the cylinders like metallic pellets of poison. The muzzle's bore appeared monstrously large, like the gun wanted to swallow me.

Now stand up.

My legs pushed me upright. My shoulders turned so I faced Jolie, and the rest of my body rotated awkwardly like I was a marionette.

Jolie pushed up from the ground, staggering as if punch drunk and braced against the adobe wall. My arm shifted and pointed the revolver at her.

Now shoot her.

My finger curled against the trigger, then stopped. The front sight danced across Jolie's body.

Phaedra's spell clasped my wrist to hold the gun steady and centered on Jolie's belly. My trigger finger started to squeeze but I fought to keep it frozen. Her spell coiled around my hand and my fingers cramped in the effort to resist. At the instant I thought she would win, I jerked to the left. The magnum boomed and spat a ball of flame. The slug chopped into the wall inches to Jolie's side.

A sharp blow clipped the back of my head. Phaedra was beside me, drawing the shovel back for another swing.

Again.

My arm grew rigid and pointed the pistol at Jolie. Phaedra's spell felt like two hands had seized my wrist to aim the magnum. My finger took up the slack of the trigger and stopped. Needles of pain sank to my knuckles, forcing the finger to tighten. At the moment when I could no longer stand the pain, I leaned backwards. The magnum fired harmlessly into the air.

Phaedra clubbed the shovel against the back of my head. Stars of pain whirled in front of my eyes.

What's the matter, Felix? She swung the shovel.

Wham! Another blow to the back of my head.

Why are you resisting me? Did you think I would ever turn out any different than this? You knew from the beginning how dangerous I could be. Yet you turned me. You could've let me die.

Another blow. This time the stars burned through my brain.

But you didn't. I guess I owe you. I should call you daddy.

Another blow. The agony clanged in my skull.

Daddy.

Wham!

Daddy.

Pain melted my resolve. Where was Carmen? Why wasn't she using her powers to deflect Phaedra's spell? Maybe Carmen was too weak. Then she shouldn't stay. She should leave Jolie and me and save herself to continue the fight at another time. And where were the crows? El Cucuy?

Words clogged my throat, and her spell loosened enough to let me talk. The words croaked free. "Enough. You win. Just don't hit me anymore."

Another blow. *Why not? I'm getting the hang of this.*

Phaedra's spell evaporated from me. Jolie's aura flashed in pain, and she crumpled to the ground.

I had only managed a quick pulse of relief before the spell returned, plunging back through my kundalini noir and taking control of my arm.

I jerked the trigger twice and the two bullets ricocheted against the wall.

Four rounds expended, two remaining.

Phaedra hit me again with the shovel. *Goddammit, what is wrong with you?*

I wanted to drop from the pain but her spell kept me from toppling over.

You don't want to play, then fine. My spine straightened like a string pulled me upward by my neck. My arm twisted and brought the pistol back to my head, then pressed the end of the barrel against my temple. The more I wrestled to regain control of my arm, the harder the muzzle pushed. My consciousness shrank around the ring of steel digging into my skin. My kundalini noir quivered like it was going to shake itself to pieces. At any instant, the depleted uranium slug was going to blow my skull apart and paint the adobe with my brains. The tension of my impending death made my mind scream.

I waited. Phaedra's hold on my kundalini noir tightened and relaxed. It tightened again, but not as strong. Something was happening. I was able to swivel my eyes and caught that Phaedra was watching one corner of the enclosure. I panned my gaze to see what.

Carmen staggered around the corner of a wall, tramping step-by-step as if advancing through a gale-force wind. She and Phaedra locked eyes. Spikes of hatred jutted from both of their auras.

Carmen raised her hands. Claws extended, she advanced on Phaedra, who staggered backwards and cocked the shovel to swing it like a club.

The spell on me weakened. And on Jolie. She rolled onto her belly and inched toward Phaedra. My arm dropped into my side. It felt rubbery and useless so I snatched the magnum with my other hand and aimed at Phaedra.

Jolie extended an arm and snagged Phaedra's ankle. I held the pistol as steady as I could and fired. The bullet smacked Phaedra's shin. She cried out, dropped the shovel, and collapsed onto her back.

The spell vanished and I sank to my knees. Too weak to raise the magnum, I watched Phaedra try to kick free of Jolie, who dug talons into her ankle. Blood gushed from the wounds.

Carmen shambled toward them. Phaedra tried to crawl backwards but Jolie held fast to her shattered, bleeding leg.

I reached deep and rallied my strength. I aimed the revolver at Phaedra's torso and squeezed the trigger. The pistol barked flame. Phaedra shook as if kicked. She fell flat and lay still.

Then her head raised. Her eyes burned bright as a welding torch. Her lips parted wide, displaying her fangs. The back of her mouth began to glow and a shriek and a flame of sparks blasted out. She raked this flame at Jolie, then me. The sensation was like my kundalini noir was pelted by screaming, red-hot ball bearings.

Cringing, I brought my hands up to shield myself.

She aimed this flame at Carmen, who staggered backwards from the blow. The sparks ricocheted off Carmen like a stream of water striking a pole.

The flame and the shriek stopped. Phaedra stared at us, looking haggard, her face creased with wrinkles like this last attack had drained years from her spirit.

Carmen spied one of the surveyor's stakes, dragged her feet close and yanked it free. She lifted it to her chest. Phaedra watched, too weak to move.

Jolie crawled forward and grabbed Phaedra's left wrist and pinned her arm to the ground. I pushed myself toward our young monster and seized her right wrist. She tried to pull free but my fingers became like iron.

Phaedra scowled at us. "All of you, you're going to eat shit in hell. You think this is over. I'll come back. I'll find a way." She let loose a string of curses that would've burned the ears off a stevedore.

Carmen held the stake firm, the point away from her body. "Bitch, shut the fuck up." She positioned herself between Phaedra's feet and let herself topple forward.

Phaedra jerked her arms, but Jolie and I held firm. The stake punched into her sternum. She bellowed in pain. Blood spurted. Carmen fell flat against her. She pushed up to straddle Phaedra's hips. Carmen's hair swayed in greasy strands. Tendrils of rage lashed from the penumbra of her aura like she was channeling the fury of a lightning storm.

With a grunt and a sneer of contempt, Carmen shifted her weight against the stake and it sank deeper, crunching through bone, releasing another spray of blood.

Phaedra's hands curled into fists. Her thoughts screamed into my head.

Pain. Mercy. Pain.

Carmen twisted the stake and screwed it in deeper. More blood gushed upward. She grunted again and gave the stake another twist.

Phaedra's fingers slowly unclenched.

Pain. Pai—

Her aura contracted and dimmed. Carmen gave the stake one more twist. The aura disappeared as if Carmen had flicked a switch.

Carmen scooted off Phaedra and plopped against a wall. The dust of dried vampire blood sloughed from her face and hands. Jolie dragged herself to Carmen and wrapped an arm around her waist. She rested her head on Carmen's thigh. Carmen closed her eyes and stroked Jolie's hair. A dozen crows crept from the shadows and formed an arc around them.

A skin-walker sauntered into the enclosure like a bizarre caricature of a horse entering a stable. An iridescent gloss scrolled though his hide and his outline shrank into the shape of a man. Yellowhair-Chavez. He looked at Carmen and Jolie, then cocked his head to study Phaedra's corpse.

"Any final words?" I asked in a raspy voice.

"I've dated worse." He turned and walked away.

Too weak to do anything but rest, I lay on the ground. The back of my head ached. I could use aspirin. Better yet, morphine.

Staring at the stars, I remembered all of the vampires who had fallen in this war. I also remembered the four chalices on D-Galtha who had sacrificed themselves: Toby, Irsan, Cassie, and Juanita. I set aside my grief to chuckle sardonically that despite the odds, we had triumphed.

Chapter Fifty-One

The western horizon brightened from indigo to azure. In a few moments the morning sun would crest the mesa and its rays would blast over us.

Carmen, Jolie, and I stood beside the Cress Tech Humvee. The Chaco Ruins were between us and the rising sun. We were dressed head-to-toe in thick clothing that included hoods, gloves, and welders' masks. A dozen other vampires, similarly clad, stood alongside us. Soon after Carmen had killed Phaedra, vampires converged upon our location in a fleet of Humvees and MRAPs. They were the rest of Antoine and King Gullah's force and had arrived too late to help us fight. The force was led by Mel Moretti, the whiskered leader of the Denver nidus, and Dan Sky-Pony, an old friend of Carmen's I hadn't seen for years. They shared their stash of heavy clothes so we could join them at this funeral.

Our vehicles were scattered along of the bottom slope of the mesa. Fifty yards away, Phaedra's naked, headless body lay close to the rim of a kiva in the center of the ruins.

Mel and his vampires had rounded up Phaedra's human minions, fanged and turned them, then cut off their heads. As dead vampires, they would be easier to dispose of. Their naked, decapitated bodies lay beside hers, all lined up like the catch of the day. The other headless bodies belonged to the remaining rogue vampires, also captured and executed. All the severed heads had been collected into a pyramid, Phaedra's on top. The remains of the suicide-bomber vampires—torn limbs, fragments of torsos, assorted organs—had been likewise gathered for destruction.

Off to the side lay another line of undead, mangled remains. These belonged to Antoine and King Gullah and the rest of the crew we had scraped from the debris of their doomed helicopter.

To protect the Great Secret, we presented what was left of our bloodsucking kin—friend and foe—to be ravaged and consumed by the rising sun. Standing ramrod straight, we resembled stone sentinels jutting from the hard-scrabble landscape. Normally we vampires hid from the deadly reach of the dawn's rays. But when it was time to offer our fellow vampires to the sun, especially en masse as we were doing today, we did so in a ceremony to pay homage in this final *adios amigos*.

A flock of crows landed among us. They turned toward the sun and held still.

The sun peeked over the horizon. The tinted lens of my visor dimmed the harsh light. A faint hum echoed through me, a noise that didn't register in my ears but instead quivered through my nerves.

The sun floated above the horizon, its light exploding in nuclear brilliance. The humming sound raked needles across the inside of my skin. My kundalini noir vibrated like a crystal goblet on the verge of shattering. The mask became stifling hot. I squinted, then clenched my eyes. I saw red through my eyelids, then orange, and when the light threatened to burn my retinas, I raised a gloved hand to shield my face.

The sun's rays baked my hand and shoulders, then my chest. The humming noise sharpened to a whine. The sun rose and levered a wave of heat down my body. To my belly. My hips. My thighs. Shins. Feet. The heat cooled. I opened my eyes and dropped my hand. All the other vampires were also lowering theirs so it appeared as though we had just finished saluting the sun.

The white edge of sunlight crept from us to the corpses at the ruins. The instant the light touched undead flesh, the skin crinkled and smoldered. Phaedra's belly tore open, spilling guts that writhed and shriveled in the dirt. Like the others, her body crumbled, revealing bone, which broke apart and disintegrated into ash.

The light reached the pile of heads. Phaedra's faced the sun, so all we could see was the back of her cranium. Her hair burst into smoke. Flames jutted out her ears. Her skull softened, then collapsed as if it were a rotting pumpkin. The mass of heads beneath her crumpled, and the burning skulls scattered like loose melons. Tongues of fire licked from eye sockets, ear holes, mouths, and neck stumps. The air stank of burning meat and scorched bone.

I felt no satisfaction at seeing Phaedra incinerate. All the misery she had caused was too high a price for the cheap thrill of watching her roast.

The whine softened to a hum, then dwindled into silence. Smoke braided over the piles of ash. The mysterious wind that always appears afterwards swept from the south and kicked up the soot. Twists of gray corkscrewed into the sky, fading, dissolving to nothing. Some of these vampires had lived for centuries, dined on the necks of kings and queens and lorded over empires. Now nothing remained but their memory. Chaco Ruins and the surrounding mesa appeared suddenly vast and I felt incredibly small.

The back of my head still smarted. Jolie, Carmen, and I moved like our bones were connected with rusted hinges. Our kundalini noirs were tender like the raw flesh under a scab. Even with our vampire recuperative powers, we'd still need days of rest and a diet of fresh human blood to get back our undead mojo.

The sun climbed high enough to weaken the dawn's light. I lifted the welder's mask to slide sunglasses underneath and cover my eyes. Oven-hot air toasted my skin. All of the vampires removed their masks and began to unfasten the protective garments.

As one, the crows leapt upwards. They scattered in groups of two and three and flew in all directions. Their cawing filled the canyon with a melancholy echo.

Mel's assistants collected the masks and clothing. Jolie donned wrap-around shades and smeared sun block to touch up the back of her hands. She offered some to Carmen, who refused with a shake of her head. Jolie held the tube for me, but I didn't need it. She tucked it into a jeans pocket and fished out loose cartridges to top off the magazines of her .45s.

Carmen rubbed her side like she was massaging a cramp.

"You okay?" Jolie asked.

"My kundalini noir has stopped hemorrhaging, but it will be days before I'll feel normal." Carmen lowered herself onto a large rock and sat, her expression shrinking into a thousand-yard stare. Like her, for the moment, I was done with fighting. All I wanted was to sit beside her and process all the drama and heartache we had gone through.

I put my hand on her shoulder, and she patted my fingers. Her mirrored sunglasses reflected the mesa but of course, not me.

Mel trundled over to us, Ray-Bans on his face. In his padded suit and thick boots, he looked like a deep-sea diver. He asked, "Everybody up and at 'em?"

Carmen nodded and raked fingers through her stringy, sweat-matted hair. Jolie and I helped her up.

Mel set his helmet on the ground and unzipped his suit across the front and down the legs. He shrugged out of it and kicked his boots free. He slipped a cigar from his shirt pocket and stuck it in his mouth. A crow landed by his stocking feet.

"Now that we're done with this business, the real work starts." He mumbled around the cigar. "First order of business is to reconstitute the Araneum." He pulled a memo pad from the pocket and flipped through the pages. "Now raise your left hand."

We raised our left hands.

"Now bare your fangs and repeat after me. *Tenebras et perpetuam noctem copias obtestor, meos immortuorum ad fidem Araneum et in perpetuum defendat, Magni Secreti.*"

I hadn't recited those words in years, not since I was enlisted as an enforcer for the Araneum. Not every vampire swears allegiance to the Araneum, but every undead bloodsucker must protect the Great Secret. If they didn't, they answered to killers like me.

Mel plucked a fountain pen from his pocket. He jotted our names onto a page of the memo pad and tore it free. The crow extended one leg, a message capsule clipped to its ankle. Mel crouched to remove the capsule, unscrewed the top, and inserted the page. He replaced the top and clipped it back on the crow. It jumped past his head, circling upward, and flew toward the east.

Wisps of smoke ribboned in the canyon from fires north of us, the wrecked vehicles from last night's fight between King Gullah's vampires and Cress Tech.

"What a mess," I said.

"Of course it's a mess," Mel replied. "What else would you expect from the federal government? It's such a big, goddamn mess they haven't yet figured out what to do. Right now Cress Tech and the feds are so busy pointing fingers that it'll be a few hours before any help shows up."

"There's going to be a huge investigation."

Mel laughed. "Fuck yeah." His cigar balanced on the edge of his bottom teeth. "The 'huger' the better." He pointed to the line of towers in the distance, so far away they resembled a faint line of toothpicks. "Cress Tech and their buddies in the NSA and CIA cobbled together this scheme to discover psychic powers and communicate with aliens. And what did they get? One big goat screw. A shoot-out between friendly forces. Untold numbers of casualties. Dozens of wrecked vehicles and helicopters. Millions and millions of dollars lost. And for what?" One of Mel's bushy eyebrows danced like a spastic, hairy caterpillar.

I couldn't see what Cress Tech had learned. "Nothing?"

"Exactly. Bupkis. Imagine how bat-shit crazy this expensive cluster fuck is going to sound to Congress."

"If it gets that far," Carmen added.

"So no more psychotronic research?" I asked.

"For now." Mel flicked a vintage Zippo and lit the cigar. His hamster-like cheeks bellowed as he puffed, causing his steel wool-like sideburns to bristle.

"Then are we done?" Jolie asked. "We have other business to attend to."

Mel snapped the Zippo closed. He tipped his head to the mesa behind us, in the direction of Coyote's home. "Yeah, sure. Give my regards." He saluted with his cigar.

We returned to the Humvee and climbed in. Devane was where we had left him, balled up in the rear seat and covered by a tarp. When the poor guy finally came to, he would be groggy and stiff for another couple of days. His memory of the big, bad Cress Tech shootout would be one blank stretch of amnesia.

Jolie did a sharp U-turn, and we four-wheeled up the mesa to Coyote's home, or what was left of it.

A long, gleaming Airstream trailer was parked beside Coyote's burned-out doublewide. A Ford F-350 idled by the fence. Yellowhair-Chavez and his Navajo buddies—skin-walkers for sure—were double-checking the leveling jacks at the corners of the Airstream. They hadn't wasted time finding a new crib for Coyote and Rainelle.

Jolie parked, and we got out. Carmen limped a couple of steps until her gait strengthened. From somewhere around the trailer, a generator purred. Yellowhair-Chavez ceased his work and his gaze followed Jolie.

"Your secret admirer and his leveling rod want attention," I said.

She shot me a dirty look, then smiled warmly at the skin-walker. He returned to inspecting the jacks.

The door to the Airstream opened. Rainelle stepped onto a makeshift porch and waved a cheerful welcome. "Coffee's ready. And I have tamales. Fry bread. Some fresh Type A Positive." She made no mention that we had just survived the worst fight of our supernatural lives and acted like we had stopped by for a Sunday visit.

"How is Coyote?" I asked.

She held the door open for us. "Doing better."

"How about Doña Marina?" Carmen climbed the steps.

"She's inside, with Coyote."

"And El Cucuy?"

"Gone," Rainelle answered. "It's daylight, remember?"

The Mexican boogieman had been a good ally, but I didn't appreciate how he and Doña Marina had used us to distract Phaedra. If I met him again, I didn't know if I would shake his hand or kick him in the balls.

We filed into the crowded kitchen and removed our shades. Warm, homey aromas from the stove and plastic, new-trailer smells greeted us. Rainelle told us to go to the right through the dining area. The narrow door at the end stood open.

Coyote lay on the bed, propped up on a stack of pillows. He was dressed in clean clothes, even clean socks. Doña Marina sat beside him on the mattress, dressed in a purple velour tracksuit. She was stirring a cup of porridge that smelled like raw, bloody liver. My mouth watered.

My undead trickster friend grinned. His aura rippled around him.

I stepped forward, but he waved me back, "Where are your manners, *cabron?*" He extended his hand to Jolie and Carmen. His withered face bunched around his smile, fangs jutting between thin lips. Jolie and Carmen took turns leaning over him to receive quick, grandfatherly pecks on their cheeks. He didn't leer or try to cop a feel. I blinked in astonishment.

Doña Marina handed him the cup, and he spooned the liver porridge into his mouth.

"How are you doing?" I asked.

"Needs cilantro. And rat," he commented, then looked at me. "*Mejor*, for sure."

His mother stood from the bed. "Now that Phaedra is dead, *mijo*'s wounds can heal."

I gave her a cross stare. "What about a thank you?"

"I saved him, not you." Doña Marina's quick reply told me she knew exactly what I was getting at.

"By playing us," I replied.

Carmen tugged at my arm. *Let it go.*

I wanted to box Doña Marina in and make her squirm in remorse. Instead she smirked. "Men and their pride." She presented her open hands and bowed. "*Gracias, mi valiente.* It's not enough to be grateful that we won, and that my son and Carmen are safe, but I must acknowledge that your feelings are hurt. My apologies."

I wasn't shamed, only more angry, mostly at myself for thinking I could best a woman in an argument. I glanced at Coyote for guidance. He scraped his spoon inside the cup. The only way for me to save face was to beg pardon from his mother.

"Doña Marina," I began, faking sincerity as best I could, "forgive me for …" She was gone.

Carmen and Jolie's eyes widened in surprise. Their gazes

searched the compact bedroom as if Doña Marina could be hiding in a corner or had tucked herself into a drawer.

"How did she do that?" I asked.

Coyote lapped crimson pudding from his spoon. "After all this, *ese*, haven't you learned a thing? Summer school for you, *pendejo*."

Rainelle called for us from the dining table. She had steaming cups of coffee and a carafe I hoped was filled with blood. We began to retreat from the bedroom.

"*Vato*," Coyote said, "I owe Rainelle a romantic getaway to show my gratitude. Someplace fancy. Maybe the Travelodge in Farmington. But I'm a little short. Could you spring me some *ficha?*"

I pulled my pockets inside out. "I'm broker than you are. The last of my cash was burned up in your doublewide."

"So'kay. You can mail a check when you get home. Or better yet, use PayPal."

Chapter Fifty-two

I was back where this adventure had begun, in my office on the second floor of the Oriental Theater. Jolie remained in New Mexico with Yellowhair-Chavez, no doubt working overtime at keeping his wigwam warm.

Carmen lay beside me, hip to hip, shoulder to shoulder, hands clasped, both of us still clinging to the ebbing orgasm. The ceiling fan swirled above and its wash cooled our sweaty bodies and the moist funk between our legs. The office lights were off, but the neon glare from the marquee stuttered through the windows and bathed us with a wandering, fiery glow.

During sex Carmen and I clutched one another like shipwrecked survivors on a raft. Release wasn't so much a surrender to pleasure as a respite from the anguish shrouding our minds.

Guilt wormed through me. How much of the recent disaster had been my fault, and how much of it was inevitable? Against my better judgment I had turned Phaedra and created the monster that tore the Araneum apart and almost killed us. Before that, I had let Carmen get kidnapped by the aliens. In a curious and tragic way, the two events had coiled together, the universe undoing one mistake with another ... at a price.

Phaedra's insurrection caused Coyote to look for help in the psychic realm. That was where he pinpointed Carmen on the far side of the galaxy. Her extraordinary empathetic powers made her a valuable treasure to the aliens. Those same powers made her a threat to Phaedra.

I would get through this. Time heals all wounds, just as it wounds all heels. Carmen had to cope with the memory of years spent as a pet to her alien masters, never knowing if return to Earth was possible. Plus she bore the injuries inflicted by Phaedra's psychic blasts. As did Coyote.

The minus column to this disaster included the untold number of vampires murdered. A lot of humans had also been killed, but they were only an asterisk to the carnage. Plus I couldn't forget the disastrous end to the Nancharm. And Che, Coyote's fearless dog. So much bloodshed only to circle back to where we had started—with the Araneum again firmly in charge.

Carmen was resilient, perhaps the strongest vampire of them all, and yet when she rested her head on my naked chest, I could feel the dissonant vibration of her damaged kundalini noir.

We didn't talk about how we felt. Why bother? We had to process the trauma on our own and shovel it into a corner like so much manure, to use either as compost for lessons learned or remain as shit to stink up our minds.

On some nights, Carmen and I climbed on the theater roof to study the sky and sift through our recollections of D-Galtha, which was fading into dream-like memories. We stared at the stars and tracked the occasional moving lights, certain they were satellites or airplanes but secretly wishing Blossom would drop by for a visit. A very short visit, only long enough to keep us posted. Had the Wah-zhim succeeded in overthrowing the Nancharm or did the civil war within the Galactic Union continue? My kundalini noir flinched in remorse for my part in killing Moots.

The cheerful jangle of noise from a First Friday Art Walk carried through an open window. As did the aroma of carnitas and beef, onions, and cilantro. Carmen raised her head. She let go of my hand and rose to her feet in one fluid lift.

She grabbed a wine glass and filled it from an open bottle of pinot noir on my desk. Glass in hand, she sashayed to the window, anchored her elbows on the sill and looked out. She was haloed by the flickering light from the phallus-shaped marquee. I wiped myself with a hand towel, then rose from the rug to join her.

We looked down on the sidewalk. About twenty people milled between the entrance of the theater and a taco truck parked against the curb. Even if anyone bothered to look up, I doubted they would've noticed us in the darkened window.

Smoke rising from truck roof vents brought the delicious smells. I could use a snack. "Hungry?"

Carmen sipped from the glass. "Maybe later. I still feel a little stuffed from my all-meat diet." She bumped her hip against mine.

From the window we overlooked this area of the west Highlands neighborhood. Clusters of people strolled along the sidewalk, making the circuit among the few remaining galleries. In the short years that I'd been here, gentrification had swept out a tamale shop, a comic-book store, various art studios and replaced them with a hipster barbershop, wine bars, craft breweries, upscale eateries, and one real estate office after another. On either side of the commercial strip, a rash of McMansions stood where century-old bungalows had been scraped away.

Thankfully, the blunt-tooths remained clueless to the recent supernatural war. Just as Mel had predicted, the feds were doing their best to hide the Cress Tech fiasco in a file classified *Top Secret-Never Mind*. The media carried the official version—that the many casualties and the loss of equipment had been caused by a live-fire exercise gone wrong. Better to blame incompetence than admit the truth about their aborted search for psychic energy and alien contact.

The psychotronic towers had been torn down and hauled away. The explanation for their existence was that they were temporary antennae erected for America's perpetual GWOT—the Global War on Terror, a.k.a. the never-ending cash cow for the military-industrial complex.

A crow fluttered through the darkness. Carmen and I backed away to let it land on the windowsill. A message capsule glittered on its leg. The Araneum was back in business. Duty called.

I reached to remove the capsule. The crow snapped at my hand and squawked. It stared at Carmen and raised the leg with the capsule.

"Be my guest," I said.

Carmen unclipped the capsule and unscrewed the ruby-encrusted cap. Out burst the stench of rotting meat, the telltale stink of the flayed vampire flesh the Araneum used as parchment. She extended a talon from her index finger and hooked a roll of parchment from the open capsule. Unfolding the roll to the size of a postcard, she turned her back to the neon light to better illuminate the message. The light made the translucent parchment glow. When I squinted to read the words the crow nipped my arm, warning me to back off.

As she read, Carmen chewed on her lower lip. She balled the parchment and offered it to the crow. If this was daytime, she could toss the parchment into sunlight and watch it disappear in a puff of smoke. But as it was night, the crow would have to eat it. The bird sighed and took the message from her fingers. He tossed his head back to gulp it down. The crow shut his eyes and bowed. His belly rumbled. He winced and coughed smoke, a gross stinky odor.

Carmen replaced the cap and clipped the capsule to the crow's leg. It turned around and flew off.

"Well?" I looked at Carmen.

She downed the last of the wine and returned the glass to my desk. "The Araneum has appointed me to the Central Plenum." She wandered about my office to collect her clothes from the floor and the furniture.

"Congratulations. It's quite a promotion. If that's what you want." Soon Carmen would be gone. Again. I grasped the wine bottle but set it back down. Suddenly I wanted something stronger. Scotch. Rye. A neck teeming with Type O Negative.

"I know you're no fan of authority, but the Araneum needs me." She bunched her clothes. "I'm the only vampire with so much first-hand knowledge about the aliens."

"Who's holding you back?"

"You won't miss me?"

"Silly question. Plus there are a couple of bennies for me in this. One, it wouldn't hurt to have an ally among the hallowed ranks of our superiors. And two, with your elevated pay grade it'll be easier for you to spot me a loan."

"That's worrisome." Carmen laughed. "You sound a lot like Coyote."

"You're right, that is worrisome. When are you going to tell Jolie?"

"Soon. I'll sweeten the news with a romantic getaway."

I chuckled. "First you'll have to pry her loose from her Navajo stud."

"That's your job." Carmen dropped the ball of clothes on a chair.

"Whattaya mean?"

She walked to me. "You have a vested interest in pulling them apart because that romantic getaway includes you." Carmen gave a smile that was better than Viagra.

Acknowledgments

I feel like Lazarus with this book, and that's a very good thing as I've been gone a while. First on my thank-you list, Kevin J. Anderson, the honcho at WordFire Press, and Peter Wacks, his over-worked and relentlessly optimistic editor, plus the behind-the-scenes elves who keep the gears oiled and turning at WordFire. My critique group, who make literary beat-downs something we all look forward to: Jeanne Stein, Warren Hammond, Angie Hodapp, Aaron Michael Ritchey, Travis Heermann, Tamra Monahan, Lou Berger. And Terry Wright. A special nod to those great folks at Lighthouse Writers for allowing me into their tribe of awesomeness: Andrea Dupree, Michael Henry, Nick Arvin, Dan Manzanares, Kerry Booth, and the rest of those amazing word scribblers. Su Teatro for keeping me in the loop. Rocky Mountain Fiction Writers, my literary home. A special mention of Eric Matelski for nailing the cover art. Jen Mosquera and Eric Jaenike for never letting me forget my shortcomings as a human being. Mark Graham, Manuel Ramos, and Rudy G for their props and support. My sister Sylvia and her partner Janet for keeping the faith. My sons Alex and Emil for putting up with me. And lastly, to my fans, for stoking the fires and bombarding me with, Where the f*ck is Felix? I hope this story was worth the wait.

About the Author

Mario Acevedo is the author of the Felix Gomez detective-vampire mystery thrillers. A former helicopter pilot, paratrooper, engineer, and art teacher, Mario lives and writes in Denver, Colorado. He takes his orders from Scout, a Shiba Inu.

Other WordFire Press Titles

Our list of other WordFire Press authors and titles is always growing.
To find out more and to see our selection of titles, visit us at:

wordfirepress.com

CPSIA information can be obtained at www.ICGtesting.com
Printed in the USA
LVOW06s1928170915

454607LV00001B/75/P

9 781614 753070